Another heart-warming
Ireland, set on the

'Unexpected Truths made me dream of ...,
escape – and romance. Five stars!'
Leah

'Lamorna has done it again! This time she brings the Cornish
coast to life, a new set of characters to love and adore.'
Lynn

Also By Lamorna Ireland

Lamorna would love to hear from you. Find her on:

 Facebook.com/LamornaIreland

 @AuthorIreland

 www.LamornaIreland.co.uk

Unexpected Truths

Lamorna Ireland

AUTHOR

To Mevagissey and all the people who keep its heritage alive.

Lamorna Ireland

x

Prologue

It was a mild and peaceful winter's morning. The darkness that sat like a heavy blanket on the sleeping village was yet to be pierced by the first beams of morning light. The gentle lapping of the water and click-clacking of the boats bumping against each other soothed Elaine Waters as she filled her lungs with the sea salt air, the easterly chill waking and alerting every part of her.

It was a tradition of hers, every morning. She never slept well anyway, so for her there was nothing better than to see her little world wake up right before her eyes, to watch the fishing vessels set off beyond the harbour wall for their day's trawl, to see each little window light up with life as residents started preparing for their day ahead. This time of year though, there were less windows lighting up. With more and more homes being subjected to the second-home status, in the winter Mevagissey was a ghost town.

These days, the piercing cold seeped into her joints, and she cursed her aging body as she struggled her way down the little stone steps that led to the tiny patch of beach just behind the fish market, one gloved hand clutching her flask of tea with determination. She longed to free her feet from her wellies, to twitch her toes into the sand and feel the sea water rinse over them, but it would be foolish to do so in her current condition. Once upon a time she would have done, no matter the time of year. It was, after all, this very beach where her Mevagissey story began, where she'd met the first love of her life.

She'd been eighteen years of age and she'd ventured up to Mevagissey from Newlyn with her good old dad, who was looking to buy a new otter trawler to join the Newlyn fleet. Leaving the men to bargain with numbers, she'd occupied herself by finding sea glass in the shallow waters - her favourite pastime - when a young fisherman approached. He was slight in stature, his waders drowning him, but the kindness in his eyes captured Elaine the very moment he said hello, descending the steps to join her on the sand.

"I'm Jacca," he'd said, one strong hand outstretched in offering, the other removing his woollen hat, releasing a head of unruly black hair.

"Elaine," she'd replied, placing her hand inside his, his warmth spreading through her like a warm cup of tea.

Suddenly, Jacca had found every excuse under the sun to visit Newlyn, often stopping in after a long-haul fishing trip to spend time with her. They'd courted and were married within the year, Elaine going against her parents' wishes and joining the Mevagissey community, rather than settle for one of the young skippers in her own birth town. Not dissimilar from Newlyn, Mevagissey had enchanted Elaine right away and she'd rooted there without hesitation.

Looking back to that very first year, stood on that very beach, with over forty-something years behind her now, Elaine would never have imagined the journey life had had in store for her. The good, the bad, the wonderful, the utterly tragic. Elaine never thought that a heart could swell with so much happiness whilst being on the brink of breaking, all in one go.

She was pulled out of her thoughts for a moment as she heard footsteps approaching along the quay, the sound ricocheting off the early morning darkness.

"Hello Bill," Elaine said as soon as she recognised the mane of grey hair and the distinctive smell of pipe tobacco.

"Morning Elaine, m'love," Bill said fondly. "How you feeling today? Some morning!"

"Isn't it, just? I'm alright. Don't fuss."

"You take it easy," Bill pointed a warning finger as he hauled some rope up onto his other shoulder. "I shall be telling Jacca you've been out and about, you naughty girl."

Elaine laughed, knowing Bill well enough to know

7

that he had his heart in the right place. Only five years her senior, the closer side to the seventies than her, she always took his 'naughty girl' comment in good jest.

"Ooh, don't you start. Dear Jacca has already threatened to move me back in with him."

"Yes well," Bill nodded, a slight sadness caught in his expression, "given the chance, I think he'd have you moved back in with him any day of the week. Right, must crack on! Don't want any other bastard beating me to the wreck netting. Cheers, m'love."

Smiling and waving a farewell, Elaine turned her attention to the flask of tea, which had now cooled to a drinkable temperature. Bill was right, of course. Her darling ex-husband would see to it that they were not only living together again, but that they were remarried as well. The very idea warmed her through, but somehow, given the circumstances, it just didn't seem right. She loved Jacca with all her heart, but after years of hurt and grief, she didn't want to unsettle the boat that had finally begun to work with the choppy seas of their life together. Of course, then there was Paige, their fiery daughter. She had not done well with Elaine and Jacca's divorce, and somehow Elaine didn't see her doing well with the confusion of her parents returning to one another again. No, best they left things the way they were.

She'd give Paige a call later, she decided. It had been a week or two since she'd spoken to her last, and she was always curious to hear about the things her daughter got up to in Bristol. Their relationship was strained at times, it had been ever since... well, even now Elaine struggled to think about it. But they made the effort to stay in touch. Sometimes she even took her iPad over to Jacca's and they chatted with Paige over that video chat thing that so many people used these days. She marvelled at the ways technology kept people in contact and was grateful for it as a way of keeping Paige in their lives. She'd been so proud of her daughter's boldness to seek her own culinary career, even if the opportunity had had Paige packing her bags and flying the nest sooner than Elaine had hoped. Now a sous-chef in a successful city restaurant, Paige had made a good name for herself, her reputation preceding her. Secretly, Elaine had hoped Paige would join her in the equally successful running of Giuseppe's, the Italian seafood restaurant looking out on the quay that she could now call her very own, thanks to the pure generosity of her dear friend Giuseppe himself.

Giuseppe.

The second love of her life.

He had been both her saviour during the darkest of times and the spanner in the works. When it had seemed her whole world was crumbling around her, Giuseppe had been there to pick up the pieces. They'd had five wonderful years together.

The first sign of light was seeping up over the horizon now and the seagulls were unsettled in their nests above. She knew that any moment now Jacca would be coming out of his cottage on the other side of the harbour to get his boat ready for another cold, wet trawl just off the bay. No doubt he would clock her as soon as he stepped outside and would rush over to make sure she wasn't overdoing it. She'd been unwell for weeks now, putting it down to age. But since her fall last week in the restaurant, Jacca and some of her other close friends had been intolerable, fussing over her like she was glass ready to shatter.

Then again, that numbness in her arm had returned again. She steadied herself on the metal rail of the steps leading back up to the quay, tired and a little disorientated. She'd rest for a moment, then finally do as she was told and return to the warmth of the restaurant. It wouldn't be long until Nick, her trusted head chef, was there to begin preparations for the day ahead.

If only she could move that blasted arm.

Chapter One

It was another thriving night of reservations at Garlands. Chefs and kitchen staff alike bustled and manoeuvred around each other like practised choreography. A symphony of clinks and scrapes against dishes; the rhythmic thud of knives against chopping boards and the sizzling of fresh ingredients hitting the hot pan. On the odd occasion, the beeping of a timer and the dinging of the bell signalling the waiting staff. A feverish murmur amongst the hierarchy of chefs as orders were chucked into the organised chaos.

"Gary! Get on the line!"

"Yes, chef!"

Paige Yelland's brow creased as her hands worked busily on the presentation of her current dish. Ignoring the shooting pains coursing through her neck and lower spine, a tell-tale sign of RSI, she placed the steak on top of polenta and carefully leaned three asparagus spears against them. Forty-five-degree angle - that's what she was always told. Hurrying to the next stage, she created accent dots on one side of the plate with two types of sauces, admiring the bursting contrast of colours surrounding the pinky-brown of the meat centring the plate. Conscious - as always - of time, she garnished the steak with flash-fried basil leaves, like three little pieces of stained glass, and dinged the bell - declaring the dish finished.

"Paige! Phone!" Tim called from the office.

"Take a message!"

Garlands wasn't at the top of its game, winning multiple food awards, for nothing, and Paige certainly hadn't climbed the kitchen hierarchy without going full pelt on every single shift. Each second counted and it was her role as sous-chef to ensure that the kitchen worked like a well-oiled machine.

At ten o'clock, the clean-down process began and the atmosphere in the kitchen became considerably lighter. Paige finished wiping down her station, passing Matthew on her way to the office.

"Fancy staying at mine tonight?" Paige offered, brushing her shoulder against Matthew's back in a tired, half-hearted attempt at teasing.

"No way," Matthew replied, pulling a face. "I'm bloody shattered."

Paige's arm fell to her side with a slap as she threw him a sour look. "Charming. You're allowed to do that thing called sleep at mine too, you know?"

"Don't be like that," Matthew soothed, planting a kiss on her forehead before heading to the office. "You know I don't sleep well at yours."

To be fair, neither did Paige very much. Her two lavish roommates were halfway through their degree courses and seemed to spend more time partying than revising these days. It was a Saturday night, so no doubt they'd fall through the front door at some point in the small hours of the morning, a tangle of legs, hair extensions and heels. Perhaps Matthew had a point.

"On second thought, can I stay at yours?" Paige pleaded. Matthew chuckled as he rooted through this morning's invoices, knowing exactly what she was thinking.

"Maybe it's time you found new room-mates," Matthew suggested, mock pity in his ice blue eyes.

"Maybe it's time we moved in together."

Matthew looked up from his invoices, his brow furrowed. "You're funny, Paige."

"I wasn't trying to be."

"You going to call your dad back or what?" Matthew waved the post-it note that Tim had scribbled the message on, a clear distraction from a topic he wanted to avoid, at all costs.

"Dad? He never calls. Oh bloody hell, I hope Mum hasn't fallen over again," Paige groaned in exasperation.

Paige felt a tinge of guilt as she was reminded of her feeble attempt at daughter duties, to go and see her mother since her last fall. She hadn't even had a chance to speak on the phone with her much since the evening of her incident, where Paige had at least managed to squeeze in a video chat. Her mother had been terribly tired, her speech slurred from the exhaustion of the day she'd had.

"I'll check the coffee machine is still on and get the girls behind the bar to make you a coffee," Matthew said, offering Paige the desk chair and rubbing her arm in sympathy. "You call your dad."

As Matthew took off on a hunt for fresh coffee, Paige's foot tapped involuntarily on the office floor, under the desk. She flicked the post-it note in agitation, a trickle of shame causing her to hesitate in picking the phone up right away, before giving herself a shake and grabbing the receiver. Cop-out text messages weren't going to cut it this time. If her mum had had a fall again, maybe this time she'd best step up and take a trip to Cornwall to check she wasn't needed.

She wasn't going to be needed, that was a given. Her parents had coped fine in her absence for the last ten years, the tight Meva community looking out for them in her place. Her parents didn't need her coming down and spoiling the status quo of their now settled but strange lives as a separated couple.

"Hi Dad, it's me. Did you call earlier?"

It only took three words. Three words.

"Paige, my love…"

As her father's voice seeped through the earpiece, the office walls closing in, her limbs became numb and heavy barely able to hold the phone in place. This feeling was familiar and yet different at the same time.

She was gone.

In one phone call, the world had stopped making sense.

She couldn't be gone.

Grief doesn't come in one size. In fact, grief is one of

12

those things that hits us all in very different ways. It is also something that we all know is an experience we will have to endure one day, and yet we all enter it completely unprepared, no matter how expected the death of a loved one was going to be. We're reminded briefly of our mortality and promise to seize the day, for some of us only to hastily return to our monotonous routines, clinging to it like a safety blanket.

For Paige, the unexpected and sudden death of her mother Elaine shook her to the core, the paralysing guilt of not seeing her sooner all-consuming. She thought of her dad, the weariness and sheer sadness in his voice haunting her since that phone call. Days went by and her stomach became more hollow at the memory of it all.

It wasn't long until the restaurant became her safety blanket, upping her hours just so she could avoid being at home alone with her thoughts, or worse home alone with her roommates, who would overcompensate the urge to rid her of her sadness.

"Aww, babes. D'ya know what you need, yeah?" Carrie said, throwing herself on to the sofa opposite Paige one particularly dreary afternoon, her long fingernails clacking against her phone screen as she typed out a message in record time. "You need a night out."

The standard prescription from these two, who thought anything could be solved with a night on the town, quite often resulting in a broken heel, their make-up halfway down their face and finishing up with a kebab, despite them both claiming to be vegetarians. Paige being more of an introvert, having barely hit a pub in the last six months let alone a night out, found this her idea of torture at the best of times, let alone when she was in danger of collapsing into uncontrollable sobs at any given moment.

"Definitely not," Paige responded, firmly.

"I always find, when I'm feeling sad, getting pissed makes me feel so much better," Georgina declared from her station at the mirror, as she carefully curled her long, platinum hair.

13

"That's a slippery slope right there," Paige muttered, thinking of someone else in her life whose loyalty and dependency to the booze had had a lot to answer for. She rubbed her temple in irritation as she tried to focus on a programme on TV, which she only had a slight investment in. Still, she needed something to put her focus to while the girls yapped on about absolute nonsense. Despite her best efforts, she found herself reaching for her phone to call the restaurant.

"Need spare hands?" Paige asked down the phone to Matthew, two seconds later. "Please?"

The usual unhealthy coping strategies continued and for the hundredth time one evening, during a particularly busy Friday night shift, Matthew ordered her to go home.

"Tell me to go home one more time Matthew and I'll ram this spring onion somewhere dark and painful."

"We're getting backlogged with orders! I get that you want to keep busy, but you're not... thinking straight."

"Speed up, Paige," Paige translated, giving herself a shake and picking up a knife to begin chopping. She choked on a sob and Matthew tutted... actually tutted. White anger coursed through her body as Paige slammed the knife down, barged past Matthew to the office and grabbed her coat.

"What are you doing now?" Matthew asked, incredulous.

"You've told me to go home, I'm bloody well going home," Paige cried, forcing her arms into the in-turned sleeves, ferociously ignoring the stares from her brigade of chefs and slamming the side door out into the alley behind her, shutting out the expletives coming from her hot-headed boyfriend.

That's another thing that grief never prepares you for. The absolute rollercoaster of emotions. The aching need to crawl into bed, your head full of cotton wool, unable to piece together the day ahead, all the way to the impulsive desire to slam someone's head in to a wall through anger over the unfairness of the world.

14

But she didn't deserve to feel like this. She should have visited her mother sooner.

Paige was at least relieved to find that Georgina and Carrie had taken themselves out for yet another night in the city, giving her the whole apartment to herself for complete self-pitying and wallowing.

She'd had so many opportunities to visit her mum. She could use work as an excuse all she liked, but she'd had time. The truth was, over the years, returning to her childhood home to visit her parents had become harder and harder. It seemed that the longer you left things, the more impossible it got to face them head on. And the more you stewed over the problem, the more you questioned your own credentials. She didn't want to admit that the time to forgive and forget had been overdue long ago and now it would never be able to happen.

Later, and to her mild surprise, Matthew arrived at her door with leftover food. By now, Paige was calm and numb, her hands poised on the stem of her wine glass. She eyed him warily as he let himself in, pulled his coat off and poured himself a glass of the same red. The silence between them stretched and stretched, making Paige itch. Finally, Matthew sat down at the opposite end of the breakfast bar and released a long sigh through his nose.

"Calmed down now?"

Matthew often did this. At a moment where he should perhaps have been finding something comforting to say, instead he'd settle for something that can only ever come with an accusing tone. Paige chewed the inside of her mouth, something *she* always did when she wanted to chuck a clever retort back at him but was too foggy minded to piece one together.

"The funeral is on Monday," Matthew continued, once it was clear that Paige wasn't going to retaliate. "I've covered your hours for the weekend. Why don't you head back early tomorrow morning? See your dad. Catch up with some friends. Gather your thoughts. I'll join you first thing

Monday morning for the afternoon service."

Paige nodded mechanically, agreeing with him for the sake of it. She didn't have the energy to argue. Then just as a fresh, nauseating wave of guilt washed over her, she rubbed her face down with her hands and groaned with the pain that ached her heart.

"You're tormenting yourself again," Matthew tutted, not unkindly. "You've got to stop tormenting yourself. Nobody, including you, knew that your mum would pass away from a stroke."

"That fall she had all those weeks ago, that was a warning sign," Paige sniffed. "I didn't even get myself down to Cornwall -"

"You couldn't, Paige. You were working double and back-to-back shifts."

"That doesn't matter," Paige countered, crossing her arms on the breakfast counter, a shiver running through her, despite the toasty warmth of the apartment. "I should have made more of an effort to check on her - at least called her more than once. All I did was text her and Dad every now again, as if that was my duty done."

Matthew sat in silence, knowing that anything he said would be countered or dismissed, as Paige drained her wine, feeling utterly miserable.

"I'll go and pack," Paige muttered, sliding off her stool and shuffling to her bedroom.

That night brought on dreams of crashing waves, the cawing of seagulls, the click-clacking of the fishing boats in the harbour and her mother's facial features blurring into non-existence.

"I found one! I found one! Look Mummy!"

Paige's little voice travelled around the village on the eastern wind, pure jovial excitement in her tone. Her inky black hair blew wildly around her head as she cupped her hands with a gentleness beyond her years. She shouted for her mother again.

"Look at that!" Her mother gasped, plucking the

smooth sea glass from her daughter's little hands and holding it up to the sun. "Paige, my sweetheart. You've found a rare one here. I seldom find red ones!"

"Mummy, let's find some more!" Paige cried, gleeful as she frolicked through the breaking waves, her shorts soaked as she went too far. It wasn't very often that they hunted for sea glass on this beach, given that it was usually too wild and under water for them to get past the bottom steps. Her mum was usually found on the little patch of beach on the other side of the harbour, nestled in the corner of the outer wall. That was where her mummy and daddy had met many years ago. She had been told that story almost a hundred times before.

"Paige! Look!" Elaine shouted in whisper, pointing beyond the jagged rocks just yards in front of them. Paige followed her line of vision, just in time to see the smooth grey head of a seal disappear under the water's surface.

"Stay very quiet, m'love. He might come up again. Yes, there he is - look!"

Paige's little body was rigid, afraid that she would scare her little sea friend off from the slightest of movements. Her mother's hair tickled her ears as she crouched beside her, watching with anticipation as the seal circulated around the rocks, looking for its next meal. Her breathing was unsteady as her body practically hummed with excitement and juvenile energy. The sea always called out to her, just like her fisherman daddy, and today was no exception as she longed to dive right into the water with her new little seal friend.

A few more bobs under the water, the seal finally surfaced for the last time before disappearing completely, most likely to a quiet little cove to rest on a full belly of fish. Paige clucked her tongue in disappointment and resumed her frantic search for more sea glass.

"Five more minutes, sweetheart. Then we must head home to put dinner on."

"Mummy," Paige said, dipping her tanned arms into the cool water and scooping her fingers through the

17

shingles, her eyes on the constant look out for colour amongst the browns and greys.

"Yes, my darling," her mother cooed, her own hands sieving delicately through the stones on the sea bed. She pocketed two more murky green sea glass, pleased with today's finds.

"I'm going to live here forever and ever," the little girl declared. Her mother watched her proudly, a replica of herself.

"There's definitely worse places to be, m'love. Now come on, time to head home. It will all be here again tomorrow."

Chapter Two

The pungent smell of fish and dried seaweed mixed with the aroma of fresh chips assaulted Paige's nose as she walked through the narrowing streets of Mevagissey. Her suitcase trundled noisily behind her against the old cobbles as she fumbled with her phone in the wet drizzle, her damp fingers slipping and sliding across the screen to send a text to Matthew, notifying him of her arrival. Without a parking permit to grant her access to a space on the harbour below her dad's cottage, Paige had circulated the village one-way route at least twice in search of a free space, before admitting defeat and claiming one of the council Pay & Display spaces on Church Street.

Now on foot, Paige took a sharp left, past the Fountain Inn and along Cliff Road, merging on to Old Road, where her dad's old fisherman cottage sat looking over the harbour. It looked the very same as it always did. Like it had done for as long as Paige could remember. On a particularly miserable day like today, the grey pebbledash and dark wood-stained trim made Jacca's cottage look pretty grim by Paige's standards, who had become so accustomed to the high ceilings and crisp, white decor of the Georgian townhouse her apartment was situated in. Nets and buoys hung from the balcony on the second floor and the storm porch underneath cluttered with stacked crab pots, old footwear and a set of waders.

Paige rapped on Jacca's front door impatiently, the mild drizzle increasing rapidly to more of a downpour. Her raincoat was perfectly practical in normal wet weather, but here the rain seemed to come in sideways. She banged on the door one more time. Nothing.

There would only be two places that her dad could be. On the boat or at the pub. Given it was only one in the afternoon, Paige quietly hoped it would be the former. She leaned over the jagged top of the Cornish dry wall and peered down to the harbour below, scanning the litter of boats and looking out for one particular little vessel.

Jacca's boat was seen bobbing up and down outside the fish market, his white hair and his bright yellow waders making him hard to miss. Paige waved him down as she eventually got herself on to the waterfront, negotiating piles of rope and tangled netting as she went.

"Y'alright, m'love? This is a nice surprise!" Jacca shouted, as he steered his boat closer to the quay.

"Is it? Did you not get my message?" Paige shouted back, her face now saturated from the rain. She waited patiently for Jacca to get closer. "Dad, I messaged you saying I'd be arriving today."

"Oh, you know I don't check my mobile," Jacca retorted, heaving himself on to dry land and wrapping his daughter in a warm embrace, enveloping her in the familiar smell of tobacco and fresh fish. "Lovely surprise all the same. How are you?"

"Crap," Paige replied, wrinkling her nose in an awkward grimace. "You?"

"Yeah - crap is pretty spot on. Your mother and I may not have been married anymore but 'twas still hard to wake up one mornin' and find she wozzent living across the harbour from me. Know what I mean?"

"I know, Dad," Paige nodded, rubbing his arm and batting down the perplexed frustration she often felt with her father's affection towards her mother. She did, after all, break his heart.

"Shall we head back to mine for a cuppa? Where've you parked?"

"Church Street," Paige fell into step next to her dad, her hands in her jacket pockets.

"Ooh, bleddy hell. We'll move you later. Will cost you a bleddy fortune paying council rates all weekend. I'm sure Sandra up the road will lend you her driveway while you're here."

Paige did her best to avert her gaze as they walked past Giuseppe's restaurant on the waterfront. That was something she couldn't deal with right now.

Up the steep footpath, just past the ice cream parlour, it led straight back to Jacca's front step - a convenient location in which three generations of fishermen had lived to be in close proximity to the harbour office and fishing market. The house attached to Jacca's looked relatively fresh in its new white paint, a new wooden balustrade leading to the front door which sat adjacent to Jacca's balcony on the second floor. Paige didn't recall this house looking so fresh. Probably a holiday home now.

"'Scuse the mess. Haven't had much time to tidy up this week," Jacca grumbled as they fought their way through the tired front door, just one of many things that desperately needed a lick of paint.

A week? There was no way this level of mess was created in one month, let alone one week. Paige followed her dad through the newly cleared track that he was creating, passed old newspaper mountains, discarded fishing equipment and dirty dishes. This was just the living room; Paige shuddered to think what the rest of the house was like. A sudden pang of guilt hit her square in the chest. There she was, keeping a blissful distance with her life in Bristol, whilst her dear old Jacca slowly buried himself in his very own tip site.

"Dad, have you thought about hiring a cleaner?" Paige tried to sound tactful but knew she'd failed.

"What do I need one of those for? Not that bad, is it?" Jacca stood in the doorway to his kitchen, his hands on his hips as he took a sweeping look around. "Anyway, tea? Coffee?"

"Tea, please," Paige replied, trying to find a place to sit amongst the clutter. She eventually settled for a precarious perch on the arm of the sofa.

"So, where's that boyfriend of yours? Still seeing each other?"

Paige rolled her eyes to the ceiling and sighed with

exasperation. Her parents had only met Matthew a handful of times each in the last two years of Paige and Matthew's relationship, but she could always trust her dad to be two scats behind on her life.

"Matthew's fine, thank you," Paige replied.

"Moved in together yet?"

"If we had, don't you think I would have told you?" Paige pointed out.

"Your mother and I were married by now - you two need to crack on!" Jacca called from the kitchen whilst Paige's eyes rolled up to the ceiling for a second time at the irony of his comment.

Jacca appeared in the doorway with his usual two RNLI mugs, both steaming with the hot beverage, and looked around his living room again.

"Shall we take these teas onto the porch? This place is a shit-hole," Jacca relented, leading the way back through the front door, shifting his fisherman paraphernalia out of the way and clearing space on the little bench for them both to sit on.

The sea was crashing and sloshing ferociously beyond the wall, but the rain had mellowed back down to a gentle mizzle. Popping his tea down, Jacca leaned into the house to grab a blanket from the back of the armchair, then offered it to Paige to drape over her lap. Although her heart was heavy with grief, tears threatening to fall any moment now, Paige found herself closing her eyes and savouring the moment. This used to be one of her favourite things to do, to sit out in the porch with a hot drink - often it was a hot chocolate - and hear all about Jacca's recent fishing trip. Once upon a time he'd have been animated through his storytelling, giving his young daughter the more mythical version of his travels. Now, Paige's moment of luxury lasted for about a second before Jacca's lighter clicked to life, igniting the cigarette in his mouth. Jacca attempted to blow the smoke discreetly away from his daughter, only for the breeze to blow it straight into her face.

"Thought you'd quit smoking," Paige waved the

smoke out of her face with a tut.

"Old habits die hard," Jacca replied sideways through his mouth.

Conversation was strained, as it always was. Seagulls cawed nearby and a symphony of more delicate songbird noises lay in the background.

"So, how's the restaurant?" Jacca asked, taking a swig of his tea.

"Fine thanks, Dad."

"You got the time off OK?"

"Yeah, Matthew covered my shifts until Tuesday evening. I'll probably head home that morning."

Jacca nodded and stared towards the sea, almost with a longing. Paige bit her lip as an awkward silence fell between them again and realised she needed to put more effort in for her old dad.

"The garden's looking lovely, Dad! Caught a glimpse of it back there when you were making tea."

"Thanks, Bird. It's coming along now. Was looking a sorry state other side of Christmas, what with the old decking rotting right through. But Nick gave me a hand a couple of weekends ago to replace the planks. I'm gonna put some decking rope around there at some point - and got to treat the wood. It's getting there. Come and have a look."

Paige smiled fondly as her dad led her through the house and into the back garden, pointing out little projects that he had planned, his awkward demeanour suddenly replaced with that of enthusiasm and passion for his green-fingered hobby.

"Keeps me out of trouble anyway. You know me, Bird. Can't stand being cooped up indoors for too long. Even in this weather."

Paige was starting to understand the state of the house now and a fresh wave of guilt washed over her at her absence in her dad's life. She tried to stuff that unpleasant feeling to the back of her mind as she sipped her tea tenderly. Jacca must have shovelled about three tablespoons of sugar in it despite her declining the offer of sugar at all.

"Nick said about putting a pergola here and boarding this side to block off the east wind. Gets a bit nippy up here. Best do that nearer springtime."

"Who's Nick?" That was the second time Jacca had mentioned this Nick bloke and for some reason the second time made Paige bristle.

"You know - Ted's boy! Stone. Nick Stone!" Jacca offered, impatiently. "Nick, Nick!"

"You can keep saying his name, but penny isn't dropping Dad."

"You went to school with him, I'm sure. Ah no, you went to school with Laura. His sister. Nick is a bit older."

Laura Stone. That name she knew. They had indeed gone to school together. Laura had always been one of the timid ones in their year group, often tucked away in the library somewhere keeping out of the way of the more brash students. She'd always liked Laura in passing conversations during lessons or school trips, but once college started they never crossed paths.

"I remember Laura. Gosh, haven't spoken to her in years."

"Why don't you meet her for a coffee while you're down. She'd love to catch up, I'm sure."

"Yeah...could do," Paige said, non-committal. Matthew had said to use this time to catch up with family and friends, but she only had Jacca in terms of family - and friends? She'd never been great at nurturing friendships. Trying to rekindle old ones didn't sound very appealing given the circumstances.

"Then again, you'll see Laura on Monday. At the fu - " Jacca's voice fizzled out and his face sank glumly, his focus suddenly on rolling a fresh cigarette.

Another painful silence sat loudly between them. Paige turned her gaze awkwardly back out to sea, squinting into the sun that was attempting to break through the clouds.

"Everything sorted for Monday?" Paige broke the

silence.

"Think so. The staff at your mother's restaurant are sorting the food. Ted's helped me with the arrangements with the funeral director because, as you know, he lost Fiona a few years ago."

Paige didn't know this, but she kept quiet and nodded along all the same, her guilt growing by the minute as she realised she'd contributed to absolutely nothing towards her mum's funeral.

"What about flowers?" Paige added, her heart sinking as she realised she hadn't ordered her own arrangement. She'd been too busy masking her grief with double shifts at work. She was feeling more selfish and wretched by the minute.

"Oh, Bev is doing it. You know, Bev's Flowers in St Austell?"

No? But again Paige nodded, pretending she knew all these people that her dad seemed well acquainted with.

"I'm sure she'll add an arrangement to the order if you wan' to?"

Paige nodded and made a mental note to call Bev when she had a quiet moment. She was suddenly feeling a heavy sensation of estrangement. The fact that Jacca hadn't asked if she wanted to contribute to the flowers, or any part of the funeral for that matter, made Paige feel both put out and guilty. She'd clearly detached herself from everything in this little village more than she'd thought. That had been her plan all along, so why did it hurt so much to feel like the outsider looking in on Jacca's little life in Mevagissey?

"How's it going?"

"Awful," Paige replied curtly down the phone to Matthew as her wellies clopped against the wet tarmac on her way down to the harbour. Jacca had taken himself to the social club for a few drinks with his usual lot and Paige already needed fresh air from the stifling mess that was her dad's house. "Dad's in total denial of the pigsty he's living in. I just had to wrestle my way up the stairs to the third floor where my old bedroom is because it was blocked off from just utter crap. How's the restaurant?"

"Still here," Matthew joked. "Hasn't changed much since yesterday. Stop worrying about the restaurant and just take the time to relax."

"I'm here for my mum's bloody funeral, Matthew. Not for a seaside break."

"I'm just saying," Matthew huffed. "You're usually there for Christmas and birthdays, your visits are fleeting and you barely give yourself time to catch up with people. This weekend is going to be hard on you, Paige. Be kind to yourself. Get the ice-cream and the flake!"

Paige thawed and smiled at this last bit. "There's an ice-cream parlour here on the harbour, as a matter of fact. Aw man - they do hot waffles."

"That sounds amazing! Even better. Sample some flavours for me and tell me the best one on Monday when I get down to you."

"Will do," Paige smiled into the phone, the conversation with her boyfriend calming her tempered disposition.

"Best crack on. Busy night tonight. See you on Monday, Babe."

The phone call terminated, Paige pushed her phone into the back pocket of her jeans and decided to do as she was told for once, walking into the ice-cream parlour for her waffle sundae.

Within ten minutes she was walking back out into the dull, damp air, with an ice-cream and waffle sundae the size of her face. Her eyes popping, she gingerly dug into it with the complimentary wooden spoon, a little embarrassed at her gluttony. She'd have to jog off the calories later on her evening run.

"Paige? Paige Yelland!"

As Paige was heading for the harbour wall, a woman with shoulder-length blonde hair, and a little girl in tow, rushed towards her, waving her down. It wasn't until the woman was much closer that it twigged to Paige who she

26

was.

"Oh, hi Laura! Sorry, I didn't recognise you for a second."

Laura was practically a shadow of the person Paige remembered back in their school years. She had always carried more puppy fat in their youth, but this Laura standing before Paige had lost more than just puppy fat, looking almost gaunt in the face - a shadow of a person she once knew.

"How are you? You're looking fantastic," Laura remarked, a wistful tone about her. "You always did have gloriously tanned skin, even this time of year."

It was true. Paige had inherited her mother's natural olive skin, which turned a golden brown in the summertime, along with the family's signature black hair, hers making it all the way past her ribs.

"Thank you," Paige replied, smiling. "You're looking well."

"Oh, don't be polite. I look like crap. But single-parenting and night-shifts will do that to you."

Paige noted Laura's uniform.

"You're a nurse?"

"Yes. On my way to work now actually. Just dropping madam here to her uncle."

Paige smiled down at Laura's daughter.

"Hello. What's your name?"

"Lilly," the little girl replied, articulate but shy.

"And how old are you, Lilly?"

"I'm seven. I'll be eight soon. Your ice-cream is melting."

Lilly giggled as Paige attempted to lick up the sticky mess that had dripped down all over her hand, the hot waffle melting everything before she had a chance.

"Sorry, we'll let you get down to business with your dessert. We must catch up while you're down. Oh shit!"

Paige exchanged bewildered looks at Lilly, who covered her ears from her mother's expletives.

"There's me blathering on like an idiot! Your mum

was such a lovely person. I'm so sorry for your loss."

Laura grabbed Paige for a hug, Paige desperately trying to keep her melting mess of a dessert away from Laura's uniform.

"Of course, you won't want to meet for cheery coffees and stuff. You'll want to spend some time with Jacca and prepare for Monday."

Paige felt a little sorry for Laura as she stumbled through her words and was reminded of their old school days where Laura had always been eager to please anybody and everybody. Paige still found it frustratingly endearing, even now. "No, I'd love to meet for a coffee. It will keep me busy and out of Dad's way."

Laura's tired face lit up and Paige almost saw a glimpse of the rosy Laura she once knew very well. "Really? That would be lovely! Why don't we meet at Giuseppe's tomorrow morning for breakfast?"

Paige's eyes darted nervously over to the restaurant in question across the harbour, her heart pounding against her chest at the very thought.

"Is there a coffee shop we could meet in?" Paige suggested.

"Not for the time I was thinking."

Laura must have seen the flash of darkness cross over Paige's face at the suggestion of meeting in her mum's restaurant and she regarded her with concern.

"That's alright," Paige shrugged, a feeble attempt at being coy. "But won't you have just finished your night shift? And is the restaurant even open for breakfast?"

"I will have, but my brother always gives us a decent breakfast before I head off to bed and before Lilly goes to school. He's the head chef there, hence we get early access. Are you OK with early mornings?"

"More than fine."

Early mornings she could handle; stepping foot in Giuseppe's restaurant again after all those years, not so much.

"Great. We'll see you tomorrow at seven. Good to

see you! Come on Lilly."

The three of them exchanged goodbyes and Paige finally got stuck into her dessert which was now more of a soggy puddle of stickiness. As she walked towards the harbour, Paige tried not to think about her new plans for tomorrow morning. It would be really good to catch up with Laura after all this time, but the chosen location was going to throw up more emotions than Paige knew what to do with. She glanced across at the lighthouse on the outer harbour wall as she settled herself against the black railings, giving the weekend ahead of her careful consideration. With a new sense of determination, she decided that the weekend was pretty rubbish by average standard anyway. She may as well kick up some old dust while she was here and enjoy a well overdue coffee with an old friend. With that decided, she dived into her cold, soggy dessert with gusto and drank in the scenery.

Chapter Three

The flowers now ordered with Bev, Paige had spent the rest of the afternoon clearing the stairs that led to her old room on the third floor. After almost breaking her neck twice, she'd decided enough was enough and had grabbed some bin liners from under the kitchen sink. She'd tutted and huffed over her dad's sloppiness but quietly kicked herself for not seeing this issue sooner. She'd last been down to visit over Christmastime but hadn't actually gone into Jacca's house. In fact, Matthew had been frustratingly accurate with his comment - her visits were almost always fleeting.

When Jacca had returned home from the social club, he'd shuffled into the kitchen and offered them both beans on toast for dinner. She'd accepted and ate the food with no quarrels, but after checking the contents of his cupboard she'd realised this was probably on the menu most nights. She'd made a mental note after that to head to the supermarket the next morning to fill his cupboards up and make him a decent meal. Perhaps she would head there after meeting Laura.

Now, with Jacca fast asleep on his armchair in front of the TV and Paige feeling irritable at best from the dusty chore of clearing the stairs and giving her old room a bit of a spring clean, she felt the usual daily pull to don the trainers and pound the pavements.

It was pitch black outside and taking the coastal path was out of the question, so for now Paige would have to make do with lapping the crescent shaped route along the quay, from one side to the other. Spinning around at the lighthouse and starting her second lap, she started to feel herself again as she fell into her natural rhythm. She breathed in deeply through her nose and exhaled with mild contentment through her mouth, a plume of hot mist hitting the biting cold air, her muscles unleashing lactic acid. To Paige, running was like a drug and it instantly calmed her.

The streetlights paved the way for her, the village sleeping in a heavy silence despite it only being 8pm. The sound of her trainers on tarmac echoed across the harbour and soon she was so engrossed in her to-ing and fro-ing that she could have been the only human being left on earth. She was so used to having to share her running route back in Bristol, that this felt rather luxurious, even if every now and again the sea threatened to nip at her legs with the occasional drenching.

By the time she was nearing a suitable number of laps to constitute as miles, Paige felt her mood lighten, her limbs deliciously tired from the exertion. Giving the white lighthouse a gratifying pat, she was just considering whether she could fit in a morning run before meeting Laura tomorrow when a large black Labrador came bounding towards her, all limbs and chops, the biggest grin on its face. A man was bringing up the rear, roaring the dog's name into the salty air.

"Bear! You stupid bloody dog! Get back here now!"

Realising the situation, Paige made herself bigger with her arms and attempted to block the dog's path, only to find herself knocked flat on her back with thirty-five kilos of black mass trampling her down, her feet slipping on the wet ground. She gripped the dog's collar, wincing as it dragged her cold, bare legs against the cobble. Bear was unbelievably strong and Paige was only too glad when the man finally caught up and relieved her from his pull.

"Christ sake, Bear! You big oaf! I'm so sorry." The man buckled Bear safely on to his lead, freeing Paige's hands to wipe the excess mud from her jacket and assess the damage on her legs, which was hard to do when they were caked with dirt. "He is *not* my dog. Elderly lady, two doors down from me. Why she got a sprightly Labrador of all breeds, I'll never figure out. Just wanted to make it very clear that I am not responsible for his behaviour. Are you alright?"

"Yes, I'm fine," Paige chuckled as she brushed herself down. She looked up and her laugh almost morphed into a weird sort of squeak as she took a good look at the man. His piercing grey eyes met hers and she suddenly felt completely foolish in a heap on the floor, covered in dog hair, dirt and slobber. She clambered up, her cheeks blazing as she struggled to find a place to avert her gaze. "Right, well. Glad you got your sister's dog back."

Paige started walking away, trying not to let a slight limp in her left step show. She must have slightly twisted her ankle on her way down and now that she had stopped running, she felt cold to the bone in her stupid running shorts. How humiliating.

"Hang on, you're limping. Let me walk you back," the man offered his arm, his expression a mix of guilt and mortification. "It's the least I can do."

Paige hesitated at first, then gave in to the offer. Her ankle really was starting to hurt. She slipped her arm through his and immediately blushed at the hardness of his muscles. With a cheeky side glance, she noted that he must be well over six foot given that he was towering over her own five-foot-eleven stature.

"Are you training?"

"Sorry?"

"The running. Are you training for a marathon? You must be freezing in those shorts."

"Oh. No," Paige replied, stupidly. The pain was fogging her response. "No, I just like running."

"Fair enough. Never saw the appeal, personally."

Paige felt the man's eyes appraising her. She then realised that she was walking on a baron harbour, in the dark, by the arm of a strange man. She didn't even know his name.

"Are you down on holiday? I don't recognise you."

"What, do you usually recognise every resident of Mevagissey?" Paige arched an eyebrow.

The man chuckled. "It's a small village. People who

don't live here usually stick out." Paige noticed the second glance at her shorts.

"You implying I'm an emit?"

Nick's eyebrows wiggled slightly in response.

"Oh, well your radar is all out then, because I grew up here. I'm Cornish."

Nick thought about this for a moment before responding. "How long you been over the Tamar?"

"Ten years," Paige replied, warily.

"Ah... well, I'm sorry to say you've been over the border for too long."

Paige felt the unfamiliar sensation of a smile creeping on to her dry, chapped lips, her eyes twinkling in amusement.

"What a shame. Thankfully, I won't be here long. I'm just down... visiting family." She wasn't about to go into detail about her mother's death and the fast-approaching funeral. The last thing she needed was stranger pity. Paige silently and vaguely gestured towards the direction of Jacca's house. As they passed her mother's restaurant, which was obviously closed this evening, a wave of nausea washed over Paige from the growing pain on her ankle.

"Sorry, can I just stop for a moment?" Paige groaned, sitting on one of the nearby benches.

"I'm going to touch your ankle," the man announced. "If that's okay."

A smile crept on Paige's face involuntarily and she nodded her consent. This was turning out to be a very strange evening, she thought to herself, as the man lifted her bad ankle up and rested her foot on to his knee. Bear was all out of steam from his excitement and was sitting patiently, his eyes half-closed in lazy contentment and his tongue lolling out to one side. Paige tried not to gasp as she felt the man's fingers prod gently around the ankle. His touch was tender and intimate, and she suddenly found herself fascinated with a coil of old rope to the left of her.

"I'm Nick, by the way."

"Oh. Hi, Nick." She couldn't have been more

wooden in her response.

Moments later, she gave in to temptation and took a better look at him. His shaved short hair was dark and even in the poor light of a nearby streetlamp she could see that he sported a weathered tan, showing the time he spent outdoors. Long, rugged stubble hugged his chiselled jawline and wide shoulders bulged underneath his jacket.

"I doubt it's broken. You've probably pulled a tendon. Is it far to where you're staying? I can always get my car."

"It's just up there. On Old Road."

"Great, that's where I live. Best crack on - I've left my niece fast asleep in bed to catch this bloody dog. Up you come."

Without much say in the matter, Paige was hoisted up and supported into a standing position, Nick's arm clasped firmly around her waist. This bloke didn't waste much time with appropriate introductions.

"Are you always this hands-on with visitors?" Paige huffed indignantly, concentrating hard on not letting the closeness of his hard body affect her as they ascended the steep walkway up to the houses.

"Only the good-looking ones. Oh, that came out wrong. Now I sound like the village pervert."

Paige snorted a laugh and wriggled out of his supporting arm, pointing to Jacca's house. "This is me."

The boyish grin playing on Nick's face faltered and he looked up at the house, his brow creased in the middle in confusion. "You're staying here?"

"Yeah. This is my dad's house," Paige replied, hobbling up the step to the front door whilst fumbling in her pocket for the spare key.

"Oh, of course. You're Jacca's daughter."

He wasn't smiling anymore, and Paige felt his warmth evaporate, even from where she was standing.

"Yep," Paige said awkwardly. "So, nice to meet you. Thanks for walking me back."

"No problem. Put some ice on that ankle," Nick

34

added, the smile still not returning. What was his problem?

Paige crossed the threshold, into the warmth of her dad's cottage and didn't dare look out to see if Nick was still there, in case his death stares officially turned her into a block of ice.

Paige would have dwelled on Nick's sudden change in tune further, but after some pain killers and a warm bath, it didn't take long until she was fast asleep from tonight's escapades.

The next morning, Paige tested out the strength of her ankle, gingerly placing weight on to it to see if she could walk rather than limp. The swelling had gone down considerably since last night and a long soak in the bath had helped to sooth any extra aches and pains from the fall. Even if it had resulted in Jacca moaning about her using up all the hot water.

"Get a new boiler system then," she'd retorted back. "You don't have to live in the stone age."

At 7am on the dot, Paige arrived outside Giuseppe's, her ankle now throbbing again from the gentle hobble down the slope to the harbour. She chewed on her lip and tapped her hand against her crossed arm in agitation as she glared at the red brick arched windows and terracotta orange entrance, a fake olive tree sitting out of place on the dark, cobbled street. This place had always had the ability to put her in a bad mood, like a bear with a sore head. This was the place responsible for her dad's heartbreak and her parents' resulting separation, and she hated everything about it. Even if - at this very moment - it looked frustratingly inviting, the warm Mediterranean colours inside glowing in contrast to the achromic streets on the outside, a thick fog sitting in place and making visibility poor for the fishermen now preparing their vessels for the morning trawl.

She'd be here on Monday for the wake anyway, so she may as well get on with it. She caught a glimpse of Laura inside, waving her in frantically, so Paige slapped on a cheery expression and pulled the handle, letting herself in.

35

Inside, the interior was just the same as it always had been. Red and white chequered tablecloths and bamboo dining chairs included. In fact, the decor hadn't changed one bit in the last ten years, that she could remember. The Venetian carnival masquerade masks still looked down at her from their very same spot on the walls around the restaurant and - yep! - still gave her the creeps.

On one of the round tables nearest the window, Laura and her daughter Lilly sat ready for some breakfast. Lilly was all ready for school in her uniform and Laura was cradling a coffee, looking drained but pleased to see Paige.

"I didn't realise we'd be the only ones here," Paige whispered, like they were trespassing, as she eased herself on to a chair right next to the window, shaking her wet coat from her shoulders. She smiled warmly at Lilly, who was reading a school library book. "Morning Lilly."

Lilly smiled over the top of her book, returning immediately to her written words.

Laura rolled her eyes at her daughter, stirring an extra sugar into her coffee. "It doesn't open until lunch time, but Nick had Lilly last night and starts work at six. So it just makes sense to meet him here. It's become a bit of a tradition, hasn't it Lilly-Pops?"

"Nick?"

"Yes, my brother. He's the head chef here." Laura was frowning over her coffee. "I would have thought you've already met. Nick has worked here for years."

Paige didn't want to admit the reason why she didn't know very much at all about her mum's restaurant, so opted for a simple shrug whilst pondering over the possible coincidence of there being two Nicks in the vicinity.

"So, what do you do for a living now Paige?"

"I'm a chef," Paige replied, raising an eyebrow wryly. "Sous-chef in Bristol."

To Paige's surprise, Laura threw her head back with laughter. "That's hilarious!"

"Why?" Paige smarted. What was so hilarious about her being a sous-chef?

"Oh no, not like that!" Laura had the good grace to look bashful. "That's awesome! No, I just think it's funny that Nick doesn't realise yet that he's cooking breakfast for a professional chef. Ah, speak of the devil. Nick, this is Paige. She's a professional chef from Bristol."

"So I hear," Nick humoured, rubbing his hands in a tea-towel and flinging it over his shoulder. "How's the ankle?"

And there he was. All the warmth and friendliness that Paige had received from Nick had evaporated the moment he'd found out she was Jacca's daughter. Today was no exception, and he stood by their table, legs wide and arms folded, his chef whites straining under the tension of his muscles. Not that Paige had noticed.

"The ankle is fine thanks. How's Bear?" Paige leaned back, a coy smile playing in the corner of her mouth. Nick's eyes flashed for just a moment before he recovered himself.

"Bear's fine. Edith's stupid dog escaped last night and trampled Paige over by the lighthouse," Nick explained to his sister, who was now looking utterly confused.

"Oh god. That dog is such a lummox. Honestly, why did she get a Labrador?"

Paige shrugged and waved off the situation whilst Nick burned a hole in the side of her head from the death stares he was currently shooting her way.

"Right, what are we having for breakfast?" Nick clapped his hands loudly. "Lilly? Are you with us?"

Lilly looked up from her reading book, pretending to seem annoyed. She was a very striking girl of her age, with long, sleek blond hair and glass-grey eyes, like Nick's. Paige wondered what features Lilly had inherited from her father - wherever he was - because it was clear she had inherited most of Laura and Nick's defined family characteristics.

"Pancakes? Bacon buttie? Toast? Give me a sign!" Nick grabbed his niece's shoulders and shook them playfully, causing her to erupt in a fit of giggles.

"Pancakes, please."

"Pancakes for the princess! Laura? The usual?"

Laura nodded, yawning and stretching over her coffee.

"And for you?" Nick turned to Paige. "Nothing posh, I'm afraid."

"Thought you were the head chef," Paige retorted, immediately regretting it. She'd been going for a bit of light banter, but it hadn't come out that way at all and now Nick was glaring at her, his jaw rigid.

"I am. And a very good one, thank you. But breakfast isn't actually on the menu here and I don't have time to whip up something fancy. I have lunch reservations to prepare for."

Well, that told her.

"Yes - sorry. I'll have some pancakes with Lilly, if that's OK."

Nick turned on his heel and stormed into the kitchen, leaving Paige feeling suitably bashful for her rudeness.

"Sorry. I didn't mean to upset him," Paige turned to Laura.

"Oh, don't worry. He's been a bit out of sorts since Elaine died. Took her death really bad, actually."

Paige was surprised and equally irritated. Funnily enough, she wasn't taking her mum's death too well either. Where was her sympathy? Weren't people supposed to be ultra-nice to those whose mother just died? Without really knowing her, this Nick had made some wild presumptions of her and, whatever those were, he was punishing her for it. While she sat there steaming a little over the injustice of the treatment received, Laura had got up and poured Paige a coffee, unaware of the little battle going on in her mind.

"Sorry, it's filter coffee. So tell me about your restaurant in Bristol."

Within twenty-minutes, Nick had placed a stack of fresh, fluffy pancakes in front of Paige and Lilly, glistening in drizzled maple syrup and scattered with a selection of berries and sliced banana. Laura's weary eyes widened with pleasure as her brother placed a door-wedge sized bacon sandwich in front of her, his large hand squeezing her shoulder to jolt her awake. Paige watched his retreating back as he returned to the kitchen, regarding him with interest.

She speared the bottom layer of pancakes with her fork and ran a knife through. They were spongy and perfectly moist with syrup. She closed her eyes euphorically as the sweetness of the maple syrup and the tang of a blueberry hit her taste buds. It was the best pancake she had ever tasted.

Paige and Laura nattered between mouthfuls of their breakfast, catching up on old times and filling in the gaps from when they'd last seen each other. Paige listened with sympathy as Laura talked her way diplomatically around the details of her failed marriage. It was clear that she was being careful about what she said of Lilly's father in front of her and Paige didn't probe further with any questions.

"So that's why Nick has Lilly a few nights a week. Being a nurse, I can't really pick and choose my shift patterns. And unfortunately Scott has chosen to be - shall we say - a very absent father."

Laura stroked her daughter's hair, Lilly suddenly extra invested in her milkshake and consuming it in large gulps. Paige was quietly appalled for Laura, both impressed and frustrated with her cool attitude towards the bloke's pathetic contribution as a parent. She wasn't naive to the reality that not all marriages were built to last. In fact, she knew all too well what could happen to a family when a marriage broke apart, having first-hand experience in the matter when her parent's relationship did just that. But no matter what the quarrels between parents, you showed up for your children - right?

"Oh! Look at the time! I said I'd drop Lilly to my dad's about now. And I need to head to bed." Despite her fatigue, Laura bounced into action, clearing the table and taking dirty dishes into the kitchen. As she returned, she shot Paige an apologetic look. "So sorry to cut this short, Paige. Really lovely having this catch up."

"It was lovely," Paige replied with earnest, feeling a little deflated that it was over so quickly.

"I suppose I'll see you again tomorrow," Laura winced, smiling with sympathy as she slipped her arm into her jacket.

"Yes," Paige sighed. "Yes, see you then."

As soon as Laura and Lilly had disappeared from view, Paige was once again left alone with her thoughts and a very heavy heart. At this point, she could curse Matthew for his ridiculous suggestion that a weekend in her old village would be a welcome distraction. Work would have been the welcome distraction - keeping her busy and without time to even indulge in any mournful thoughts. But here she was, idle and lonelier than ever. She had her mum's previous life on show here, practically shoved in her face as a reminder of how disjointed their relationship had become in the end. A cruel reminder that anything they might have wanted to resolve now would never be able to happen.

She was just about to leave the restaurant, suddenly feeling that she had spent enough time there for one day, when her phone came to life in her coat pocket. A quick glance at the screen told her it was Matthew. A wave of relief came over her at being able to connect with her life back in Bristol for just a moment.

"Hey," Paige cooed down the phone, smiling at the thought of hearing his voice despite wanting to curse him a few moments before.

"Babe, have you got a moment to talk?" Matthew's voice rang through with a tone of apprehension.

"Yeah," Paige checked her surroundings, confirming that she was alone and returned her attention to the call. "What's up?"

Matthew sounded wretched, huffing and puffing like he did when something was bothering him. Paige could imagine him running his hands through his thick, dark curls, pacing the kitchen in full Gordon Ramsay style. Perhaps it was one of the kitchen porters failing to turn up for a shift again. What if it was a food critic choosing to visit the restaurant tomorrow of all days?

"Paige, I don't know how to tell you this. Oh god, you're going to hate me."

Paige kept silent, worrying her bottom lip in anticipation of what he had to say. The pregnant pause continued and she was about ready to shout down the phone to him to spit it out.

"Paige, I can't make it down to Cornwall tomorrow. I'm sorry."

Her heart hammered against her chest and immediate anger rose like bile in her throat. Her next words were quiet.

"What do you mean you can't make it?"

Paige heard Matthew swear and the sound of a saucepan crashing into a sink told her he was taking his frustration out on the restaurant kitchen, like he often did.

"Look, something has come up. Something important, and I need to be there by 2pm tomorrow."

"You're being very cryptic here. Need to be where?"

Another exasperated puff down the phone.

"I can't say too much now. I don't want to jinx anything, but I had to tell you that I wouldn't be there tomorrow."

Another agonising pause.

"Look, I know it's not a lot to go by-"

"It's *nothing* to go by, Matthew," Paige hissed down the phone. "You're abandoning me on the day of my mum's funeral and you won't even tell me why!"

"I know. I'm sorry. I really wish I could explain everything. I will though. I promise."

Paige felt four little walls form an emotional barrier around her, something she always did when someone let her down. She chewed on her lip now, a bitter grimace set on her face.

"Can't wait," Paige replied, deadpan.

"Please Paige. Don't be like that. I'm sorry."

41

"Yep."

With that, Paige thumped the red button on her screen and stuffed the phone into her jeans pocket, willing the tears in her eyes to retreat back from where they came. After a few moments of cleansing expletives muttered under her breath, she turned to leave once more, when a framed photograph caught her attention above the bar. Edging closer, Paige soon recognised the faces looking back at her and regretted the moment of curiosity almost immediately. The small huddle of kitchen and waiting staff smiled widely, creases in their eyes suggesting they had just finished laughing at something together. A younger version of Nick smiled at her with ease, his hair longer and his face clean shaven, a sheer contrast to the shaved head and wild beard that he wore these days.

Paige felt her lungs restrict and her heart squeeze painfully in her chest as her eyes locked on to her mother's. Wedged in tightly under the large, tanned arms of her partner Giuseppe, and surrounded by her beloved restaurant staff, Elaine looked radiant with happiness. And neither Jacca nor Paige were there to spoil that bubble. Paige's fists tightened and she chewed her lip, her mouth contorted into a hard line.

Sadness engulfed Paige at that moment and her fists fell limp at her sides. She would never be able to repair the years of damage in their relationship. This was it. They'd missed their window. For a moment Paige forgot herself and succumbed to the tears that had threatened to fall for Matthew, clutching the counter to steady her balance. A few minutes later, Paige was recovering herself and about to skulk out of the door when a large silhouette in the doorway to the kitchen made her jump. In her grieving state, she had almost forgotten that she wasn't alone, and Nick's eyes were now burning a hole in the back of her head as she hastily grabbed her stuff and bolted out of the restaurant door.

Chapter Four

On the day of Elaine's funeral, the weather was suitably avoiding clichès, with clear, blue skies, the sun shining down on the sea of black descending upon the church, breaths puffing like clouds into the frosty air. Paige and Jacca had driven in silence in the funeral procession which, led by the hearse carrying her mother, had taken them through the streets of Mevagissey, shopkeepers and residents paying their respects as they watched the convoy make its way to the Parish church. It seemed that the whole of Mevagissey had been on their doorstep this morning, and yet the church yard was packed with more mourners. Paige had always known how loved her mother had been but seeing the sheer volume of people waiting for them at the church had moved her beyond words.

By the time they had arrived back at the restaurant for the wake, everything from the eulogy to the words of conciliation was a hazy blur. Initially, Paige had planted herself by Jacca's side, naively thinking she was there to pick up the broken pieces, however it didn't take long for her to realise that her presence there was pretty much redundant. Jacca soon drifted off to have a few drinks with his fishermen buddies, a half-arsed introduction made between his friends and his daughter before setting to work with his pint, leaving Paige standing awkwardly on the side-lines. She listened to stories being told of Elaine's kindness and her contribution to the Mevagissey community, painfully aware that none of these stories crossed over with any part of Paige's life. They really were two very separate entities.

"Thought you might need some company," Laura squeezed in next to her, wrapping her in a quick hug, which Paige returned gratefully. "How are you feeling?"

"Like the new kid at school with no friends," Paige

joked, her smile not quite reaching her eyes. "There was me thinking I'd be looking after Dad all day and he's buggered off to find the bar with his mates."

"Oh, well Nick's just brought out the Trengrouse cider, so no doubt they've all started that already," Laura tutted, leaning against the counter. "But honestly, how are you? You're handling all of this very well."

"Am I?" Paige asked, unconvinced. She rubbed her eyes, wearily. She hadn't bothered to wear mascara today. The pre-empting of tears being shed today made the whole idea of covering her eyelashes with a black paste completely ludicrous, so she'd decided natural and haggard looking was the most comfortable option for the day.

"Sorry if this is a sore subject but," Laura dropped her voice to a whisper, "where's your boyfriend? Didn't you say that he was coming today."

"Mm-hmm," Paige replied, her mouth set in a grim line. "He had other commitments...apparently."

"Dick," Laura breathed over her cup of tea. This made Paige smile and she felt an instant warmth towards Laura. "Men are such dicks. Oh, apart from you - you're alright."

Paige turned to see who Laura had directed this last remark to.

"What's this?" Nick appeared from his usual hiding place, throwing his signature tea-towel over his shoulder, his black tie slightly loosened on his shirt collar.

"Paige's boyfriend made other plans today. Of all days! Can you believe that?"

"Jesus." Nick's eyebrows shot up as he crossed those big arms. "That's crap."

"Laura! Do you mind?" Paige cried, gaping at her friend incredulously, before getting distracted by the slightest glimpse of ink poking from under Nick's sleeve.

Laura looked confused for a moment. "Oh, don't worry about Nick. I tell him everything."

"I'll remember that," Paige said, as she shook her head in mild amusement.

44

The three of them stood by the counter for a moment, watching as the subdued crowd hitched it up a notch and started turning more into a celebration of Elaine's life, thanks to the arrival of alcohol.

"'Ere - anybody hear about the new vessel joining the fleet?" One of Jacca's friends, previously introduced as Bill, announced to the whole room.

"Eh? You sure, Bill?" Another old fisherman piped up in the corner.

Bill grunted in confirmation. "Joining us next week apparently. Another otter trawler."

"Local?" Jacca asked, his glasses slightly askew on his nose.

Bill shrugged, and there was an uneasy murmur amongst the old fishermen.

"Just as long as he don't try to pick no bleddy scallops," another cried, spilling his cider. "That's my turf."

Laura and Nick tutted in unison, confusing Paige for one moment before Laura muttered, "Oh Dad."

"Shouldn't they be pleased about having another fisherman on board?" Paige asked Nick and Laura quietly.

"It's a bit first come first served out there at the moment," Nick explained. "Protecting the stock has become a bit of a priority, so they might be worried about someone new coming in and putting added pressure to the bay. That, and they're a territorial bunch."

Paige hadn't thought of that. She knew stock was much more of an issue now than it had been twenty to thirty years ago, going by what her father often told her, but she'd also got the impression from the same man that they needed more fishermen out there to protect the industry and the working harbour.

"Oh, it's three o'clock," Laura groaned. "I need to fetch Lilly from school. Nick, look after Paige will you?"

"It's OK. I don't need looking after," Paige reasoned, after Laura darted out of the front door. "I'm sure you have enough to do today."

She was being polite, though secretly pleased that

45

she'd engaged Nick in a fairly civil conversation after yesterday's disaster.

Nick appraised Paige for a moment, looking down at her with those piercing grey eyes, the breath catching in her throat as she felt herself falling into the depths of them. Finally, breaking her out of her strange trance, he shrugged. "Fair enough."

And with that, Nick strode back into the depths of the kitchen out back, leaving Paige to flounder once again in loneliness on the edge of a once familiar crowd.

For a small-framed man, Jacca was surprisingly heavy and it took all of Paige's strength to heave him up on to her hip, his floppy arm draped around her neck. It was now six o'clock and Jacca had wasted no time in finding the bottom of the Trengrouse cider keg. Thank god the restaurant was closed to the public today, Paige thought to herself. She'd endured a few public embarrassments from her dad's over-drinking in the past and didn't fancy repeating it today of all days.

"Dad, help me out here will you?" Paige puffed, straining under the weight of her paralytic father as he started to slide down her side like a floppy salmon. "For God's sake!"

"Here, let me help you," Nick came out of nowhere, grabbing Jacca's other side and hoisting him back up to a more helpful position.

Paige said nothing, quietly grateful that Nick was there before Jacca ended up a heaped mess on the restaurant floor. Between them they managed to get him up the walkway to Old Road and through Jacca's front door. The sofa would have to do; both Nick and Paige were sweating from the excursion of carrying Jacca's dead weight between them.

Jacca groaned as his head landed with a plop on the cushion, his body convulsing from the sudden movement.

"Sorry, this is a bit embarrassing," Paige said to Nick as she draped a blanket over her father.

46

"No it's not. We're used to this nonsense, aren't we Jacca?" Nick raised his voice playfully in Jacca's direction. "Best have a bucket or something on hand."

Paige watched Nick's retreating back in utter confusion as he took himself off into Nick's kitchen to retrieve the washing-up bowl and an old towel from under the sink. After propping them in place on the floor next to Jacca, he loosened his tie enough to slip it over his head and removed the navy pin-striped apron he was wearing around his middle.

"Right. Coffee? Tea?"

"Oh. No, I'm fine thank you. I think I might head up and have a shower now. Wash the day away, so to speak."

"Suit yourself."

Nick's continued blunt attitude made Paige feel like a scolded child. She was relieved to hear the front door slam shut, announcing Nick's departure as she made her way up to the second floor for her shower. With Nick gone and Jacca out for the count, she could have the quiet night in she so craved after a day like today.

Feeling marginally better for getting out of her restrictive funeral-wear and having a warm shower, Paige tip-toed downstairs in her towel not long later, rubbing her hair dry with another, to check on her father. The last thing she had expected to see was Nick making himself at home, cooking something that smelled absolutely delicious in the kitchen.

"Shit," Paige breathed, checking the security of her towel as Nick's eyes clapped on to her damp body, a twitch of a smile pulling up on the side of his mouth. "I thought you left."

"I did. To lock up the restaurant. Need to make sure Jacca eats something," Nick's eyes finally stopped wandering and he met her gaze. "You look like you could do with something as well. I didn't see you touch the food at the wake. Croque monsieur alright with you?"

Paige nodded a reply. "I'll just... put some clothes on."

47

Suddenly unsure as to what to wear and feeling somewhat irritated that her chances for a quiet evening had slipped through the net yet again, Paige finally settled with her grey running leggings and a navy cable knit sweater, her long black hair beyond help but mascara firmly in place to avoid the raddled look she'd settled on before now.

Back downstairs, Nick was encouraging Jacca into a sitting position and forcing a glass of water into his hands.

"Jacca mate, have a sip of this."

There went Paige's theory that Nick's behaviour the other day was due to his hang-up with her father. He seemed quite at home here and his patience towards Jacca's current condition suggested otherwise. In fact, if she didn't know any better, she might even believe that Nick cared for her father in some way. He looked up at Paige and nodded towards the kitchen.

"Your dinner is being kept warm in the Rayburn."

"Thank you."

"Right Jacca, do you reckon you can manage a bit of your favourite?"

Jacca grunted in response.

"Come on you old fart. You need to eat something."

Nick slipped past Paige in the doorway as she was making her way to the dinner table with her meal, his firm chest brushing against her back and sending electrical currents to somewhere in her navel. As Paige took a delicious bite of her croque monsieur, Nick's phone trilled in the kitchen.

"Hi Dad… Yeah, he's fine… Yeah, too much to drink… No, I've locked up for now. I'll sort it out later… She is."

Paige glanced up just as Nick looked over his shoulder in her direction.

"I doubt it," Nick muttered down the phone, causing Paige to prickle slightly. What were they saying about her?

Nick brought the conversation to an end and took Jacca's dinner to him, waking him up for the second time.

"This is delicious. Thank you," Paige said, trying to fill a silence.

"S'alright. I'm going to make sure Jacca eats this, then I need to go back and clear up."

"Don't you have porters for that?"

Nick turned in his seat, giving Paige an incredulous stare. "It's a small brigade, but I do. I gave them all a day off seeing as I had to shut the restaurant off to the public today. Most of them were attending the funeral anyway, being very close to Elaine and all."

He was certainly good at making Paige feel about an inch tall.

"You know you're speaking to Elaine's daughter, don't you?" Paige blurted out, dropping her grilled sandwich on to the plate.

"You wouldn't think so," Nick muttered.

"Excuse me?"

Nick didn't respond, laying Jacca back down on the sofa.

"I don't think Jacca's ready to eat yet. I'll put his food back in the Rayburn. When he stirs, give him a sip of water and get him to take small bites. Not too much else he'll be sick."

"Thank you," Paige snapped, her heart thudding against her chest and her hands shaking in fury. "I'm sure I'm capable of looking after my own father."

"Capable, maybe. Willing?" Nick shrugged and left before Paige could retort back.

Paige seethed for the rest of the evening. Jacca finally stirred around 9pm, so she decided to dump Nick's cold croque monsieur in the bin and make him buck rarebit instead. Nick could shove his stupid French grilled sandwich somewhere painful.

After tentatively eating his rarebit and sipping his way through his glass of water, Jacca had crawled up to bed. Paige was disappointed but not surprised by this end to a horrible day. A large part of her knew that there was no way Jacca would be compos mentis past 6pm, but the smaller part of her had hoped she could rely on the comforting company of her father on the evening of her mother's funeral. As she settled herself under the blanket on the sofa, feeling utterly miserable as she attempted to find a decent channel on Jacca's archaic TV, she wished more than ever that she was back at Garlands, in the full bustle of a busy shift and with absolutely no time to brood. A quick check of her phone confirmed to her that Matthew had also not bothered to message since his flaky 'hope today goes well' text this morning.

Hope today goes well - What kind of message was that? Yes, my mother's funeral went swimmingly thank you. Bloody marvellous.

His reasons for leaving her in the lurch needed to be spectacularly justified because at this moment in time she was pretty sure she would never let him live this one down.

Bringing her feet up and under her bottom and chewing nervously on the side of her thumb nail, Paige racked her brain through all the possible scenarios that could have led her boyfriend to be absent today of all days. Under the exasperated guilt he had dramatised on the phone, there had been the unmistakable buzz of excitement in his voice. She'd just have to find out for herself tomorrow evening.

Paige left with little fuss early the very next morning, after a brief and silent breakfast with Jacca. She was working the evening shift tonight so wanted time to get home and freshen up in a fully functioning shower. She was quite happy to put some distance between her and Mevagissey again until the next family obligation summoned her down, though leaving Jacca behind to rattle around in his house by the harbour was becoming more and more difficult. Nick's words the night before, suggesting that she was a bad daughter, had irked her beyond measure and now she felt incredibly sad that someone she hardly knew had voiced her own guilty concerns out loud. She arrived back in Bristol feeling thoroughly ashamed and wretched.

Paige always relished in the opportunity to step up

and run the kitchen as her own in Matthew's absence - despite her annoyance on this occasion - so it didn't take her long to get lost in the job she loved, perfecting every dish that left the kitchen and overseeing every creation from her crew. She soon detached herself from the niggling emotions that had lingered from her three days in Mevagissey, like a bad after-taste, and kept her focus purely on the food that went out to this evening's diners.

"So," Abigail asked towards the end of the shift, when orders were thinning out enough to hold conversations between prep. "Are we going to tackle the elephant in the room? Or just let it bounce around, causing havoc?"

Paige took her eyes from the plate she was dressing long enough to give Abigail a bemused look.

"What elephant in the room?"

"Matthew? In London? Without you?"

Paige immediately worked on rearranging her facial expressions, not wanting to give away the irritation and hurt she felt towards the staff at Garlands knowing her boyfriend's mystery whereabouts. Matthew had only just felt obliged to share this with her recently, but it appeared she wasn't as privy to that information as she had thought.

"He's allowed to go to London on his own. Doesn't bother me."

It was mostly true. Paige wasn't the kind of person to pine after her boyfriend if he went away without her. No, what did bother her was the secrecy and allowing whatever it was to come before being there for her at her mother's funeral. *That* bothered her.

"Yeah, but how do you not even know what it's about? We're all dying to know and thought maybe you'd at least be able to shed some light," Abigail's face furrowed in worry. "But you don't, do you?"

"Well, never mind," Paige straightened up, wiping her hands on the cloth draped in her apron pocket. "I'm sure we'll find out soon. Get back to your chocolate ganache before you curdle it."

Later that evening, Paige shuffled into her apartment, desperate to just collapse into bed after the busiest night of the year so far. It wasn't just the physical tiredness that drained Paige. It was the emotional exhaustion that still clung to her like a leech.

"Hey girl!" Georgina trilled from behind the kitchen counter, a concoction of mixers and spirits laid out in front of her. "Haven't seen you since you got back. How was it?"

"As expected. All done." Paige removed her coat and clambered on to the breakfast stool. "What are you making?"

"I've got a job interview next week," Georgina bit her lip in a mixture of excitement and nerves.

"That's great," Paige managed, forcing her tired facial muscles to resemble something like a smile. Paige knew that so far Georgina had struggled to hold down a job given that the very thing got in her way of a good Saturday night, after a week of hard studying and constant testing. She'd even flaked out on a waitressing job at Garlands, which Paige had arranged for her only to be let down spectacularly by her own roommate. Paige did her very best daily not to bring her up on that. "Where to?"

"God, you're proper Cornish aren't you?" Georgia pointed out in delight, her own Essex accent not quite pulling off the 'proper'. Paige threw her arms up in the air in exasperation and gestured for her to answer the question. "The Vincent is looking for a weekend mixologist, so I've applied telling them I'm experienced, but really I've never made one in my life."

"Well you drink enough cocktails so I'm sure that makes you qualified enough," Paige teased, dodging an ice cube that had just been chucked her way.

"Cheeky. Right, for that you can be my guinea pig. Porn star? Cosmopolitan? You look like shit, so Espresso Martini?"

Sending a rude gesture in Georgia's direction, she didn't necessarily disagree with her. She was dog-tired. "Go on then. Coffee and alcohol. Perfect."

As Georgia busied herself with the ingredients for Paige's martini, Paige could barely register her phone vibrating in her pocket and groaned at the sight of Matthew's name sprawled across the screen. She was too tired for this conversation.

"You're through to the semi-finals of the National Chef of the Year competition?" Paige echoed Matthew moments later in the privacy of her room, after he'd finally revealed his reasons for being in London.

"Can you believe it?" Matthew's euphoric voice bounced out of the phone speaker. "Babe, this is going to open so many doors!"

Silence. Paige didn't know how to respond. She simply stared ahead, her attention slightly caught by a house fly buzzing around the window, crashing aimlessly into the glass pane. She considered joining it, smacking her own head against the window in complete frustration.

"Hello? Babe, you there?"

"Yeah. Yeah, I'm here. Congratulations." The flatness in her voice gave her away.

Another silence fell between them.

"Are you not happy for me?" Matthew said, hurt pulling through in his tone.

"Of course I am. Of course. I'm just a little blindsided right now." Paige chewed her lip, her stomach churning at the growing mix of emotions festering within.

A cooking competition. That was the big secret? That was the thing he chose over being there for her when she needed him most?

She picked her next words carefully. "Why didn't you tell me?"

"Because!" Matthew's voice burst through the speakers again, impatient and exasperated. "Because I didn't want to make you feel even more shit than you do already. With your mum, with your job."

Paige pulled an affronted face, glaring down at the phone which she had now plonked down on her chest of drawers, loudspeaker doing the work for her. "My job? What's that supposed to mean?"

"I didn't know whether you'd be... funny about me... you know -"

More exasperated sighs followed.

"No Matthew. I don't know. You're making no fucking sense."

"I didn't know whether you'd take it badly that I'm... progressing in the industry. It bothers you."

"No, it doesn't! When have I ever given you that impression? Matthew, none of this explains the secrecy. Hang on... you're in the semi-finals." Realisation dawned on Paige and she felt sick from it. "This will have been going on for months!"

"November," Matthew said, quiet and still.

This had nothing to do with him protecting her emotionally whilst she was grieving and everything to do with him simply not trusting her to be supportive enough.

"I'm sorry Paige."

Trust. That's what Paige wanted in a relationship. Needed in a relationship. Whatever foundations of trust Paige and Matthew had built theirs on the last two years was slowly crumbling under the strain. Those emotional barriers were notching up a few rows, little bricks of bitterness and resentment stacking on top of one another, fighting for the top space. Paige had been here before and didn't like the person it turned her into at the end of the day.

"For what?" Paige replied coldly, shrugging despite Matthew not being able to see. "It's late. I'm going to bed. Congratulations again."

Paige ended the call and pushed the phone away as if it had burned her. Whatever words of apology or frustration Matthew was about to send through in his barrage of messages, Paige didn't want to know, so she stuffed it into a drawer for good measure just as Georgina shouldered her way in cautiously, a martini in both hands.

"Thanks Georgina," Paige said, relieving her of one

of the martinis. "Don't suppose you need to practise making shots?"

The next couple of weeks trudged by uneasy, strained and with just a hint of acrimony - on Paige's side anyway.

Everyone back at the restaurant had, of course, been over the moon for Matthew and had practically showered him in praise on his return from London, leaving Paige decidedly disgruntled. It wasn't like she was jealous or anything. She couldn't think of anything worse than having to prepare her speciality dish with cameras in her face and somebody firing questions at her every two seconds. Actually, Paige didn't quite know why she was so pissed off. She just knew she was, and she was going with it.

Matthew could have told her.

He could have trusted Paige enough with a minor piece of information like entering one of the biggest national chef competitions in the country - and actually getting through to the semi-finals! Was that not something you shared with your girlfriend pretty much from the beginning?

He could have done with not using her mum's death as a cop-out excuse for keeping such a big secret from her, given this had been going on way before Elaine had departed from this world. Better yet, she would have liked his support on one of the toughest days of her life. He'd barely even asked how the funeral had gone and this hurt Paige to no end. As always though, she didn't tell him this - acutely aware of how hypocritical she was being by not being transparent in their relationship.

She was starting to get really fed up with her own miserable company one afternoon. Returning from a run and checking the letterbox, one particular letter amongst the usual pile of junk caught her eye. The envelope was of a good quality and branded with the logo for Morgan & Gilbert Solicitors. Her curiosity piqued and Paige couldn't tear the envelope open fast enough. She'd never received anything so official in the post in her life.

Dear Miss Paige Yelland,

As you may be aware, your mother, Ms Elaine Waters, sadly passed away February 8th. We are acting in the administration of her estate and you are a beneficiary under her Will. Please would you contact us...

Paige didn't finish reading the rest of the letter, having read enough to make her mind spin.

Beneficiary? Elaine's estate?

Elaine didn't own property! She didn't own very much under her name after leaving Paige's father, having left everything they had built together as a family with Jacca - out of guilt, Paige supposed. What on earth could there be of Elaine's this big that Paige would be receiving this letter?

Unless...? No, surely not.

Chapter Five

"You've inherited the restaurant in Mevagissey? Your mother's restaurant?"

Matthew had come over from the gym about an hour ago after she'd called him in a frantic state, to find Paige pacing a track in the living room carpet with nervous energy. The phone still in her hand from the conversation with a Mrs Katrina Jenkins from Morgan & Gilbert Solicitors in Truro. After a long-winded procedure of passing over identification information over the phone to prove that she was indeed Paige Yelland, daughter of Elaine Waters and a beneficiary under her mother's will, Katrina had proceeded to drop the bombshell that Paige was to inherit Giuseppe's restaurant in Mevagissey.

"What are you going to do?" Matthew continued, his one-sided dialogue falling on deaf ears as Paige zoned out for the hundredth time. "Paige!"

"What?" Paige jolted, her hands on her hips as she resumed her pacing.

"What are you going to do?"

Paige threw her shoulders up in an exaggerated shrug. "I don't know. What do I do? I don't bloody want it!"

"What are you talking about?" Matthew was incredulous. "Of course you want it! You're being given ownership of your own restaurant. Do you know how many chefs would kill for that to just be dropped in their laps?"

"Don't say it like," Paige said with disdain. "This is a result of losing Mum in the first instance. Don't make me sound lucky and ungrateful."

"Yeah, alright - you're right. It's not quite like that. But you have been given a good opportunity here."

Paige regarded Matthew, eyeing him suspiciously.

"You seem very keen for me to go for this."

"Of course I am. Paige, this is a big - "

" - opportunity. Yeah, I heard you the first time."

"Christ, girl. Even with a bloody restaurant thrown at you, you seem to have this chip on your shoulder. What the fuck is the matter?"

Paige could have slapped him. "Forget it."

A lot of their conversations were like this these days. Matthew was quick to resort to anger towards Paige's temperament, and she had to admit - she didn't blame him. She annoyed herself. It seemed something had shifted between them recently and they were no longer able to understand each other's perspectives. Paige was exhausted trying to explain herself all the time so she decided to take herself for some fresh air, despite having been for a run earlier.

It was a cold winter's evening but the full moon shone brightly in a clear starry sky over the nearby park, making for pleasant conditions for couples, dog walkers and runners alike. Paige had already been on a run once today and the park seemed none the quieter now than it was in the middle of the day. It seemed running was the only thing keeping Paige sane at the moment so she fell into step for the second time that day and exerted her frustration through measured breathing, arm pumping and pavement pounding.

Paige was neither glad nor surprised to find a note from Matthew on her return, informing her that he had 'gone out for drinks with the lads' and that he would see her at work tomorrow. The fact she was glad of his absence for another evening made her a little uneasy how relieved she felt not to endure tense silences between them, unspoken words bouncing between them like little angry pinballs. Instead, she could have a long bath and watch a film, in quiet and blissful isolation.

She had promised Katrina from the solicitor's office that she would notify her of her decision in a week's time. She wasn't going to torture herself with this decision-making tonight. Perhaps instead, she would try to switch off entirely and let the works of Richard Curtis in *About Time* ease her mind and soul.

Maybe if she wrote a pros and cons list?

It was two days later and Paige was contemplating the decision she needed to make whilst doing the orders in the office at Garlands. Matthew's roaring laughter could be heard in the kitchen as he joked about with Stuart, one of the station chefs.

Communication between him and her had been limited but bearable since the evening Paige had discovered her inheritance, and occasionally Matthew made a gentle probe to ask whether she had made her decision yet. Matthew had also received information on the next stage of the Nationals competition and a brief on what he would be asked to prepare in the finals. Since then, he'd spent longer hours in the restaurant kitchen, using Stuart's expertise as a former Pâtissier in Paris. Not once had Matthew asked for Paige's opinion on his dish choices, nor had he involved her in any way when it came to the competition. Paige pretended this didn't bother her, knowing that she had brought this upon herself. She should perhaps have been more supportive.

"How's the choux pastry going?" Paige asked as way of a conversation opener, emerging from the office.

"Fine," Matthew muttered, his full focus on the stacking of his choux pastry puffs.

"Is croquembouche not a little outdated?"

Paige tried to hide her wince as Matthew's hands dropped to his side and his face pinched into a deadly glare.

"I did say that, yeah," Stuart said bashfully, biting the side of his thumb.

"You said it was a show-stopper, mate!"

"It is, boss," Stuart countered shyly. "It'll look epic. They were all the rage when I worked in Paris."

"So, what's the problem?" Matthew snapped in Paige's direction.

Paige shrugged, choosing not to rise to Matthew's

attitude. "I just wonder if they'll be looking for something that demonstrates more of your skills. Croquembouche looks good and all, but at the end of the day it's just choux pastry stacked into a cone and some spun sugar."

Stuart gaped at Paige like he had been slapped and Paige shot him an apologetic look.

"I just mean that this is the Nationals, Matthew. I'm pretty sure they were tasked to make one of these on The Great British Bake-off."

Matthew threw a choux pastry puff over his shoulder. "That's it - I'm choosing something else. You really know how to piss on people's fireworks, Paige."

Leaving Paige rooted to the ground and blazing in the cheeks, Matthew took a wide sweep around her, into the office and slammed the door shut. Feeling decidedly ashamed, she glanced at Stuart who really didn't know where to look.

"Sorry," Paige muttered, unsure whether she was apologising for her dig on his choice of showstopper or her blame towards Matthew's outburst.

"No problem," Stuart waved a hand, his smile not quite reaching his eyes as he rocked on the spot awkwardly. "I'm just going to start on the filo pastry for tonight's desserts."

With Stuart gone, Paige took a deep breath and knocked on the office door. If Matthew had replied, she didn't hear it, so decided to let herself in anyway.

Inside, Matthew sat hunched over the desk, his head in his hands, a posture of utter defeat. Horrified, Paige slipped into the office and closed the door to give them privacy. The little cupboard of an office was a squeeze, but she slipped into the spare seat which was tucked into the corner between the desk and the wall nearest the door, waiting patiently for Matthew to rise from his hunched position.

When the silence became too much, Paige decided to go first. "I'm sorry."

Matthew rubbed his face and sat back in his chair, a

heaving sigh escaping through his nostrils. "Me too. Paige... I don't think I can do this much longer."

"Do what?"

"This," Matthew gestured his hands between them, his eyes finally rising to meet hers. "We're horrible to each other at the moment. I hate it! You're grieving and I should be looking after you in this shitty time, but instead we just argue."

Paige stayed silent, watching Matthew battle with a bag of emotions. So far, he wasn't wrong.

"I feel like you resent me for doing the Nationals, and actually doing well. I tiptoe around you. I don't feel like I can celebrate my successes around you. This competition is important to me. I don't know, Paige. I'm not sure we're good for each other anymore."

Paige waited to get upset, for the expected tears to come flooding in at what Matthew was suggesting, but instead she found herself nodding slowly, her eyes slightly glazed and staring at a slight dink in the paintwork of the wall just to the side of Matthew's head.

"I'm sorry, Paige." He looked wretched, dragging his hands through his thick curls and across his stubbled face. "I'm so sorry. This is awful timing."

"No, you're right. I've been wrapped up in my little bubble since Mum died and I haven't supported you with this competition -"

"Paige, we haven't been right for a while now," Matthew said, gently. "I think we've just been coasting. I still care about you Paige, but I feel more like a nuisance friend than your partner these days."

In a strange way, Paige understood what he meant by that. He was right. They had been coasting for a long time, it seemed. Underwhelmed in each other's company, and somehow drifting apart even though their paths literally criss-crossed each other every day as they worked together and lived in each other's apartments. Perhaps that was half the problem. Some sort of tightness in Paige's chest loosened and she was surprised to feel a small blast of relief at this realisation.

"Do you hate me?" Matthew asked, wincing at Paige's silence as she drifted deep into thought.

"No. No, of course I don't hate you. In fact, I agree with you entirely. I'm actually a little relieved."

"Crikey, Paige. Don't leave me with too many bruises," Matthew joked, rubbing the back of his neck, his eyes swimming with unshed tears.

"You know what I mean," Paige smiled. "I've just been feeling so numb recently with Mum that I suppose I didn't realise... I'm glad we're talking, rather than barking at each other or ignoring each other entirely. This makes a nice change."

Matthew smiled wryly and grabbed Paige's hand from across the desk.

"I do love you Paige. I haven't stopped loving you and caring about you. I'm just not sure the love is the same anymore."

Paige nodded again, the little prickles of feelings and understanding penetrating the numbness and giving her a little more space to breathe. She took advantage of that and drew a deeper one in through her nose, filling her lungs.

"I know. I still love you. But you're right, it's not the same anymore." She watched as Matthew's callused thumb grazed over her hand. "So, what now?"

"Honestly? I think you should accept your mum's inheritance. You've got a lot of emotional baggage down there holding you back and I think you need to face it head on. But that to one side, that restaurant is one hell of an opportunity for you. You're wasted here as a second."

"What about you? If this competition in London takes you elsewhere, what will happen here? Maybe I want to go for Head Chef here when you bugger off," Paige joked wryly.

Matthew smiled, but his eyes remained fixed with seriousness. "Is that what you want? To stay here? You're practically doing the job now Paige. What difference will a title make? The restaurant in Mevagissey though... you'll own it. You can put your own stamp on it. Please… really think about this."

"What about you?" Paige repeated, not committing to Matthew's request with a response. "What are your plans?"

"Can't you tell? I'm fidgety. This place has opened a lot of doors for me, but I'm so bloody bored. I don't know, I might see how the competition fairs out, then see where it takes me. But I won't be burning any bridges here yet, not until I see what doors open up in London." Matthew glanced at Paige, a slightly wicked smile playing on his lips. "Not everyone gets given a restaurant!"

"No! Piss off! Don't you dare!" Paige ripped her hand away and shoved him in the shoulder with it, Matthew immediately chuckling and grabbing her hand again.

"I'm joking, I'm joking! Sorry, way too soon."

"Way too soon. Dick move!"

"You always have been easy to wind up," Matthew smiled, fondly. "I'm going to miss you, Paige. Now get on to the phone to that solicitor. You've got an inheritance to accept."

With the emotional turmoil of the next couple of weeks following Paige and Matthew's surprisingly smooth separation, Paige found herself completely and emotionally drained once she'd squeezed the last of her belongings into her little Fiat, paid farewell to Matthew and driven away, set for Cornwall once more, her Bristol life now sadly behind her. Her roommates had been wonderfully supportive and mostly focused on the excitement of having a restaurant in sunny Cornwall to visit when end of term exams had been and gone.

She checked her side mirrors, her rear-view mirror compromised from her boxes of belongings obstructing her view, and caught her final glance of Matthew, still waving her off as she rounded a corner. They'd promised to stay good friends and to stay in touch, particularly as they both were to embark on exciting and terrifying new journeys that may one day find their paths crossing again.

Despite knowing that ending their relationship had been the best thing for both of them, Paige was still unbelievably sad to be drawing things to a close from her life in Bristol. Ten years she had lived there, having left Cornwall to complete a Chef apprenticeship in a highly regarded restaurant in Bristol city centre.

She had first moved into the basement flat belonging to a newly married couple, when they'd been looking for a lodger to support their hefty mortgage repayments. When the first baby had arrived, along with its relentless screaming throughout the night, she had swiftly moved on to a more quiet setting with an overly reserved law student who Paige engaged in conversation with for a grand total of about five times for the whole year of their tenancy agreement. After getting her first job post-qualifying as a station chef in Garlands, she met Matthew and a slow friendship grew. Matthew had said on a number of occasions that Paige had been a hard nut to crack and that he'd never known a girl to be so difficult to woo. Given that she rarely radiated warmth with her demeanour and chose to keep most people she knew at arm's length, she could only agree that Matthew probably had a good point.

Disregarding Matthew's brash enthusiasm towards Paige's new ownership of Giuseppe's, Paige had characteristically taken things slow and opted to request unpaid leave from Garlands for the next four weeks to test-run her new role in Cornwall. As much as it was a great opportunity for her - as Matthew kept reminding her - it was still a piece of Elaine, a piece from the part of her mother's life that hadn't involved her or Jacca. As petty and ungrateful as she knew she sounded, it wouldn't have been her first choice of restaurant.

It felt strange to be returning so soon, given that her visits to Cornwall were usually scattered far and few between across the year. Jacca, being more prepared for her arrival this time round given that Paige would be living with him for the time being, had arranged for her to have dibs on Sandra's car park space on a more permanent basis. It still meant several trips from the car to Jacca's house to get all of her belongings indoors and when she'd finally plonked the last box on the bottom step of the staircase, her skin sheening from perspiration despite the winter chill in the air, she was desperate for a cold drink.

A quick glance in Jacca's fridge told her she'd be needing a trip to the supermarket again before nightfall. She was starting to think that an empty fridge and cupboards was the norm in this house. She checked the time on her phone and decided now was as good a time as any to head to the supermarket. She could have the kitchen brimming with supplies and a hot meal on the table for both of them before Jacca returned from fishing.

Paige was just locking up the house when the front door of the house to the right flew open, followed by Nick stepping out to lock his own door. He caught sight of Paige just as he started descending his steep steps down to the walkway.

"Alright?" Nick smiled. "Back again?"

Paige nodded, no desire whatsoever to spark a conversation with him. So he was their neighbour... Great.

"I'm just heading to the supermarket," Paige said, unnecessarily. She was pretty sure Nick wasn't interested in where she was heading, so she didn't really know why she'd said that. "Dad's cupboards are practically empty again."

Nick chuckled. "That sounds about right. Hadn't expected to see you again so soon. You staying for a while, then?"

Paige was a little blindsided at Nick's sudden friendliness, or at least his much less cold demeanour from the last time she was down. She was also ashamed to admit that she was utterly distracted by those broad shoulders again, his arms practically bulging as he leaned casually against his step railings. "Um, yeah. Well, I'm moving in actually. I think."

Nick's brow furrowed as she stumbled through her

words, lowering her head and fumbling with the keys in her hand.

"You think?"

Paige sighed and bit her lip. "Yeah. Everything is a bit up in the air at the moment, so I'm just... trying something out."

It was utterly cryptic and Paige wrinkled her nose at her wishy-washy explanation, but after their last experience in each other's company, she didn't much fancy being scrutinised.

"Anyway, better get going. I was hoping to surprise Dad with a nice meal in tonight."

"That sounds nice," Nick said, rubbing his beard and looking awkward. "Guess I'll freeze his pie that I made him for dinner and save it for another night."

Paige's heart sank as the feeling of estrangement pinged back to punch her in the gut. "Sorry, I didn't realise. Forget it, you guys carry on. I'll just grab some fish and chips on the harbour and stay out of your way."

"Hey, whoa! Don't be daft. It's just something we do every now and again, when I have an evening off. My dad joins us too. Paige, why don't-"

"No, no. Honestly, it's fine. I don't want to intrude."

God forbid she was to intrude on her father having dinner with some bloke from next door who just happens to run the kitchen at her mother's restaurant - her restaurant.

That was going to take a lot of getting used to.

Feeling utterly mortified at the unexpected tears brimming and threatening to escape, Paige finished locking up and power-marched her way down Old Road towards Sandra's to collect her car. She didn't know why she suddenly had an urge to cry and she didn't know why the village suddenly started feeling small again, like the walls of the buildings were squeezing in on her. What she did know was that she had, yet again, made an absolute tit of herself in front of this Nick bloke. Her worries bolted over to the thought of Monday, where she would be meeting her team at Giuseppe's and would be announcing her position as

Nick's boss. Something in her intuition told her that he was going to be far from pleased about the prospect and if she was entirely honest, the feeling was mutual.

Chapter Six

The sky was a murky grey and the waves of the sea lapped menacingly against the outer harbour wall below as Paige scrambled down the little steps to sit and look out to the darkening sea, her fish and chip dinner wafting up and making her tummy grumble. Really, this should have been the last place she'd want to take her solitary meal, given the memories it triggered from all those years ago but there was also something quiet and comforting about this very spot. It was ironically a place she'd often occupied when she'd wanted to get away from the suffocating misery and anger during those unspeakable times growing up.

A couple of seagulls hovered in mid-flight above her, no doubt eyeing up her dinner. She smiled as she recalled Jacca's nickname for them.

Mevagissey chickens.

For a moment, it brought her back to those simple years of coming home from school, seeking Jacca out on the many vessels out on the bay, knowing they'd hit the jack pot when the seagulls were flocking around them like hungry vultures, cawing away in their territorial manner. Jacca would return home, beaming from ear to ear, inviting a young Paige to a little eye-spy game. A game which involved spotting which seagull was going to attack an emit's ice cream or portion of chips first. It often left them both going into tea, with tears down their cheeks from laughing so much. It never took long for a poor tourist to be at the mercy of one of the hungry Meva chickens.

She crossed her legs now and cradled the tray in her lap, her arms ready for the fight if any should decide to try their luck. The sea was pretty fierce this evening but layered up in her old waterproof trousers and trench coat, she felt pretty cosy albeit frumpy. Good job she wasn't out to impress, it wasn't exactly the most glamorous of outfits.

She hadn't stuck around once the cupboards were replenished with groceries, not wanting to receive an obligatory invitation out of pity to Jacca and Nick's pie party. It seemed that Nick had a much larger presence in Jacca's life than Paige had initially realised, and he was his next-door neighbour to boot.

Their next-door neighbour, Paige reminded herself.

She was living there too now. She wasn't sure how she felt about living right next door, given their peculiar introduction a few weeks ago and the very sudden change of direction in their manners towards one another.

She couldn't figure Nick out. She could scold herself for blushing like she did that evening when they first met. The way her stomach had fluttered when he'd touched her ankle, gently but firmly pressing down on her skin to check the damage. He'd been warm, welcoming and perhaps even a little bit flirtatious, and Paige annoyed herself by quietly admitting that she'd quite liked it. It seemed, however, that once he'd found out who she was, he'd wanted nothing to do with her, and had made her feel decidedly shunted ever since. The best thing to do for the moment would be to stay out of the way, and certainly not get in the way of any existing arrangements Nick and her dad had together.

Choosing a particularly chunky chip, she looked out to the vast ocean in front of her, the dark sky looming overhead as the last of the sun slipped below the horizon. She was entirely alone, in the dark, on a soaking wet harbour, but a small sense of calm washed over her for the first time in weeks. It was only a surface emotion though. She knew all too well that under that layer of calm was a storm of anguish and nerves for what lay in store, not to mention the bitter mix of grief for both her mum's death and her failed relationship with Matthew.

Matthew had messaged her earlier, asking if she'd arrived in Cornwall safely, which had made her feel both incredibly sad and relieved that they'd left things on good terms. To say she didn't miss him would be a complete lie and on the odd occasion, since they'd declared the end of their intimate relationship, Paige experienced a small pang of panic over whether they'd done the right thing. Whether she'd done the right thing.

Nothing that could be undone now.

Once she'd demolished her fish and chips, Paige bagged up the empty chip paper and trays and carried them back with her on a slow stroll back towards the house. It was now gone 8pm though the blackness of the sky made it feel much later, so she hoped she had given the men enough time to finish their meal.

"Alright, Bird? Where'd you run off to? I tried calling your mobile several times."

Though relaxed in his usual armchair with a whiskey in his hand, his face was pinched slightly in worry towards his daughter. Nick's large figure was taking up most of the sofa behind him and Nick's dad occupied the chair by the window.

"I left it on charge upstairs," Paige shrugged, putting her rubbish in the bin and washing her hands at the kitchen sink.

"Where'd you go?" Jacca repeated.

"Just to the harbour wall with some fish and chips."

Jacca nodded knowingly. "Should have guessed you'd gone there. You needn't have scarpered like that. There was plenty of dinner for the four of us, weren't there lads?"

"I did try to tell Paige that," Nick added, shrugging from his spot on the sofa. "You would have been very welcome to join us."

"Thanks," Paige smiled grimly, her mouth pinched painfully as she clamped down on what she really wanted to say. *Thanks for granting me access to dinner with my own father in my own family home, you do-gooder prick.* Instead she turned to Jacca and announced, "I've got some unpacking to do."

The next morning, after a quick but slightly damp jog

around the harbour, Paige made Eggs Benedict for both her and Jacca. Paige's early bird habits had been adopted by the many early rises with her dad, back in his prime fishing days. He had planned to retire a couple of years ago, but clearly the calling of the sea was far greater and old habits died hard. The smell of a cooked breakfast still coaxed him out of bed easily enough, and by 8am they were sat enjoying their breakfast in companionable silence.

Paige and Jacca had always been easy company for each other, having been just the two of them for many years after her parents' divorce, before shipping off to Bristol for a fresh start. Neither liked small talk and both found silence to be just as pleasing and powerful as a meaningful conversation. Paige recalled that this used to drive her mum mad, given that she was somebody who had felt the urge to fill all the silences wherever possible.

"What's the plan then?" Jacca said, after he'd finished his last mouthful of food, laid his cutlery to rest and leaned back in his seat with his tea cradled in his hands. "I didn' speak much with Nick last night about the whole ordeal, but how's this restaurant business gonna work, then?"

"Does Nick know already?" Paige asked, her eyes widened in worry.

"'Course he does. He runs the place."

"Don't know," Paige replied truthfully, a resigned sigh escaping her lungs. "I have a meeting with the solicitor this afternoon. Think I have some forms to sign and hopefully will be given more information from there."

Jacca nodded quietly and looked through his window out to sea, his usual trademark move when his mind wandered.

"I know, Dad. I know this is really weird, and I'm uncomfortable with it all too."

He nodded again, his bottom lip wobbling slightly, giving Paige the sudden urge to wrap him in a big hug. But of course, she didn't. She did what she always did and sat fastened to her seat, staring at her dad with a sense of sadness and redundancy.

"It dun't bother me, you running the place and all. Couldn't be prouder, in fact. And I do have dealings with the place. Don't go thinking I avoid it all together. Helps having Nick in there, and it'll be even nicer popping in now, seeing my baby girl in there, giving everybody what-for... "

Jacca shot Paige a cheeky grin, one that she hadn't seen in a long time, and she couldn't help but return it gladly with a grin of her own.

"So, what is it?" Paige asked, tentatively.

Jacca paused for a moment before replying, his voice thick from a sob caught in his throat. "It's just... She's really gone, in't she? Do you reckon they've found each other again?"

Eyes smarting and her heart aching, Paige leaned forward and grabbed her father's callused hands. She knew who he meant, and he didn't mean Giuseppe. "I reckon they have, Dad. One hundred percent. And she's giving him bleddy stick right now."

They chuckled softly together and returned to their own thoughts, their hands still entwined as they gazed back out to sea. If it wasn't for the list of errands Paige needed to run today, she'd have happily sat there and clutched her old dad's hand all day.

Katrina Jenkins' office was tucked away on the top floor of one of the Victorian terraced buildings on Lemon Street in Truro. It had been years since Paige had ventured into Cornwall's only city and she was quickly reminded as to why. After paying a small fortune for parking and negotiating her way through a crowded piazza, she felt a little ruffled by the time she'd taken a seat in one of Katrina's seats in front of her desk.

"Thank you for coming in, Miss Yelland. I trust the move down went well?" Katrina asked, once introductions and hot beverages had been made.

"Yes, thank you. Actually, I haven't fully moved down. A lot of my larger belongings are still in Bristol for the time being, so I've moved down with just a carload of necessities for now."

"Oh?" Katrina glanced up from her paperwork, an eyebrow arched. "Not fully committing yourself yet then?"

"It's a big upheaval from my existing life," Paige explained, diplomatically. "I just want to make sure it's the right thing before I cut ties."

"Sensible."

That was just about it. A couple of life events from her past had turned her world upside down and now she was nothing but sensible. Some called it calculated, most called it boring. Matthew especially had found this trait of hers monotonous and limiting when it came to the life they shared together. Well, she had her reasons and she was sticking with it.

"So, there are a few things we'll need to go through today. The good news is you shouldn't be liable for inheritance tax as your shares are held in a family trust. So we'll look to get those shares transferred to you in the coming weeks. We can look at Business Property Relief as well, to ensure that…"

Paige's ears were pounding as she watched Katrina's flailing hands punctuate her professional lingo, nodding weakly as if she understood a single word that this woman was saying.

Inheritance tax?

Business Property Relief?

Not for a moment did Paige recognise a single phrase, and the room suddenly became very small as she realised the enormity of what she was getting herself involved in. She couldn't do this. She didn't know the first thing about running a business. What if, financially, the restaurant was in trouble? What if she was actually inheriting a big fat load of debt?

"Miss Yelland? Have I lost you?"

Shaking herself back to reality, it was then that she realised Katrina appraising her with an odd frown across her brow.

"Sorry."

"I was just saying that it would be worth you getting in contact with your business partner. A Mr N. Stone. He owns twenty percent of the restaurant. You own the bigger share which means you hold more ground on any decision process, but it's probably best to keep on the good side of business with him."

The fuzzy, dizzy feeling circulating around her head dropped to the floor as her mind sharpened for a moment. "Business partner?"

"Yes, a Mr Nick Stone will be inheriting twenty percent of the restaurant under Ms Waters' instructions."

"That bastard gets everywhere," Paige muttered.

Katrina paused for a moment, taking in Paige's retreating demeanour. Her professional tone softened as she took pity on her. "I know this is a lot to take in. I see many people come through this office, their eyeballs practically turning into pound signs right before me. I also see people like you, whose grief is still too fresh to even contemplate getting their heads around a new business."

Paige nodded, only semi-aware that her cheeks were damp from a few pesky tears. Truth was, grief had existed within Paige before her mother's death. Grief had existed within all of them and this was partly to do with why accepting this inheritance was so damn hard.

As kind as Katrina was being, Paige didn't want to give any more opportunity for this conversation to continue, so she picked up the nearest pen, smiled weakly and took a deep breath.

"Let's do this. Show me where to sign."

After squeezing her Fiat into her tiny space on the harbour, Paige walked along the waterfront and up the steep path leading to the cottage, her head pounding and an overall numbness descending. Jacca's waders were missing from the storm porch, so Paige hazarded a guess that he was out on the boat still.

"All sorted?"

Paige's head whipped up to the front door of Nick's white cottage next door, the man in question locking his door up as he glanced in her direction.

"Sorry?"

"Are we looking at the new owner of Giuseppe's?" Nick's expression was unreadable, but oddly Paige noted a slight smirk twitching in the corners of his mouth.

"How do you know?"

Nick laughed as he jogged down his front steps cheerfully. "Crikey, you must be joking if you think that not a single person knows about it. Don't look so worried, the villagers haven't sharpened their pitchforks yet."

Paige clutched the paperwork from Katrina's office tighter, unsure how to respond.

"Well then, I'm guessing it will be common knowledge that you are twenty percent owner of Giuseppe's," Paige quipped, her tone deadpan. "Congratulations."

"Came as a shock, I'll admit," Nick replied, rubbing his beard awkwardly.

"Mmm," Paige arched her eyebrows, her tone set. "Came as a shock to me too."

"Why don't you pop down and have a look at the place?" Nick offered. "We're getting ready for evening service. I was just popping home to give my cat his Metacam." Then added, as if Paige had asked, "he's got arthritis."

Paige considered his offer, which she couldn't really refuse. But a large part of her just wanted to sink into a hot bath and mull over everything she had just signed on the dotted line for. Sighing inwardly, she locked the cottage back up and followed Nick to the restaurant.

Giuseppe's was busy and functional, a contrast to the last time she was there having out of hours breakfast with Laura. The small number of front of house staff busy setting the tables for tonight's service glanced in her direction as she and Nick entered the building from the front entrance.

"This is Paige, guys. Elaine's daughter," Nick announced, leading Paige towards the bar and offering a stool. Paige waved shyly at the staff, who now knew who she was and were looking all the more curious for it. She tried not to read their expressions. She wasn't sure she wanted to find out yet just how welcome or unwelcome she'd be. She knew, all too well, the politics involved amongst staff in a restaurant and could imagine them sizing up the new recruit and placing bets to how long she'd last - never mind her owning the place.

"Coffee? Something stronger? Got a new gin this week, if you're into that."

"I'll try a gin," Paige relented, then added for the sake of being polite, "thank you."

"No worries. You look like you might need it."

Paige's eyebrows arched up in agreement as she chanced a glance around the room, trying not to outwardly grimace at the way the young girls haphazardly rolled cutlery in paper napkins and threw them into a basket ready for the evening's service.

"Many bookings tonight?" Paige asked as Nick passed a well garnished G&T over the bar.

"Not too bad. Considering the day of the week and time of the year."

Paige nodded and sipped her drink through the straw. It was very well made, with a refreshing mix of rhubarb and raspberry. Given the time of year, she perhaps should have opted for something more warming, like a Baileys. Then again, she was half way through it already before she found something else to say to break the silence. Oh god, she was looking for small talk - her least favourite thing.

"Garlands, the restaurant I worked in back in Bristol, is busy all year round."

The floor may as well have swallowed her whole as she mentally gave herself a telling off. That hadn't even been what she had planned to say, and yet there she was saying the most pretentious thing she could have possibly opted for.

"Well, good for Garlands," Nick remarked, his arms crossing across his chest as they seemed to every time Paige managed to annoy him. "If you haven't noticed, a little fishing village that tourists are only interested in when it's sunny, doesn't get all year revenue like a city does."

Paige wanted to reply with something a little more appeasing, in the way of damage control, but she was almost too afraid to open her mouth should the wrong thing come out again. Instead she opted to hide behind the rim of her gin glass, listening to the tinkering sound of the ice cubes bouncing against the crystal. Nick cleared his throat and leaned on the bar.

"Listen, this is a tight-knit community. I know you grew up here, but you've been gone a long time. You'd do well to tread carefully and not upset too much of the status quo."

Paige's eyes snapped up to meet his, blood rushing through her ears as anger festered within and threatened to boil over.

"I know that, don't I?" Paige retorted, her resolve crumbling once again as Nick's words irked her. "Don't treat me like a complete emit. I'm very aware of this 'tight-knit' community." She doubted Nick would pick up on her quip about Nick's strange 'tight-knit' relationship with her dad.

"Yeah?" Nick appraised her, his hands on his hips. "I'm not sure you do, to be honest. I've worked here for almost ten years. Lived in the village all my life. Known Elaine and Jacca for years and yet I don't know a bleddy thing about you. You come down here, face like a slapped ass, treating this place like it's the biggest inconvenience you've ever been handed. Don't mind me if I'm slightly unimpressed by your motives."

Paige's eyes narrowed and her gin glass hit the bar with a thud. "You're a real dick, you know that?"

"And you're a spoiled brat."

Her cheeks ablaze and a tidal wave of humiliation washing over her, she caught a sob in her throat as she shot

Nick the dirtiest look she could manage before sliding off her stool and fleeing out into the early evening air.

She was vaguely aware of Nick calling after her and picked up the pace, her arms folded across her chest as angry tears smarted in her eyes.

How dare he say those things? How dare he hold some moral high ground over her, this bizarre attachment he had formed on her family in her absence. She wanted to go back and have it out with him but as usual, running away seemed to be her go-to option, and though she shouldn't allow it, his words had wounded her and taken the wind straight from her sails.

She stabbed the key into the lock of the front door, fumbling slightly with the mechanism before realising it was already unlocked, Jacca's waders back in their usual place.

"What's wrong with you?" Jacca demanded as Paige came hurtling through the front door like a thunderstorm.

"That Nick is a fucking prick!" Paige announced to the whole house, her rage taken up a notch at her accidental rhyming, before taking herself to the safety of her bedroom on the top floor. Moments later the slamming of the front door rattled through the cottage, Jacca no doubt taking himself to the social club for his usual pint or three. Entirely alone, Paige gave in to the sobs and wept. Wept until her throat was raw, her tear ducts spent and her entire body exhausted from the whole exertion.

She'd known this would be a bad idea. She'd been gone for too long and now there was no room for her here in Mevagissey. It bothered her that this man had embedded himself so far into the family, claiming weekly pie nights with her dad and somehow leeching on twenty percent of her mother's restaurant. There was somebody else who should have had those privileges. It wasn't her and it certainly wasn't Nick the Prick.

Upon returning from wherever he had disappeared to, Jacca had knocked on her bedroom door and gently coaxed her out with the promise of food. They'd had dinner together and she'd been grateful that her dad hadn't

78

probed her on the dealings between her and Nick. Jacca had then passed his daughter a beer and they'd sat silently on his little wooden balcony, a tiny space perched on the front of the cottage with the most stunning view of the harbour below. They'd remained there for the rest of the evening playing a game of cards, Paige only retreating back into the house once she'd spotted Nick walking back up to his cottage at the end of his shift, little Lilly in tow and looking suitably whacked from a late night.

Paige headed to bed, heavy and sad, with the promise of more disputes to come. She knew her own behaviour tonight hadn't exactly been business owner worthy but either way she was going to have to find a way to make this work. Or perhaps she'd be finding herself heading back to her old life in Bristol faster than she'd anticipated. But what was really left for her in Bristol?

She had to make this work.

Chapter Seven

Nick

It wasn't very often that Nick Stone woke to begin a day coated in shame and regret. He was well-known for being calculated in his manners, an easy-going nature, the gentle giant in the village.

Last night, he'd allowed her to get the better of him. He'd been preparing to meet Jacca and Elaine's daughter for a long time, promising to have things to say her that needed to be said, but in a controlled and civilised manner. He'd planned to make her see how her absence had pained her parents over the years. He'd planned to make her realise how lucky she was to have Jacca and Elaine, so fiercely loving and loyal to her, despite her lack of effort to be in their lives.

He certainly hadn't planned to call her a spoiled brat.

And he certainly hadn't banked on how he she would look. He'd seen photos of her in Jacca's cottage of course, but they'd been old photos of her as a child, some even of her as a teenager. There was very little of her as a grown woman and his first look at her had had his thoroughly planned internal narrative thrown lost into the fog of his brain.

He sat up in bed and immediately groaned, planting his face into his hands and outwardly cringing for the words that had been haphazardly chucked around within five minutes of their conversation. He recoiled at the image of Jacca, furiously storming into the restaurant last night to defend his daughter's honour.

And quite right. Nick had overstepped a line.

But it pained him to be on the receiving end of

Jacca's wrath. It pained him like a son disappointing his father, because that's what Jacca was to him. A second father. He knew, with a fresh wave of sadness, that Elaine never would have stood for it either. He needed to try harder to make this work.

There was only one thing for it. Nick was a man of action. He jumped out of bed, stirred his sleepy niece into the land of the living and headed downstairs to begin his day.

"Before you slam the door in my face, I come in peace," Nick jumped straight in as soon as the front door was ajar, his hands spread wide in front of him. "I've come to offer you breakfast. Laura and Lilly are down there and I need to make up for being a total prick last night. I shouldn't have said those things."

A little taken aback and still clearly bruised from his words last night, Paige regarded him suspiciously.

"Your dad gave me stick an' all," Nick continued, keeping his voice light, though he recoiled slightly from the memory. "Not very often I get on the wrong side of Jacca Yelland, but he came storming down and gave me what for."

The door of Jacca's cottage finally opened wide and Paige stood in the threshold, her arms folded and one eyebrow cocked sceptically.

"Is that why you're offering me breakfast then?" Paige challenged. "To keep Dad happy?"

"No! For Christ's sake," Nick huffed. How did she have such an effect on him? "I feel like a royal dick for what I said last night and want to make it up to you. I thought you might like a catch up with Laura too." His tone softened and he tried a second time at keeping things light, accompanying it with a smile. "I'll even give you an extra pancake on your stack."

Nick refrained from fist-pumping the air in victory as an involuntary smile pulled slightly in one corner of her mouth. As she rushed back in to change out of her running gear, Nick made a mental note that food was a good way to soften her sharp demeanour.

"Yay! You're here!" Laura celebrated, a while later. Refraining from rolling his eyes, he watched as his little sister welcomed Paige to their little table with open arms. He rarely saw Laura so comfortable in female company, so he had to give Paige credit where it was due. "I hope Nick has given his full apology."

"I have," Nick replied gracefully. "Whether she accepts it yet is to be decided."

"Depends how good the pancakes are," Paige quipped, a shy smile creeping on her face as Laura threw her head back in laughter. Nick rolled his eyes in good humour but couldn't help finding a genuine smile return to his face as their eyes locked across the room. She really did have the most extraordinary deep brown eyes.

Nick disappeared into the kitchen to make the pancakes before he could start embarrassing himself and heard Laura waste no time in getting straight into a good natter with her friend.

In the kitchen, he found his sous chef elbow deep in a tray of fresh fish, cutting fillets ready for the lunch sitting later.

"Alright, boss?"

"Morning, Ollie." Nick washed his hands and started making pancake batter. "You're in early."

"Only an hour or so. Is that her in there then?"

Nick paused the whisking and glanced at Ollie, who was eying the doorway into the front of house nervously.

"The new owner? Yeah, that's her."

"You making her breakfast?"

Ollie's tone was both apprehensive and - what was it? Bitter? Nick regarded his sous chef for a moment before returning to his whisking.

"Yep. And my niece. And my sister. Just the usual breakfast run after Laura's night shifts. Why?"

"No reason. Just, Lauren told me you and her had a bit of spat last night." Then suddenly, Ollie's apprehension turned into an amused chuckle. "I heard you called her a spoiled brat. Nice one!"

Nick winced at this, the shame deepening from his quick tongue last night in the heat of the moment. He flipped the pancakes in the pan, not daring to look up. "I'm not proud of that. And you lot need to stop gossiping on Messenger!"

Silence fell between him and his second, these sort of conversations never failing to remind him of the obvious fifteen-year age gap between them. Ollie's gossiping habits to one side though, he was a decent chef.

"But you've accepted, haven't you?"

Nick was on his way through to the front to ask that Laura made him a coffee, but he paused in the shadows of the doorway as Paige stumbled over Laura's direct question.

"Yes. I signed yesterday. I'm just not sure how welcome I'll be."

"Seriously, ignore Nick. I've had a stern word with him this morning," Laura said. Nick smiled wryly at this. His sister had indeed released the full wrath of her anger on him as soon as he'd foolishly filled her in on the recent events early this morning.

"It's not just Nick." Paige looked down at the coffee and wrapped her hands around it as if the conversation had made her cold. "I don't know. I'm probably just being silly. As Nick quite helpfully pointed out last night, I've had a face like a slapped ass for weeks now, and I'm getting a bit tired of being such a misery guts. I'm not sure I'm in the right place to take something this big on."

Her voice was vulnerable and Nick's heart pulled for her despite his frustrations towards her. Deciding he could no longer eavesdrop in the shadows, for fear of hearing something deepen the shame further, he retreated back into the kitchen to finish the breakfast.

On his return a while later, his arms laden with plates of breakfast, he heard snippets of Laura's stern voice towards Lilly, followed by the scrape of a chair against the tiled floor. Lilly flew off in tears, almost knocking the plates right from Nick's arms as she tore herself upstairs, Laura following closely behind.

"What's happened?" Nick asked Paige, her expression that of complete bewilderment as she stared in the direction of the stairway.

"I'm not sure. Lilly's upset about something. Not sure where she's gone though."

"She'll have gone up to the apartment upstairs," Nick said, walking to their table by the window. "Elaine and Giuseppe's apartment. Well, your apartment now."

A look of worry and what looked like a shadow of disapproval crossed Paige's features as she continued to stare at the staircase. Nick set the pancakes down and watched her for a moment.

"Elaine used to watch Lilly for me on Laura's night shifts."

"She did?" It was almost fascinating, did he not feel so damn sorry for her at this moment, to watch her expression alter again, this time with sadness. Like she'd been left out of something big. Jealousy, maybe?

"Lilly usually sits up there and watches a film while I work now," Nick continued, regarding her carefully. "But don't worry, we'll find another solution now you're moving in."

"Oh," Paige crinkled her nose up and shook her head. "No, I don't think I'll be moving in. Lilly's welcome to carry on using it."

Nick's brow furrowed at this and he noted the tone of indignation returning in her voice. He decided it was best not to push further on the subject, wanting to be on his best behaviour. Instead, he headed to the kitchen and returned with two bacon sandwiches, one for Laura and one which he immediately started sinking his own teeth into.

"So," Nick began, pausing to chomp his way through a particularly large mouthful of bacon sarnie. "When would you like to officially start?"

Paige picked at her pancakes delicately, spearing a piece of strawberry and pondering for a moment. Nick's face was having a full workout as he tried his hardest to keep his features light and nonchalant. It was almost painful not to cock an eyebrow sarcastically or frown at her with all his confused might.

"Well, do you need an extra pair of hands?" she said, finally. "I don't want to make us one too many in the kitchen, so to speak."

"You won't. I just want to clarify one thing though," Nick rubbed his hands with a napkin and finished another mouthful of food. Best behaviour or not, he needed to know. "I'll make an attempt at tip-toeing around this... I don't want to start another argument between us. I've been head chef here for well over six years... I just wanted to make sure... you know."

It suddenly dawned on Paige what he was saying and she almost jumped in to reassure him. "Oh god! I'm not going to just come in here and rip you away from your post. What kind of cow do you think I am? No, you are still head chef!"

The relief that washed through Nick almost left him breathless. That was certainly something that had been niggling him more than he cared to admit. He was almost embarrassed to question her. As she said, he had to think her a completely heartless cow to storm in and cause that sort of upheaval to the team. But then again, he didn't know a single thing about her.

He was midway through conjuring up the next question for Paige when Laura reappeared from upstairs, a look of undiluted horror across her face.

"Nick, we've got a problem."

From a very young age, Nick had felt like the carrier of the family. When his mother had first fallen ill with breast cancer, he'd been just twelve years old. When her cancer had progressed, putting her on palliative care, he'd been eighteen. Their father had been absent for a lot of it, on long fishing trips away, whilst Nick tried to keep the household together, protective of his more emotionally vulnerable little sister. Only months after the passing of their darling mother, their father showed his first signs of vascular dementia, and so began the round-the-clock care all over again.

Now it was only instinct, when it came to his little sister, to simply want to remove the emotional baggage from her shoulders and carry the load himself. He'd done it for years.

This is what he did. He couldn't help himself.

And when that distress came in the shape and form of Scott Lansdowne, it was all Nick could do not to become murderous.

Nick had known almost immediately that Scott was going to be trouble for Laura. Call it brotherly instincts. But he'd kept uncharacteristically quiet, on orders that his meddling would only ruin the sibling bond he and Laura shared.

That being said, it had been his front door that Laura had knocked on, three-year-old Lilly on her hip, to declare through ragged sobs that her marriage was officially over. It had been Nick who had accompanied Laura to every court hearing thereafter to finalise the divorce and settle the custody agreement. And it has been Nick who has been a guardian to Lilly three nights a week whilst Laura worked nights ever since.

So of course, Nick's newest reaction towards Scott was perfectly justified - in his eyes.

"I'm going to kill him."

Nick had now abandoned the last of his breakfast and was pacing the restaurant floor with vigorous aggression, Paige looking on in bewilderment.

"Lilly's admitted to being in contact with him for weeks now. On my bloody phone!" Laura cried, now pacing in opposite lines to her brother.

"Is this…?" Paige asked, still staring at Nick and Laura in total bafflement.

"My ex-husband - yeah. What am I going to do, Nick?"

Nick came to a sudden halt, hands on his hips as he

frowned up at the ceiling in the direction of wherever Lilly was hiding upstairs. He released a defeated sigh and turned to his sister.

"I hate to say it…"

"Then don't," Laura threatened, through gritted teeth.

"You'll only damage your own relationship with her if you meddle too much," Nick said gently, recalling the same advice given to him all those years ago. "But… you should call… *him.* Let the twat know that you're aware of the conversations. Stop the secrecy."

Laura nodded, rubbing her eyes and breathing heavily through her nose.

"You're exhausted," Paige soothed, her brow creased in worry. "You need to sleep. I can walk Lilly up to school…if you're happy for me to. Might give you a head start to clear your head."

Nick was suddenly grateful for Paige's presence and gave her a small smile to show his appreciation, her returning it with the smallest of nervous smiles.

Laura nodded her consent and grabbed Paige in for a gratifying hug.

"That would be amazing. I can't believe she did this behind my back. Who'd have thought eight-year-olds could be so sneaky?"

The untouched bacon sandwich sat on the table in front of Laura, as she wrung her hands in frantic worry.

"She didn't do this to spite you Laura," Nick reasoned. "She's just confused and wants to see if she has a chance at a relationship with her dad."

"You're bloody calm, considering you were ready to commit murder about five seconds ago!" Laura scoffed.

"Oh, I want to bloody kill him," Nick confirmed, his arm muscles flexing across his large chest. "If he pisses around with that poor girl one more time, I will knock him off the harbour wall."

Chapter Eight

Paige was thoughtful as she headed back to the restaurant, walking back down Cliff Road from dropping Lilly off to school and her knees protesting all the way. A small hollow part of her heart had ached to see Nick so caring and protective towards his little sister. It only reminded her of what could have been. What she would never have. But Nick's love towards his sister had been so fierce, even Paige had felt compelled to help Laura in her frantic state.

Paige knew all too well the damaging impact a divorce could have on a child. The confusion, the constant crippling worry that it was her fault, the waves of anger that her parents gave up so easily. To hear that a parent could flake out on being a part of their child's life altogether had her heart bursting for little Lilly as she walked her safely to school.

She found Nick in the kitchen along with some other kitchen staff she was yet to introduce herself to. She was surprised to find the kitchen environment calm, with Nick taking his time to show a young lad how to chop onions finely. She watched as he guided the boy with utter patience, showering him in praise and a clap on the back when he'd finished slicing the onions to a mediocre standard.

"We'll practise again tomorrow. Great job, mate. Alright Paige?" Nick finally spotted Paige hovering in the doorway. He glanced over at her with a smile as he washed his hands. "Thanks for doing that. Is she alright?"

"A bit quiet." Paige eyed up the onion mess on the cutting board, then checked the boy was out of the room. "You're not going to use that, are you?"

"God, no! It's an improvement from his last go, though. Bloody hacked that one. Jamie wants to do catering in college so I'm giving him a few lessons in knife skills."

Paige's eyebrows shot up in response and she nodded in approval before scanning around the room, taking in the kitchen space, the equipment, the ovens, the preparation area. In the thirteen years that Elaine had worked here, Paige had not once stepped foot in this kitchen, and she was surprised by the practical layout, the gleaming appliances and tools, the vast knife collection. Some of it wasn't necessarily new, but everything in this room had clearly been well looked after, well maintained and cleaned thoroughly. Paige's culinary fingers twitched and she suddenly felt the urge to don the chef whites and whip up her favourite dishes.

Then, as quick as air escaping a burst balloon, a wave of self-doubt washed over her. Not counting the catering rooms in college, she'd only ever worked as a chef at Garlands. Suddenly, she'd do anything to be there in the safe nook of familiarity. She knew the menus, she knew the dishes and she knew where every single utensil and tool was. Here, though the kitchen was designed with practicality and ease in mind, it felt as if she was starting from scratch and even making a cup of tea right now would be arduous. She realised then that if she wanted to avoid making a complete fool of herself in her own kitchen and to show her new team that they were in safe hands, she was going to need to up her game with her presence here, familiarise herself with every corner of the restaurant and study the menu and its recipes to a tee.

Clearly leaving her to her own devices, Nick had started work on a new onion, slicing and dicing it to perfection, she noted.

"Do you mind me taking a look at the menu?"

"Not at all," Nick looked up briefly, before returning to his work. "Tonight's specials are behind the bar."

The specials were printed on buff parchment paper, with the headline in a calligraphy-style font. A little outdated, Paige thought to herself. Once she glanced at the dishes on offer however, suddenly the style of the stationary was forgotten. Whoever had thought up this ambitious menu - she only assumed it was Nick in his position - had crafted the list of dishes with the current season, local produce and creativity in mind. It was a far cry from the obsolete surroundings and certainly deserved a more suited stationary style.

"What do you think?" Nick probed, hoisting himself on to a stool in front of Paige as she studied the menu.

"It's very Italian."

"No shit, Sherlock. We are called Giuseppe's," Nick scoffed. He sat patiently waiting for Paige to offer further comment.

"It's a beautiful choice of dishes," Paige added with earnest. "I'm not going to attempt the Italian names on here, but the mixed seafood linguine with chilli and cherry tomatoes sounds sublime."

"*Linguine ai Frutti di Mare*," Nick translated, with impressive accuracy in his pronunciation. Paige ignored the sudden slight pinch in her lower abdomen.

"This sounds simple but delicious. Pasta shells and beans with squid and chorizo."

"*Orecchiette con Calamari e Chorizo.*"

"Alright show off! Do you speak Italian?"

"Not at all. I've just written these menus enough times that the names stick. That one was a particular favourite with Giuseppe himself."

Paige's eyebrows arched ruefully for a moment before she returned to the issue at hand. "About the menu... the stationary, that is..."

Paige faltered slightly as Nick stood a little taller, his burly arms folding in front of his chest and the flesh between his brows furrowing in anticipated fortification.

"Do you think the style is a little dated?"

"Are we sat in a trendy restaurant, with cut lines, simplistic decor and uncomfortable modern seating?"

"Do you always answer questions with another question?"

"Do you?"

Paige steadied her resolve before continuing with the utmost patience. "Modern seats aren't necessarily uncomfortable and these old bamboo chairs are hideous."

"Oh, now you've got a problem with the furniture..."

"It's just... the decor hasn't changed at all for as long as I have known it. I'm pretty sure they're older than you and I put together!"

"And not one customer has complained about it. They come for good food. They get *outstanding* food. Full stop."

Paige took a steadying breath, her temper rising as Nick spread his feet out slightly for a stronger, more stubborn stance. God, he was infuriating.

"You're telling me you don't take environment into consideration at all?" Paige challenged.

"If the place is clean, has comfortable seating and excellent food, I'm there."

"Right," Paige pinched her lips in between her teeth and seethed for a beat, clutching the specials menu and wishing she hadn't raised the subject. If this was how conversations ended up just from discussing menu stationary, what can of worms was she going to open by attempting to change anything else? And if she was honest, there was an endless list of things she wanted to change, to erase from this place.

"That was fun," Nick grinned, his demeanour changing like a switch. "Love a good debate."

Paige's mouth opened and closed like a demented goldfish as she fumbled for her words. "I thought you were pissed off for a moment! That I'd offended you!"

"Over stationery? Hardly." Nick chuckled. "But I stand by my opinion. The menu, the dishes, the decor - all of it is authentic Italian and it works. I think you should find your feet here and get a feel for what Giuseppe was trying to create here before you come in trying to change it all. It won't go down well with the staff. Maxine being one of them. She's worked here longer than I have."

A quick glance at Maxine as she came in for the start

of her shift told Paige that she was ruthless, hardworking and a force to be reckoned with. When Nick had introduced Paige to her, Paige had offered her hand to shake in greeting, only for Maxine to merely grunt a curt acknowledgment, sizing her up as a new recruit before getting straight into her work.

"Maxine keeps the front of house lot in line. She's a bit rough around the edges but she's got a heart of gold," Nick explained after Maxine had left Paige feeling suitably shafted.

Paige exhaled in exasperation, feeling totally crestfallen already.

"You're going to have to have a thick skin to begin with. Everyone here is justifiably nervous about the restaurant changing hands and they might not all be receptive to begin with," Nick muttered into her ear, feeling like a rational conscience on Paige's shoulder.

"You can say that. Your fuzzy welcome didn't exactly pump me full of confidence."

"Well, I am sorry about that," Nick said with earnest, though he regarded her as if he had planned to say something else. "If I'm honest, I was all set up to hate your guts before I'd even met you."

Paige muttered 'Jesus' under her breath, her stomach curdling at his brutal honesty.

"Hear me out. I need to explain my behaviour the weekend you first came down. And there after really." Nick's tone was soft and apologetic as he blocked Paige's way to ensure she stayed and listened. "I'd known your mum a very long time, and to see how much your unexplained absence pained her - well, I formed an opinion of you in my head. I had it in me that if I ever met Elaine's estranged daughter, I would have a few chosen words to say to her."

Paige's foot tapped nervously on the floor, her arms across her body in defence. She really didn't want to hear this.

"But then when I realised you were her, that evening

Bear decided to practically run you off the harbour, all the words sort of just dispersed and the wind got knocked out of my sails a bit really," Nick looked down at Paige with a frown on his face, his grey eyes penetrating through her and making her squirm on the spot. "I can't quite figure you out."

She could have said the same thing about him. One minute he thawed just enough for her to feel moderately comfortable in his presence, the next he was stripping her bare and making her feel like the biggest fraud to have ever walked through this village. He also seemed to know exactly how to provoke her temper, and she felt the red mist forming behind her watery eyes at that very moment. She wasn't sure what he had tried to achieve in this disclosure of his, whether it was supposed to be some sort of apology for his behaviour or another dig at her to see how quickly she'd scarper back to Bristol. What she did know however was that she couldn't keep walking away. She'd done enough of that in the past, and if Nick really was playing some clever mind game to scare her off, she needed to make sure his plan fell spectacularly at his feet.

"Well," Paige began, when she was sure Nick was finished, "my mother always told me never to make a judgment on somebody until you had all your ducks in a row. And given that you don't know a damn thing about me or my family history, I'd say your ducks are all over the bloody shop right now."

Satisfied that her words had finally rendered him speechless, she picked up a notepad and pen and nodded at the ingredients that Nick had laid out ready to make the lunchtime special.

"Paige..." Nick growled, in warning.

"I don't want to get in the way, so I'll just watch and take notes for today if that's alright." Paige put on her best smile whilst her legs felt like jelly, her stomach doing somersaults. Nick harrumphed loudly and got down to work preparing for the lunch service.

Paige couldn't have got home and shut the door behind her fast enough that evening. Far from feeling composed and in control, she had shadowed Nick's small team of chefs, watching them prepare their signature dishes and getting an idea on each person's role in the kitchen. Keeping her distance, she also observed Maxine who was still choosing to give her the cold shoulder. That little issue to one side, she'd been happy in her success to reassure some of the more pliable staff members that she wasn't a threat to them or their jobs. It had been a relief when a couple of the young waitresses had started being friendly and even shared a few laughs with her.

The next morning, Paige's determination to break through Maxine's icy barrier and get back on good terms with Nick had her out for a run at 6am, with the plan to be back in the restaurant for the start of Nick's shift.

Everything in the harbour glistened from the winter frost, Paige's breath a white puff in front of her as she lapped a steady pace around the quay. The cold had her muscles screaming in protest and her body inefficiently using up oxygen, so it didn't take long for Paige to give in and start walking back to the cottage. She was just passing the old fish market when a voice boomed across the water.

"Paige!"

Whipping around towards the vague direction the voice had been coming from, Paige clapped eyes on a man who was geared up for a cold, wet day on the ocean, the bulk of him suggesting he had numerous layers on. Blonde hair poked out from under a burgundy beanie hat and when the man had finally reached Paige on dry land, he was beaming ear from ear.

"Paige, I can't believe it! It's been years. How are you doing?"

"Charlie?" It finally clicked for her, and suddenly her grin was matching his. "I didn't know you were a fisherman."

"I am now," Charlie said, his hands on his hips. "Started a couple of weeks ago, in my new otter trawler. Well, not brand new. Actually, old and rusty."

"Oh, so you're the new fisherman joining the fleet?" Paige nodded in understanding. Charlie's smile had always been contagious and she found her cheeks aching now as they took each other in. "I thought you went up country to train to be a lawyer."

"I did. Got my law degree. Hated it and suddenly hated the idea of any job confined to four office walls. So here I am, my new office being the entire ocean." He waved his arm out to beyond the harbour wall for good measure. "Parents weren't best pleased, mind."

"I bet," Paige laughed. "All those student debts!"

Charlie waved the worry away, something Paige remembered him doing a lot in their school days and nodded toward the restaurant. "So, the rumours are true. You've taken ownership of Giuseppe's."

"Yep. Guess so."

"And you sound ecstatic about it."

"It was my mum's restaurant. She died about a month ago."

Charlie's boyish face creased into a frown. "I'm sorry, Paige. I had heard about it from some of the other fishermen."

"Then you'll know why I'm not massively ecstatic about it."

Charlie nodded in understanding, though he seemed as if he wanted to say something else.

"Well, now I know that we live in the same village again, I would love to catch up with you properly soon. Perhaps somewhere a little warmer," Charlie added the last part, pointing out that Paige was now shivering in her running skins.

"Good idea," Paige agreed, blowing some hot air into her frozen hands. "Why don't you pop into the restaurant before you head off this morning. We'll exchange details and I'll send you off with a hot coffee. Filtered, though."

Charlie pulled a blissful face. "You always were a dream, Paige. See you in about an hour then."

Upon her arrival back in the restaurant, after she'd climbed out of her running gear, warmed up under the shower and donned her trusty chef trousers and a simple black t-shirt, Nick welcomed her with a coffee and bacon sandwich.

"Thought you might be in early. I didn't see you eat a single thing all day yesterday, so get that down you."

"Thanks," Paige said, impressed by his intuition. "I forget to be hungry when I spend the whole day smelling food. Bad habit, I know."

Nick thought about that for a moment before nodding his head. "Actually, I know what you mean. Doesn't stop my massive appetite though. You did well yesterday."

Paige looked up from over her door-wedge bacon sandwich, her eyes wide in surprise from his compliment. She chewed quietly, unsure how to reply.

"The team liked you."

"Apart from Maxine," Paige added without thinking.

"Ah. Yes, about Maxine," Nick began, taking a tray of fresh scallops from the fridge. "I think you need to have a proper chat with her this afternoon. She told me yesterday that she actually knew you very well when you were a young girl, and when you didn't recognise her and offered to shake her hand like a perfect stranger - I think she just took it to heart a little."

Paige cringed and placed her half-eaten sandwich back on its plate. "Crap. I didn't realise. She can't expect me to remember every family friend from my childhood though, surely?"

Nick didn't answer straight away, fully focused on prising the hinge of the scallop shell open with a shucking knife. "She mentioned that you used to go and play at her house a lot. I think her late husband used to trawl on the same vessel as Jacca at one point. She lives up Polkirt Hill."

"Oh!" Paige's hands flew up to her head as memories came hurtling back to her. Memories of playing in Maxine's huge back garden. Memories of having sleep overs. Maxine's children were a little older but had always treated Paige like a cousin and amused her for hours. "I remember now. No wonder she'd acted the way she did yesterday. I always called her Aunty Max. It just didn't occur to me yesterday, when you introduced her as Maxine."

"Yes, because Max and Maxine sound so different," Nick drawled, ducking as Paige flung a tea towel at his head. They chuckled for a moment, all tension from yesterday seeping away, then Paige grabbed a second shucking knife to help Nick with the scallops.

"I knew my memory was bad at times but being away for as long as I have been…" Paige paused, unsure whether to finish her sentence. "I guess I just need to be more observant. I'll talk to her when she gets in later."

They shucked scallops in silence for a bit, a task Paige had always found quite therapeutic as a teenager, whenever Jacca bought some home. Another small reminder of her childhood but enough to knock the wind out of her. Despite her concentration on the task in hand, she suddenly felt the slight prickle of Nick watching her.

"Paige, I-"

Nick didn't get a chance to finish his sentence as Chelsea, one of the front of house staff, came in to start her shift.

"Morning," Chelsea chirped. "There's a well fit bloke in there. Says he's here to see you Paige."

"Oh, that'll be Charlie," Paige replied, washing her hands and trying to tame the little butterflies fluttering around in her stomach.

"Who's Charlie?" Nick asked, harshly. "Why's he letting himself in to the restaurant. We're not open for hours!"

"Chill out! I let him in!" Chelsea cried, indignant, as she signed into the shift book.

"It's OK. He's an old friend. I said he could come in for a takeaway coffee whilst we exchanged details," Paige reasoned, drying her hands and making her way through to the restaurant leaving Nick to mutter something about them not being a Starbucks drive-thru.

Paige found Charlie in the restaurant taking in his surroundings with an air of ease and contentment, the big boyish grin returning to his face as soon as Paige came through to stand behind the bar.

"Right, what can I get you? Flat white? Cappuccino? I'm joking - it's filtered coffee or tea, I'm afraid," Paige said, her cheeks flushing a little at the sight of him. She didn't remember him ever having this sort of effect on her in school. As the saying went, he'd certainly matured like a fine wine.

"Filtered coffee, please."

"So, how's the fishing going?" Paige asked, busying herself with the coffee-making.

"Crap. But it'll get there. Just learning the ways of the ocean, I guess."

"Had you done any fishing before now?"

"Yeah! My Pappy was a fisherman here. I used to go out with him as often as Mum would let me. Do you still go out fishing with your dad?"

"Haven't yet," Paige surprised herself by saying, realising that it implied that she was at least considering it.

"You're welcome to come out with me some time. I could do with the company," Charlie said, rubbing his stubbly chin. "Wow, that made me sound pathetic."

Paige laughed. "No it didn't. A trip out on your new vessel sounds great actually. I'm supposed to be going through the rotas today with Nick. Once I've worked out my days off, I'll let you know."

Paige snapped the lid on Charlie's takeaway cup and handed him his hot coffee, just as he took his phone out of his pocket and asked for Paige's number. Once details were exchanged, Charlie gave Paige one more smile that went straight to her knees before taking his coffee back to his boat. When she returned to the kitchen, Nick looked beyond irritated and Chelsea was looking gleeful.

"Are you dating the new hot skipper in town?" Chelsea was straight in there, looking utterly impressed and romanticised.

"Oh for God's sake, Chelsea. Get a grip will you and do some work!" Nick snapped, his hands now fully emerged in the messy task of removing excess ligaments and coral from the scallops.

"You're not the only hot guy in Meva, Nick," Chelsea rebutted.

Paige was both slightly appalled and amused that Chelsea, no older than eighteen, was giving Nick such grief. She was certainly bolshie for her age.

"No, I'm not dating anybody. Charlie and I used to go to school together."

"Chelsea, stop your gossiping and get out here to clean some tables," Maxine berated, appearing from the front and giving Paige a flash memory of her and Maxine's children being scolded for hanging on their fruit trees in the back garden, snapping a few branches from their weight.

When Chelsea had made herself scarce, Paige took the opportunity to grab Maxine's attention.

"Maxine, can I have a quick chat with you?"

When Maxine agreed begrudgingly, they took themselves through the kitchen and into the storage room.

"Maxine, I'm really sorry for not recognising you yesterday."

Maxine's shoulders seemed to slump slightly and a little bit of sadness crossed her face. "I was taken aback a bit, you understand. I used to look after you most weekends, when Jacca was out on long-haul and your mum on evening shifts at the pub."

"I know. I remember it all now I've had my memory jogged. I'm really sorry."

"Well, it's been a fair few years and Lord knows you've been through a lot," Maxine reasoned, her features softening and the kind, jovial Auntie Max Paige could recall from all those years ago appeared before her very eyes. "I'm ever so sad about Elaine, love."

Paige nodded, a lump forming in her throat. Allowing a sigh to escape through her nose, she composed herself as quickly as she could. She wasn't much for crying, particularly in front of people.

"You and Mum were good friends. I never knew you worked here with her and… " She bit down on her lip, unable to finish the sentence.

"Only after Giuseppe's passing. As you know, he left everything to your mother. She was struggling. Jacca wasn't keen on the place - fair enough to him. You were off doing your training up country."

"I was in Bristol," Paige retorted, smiling to keep the conversation light. "Hardly up country."

"You might remember that my George was a fisherman. He worked on the Agnes with your dad in the nineties."

Paige nodded along, listening politely and relieved to have Maxine talking to her.

"Just like your dad, George would sometimes be gone for weeks at a time. He'd come home, give me lots of stinky washing, eat me out of house and home, and would bugger off again before we'd even had a proper catch up. It's a lonely life, being a fisherman's wife. Your mother and I relied upon one another's company a great deal."

The reality of what Maxine was trying to point out hit Paige in the gut and she suddenly fixed her gaze on the wall behind Maxine.

"I'm glad we've been able to clear the air, Maxine," Paige said as a form of distraction, feeling far from comfortable with this turn of conversation. "I had best go back and start doing some work around here. Prove myself worthy."

Maxine smiled with a hint of disappointment behind her eyes. "Welcome aboard, Paige. It's nice to see you back here. Where you belong."

Chapter Nine

The next week flew by for Paige and she soon fell into step with the restaurant's way of working. She and Nick had snatched enough time to sort rotas out between them, adding Paige's hours in, but they were still to sit down properly together to discuss long-term plans and where Paige's position was in the kitchen. She knew she was the owner of Giuseppe's, but the last thing she wanted to do was elbow her way into an existing rank of chefs and cause anybody to lose their place. She was desperate to get in to the kitchen though.

With a day off and very little to do with the weather brewing menacingly outside, Paige decided to tackle the pigsty that was Jacca's house. She'd sat amongst the worst of it that morning for breakfast and had decided enough was enough, heading straight to the shops to buy as much cleaning paraphernalia as possible. After all, if she decided to accept the restaurant and make her move permanent, this was going to be her home for a long time until she could afford somewhere else in the village.

Once she'd pressed play on her favourite playlist and worked out some sort of system in bags and boxes, between chucking, recycling, donating and keeping, she dived straight in. Jacca was going to be out fishing all day and probably wouldn't find his way home again until teatime, so she had the best part of the whole day in front of her to make a real dent on the mess. It would be a nice surprise for when her dad came home.

It quickly became apparent that the dirt, the grime and the sheer mess were something that had been building up for quite some time. Ruining numerous cloths and going through a whole bottle of Zoflora, Paige soon cut through the filth, the air in the cottage feeling dramatically cleaner and lighter. She piled the old newspapers by the door with the plan to take them down for recycling, then she started sifting through the paperwork on the dining table where Paige usually had to fight for a section of clear space. It became therapeutic work as she categorised bills, junk mail and appointments into piles ready for Jacca to check when he got home. She'd perhaps help him to sort out a filing system for all his paperwork, her heart squeezing slightly as she recalled her mother doing a similar task for him all those years ago.

In fact, the more she unearthed the cottage that she knew from her childhood, the one not buried under years of neglect and loneliness, the more memories that came flooding back. She recalled the smell of wood varnish from the old dresser, once a proud piece in the front room, now something that sat sadly under the stairs. The oak beams were as they always had been, striping the white ceiling with bold, dark lines - except now these same beams looked dusty, tired and spotted with spiders webs, the contrasting ceiling more tan than brilliant white. Paige was beginning to think that the house didn't need a clean as much as it needed to be redecorated entirely and this realisation came with a twinge of sadness.

This cottage had once been bursting with life and love and daily purpose, well-used but looked after. If Paige was to stay still enough, she could almost pluck the snippets of memories floating around the rooms from thin air.

But that was just it. They were just memories now. Fragile little memories, only to be looked at but never to return to or live in. That final thought almost suffocated Paige in grief, more so than the thick dust clouds she kicked up each time she shifted something from its spot.

Only one thing to do then, Paige thought to herself as she wiped her damp eyes with her shoulder - the only part of her not coated in dirt. Keep going until the inside of the cottage was recognisable again.

Midday soon appeared. Though the wind was kicking up a notch outside, the grime clung to Paige, her nose itching from the exposed dust, so she took herself out on to the storm porch for a cup of tea and some left-over soup from yesterday's shift at the restaurant. Despite feeling the dirtiest she had ever felt, and the easterly wind cutting through her hoodie like ice-cold blades, she felt quite content. She sipped her soup and watched, with a little flutter, as Charlie navigated his boat back into the harbour. She was yet to organise with him this outing on his vessel, and though she looked forward to a proper catch up with Charlie Eathorne, she wasn't massively looking forward to getting back on to the ocean, despite her feigned excitement to Charlie that day he'd suggested it. The ocean had a lot to answer for and Paige wasn't ready to forgive it.

"Wow, you're brave sitting out here," Nick commented, cutting through Paige's darkening thoughts just in time.

"I needed some fresh air. I'm deep cleaning."

"Oh... double brave. How did Jacca take it when you suggested he had a good clean up?" Nick perched on the half wall of the storm porch and crossed his arms for comfort.

"I didn't ask him. I just cracked on," Paige shrugged, finishing the last mouthful of soup. "I'm living here too now so he can't expect me to live like this."

"Fair enough. Good luck for his return, though. He near as bit my head off when I offered my services to give the place a good spruce."

Paige frowned at this, her initial anticipation to surprise her dad morphing into worry. Perhaps she should have spoken to him first.

"He'll be fine. Once he sees how much nicer it is, he'll be fine," Paige said with feigned confidence. "How come you're home by the way? Is the restaurant quiet?"

"Dead. It's the brewing storm keeping everyone away. I've left Ollie in charge for two seconds while I give Mowgli his Metacam."

"Mowgli," Paige reiterated, a smile pulling up on her mouth. "This is your cat?"

"Yes," Nick replied, affronted. "What's wrong with the name Mowgli?"

"Nothing. In fact, I love it. I just can't imagine a big burly bloke like yourself with a little fluff-ball for a pet."

"Little fluff-ball? I take it you haven't actually met Mowgli!" Nick laughed, holding one finger up. "Wait one second."

Nick returned with a large bundle of silver tabby fur.

"Jesus! That's not a cat, that's something from the Jungle Book!"

Nick threw his head back and released a huge belly laugh, presenting Mowgli like a proud parent. "Hence the name. He gets that reaction a lot. Mowgli here is a Maine Coone. Largest domesticated cat you can get."

"What made you decide to get a Maine Coone?" Paige asked, incredulous, as she admired Mowgli's large silvery mane and massive paws.

"Long story short, he came with the house. I bought this cottage when Maureen passed away, and her daughter asked if I would keep Mowgli because their son was allergic."

"I remember Maureen. She used to have a secret stash of choc-ices," Paige remembered, smiling fondly at another little snatch of childhood that wasn't laced in sadness or grief. "Can I hold him?"

Nick's eyebrows shot up and he jumped forward. "Yeah, definitely. He loves cuddles. Not very many people want to hold him because they're scared of his size."

"Aww, he must be the best heat source at night," Paige cooed as she took all eight kilos of Mowgli's mass into her arms, rubbing her cheek up against his fur. "He's gorgeous!"

Nick smiled and perched back down on the half wall as Paige fussed over a rather impassive Mowgli.

"So. Big and burly, eh?" Nick waggled his eyebrows as Paige's cheeks coloured.

"Don't flatter yourself," Paige retorted, smiling. "Now I've met your cat, I take it back. He's more manly than you!"

Nick released another belt of laughter and Paige was suddenly taken back to that day when she first met Nick, before he'd made judgements on who she was.

"Right, come on you!" Nick said to a sleepy Mowgli. "This old man needs his Metacam. That's the problem with big cats in their old age. Hip dysplasia."

"Ouch! Go and have your meds, old man!" Paige handed Mowgli over to Nick, who was now giving her a strange look, his features softened and a smile playing in the corner of his mouth. "What?"

"Nothing." He cleared his throat. "I'll leave you to your cleaning day. Can't wait to see the finished result."

When Nick had taken Mowgli inside the cottage for his midday meds, Paige drained the rest of her tea and returned to the warmth of inside. It really was looking and smelling so much better. If only she could give it a lick of paint, but that would be pushing it. Instead, she opted to tackle the kitchen next, immersing herself into the arduous task of sorting through Jacca's rather limited but slightly out of date cupboard contents.

She must have lost track of time as a few hours later she recognised Jacca's rather ungainly entrance into the cottage, the clock on the kitchen wall confirming it was dinner time. She'd have to grab some fish and chips for a quick fix.

"Hi Dad," Paige called from the kitchen, her head in a cupboard as she gave it a final wipe down with a soapy cloth. "I lost track of time, so I'll head to the chippy in a minute."

"What the bloody hell is all this?" The drunken snarl in Jacca's voice curdled Paige's stomach as she realised that he sounded far from pleased. She climbed out of the cupboard, her knees aching from her weight, and wiped the sweat from her brow.

"I was just having a clean-up."

Jacca swayed on the spot, his face practically purple from the rage pulsing through him. Paige's heart hammered in her chest, her mind shooting back to the memories of a little girl who used to hide in her room when her father got this drunk. He'd never been violent of the physical sort, but his whole aggressive demeanour, the way his soft features contorted in utter rage, used to scare her senseless. Now, all those years later, it still had that effect on her.

"Dad, it was just a clean-up. I haven't thrown anything personal or of use away."

"You don't just come back and start clearing my shit! You haven't been here! These are mine!" Jacca stumbled forward as he tried to gather an armful of old newspapers, Paige rushing forward to catch him. "Get off me! I never asked you to do this. You never asked!"

He jabbed the air between him and Paige with his finger, each jab sending a jolt of sadness through Paige as she gaped at him in horror.

"I'm sorry, Dad. I was just trying to help! I -"

"Well I never asked for your bloody help! You've not been here to help for the last ten bloody years - you can't just -"

"Dad, stop! I said I was sorry!"

"Get out!"

"Jacca, that's enough." Before Paige had a chance to register who the voice belonged to, Nick was towering over him, muttering to him to calm down and setting his hands on her father's shoulders as a way of soothing him. Paige flinched as more drunken expletives were shot in her direction. "Paige, go next door and make yourself a cup of tea."

Nick's orders were soft but with enough force that Paige wasn't asked a second time. She dumped her cloth and bolted out of the door. Jacca's voice carried over to Nick's cottage, but Paige tried her best to block it out as she took in her new surroundings, her throat bruised from sobs she was currently attempting to hold back.

Nick's cottage was just the tonic Paige needed after spending what had turned out to be a futile day of cleaning in Jacca's dark, damp pit of a house. In contrast to the dark, stained wood trim all over her dad's cottage, the interior of Nick's was modern, clean-cut and tastefully in keeping with what used to be an old fisherman's abode. The walls were whitewashed and the furnishings soft tones of blue and green to match the shades of the ocean. This had not been what she'd expected - but then again, what had she expected?

Discarding her trainers and suddenly feeling far too grubby to be anywhere near Nick's furniture, Paige trod carefully over the polished wooden floorboard and found the kitchen at the back of the house. A tiny little galley kitchen, with a large skylight above, it was suitably kitted out for a chef. With trembling hands and with arms that felt like lead, Paige opted for coffee rather than tea. She found Mowgli sprawled out on a rather trendy teal-blue armchair, so took a spot on the floor in front of him, taking comfort in stroking his large square head.

How had she judged the situation so tremendously wrong? Did she really know her own dad that little that she didn't realise how much this would have upset him? She sat on the floor, cradling her coffee, and feeling utterly miserable, Mowgli's purring the only thing keeping her from bolting entirely and heading back to Bristol. But then again, what good would that do at this point?

"Paige?" Nick popped his head around the corner of his front door. "Bloody hell, it's blowing a hooley out there. You OK?"

"You warned me he'd react like this," Paige sniffed, bringing her knees up to her chest. "You know my dad better than I do."

Nick shook his head and perched himself on the edge of his coffee table. "You were trying to do something nice for him. Something that needed doing. You haven't been here though - don't bite my head off! I'm not getting on at you. You just haven't, so you won't have seen that his drinking problem has been rather challenging recently."

"He's always had a drinking problem," Paige grumbled, trying her best not to feel or sound disgruntled by his dig on her absence. "You're not at the restaurant."

"It's dead again. Storm coming. But I saw Jacca coming out of the social club in his state and had a feeling things weren't going to go down well with the house, so I followed him home. I'll have to go back again in a minute."

Paige felt Nick's eyes on her as she stared into her coffee, utterly disconsolate and vulnerable.

"He's calmed down now. Why don't you grab some fish and chips for you both and have a chat over food?"

"I'm not talking to him when he's like that," Paige said firmly, hugging her knees tighter.

"He'd never hurt you, Paige."

"I know that!" Paige snapped. "But words hurt more sometimes, and he can get really nasty like this."

Nick nodded in understanding and Paige was grateful that he didn't probe any further. "OK, new plan. Why don't you go and check the restaurant is alright? I'll grab Jacca some dinner and meet you back there to make *you* some dinner."

A small trickle of warmth cut through the iciness that currently flowed through Paige from this evening's antics. A small, ghost of a smile appeared on Paige's face in gratitude and she nodded her agreement.

"Thank you, Nick."

"S'alright. You bloody Yellands and your dramas," Nick rolled his eyes, smiled and winked to show he was joking. Paige gave him a deadpan expression and took his offered hand to heave her up off the floor, the touch of his strong hands sending small electric currents down her arm.

Paige didn't stay long at the Giuseppe's that evening, only for enough time to devour a simple but nourishing spaghetti bolognese Nick had whipped up as soon as he was back from sorting Jacca out. The irony was not lost on her, the fact that the very place she'd avoided all these years was her safe place tonight.

When she returned to the cottage, everything was as she left it, with the addition of a sleeping Jacca sprawled on the sofa. She felt exhausted - not only from the exertions of cleaning all day, but from the unfortunate aftermath as well. She welcomed a long, hot shower to rid her of the day, but the sight of Jacca stopped her in her tracks. There was something vulnerable about her dear old father that immediately made her forgive him for his behaviour this evening. His once thick black hair now white and wispy, his tanned skin from years out to sea now leathery and aged. She gingerly lay a throw over Jacca's slumbering frame, careful to dodge any creaky floorboards which may stir him.

When did he become so frail? How much suffering had he done in her absence, without letting on during her short visits?

That was just it.

Her visits were so short - and she had to be honest, she was never fully there with her parents mentally. Her mind was always elsewhere. Her parents had been different people when everything went topsy turvy. She'd been a different person, but she hadn't bothered to get to know the new versions of her parents.

Paige went for her shower, not only to wash off the dirt and grime of the day, but to attempt to wash off the shame that now coated her all over. She knew what she needed to do.

"Matthew?"

"Paige? Hi! It's late, are you alright?"

The butterflies in Paige's tummy settled and she drew in a deep breath at the sound of Matthew's voice, surprised to find that when she needed it most, he still had a calming effect on her.

"Sort of. I called because… I know it hasn't been the full two weeks yet. But I'm calling to confirm my resignation from Garlands."

There was a pause on Matthew's end, and Paige bit her lip in worry.

"He wouldn't admit it, but I think my dad needs me down here. He's in a bad way, and things are doing OK in the restaurant. I just need to put my stamp on it."

"Paige?"

She stopped, knowing she was rambling.

"You don't have to justify your reasons. I think you've made a great decision. Just as long as it's a decision for you too."

"I've made enough decisions based on just me. It's time I put my dad into that equation as well."

Another pause.

"Good for you, Paige. Leave it all to me. We'll pool some of your annual leave together so you can work your notice from down there."

"Thank you, Matthew."

"Of course. Take care of yourself, Paige."

"You too, Matthew."

"Paige! Paige! Get up! Come on, girl! That's it - put some layers on!

Blurry eyed and utterly discombobulated, Paige was dragged out of bed by a frantic Jacca. It was still dark outside and the wooden sash window was rattling in its frame.

"Meet me downstairs."

"Dad, what's the matter?"

"The storm's hit. Several of the boats have broken their mooring and our fishing equipment is getting a beating. Need all hands on deck. Come on - get up!"

Moments later, with about a dozen layers on, Paige stepped out into the chaos of wild Mevagissey. The sheer noise of the storm was deafening as Jacca shouted out orders which just carried off into the wind.

At a glance, Paige saw Nick, Charlie, Maxine and some other residents she had begun to recognise. Maxine and a few others were attempting to salvage crab pots and signs, whilst Nick and Charlie were each throwing their weight into trying to pull in boats that had gone astray, as other fisherman tried to manoeuvre the vessels closer to the dock. It was all dangerous work as the boats bumped into one another in the mooring area, and Paige felt a pang of panic as the ocean lapped up menacingly against the harbour walls, soaking people as they got too close. Beyond the inner wall, the outer harbour and lighthouse looked lost to sea, the treacherous waves completely engulfing the entire thing beyond the Harbour Office.

"Paige!" Jacca roared against the wind, as it sprayed seawater into everyone's faces, soaking them within seconds. "Help Nick!"

Paige ran towards the old fish market on the other side where Nick was attempting to reconnect the boat to the cleat hitch on the dock.

"Help me pull it in more so I can get a decent knot!" Nick shouted above the racket. Paige did as she was told, her arm muscles screaming in protest as she put her entire strength into fighting against the boat and the wind. Jacca and Charlie were now doing the same, as were several other fishermen to nearby vessels, their shouts and orders carrying off into the dark night.

"Got it! Grab the next line! David, throw us the other line!"

The other bowline was thrown out and Paige grabbed it before it could slither into the water. She began to heave the boat inward immediately as Nick seized the line behind Paige, and together they secured it to the dock.

"Here, have these!" Nick put a pair of thick gloves in Paige's hands, which she took gratefully. Her freezing cold hands were burning, the skin torn from the friction of the rope. It was becoming harder to see as Paige shielded her face with one arm from the sea spray, which spattered painfully into her eyes and up her nose. The strength of the wind took her breath away as she and Nick raced to grab Malcolm, who had lost his footing and was being dragged to the water's edge by the line he was holding.

An agonising and deafening ten minutes passed with only two more boats secured to the docks, when a huge clap of thunder brought everybody to a halt, followed by a flash of lightning.

"It's getting too dangerous! Everyone in!" Malcolm bellowed.

There was a scurry of chaos as everybody grabbed anything and everything worth saving, heading in the direction of their homes just as another round of thunder and lightning rumbled and lit up the skies.

"Oh my god! Look at the harbour carpark!" Paige yelled, as they started climbing up the walkway back to the cottages, pointing at the tarmac which was being peeled away from the ground by the wind.

"Let's all head into mine!" Nick bellowed. "I've got double-glazing!"

Nick and Paige clambered into his cottage as Jacca checked that nobody else was out there in all the elements. Once the door was shut behind all three of them, Nick set to work relighting his wood burner, asking Paige to make some coffee. Jacca collapsed on the nearest armchair, assessing damage to his leg which was bleeding profusely.

"What've you done, Jacca?" Nick tutted, lighting a match for the fire.

"Bleddy scraped my leg on somethin'. Looks worse than it is, don't fuss."

"Let me take a look at it," Paige ordered, coming through from the kitchen with three steaming mugs of coffee. "Knowing you, you'll have to have stitches or something."

Right on cue, a huge clap of thunder rumbled and shook the whole cottage, followed by the window flashing white from the lightning. Mowgli raised his head lazily to see what the commotion was, quickly losing interest and falling back to sleep again.

"Don't think we'll be going anywhere, Maid. Unless you're handy with a needle and thread."

Paige wasn't quite in the right mood with her father yet to humour his jokes, so ignored him and had a look at his leg. The gash on the side of his knee was large and deep, blood oozing out thick and fast.

"Bloody hell, Dad!"

"Here." Nick handed Paige a first aid kit from the kitchen, and she set to work immediately, mopping up the dried blood with an antiseptic wipe.

"Can you wet a piece of kitchen roll, please?" Paige asked Nick. He obliged, bringing it straight through. Paige folded the piece of kitchen roll into a damp square and placed it over the gash.

"Put pressure here," she ordered her father.

"You train as a nurse whilst you've been gone or somethin'?"

"No Dad. It's just good practice for the chefs in charge to be first aid trained. The amount of cuts and falls that can happen in a working kitchen."

"You got one of them?" Jacca turned to Nick.

"Yep," Nick confirmed, sitting down with his coffee as Paige started wrapping Jacca's leg with a bandage.

"Fancy," Jacca nodded in approval.

Nick laughed and Paige shook her head in exasperation.

There was a pause as everyone simply sat and listened to the commotion causing havoc outside, the wood burner beginning to crackle. It was now five o'clock in the morning, but the wind and rain had more than blown any sleepiness away.

"You forgiven me yet, Maid?" Jacca gruffed. Paige let her working arms flop on-to her lap as she shot her father an incredulous look.

"You haven't apologised. You haven't even acknowledged your behaviour last night."

"Alright. I acknowledge I was a bit of a twat, and I'm sorry."

Paige sighed through her nose and looked at Nick for support, who was doing his best to bite back a smile. Giving in, Paige continued to dress Jacca's leg.

"Well, I guess that's as good as I'm going to get. You're forgiven, you old fart."

Chapter Ten

It was a sorry sight for the villagers of Mevagissey as morning light attempted to break through the parting clouds. The storm finally passed just as Nick and Paige agreed they should make breakfast baps for everyone at the restaurant. No doubt all the fishermen would now be returning to assess the damage of their precious vessels.

"Look at it all!" Paige gasped, stepping over the debris littering the streets.

"This is going to cost the village thousands," Nick sighed.

The wind was still strong enough to make talking in close proximity difficult, and the mizzled rain spattered on their faces as they looked out to the pile of damaged boats.

"That's Dad's boat over there!" Paige cried, pointing at Martha, Jacca's well-known vessel, a gaping hole in the side of it. "He's going to be so upset!"

Nick turned around towards the direction of the restaurant as Paige looked across the harbour in sadness.

"Ah."

Nick's following expletives made Paige turn her gaze away from her poor old dad's livelihood, immediately seeing the issue right before her.

Shattered glass littered the ground underneath the iconic arched windows of the restaurant, both now very much exposing the restaurant floor to all the elements.

"Great," Paige said, slapping her arms against her sides in exasperation. "How much is that going to cost us?"

"They're custom-made windows. So… a lot."

"I need another coffee."

Nick threw out another expletive under his breath, which Paige didn't quite catch in the wind, then patted Paige on the shoulder in sympathy. "I'll get the dustpan and brush.

You get the coffee and bacon."

Within half an hour, the harbour-front was occupied by concerned villagers, fishermen and business owners alike, all there to assess the damage and of course to claim their complimentary bacon sandwich from the restaurant.

"Pretty sure we didn't have this many people helping out last night," Nick grumbled, as he replenished Paige's platter for the second time.

"It's hardly costing very much. Besides, wasn't it you who told me about the community spirit around here?" Paige grinned as Nick shot her a deadpan look. Her grin soon faltered as she clapped eyes on her father, Malcolm giving him a consolatory slap on the back. "I'm just going to see if Dad's OK."

"Go for it," Nick's voice softened as he took the platter out of Paige's hands and gave her an encouraging nod.

"Dad? Are you alright?" Paige asked once she'd reached her father.

"Not really, m'love," Jacca shook his head, his eyes on the cigarette he was rolling. "I prepared her for the storm. She still gets damaged because some other pillock didn't prepare theirs! Dun't seem fair, really."

"We'll have a look at the CCTV later, Jac. I'll have a word with the fleet anyway. We weren't prepared enough for this storm," Malcolm went on, then turned to Paige. "Worst one we've seen since the 70s."

"I remember a fairly bad one just before Christmas when I was about ten years old," Paige recalled.

"Nineteen ninety-nine!" Malcolm bellowed, his thumbs tucked behind his bracers, his flannel shirt straining against his swelled belly. "Yes, that was bad enough. But damage was mild. Last night's one buggered us right up. Look! The wall's bloody gone by the toilets. And see that?"

Malcolm pointed towards a big pile of metal stranded on the outer harbour wall.

"Bleddy fuel berth, that is!"

Paige allowed Malcolm to continue to rant, mostly

to himself, as she turned her attention back to Jacca who was now lighting his cigarette and looking very solemn.

"We'll get Martha fixed, Dad. We'll get her sorted."

"You probably think I'm just being soft," Jacca took in a long draw from his cigarette and sniffed sadly. "But a boat to a fisherman... you earn your livelihood with them and they keep you alive at sea. It's something special, you know?"

"Dad, you don't have to justify it," Paige wrapped an arm around her father's brittle shoulders. "I get it. I get it, one hundred percent. We'll get her sorted."

"And I am sorry, for last night. I do remember mostly what I said, and t'int right."

Paige smiled fondly as her dear old father stumbled through his words, not one to show this much emotion in one go.

"Well, got to say - the house is looking and smelling 'ansome. So, if you're happy to carry on, I won't bite yer head off this time."

"You can help, you know?" Paige teased. "Don't think I enjoy clearing up your crap. I'm doing it so I don't break my neck tripping over something."

Jacca chuckled and wiped his nose with his handkerchief. "Right you are."

"Right, with that settled - come and get some breakfast. I have a phone call to make. Know anyone who fixes windows?"

With the broken windows exposing the restaurant to the still lingering easterly winds, and with enough to do in clearing the mess left over from last night's storm, Paige and Nick agreed that it was only best to close the restaurant for the day and pitch in with the big clean-up. Jacca was already having his beloved boat hoisted out of the water for repair by early afternoon, thanks to some handy contacts, and Malcolm was happily bellowing out orders to everyone and anyone that would listen.

By early evening, Paige was dog tired.

116

A day of deep cleaning on her hands and knees yesterday; the fight with a storm early this morning; and then a full day of lugging debris, damaged equipment and goodness knows what else across the harbour and into the skips provided by yet another handy contact - Paige wasn't entirely sure how she'd made it back to the cottage without collapsing in a sleeping heap on the cobbled streets of Mevagissey.

Jacca had taken himself off to the social club but not before receiving a little lecture from Paige.

"You've had a rubbish day. I don't want to be peeling you off the floor later because you've drowned your sorrows," she had said, sternly.

With Jacca given clear instructions to be home by seven, and Nick invited over for dinner to say thank you, Paige set to work getting a simple but warming stew cooking on the Rayburn. She counted her blessings that at least Jacca's kitchen was well equipped with utensils and decent pots and pans. It was going to take a week or two more to fully stock Jacca's cupboards enough for them not to dwindle down to a mere can of beans every few days, so with an extra delivery booked with the restaurant wholesaler, she raided the larder and brought some ingredients over to the cottage to make do.

It occurred to Paige, as she diced the beef skirt, just how little cooking she had done in the last few weeks, and how much she missed it. She hadn't wanted to jump straight into Nick's kitchen and upset the balance, and with them both singing fairly well from the same hymn sheet, she'd been quite happy to just get to know her new business from a different angle. As it was, working more from a manager's position on the shop floor, she'd built common grounds with Maxine, got to know her front of house staff and developed a whole new respect for the front of house responsibilities where customers were concerned. It turned out, where patience was needed with a certain type of customer, Paige had none.

"Bloody hell, girl!" Maxine had hooted at Paige one

evening, when Paige had inelegantly dealt with a rude and demanding customer wanting to change their dish half way through eating it. "You've got none of the grace and charm from your mother when dealing with customers, have you? Best get you back in the kitchen!"

She'd liked the sound of that, but she was also fully aware that Nick's sous-chef was starting to get a little prickly with her small presence in the kitchen, so planned to reassure him that she wouldn't be pushing him out of his position.

"I come bearing gifts!" Nick announced, as he let himself into the cottage, his height and size immediately making the place seem smaller than it already was. In one hand he had a bottle of red, and in the other an Apex dish with dessert. "It's a crumble. Nothing fancy."

"It's a stew. Nothing fancy," Paige imitated, gesturing to the pot on the hot plate with a wooden spoon.

"It's nearly seven. Shall I go and haul Jacca out of the club? No doubt he's pissed as a fart by now."

"I gave him strict instructions to take it easy."

"Don't tell him that!" Nick scolded in jest, placing the bottle on the table and bringing the crumble into the kitchen. "He'll have had double the amount now!"

Paige chuckled, though she knew his joke had a little bit of truth behind it.

"Before you go and get him... there's something I wanted to tell you," Paige said, feeling a little nervous. "After the little... situation with Dad last night, it kind of pushed me to make a decision."

"Oh. Has his behaviour made you want to run a mile, then?"

"Not exactly. Quite the opposite actually. Us Yellands are stubborn like that."

Paige was surprised to see Nick's face split into a grin, one that met his twinkling grey eyes. "You've decided to stay?"

"If it's all the same to you," Paige said shyly, the kitchen suddenly feeling ten times smaller, the small proximity between them halved again. "I spoke to Matthew last night and officially handed my notice in at Garlands."

"Yikes," Nick pulled a face, folding his arms and leaning against the counter. Paige detected the smallest hint of aftershave - a musty, citrus smell. "This is your ex? How did he take it?"

"Oh, fine! No, we left things on really good terms. He was really happy for me actually."

Paige suddenly didn't know where to look, feeling a little exposed all of a sudden. She busied herself with giving the stew a stir, still sensing Nick's closeness even with her back turned. "I know you didn't like me very much before I came down. And you're right. I haven't been here for my parents."

"Paige..." Nick began to argue, looking bashful and sympathetic. "I told you, I was quick to -"

"No, but you were right. I'm seeing this as an opportunity to make amends, and I'd like to be here for Dad. I owe him that much."

Nick nodded, though his brow was still creased in a frown. "Alright. Well, I officially welcome you aboard..." his hand closed around Paige's in a handshake. "... boss."

Paige, previously distracted by the largeness and warmth of his hand, screwed her face up and shook it defiantly. "Don't call me that."

Nick bellowed with laughter before giving Paige a dazzling smile that went straight to her knees, ducking his head through the archway from the kitchen and setting off back into the dark to retrieve Jacca from the club.

As it was, Jacca was surprisingly compos mentis when he and Nick returned back to the cottage and the evening quickly made up for the rubbish start to the day. With the fire crackling away, the rain spattering on the old sash windows, and the stew warming them through, it felt for a moment like one of those old winter days back in Paige's childhood where she didn't have a single worry on her mind. Paige was beginning to understand the relationship between her father and Nick - she was grateful

119

that Jacca had this. And though the company kept between herself and Nick was purely platonic, she wasn't completely unaware of the slight fizz between them when their eyes met or when skin made accidental contact.

It didn't take long for ten o'clock to trickle along, by which time Paige could barely string a sentence together, she was so tired.

"I'm going to bed," Paige announced to Jacca and Nick, who were immersed in a game of cards. Jacca mumbled goodnight, his eyes never leaving the cards in his hands, whilst Nick's eyes flitted up to Paige's with warmth that struck right through her.

"Good-night, Paige. See you in the morning."

"Good-night."

Her head finally hitting the pillow moments later, Paige's mind reeled over the last twenty-four hours. Her decision made to stay in Cornwall, that era of her life in Bristol coming to a swift and confirmed end. The storm. Her father. Nick.

Something between her and Nick had certainly shifted and for the first time since she'd inherited her mother's restaurant, she was looking forward to work the next day - even if it did mean handing over a colossal cheque to the person repairing her windows tomorrow. She just needed to convince a few more of the kitchen staff that she was there to take ownership of the restaurant, not their ranks.

Listening to the oddly comforting murmurs of Nick and Jacca's voice two floors below, Paige finally fell into a deep and dreamless sleep.

"Ollie, can you make up the dough for tonight's service, please?" Paige asked Nick's second the next morning. It had been a busy start to the day, with them playing catch-up from having to be closed the day before. They were fairly booked up for the evening service and had already had a fair number of bookings for lunchtime considering the winter day ahead.

There was a pause following Paige's polite request as Ollie shot Nick a warning glance, showing no signs to committing to the task. Paige looked up from what she was doing to see non-verbal communication rippling between them.

"Ollie? Can you do the dough please?" Paige asked again, her patience straining.

"Nick, mate. Do you need me to do the dough?" Ollie turned to Nick, his shoulder turning in to block Paige from view.

"No, *I* need you to do the dough. That's why I asked - twice!" Paige snapped, looking at Nick for back up. "Ollie, what's the problem?"

"Nick is my head chef. I take orders from him." Ollie's resolve wobbled, his eyes flitting nervously but with enough arrogance for Paige to want to throttle him from where he stood. She took a deep breath as Nick appeared to contemplate his best move.

"I understand that Ollie. But I'm just asking you to make some dough."

"Yeah, well," Ollie stumbled, his cheeks blazing. "It's going to be confusing having orders fired from both of you. Forget it, I'll go and make the sodding dough."

Before Paige could retaliate, Ollie stormed out of the kitchen, leaving Paige incredulous and Nick rubbing the back of his neck awkwardly.

"Well, you were as much use as a chocolate teapot. Thanks for the bloody support!" Paige snapped at Nick at the first chance.

"What was I supposed to say? I could hardly take sides! You both had valid points and I didn't want to step on your shoes."

"For God's sake!" Paige buried her face in her hands, leaning on the counter in defeat. "This isn't going to work. I desperately want to get back in the kitchen, but I'm going to bugger up the ranks in here if I do. I get that Ollie's worried, but does he have to be such a twat about it? I said 'please'! That's bloody polite for me in the kitchen!"

Nick chuckled and squeezed Paige's shoulder sympathetically, a small affectionate gesture which sent her entire body on high alert. If she wasn't so frustrated at that moment, she'd be battling with butterflies.

"Do you think maybe we should have a staff meeting at some point? Clear the air a bit. Let the staff have their rant, ask some questions - that sort of thing." Paige was aware of how fast she was talking as she bit the side of her thumb, something she did when she was irritated.

"I think that's a great idea. Why don't we put on a pizza spread for everyone?"

"Good idea. Maybe they'll be less savage toward me with food in their hands." Paige paced the floor, her hands on either side of her waist. "Or maybe they'll just use it to chuck at me."

Her pacing was compromised as Nick's large body stood in her way, his hands on either side of her arms, clamping her in one place. Her eyes flitted nervously up to his before settling awkwardly on his beard, unable to hold his intense gaze.

"Ollie is one person in a team of about twenty staff here and he is feeling out of sorts at the moment. I'll talk to him, but you don't exactly have a mutiny on your hands here. It's going to be fine."

Paige nodded, still a little unconvinced but slightly soothed all the same. "Please, just let him know I'm not here to do him out of a job."

"I'm sure he knows that already," Nick assured her, removing his hands from her arms now that he was sure the pacing had stopped. "Honestly? And don't go starting a bloody argument with him over this..." Nick looked around him to make sure Ollie wasn't in ear-shot. "I don't think he's used to having a woman in the kitchen giving him orders."

"Seriously?" Paige seethed. "What century is he living in? Isn't he a bit young to have those chauvinistic attitudes?"

"Just the messenger! Don't bite my head off!"

"Nick!" Laura's voice sounded from the restaurant.

Sensing from her tone that she wasn't particularly happy, both Paige and Nick went through to see her.

"Hello stranger," Paige smiled, giving Laura a hug and immediately noticing that her expression matched her tone. "Haven't seen you for a while."

"Work's gone a bit crazy," Laura puffed. "A couple of people on maternity, along with others off sick. Speaking of which - Nick, can you have Lilly again tonight?"

"Of course. Are you alright?" Nick looked down at his sister, a protective stance that warned her not to lie to him.

"I'm tired. And things with Scott have got really complicated," Laura rubbed her face in exasperation, before eying up the coffee pot. Her voice was small and thick. "Can I have a coffee please?"

"I'll make you both one. Why don't you and Nick grab a seat and have a chat."

Laura mouthed her gratitude, whilst Nick squeezed Paige's shoulders for the second time that day, and this time she wasn't distracted enough to not notice the explosion of butterflies take flight in her stomach. What was going on? Paige could almost have sworn that her reaction didn't go unnoticed by Laura either.

Once she'd made them both a coffee and left them to discuss the Scott fiasco in private, Paige took herself back into the kitchen to make a start on the pasta dough for tonight's dishes. Making fresh pasta was still a fairly new skill for Paige given that pasta dishes were rarely on the menu back at Garlands. It was something she had done back in culinary school but getting to know Giuseppe's old recipes and using his old pasta roller had been a new learning curve the last couple of weeks. Taking herself into the back store cupboard to retrieve said machine, she was immediately distracted by the sound of Ollie having what sounded like a complete rant down the phone, just outside the back door. The smell of cigarette smoke confirmed that he was not making the pizza dough for tonight's service, but instead taking an unscheduled break and smoking on premises, both issues that she would be raising with him later. She was about to leave him to his ranting, to get back to finding that pasta roller, when the mention of her name had her pausing again and hiding out of sight to hear more.

"Paige. Yeah, the new owner. She's a bloody bitch, mate. Thinks she's the bloody cat's meow because she was a bloody city chef." There was a pause as the person on the receiving end said something that made Ollie bark with laughter. "Yeah right, mate! Class! Yeah, yeah - pop down first thing tomorrow."

Her heart hammering in her chest and blood pumping noisily in her ears, Paige hid herself further as Ollie looked around to check he was alone.

"Nick and Paige don't get in until seven, so meet me with your van in the back at five. Because of the lights mate. They live right opposite. I'll sort you out mate. Nick and Paige? Don't know, mate - probably trying to get in her pants so he can convince her to sell to him. He was going to buy the restaurant - before she came along. I'd be furious."

Paige had heard enough. Deciding that retrieving the pasta roller would be too noisy and would give her away, she abandoned all plans of making pasta and sneaked back out into the main kitchen, well out of earshot of Ollie's conversation.

Her mind was reeling. She knew he was a stick in her side, but she'd never pinned him down as trouble like that. This little deal he was sorting his mate out with at five tomorrow morning, she could only guess it had something to do with the restaurant, and if he was stealing from them then she needed to find out as soon as possible. As for Nick... had this been the real truth behind his hostility all those weeks ago? That he and Elaine had it all in place for him to buy Giuseppe's, only for the whole thing to collapse upon her mum's unexpected death and Paige's more unexpected return home? And was Nick's warming to her recently more of a ploy to make her more malleable to the idea of selling up and getting back out of the way of his plans?

Later on, during the lunch service, Paige found a

quiet moment with Nick and out of Ollie's earshot.

"Do you do regular stock-takes here?" Paige asked, casually.

"Yes, monthly. Why?"

"Just wondering. How are they?"

"You'll have to speak to Ollie about that. That's his domain."

Without thinking, Paige hissed 'shit' under her breath and Nick shot her a suspicious look. She'd had a horrible feeling that it was exactly what Nick was going to tell her, given that she also used to be in charge of the food audit back at Garlands as sous-chef.

"What's the problem?"

Paige considered her answer for a moment, her head telling her that accusing Nick's longstanding sous-chef of stealing wouldn't go down well, but as usual her tongue got the better of her.

"I think Ollie might be stealing," Paige whispered, checking her surroundings. She jumped as Nick threw a saucepan into the sink with a loud clatter.

"Really, Paige? Jeez, I know you two have got off on the wrong foot and all, but no need to jump to those sort of conclusions!"

"I'm not jumping to anything," Paige bit back, keeping her voice low for fear of being overheard. "I heard him say something to a mate on the phone. He's definitely up to something."

Nick threw his arms up in the air in exasperation and waved Paige off, dismissing the conversation. Paige decided to drop it for now, realising that during a shift wasn't the best time. Whether he wanted to accept it or not, Paige was going to find out what Ollie was up to. Even if it did mean a dark trek down to the harbour at 5am tomorrow morning.

Nick was curt with Paige for the rest of the day, from the lunch shift through to the evening, so Paige decided to leave him to his devices and spent the rest of the day with Maxine at the front of house. When she asked Maxine whether the food audit included the alcohol behind the bar, she was told vaguely that she wasn't sure and that Ollie was the person to check with. This time, Paige kept her reaction nonchalant and confirmed that she would indeed check with him at another time. She now knew that she needed to get to the bottom of this as soon as possible.

When Nick had retrieved a very sleepy Lilly from the apartment above the restaurant at the end of the shift, the three of them set off in the cold, dark evening to the cottages just across the way from the waterfront. Mevagissey was silent and only the slight clinking of the boats and the swill of water lapping against the wall could be heard. Only a small number of windows were lit up in the houses behind theirs, making the little village look almost deserted.

"What film did you watch this evening, Lilly?" Paige asked brightly, despite her exhaustion and Nick's continued prickliness.

"Mamma Mia," Lilly replied through a yawn. The poor girl was exhausted and no doubt would have happily fallen asleep upstairs if it wasn't for the fact she would be dragged back out in the cold by 10pm to head back to Nick's cottage.

"Oh, I love that film! The first one?" Lilly nodded to confirm. "I should have come up and joined you. Sounds like a perfect evening."

"Mummy says it's your apartment anyway, so you should."

"Well, I think I'd get into trouble with your uncle Nick here if I skived off from work to watch a film, as tempting as that sounds."

Paige caught a little smile on Lilly's tired face under the streetlamp, but when she saw that Nick's expression hadn't done so much as move since they'd left the restaurant, she grabbed her opportunity to get straight down to the source of the issue.

"Nick, can I have a quick chat with you before we call it a night?"

Nick gave Lilly his front door key, "Lilly, you head up

126

and brush your teeth. I'll be there in a minute."

When Lilly had closed the door behind her, Nick turned back to Paige with a daring glint in his eye.

"I know you think I'm just stirring things up with Ollie, but please will you just humour me tomorrow morning?" Paige begged. "He told this mate of his 5am, at the back of the restaurant."

Nick stood tall and silent, his arms across his chest in his signature 'pissed off' stance.

"Please Nick. If I'm wrong, Ollie will be none the wiser of my suspicions and I'll drop it."

"I've got Lilly!" Nick argued, whispering furiously into the dark night.

"She'll be fast asleep, and Dad will no doubt be up so I'll ask him to listen out for her while he makes his crib, if that helps. But I need to check, and if for any reason I do catch him doing something, I'd rather not be alone in facing it... down a dark street... with no witnesses."

The last part was a ploy. She knew, in the short time she'd been acquainted with Nick Stone, that he would never allow a woman to be endangered in anyway.

Like a true, old-fashioned man of chivalry, Nick swore under his breath and loosened his arms down to his hips. "Fine, I'll come down with you at ridiculous-o'clock in the morning, but if you're wrong, I'm never letting you hear the end of it. I hate early starts at the best of times."

"Thank you. I just need to check it out. It's worrying me."

Nick's face softened slightly under the glow of the nearest streetlight as he noticed the worry creases on Paige's brow and the way she bit the side of her thumb anxiously.

"We'll check it out, and hopefully put your mind at rest. Now, off to bed. I'm bloody shattered."

Paige considered asking whether it was true that he had planned to buy the restaurant, but that was a conversation she was not ready to have. And this certainly wasn't the right time to bring such a delicate topic up.

Instead, they both said their good-nights and agreed to meet in that very spot in just seven hours' time, after hopefully a decent night's sleep - though, Paige didn't count on getting a decent sleep with the worry churning around in her restless mind.

Despite that, no sooner had Paige's head hit the pillow, did her alarm wake her up 4:45am to get ready for their early morning hustle.

Shoving on some jeans and a thick fisherman's jumper, Paige met a very surly version of Nick back outside the cottages moments later. He was a man of his word, though it was abundantly clear to Paige that he was regretting his word deeply. They didn't exchange too many words and instead set straight off to make their quiet way to somewhere concealed nearby the restaurant. It felt utterly ridiculous as they sneaked their way down the walkway and against the buildings facing the harbour, until they found themselves hidden behind the stack of blue fish boxes.

"Feel like a right bloody tit!" Nick grumbled as he fidgeted into a squatting position behind the wheel of a neighbouring car, taking the odd glance over the bonnet to get a good view of the back alley of the restaurant.

A part of Paige hoped she was wrong, and that her current sous-chef hadn't not only lied and deceived Nick but also her own mother for goodness knows how many years. Her hopes fizzled to nothing as she immediately clocked Ollie coming out of the back door of the restaurant, lurking by the empty kegs and with his hands deep in his pockets. He was looking around him frantically, the back door into the restaurant wide open behind him.

Paige glanced at Nick whose expression was like thunder, her stomach churning and her heart hammering in her chest. A shiver ran through her which she knew wasn't fully down to the winter's chill. They watched in tense silence as a van reversed slowly up from the other side of the little side street, its back doors stopping just outside the restaurant door. Ollie greeted a man, whose face was hidden in the shadows of a hood, and they watched as he led this strange man into the restaurant. Her restaurant.

She felt sick - physically sick - as she clutched her stomach, which was at this point doing complete somersaults. She went to stand up when Nick grabbed her arm and held her down.

"Not yet. We'll wait until they bring something out. Wait until they commit the actual crime."

"Then what?" Paige whispered, wiping her nose with her sleeve as tears began to roll down her cheeks. Despite his white rage, Nick reached out and wiped the tears from her cheek with his thumb.

"Then I kill him."

It was ten long, painful minutes until Ollie and the strange man reappeared from the storeroom, both with their arms bearing heavy boxes full of what looked like meat. Paige felt her heart drop to the floor, and no sooner were the boxes in the back of the van Nick was scrabbling to his feet, a bull ready to charge.

"Ollie!"

Her legs stiff from crouching down behind the car for so long, Paige struggled to keep up with Nick who was clearly a man out for Ollie's blood. Nick reached a bewildered Ollie with ferocious speed, whose hands had shot up in the air as if surrendering at gun point. Nick jabbed a finger at the small space between him and Ollie as the bloke in the hood was now trying to shut his van up for a quick exit. Suddenly, Paige's sadness turned to pure anger as she went straight for the driver's side and yanked the keys out of the ignition.

"You sneaky little shit!" Nick hollered, jabbing his finger into Ollie's chest, a constant murmuring of apologies erupting from what Paige could only see now as a foolish boy. "How long has this been going on? How long?!"

"I-I don't know. Not long. Nick, I'm sorry."

"This is beyond solving with a naff apology, Ollie!" Nick growled at him, before rounding on the hooded man with equal aggression. "And who the bloody hell are you?"

Nick towered over both young men, who both looked like juvenile teenagers getting reprimanded for antisocial behaviour. Without his chef whites to cover up a lot of his physique, Paige realised just how large and powerful Nick was. She gave herself a mental shake from the distraction and started removing the meats from the van.

"Oi! You can't just go into my van! Give me my keys, you b-"

"Who do you think is going to be in more trouble when the police turn up?" Paige snapped, rounding on the hooded bloke. "I'm the owner of this restaurant, and you're stealing from me, mate!"

"I had no idea it was stolen produce! Honest!" the man whimpered, both he and Ollie cowering against the wall away from Nick.

"Great friends you keep, Ollie," Nick sneered. "Happy to commit a crime with you but throws you under the first bus that comes!"

"Please don't call the police, Paige," Ollie pleaded, looking younger than ever as tears pooled in his eyes. "I'm just trying to make ends meet with my bills. My wages don't stretch far-"

"Don't you dare push the blame on us and say you don't get paid enough!" Nick roared, his voice echoing down the street and around the deserted village. "You're paid way over national, and I see you constantly splurging on stuff. So don't you make yourself out to be hard done by."

Nick's anger was now palpable as he snarled in Ollie's face. "You've disrespected me. You've disrespected Paige. You've let down the team. But worse? You've completely dishonoured Elaine's memory," Nick lowered his voice to dangerous levels. "You should be ashamed of yourself. Paige, go into the office and call the police."

Legs heavy and heart still racing, Paige took wobbly steps towards the back door of the restaurant just as the hooded man took his opportunity to wrestle the keys from Paige's hands, his fingers scrabbling desperately and his shoulders barging against hers, causing her to bounce against the restaurant wall. Nick was there in a flash, grabbing him by the scruff and pinning him against the wall.

"Nathan, mate - stop!" Ollie begged, his hands clasped to his head in horror. "Nick… Paige… please, I'm so sorry."

"Just how long has this been going on for?" Nick demanded, his hands still compromised around Nathan's scruff.

"A few months," Ollie answered, his head hanging in shame. "I'm so sorry, I'll pay it all back. Just please don't call the police."

Nick looked at Paige, whose mind was now so foggy that she couldn't think straight. She nodded once; it was feeble and meekly. Yanking Nathan's hood down to reveal his face, Nick snapped a shot of him on his phone before whipping around and doing the same to the registration plate on his van. Paige retrieved the remaining boxes from the back of the van and threw the keys at Nathan with contempt.

"Get out of here," Nick snarled at Ollie. "Don't bother coming back to work. Your employment here is terminated. Any funny business, and we're going to the police."

Ollie and Nathan disappeared without a trace and Paige was grateful to be stood near Nick at that moment as her legs finally gave out on her.

Chapter Eleven

"Jacca has already started some porridge for him and Lilly back in the cottage," Nick said, as he came through from the kitchen. "Here. Get this down your neck."

They were in the restaurant and Paige was sitting in her favourite spot by the bay window, looking out to the harbour, which was slowly coming into view with the rising sun. Nick placed a sugary tea on the table in front of her and disappeared back into the kitchen. He had insisted she sit down, declaring that she had perhaps gone into shock, and was busy making them breakfast. Moments later, he was sat unusually close to Paige, two pancake stacks oozing with syrup and fresh fruit in front of them, and a lazy arm draped over the back of Paige's chair. If it wasn't for the fact that Paige was upset and totally exhausted from the morning's events, she would have analysed this intimate gesture further.

"We should have called the police," Nick huffed, following Paige's eye trail to the harbour, which was looking quite glorious in the sun, its warmth cutting through the frosty air.

Paige shook her head and bought the sugary tea to her lips. "No. Once we pressed charges, it would have gone on forever. Potentially court and everything. I just want him gone."

"Well, he's not having his wages, that's for sure," Nick crossed his arms defiantly, the absence of his arm leaving her feeling cold. "How did I not pick up on this sooner?"

"Don't start blaming yourself," Paige scolded. "I just can't believe somebody would do that. Do you reckon it was only going on for a few months? How long has he been your second?"

"Only a year. I have a horrible feeling it's been going on longer. The more I think about it... he was quite territorial of his stock taking responsibility. We had a student from one of the St Austell schools here last summer for work experience, and he wouldn't let her shadow him for the stock taking. Made some excuse about not wanting to be distracted while he counted." Nick rubbed his face with his hands. "I'm a bloody idiot."

"No, you're not," Paige said firmly, shaking her head and popping a blueberry in her mouth. "You trusted him to be a decent human being. You were brilliant this morning by the way. Far from being an idiot. God knows what would have happened if I went down there alone." She rubbed her sore shoulder absentmindedly, a shiver running through her. It was true - the two men had been afraid of Nick and his sheer size but would quite happily have barged right through Paige to get what they needed.

"I'm glad you didn't go alone, and I'm sorry I didn't believe you," Nick said huskily, his arm returning to the back of her chair, providing warmth that she didn't know she needed.

They held each other's gaze and the moment hung in the air, until Paige's eyes filled with tears and she redirected her gaze down to the table, picking apathetically at the pancakes.

"Are you alright?" Nick asked, his voice soft and tender.

Paige sniffed and wrapped her arms around herself, feeling small and vulnerable. "I'm just thinking of Mum. She'd have been devastated."

Suddenly, it all caught up with her and the thought of her lovely mum dealing with such a horrible situation had turned on the tap of tears. Mortified, she hid her face in her hands as she succumbed to sobs, just as Nick closed the small gap between them and wrapped his arm around her, bringing her close to him. How could she fully focus on her grief when Nick's close proximity and intimacy now had her emotions whirling around in her stomach like a little tornado? Her sobs surpassed, her tummy clenched, and her heart raced against her chest as Nick's thumb stroked her sore shoulder and his breath caressed her hair. Her face pressed up against his chest, she tried not to think about the firmness of his physique. A part of her wanted to rip herself away, run a mile and stand under a cold shower. Another part of her wanted to stay there forever. Finally, her head won over her heart and she tore herself away.

"Sorry about that," Paige sniffed, rubbing her eyes and her face, hoping she didn't look as red as she felt. "I just miss her. God, I never cry in front of anyone. What's the matter with me? Even my ex-boyfriend used to joke about me being the Ice Queen or something, because apparently I never show emotion."

She was rambling again, something she seemed to do a lot around Nick. There was something about the calm force around him that made her a jittery mess. Nick's eyes were set on her, burning into her and exposing her for everything she was, and she willed him to look away.

"What?" Paige sniffed again, hoping her face hadn't gone too red and blotchy.

"You're just... not what I expected," Nick muttered, his eyes still trained on hers.

Paige shuffled in her seat, feeling suddenly scrutinised. "What is that supposed to mean?"

"I don't know. Sorry... forget it. Eat your pancakes up. They're going cold."

Before Paige had a chance to respond, Nick shot up out of his seat whilst clearing his throat, the crackling tension between them replaced with that of total awkwardness. She decided not to mention it again, though her mind raced and tortured her for the rest of the morning.

They agreed that they would do a proper stock take today and start from scratch in ensuring their produce was counted correctly from then on, Paige delicately sharing with Nick how they kept track of stock-takes back in Garlands. She dreaded to think of the losses that would have racked up over the months.

They were starting to get ready to open for the lunchtime sitting, when Charlie walked in, his usual boyish smile set upon his lovely, tanned face. His iconic blonde surfer hair was sticking out in different directions under his beany hat, and his usually large physique was lost under layers of waterproofs, ready to hit the hard sea.

"Morning Charlie," Paige smiled, as Charlie returned the greeting, releasing his head of hair from his hat and shaking out the seawater. "Can I get you anything warm to drink?"

"Ooh, yes please Paige. Coffee, if you don't mind. I was actually here to pick up on my offer all those weeks ago… which we still haven't seen through yet."

Paige looked at him a little vaguely, as she tipped some coffee into the filter machine.

"When is your next day off? I was wondering if you'd like to join me on the boat one morning. Maybe grab some lunch in another village down the coast."

"Oh."

It wasn't the best reaction, and Charlie's nervous chuckle told her it wasn't the response he hoped for either, but she didn't know what else to say. For some reason, her mind flicked to Nick, not Matthew - which confused her on a whole new level.

"Crikey, Paige. Don't leave a man hanging like this, will you."

"Sorry. Yes, of course. That sounds great. I have Friday off - any good?"

"Perfect. Make sure you wrap up warm."

Paige shot him a challenging look; one eyebrow arched. "Really Charlie? You're talking to a fisherman's daughter here."

Charlie chuckled, and they finalised their times and plans before he threw his hat back on, gladly accepted his warm coffee and faced the chilly air.

She knew a day out with Charlie was guaranteed fun, and she could do with a day of laughter and silliness. She just knew that there had been times in the past when

Charlie had wanted a little bit more than just a fun time with a friend. She certainly was not ready for something like that after Matthew, and even more so, she did not have the energy in her to have to deal with it if Charlie did get the wrong idea. She'd need to make it very clear from the get-go that their fishing day out was simply platonic.

Friday came about quickly, and Paige had found that trying to cut Ollie from the restaurant had been more complicated and felt amongst the staff than she had realised. It wasn't until Nick had firmly put certain members of staff back in place with the truth behind Ollie's sudden end to his employment, that they stopped giving Paige a hard time.

"Love how I get it in the neck, when it's their precious Ollie who was stealing from us," Paige moaned to Nick one evening, after a rather cold-shouldered shift with some of the younger female members of the team.

"I'll have a word with them. It's only because they fancied him," Nick had scoffed, rolling his eyes as he sharpened his beloved knife set.

Now, at an ungodly hour for her one day off for the week, Paige was scraping her long black hair up in a ponytail, threading it through the back of her old trusty baseball cap, and heading out into the morning darkness with as many layers as she could possibly manage whilst still achieving full movement in her limbs.

"So this is the newest member of the Meva fleet!"

Paige was admiring Charlie's boat, running a hand along the flaking paintwork and negotiating her way around the fishing equipment littering the main deck.

"Yeah. She's a bit of a fixer-upper, but she's earning her keep," Charlie said proudly, leading Paige into the cockpit, where an array of different buttons, levers and controls lay dormant, waiting to be switched on. Turning on a makeshift light which hung from the ceiling above them, Charlie turned the key and the engine chugged to life. What little glow was coming from the light made their breaths visible, puffs of white vapor filling the small cabin. The village was still very much plunged into darkness.

"I'm impressed that we're out before Malcolm... and even Dad," Paige commented, blowing her hot breath into her gloves and watching patiently as Charlie flicked switches and readied the engine.

"Early bird catches the worm, so they say," he smiled, giving her a cheeky wink and reminding her of their school days. She blushed at the memory as Charlie continued to press buttons and flick switches here and there.

"You OK there, Skipper?" Paige smiled, as Charlie finally succeeded in whatever he was trying to do on the dash.

"Trying to get used to all the electrics, and the way the autopilot works -" Charlie paused and stared at a flashing red light. "Not sure what that failure says... be alright."

Paige chuckled nervously as Charlie gently but noisily manoeuvred the boat out of the harbour. Once they were out on open ocean, Charlie sparked up more conversation, no longer needing to put so much concentration into the steering.

"Sorry to hear about your dad's boat."

Paige glanced up at Charlie, surprised by his thoughtfulness towards her dad's misfortunes. "Thank you. Martha's on the mend. She should be back on the water soon enough."

"Still. I'd be fuming. Accidents happen and all that, but even I was smart enough as a new skipper to secure my boat for the storm. Think Malcolm found the culprit anyway and threatened to remove him from the fleet."

"Really? Who was it?"

Charlie drew in a sharp intake of breath, a smile playing in the corner of his mouth. "Couldn't possibly say. I know how fierce you can be Yelland!"

Rolling her eyes and punching him lightly on the arm, Paige readjusted her cap and looked out to the dark ocean ahead. "What we catching this morning, then?"

"Otter trawling today. We'll see what it catches us. Good time for sardines, mind. Hopefully we'll get a good run on those before daylight hits and the shoals scatter."

Paige got stuck in straight away. Years of her childhood spent on Jacca's boat came flooding back and soon enough Charlie was gaping in approval at her competency and familiarity around the boat and its equipment.

"You must have spent thousands on kitting her out!" Paige remarked an hour later, when Charlie was pouring them both a quick cup of tea from a flask. Despite the thick gloves, Paige's fingers were numb from the icy cold, and she quickly wrapped them around the little plastic flask lid to thaw them out.

"Yeah. Boat is old, but all new gear. New winch. Net drums are all new. Bridles and warps. All new. Not going out here with all worn-out stuff. Won't do me no good," Charlie lowered himself onto an upturned container, slurping his tea and looking far beyond his years all of a sudden. "But yeah, thousands. No pressure to make some money on this thing, eh?"

Despite the lack of light in the cockpit, the darkened expression of worry that crossed Charlie's face didn't go unnoticed by Paige.

"Come on then!" Paige plonked her cup on the side and patted Charlie's leg in motivation. "We'll catch bugger all sat here drinking tea! Let's get the otter doors back in."

Charlie chuckled and they both sprang into action. Paige boldly jumped up onto the side of the boat, the sea spraying her already-soaked legs, to tease the blue netting from the drum, as Charlie electronically fed it into the water.

"There was me thinking I was just taking you out for a jolly. Didn't expect you to be so hands on," Charlie said, another half an hour later, as they separated the catch into different containers of salt and ice.

"Fisherman's daughter!" Paige repeated her remark from the previous day, pointing two frozen thumbs at her chest. "Don't take this the wrong way, Charlie but how are you doing all of this on your own? Otter trawling is a two-person job at best."

"Yeah, well - I get by. It's hard work, but I can't afford a crew."

Paige sympathised with Charlie. She knew all too well that a fisherman's income was unpredictable and fluctuated each month depending on weather and fish stock. But she worried over the thought of Charlie being out on the merciless sea, every day without anybody else on board to help if anything were to go wrong.

"Fishing is dangerous business," Paige voiced her concerns out loud. "Speak to Dad or Malcolm. There might be a solution to getting someone on board with you."

With another healthy catch and another hour of picking through their winnings, Charlie soon announced the end of their outing.

"I was going to take you out for lunch, but I didn't expect to catch quite as much as this. We need to get this back to Meva," Charlie apologised.

"Absolutely! Don't look so sorry, Charlie. This is a great morning's work."

Paige felt liberated as she wiped the sea spray from her face and wrung it out of her long, bedraggled hair. The early morning start, the watching of the sunrise and a familiar couple of hours catching fish had her soul dancing and her eyes sparkling. She was freezing cold to the bone and felt like a drowned rat, but she couldn't remember the last time she had enjoyed herself so much.

"I still can't believe how hands-on you are out here. What a woman!" Charlie bellowed, pretending to serenade at her feet. "Let me at least grab you some lunch back in Meva. It's the least I can do."

"Go on then," Paige smiled.

Back on the harbour, Charlie passed Paige a steaming tub of hot soup from the same ice-cream parlour where she had bought her waffle weeks ago. It was a much earlier lunch than Paige was used to, but after an early start and a morning of laborious work, she was famished.

"That place does everything!" Paige exclaimed, impressed and gluttonous over the rich smell of tomato and basil soup - a perfect remedy to thaw out every frozen part of her. The heat blissfully burned through the cardboard tub and into her fingers, and at that moment she couldn't care less if it set her hands on fire she was that cold. "Thank you so much. The perfect lunch after that trek."

"You're very welcome. Least I could do."

They grabbed a seat on one of the benches perched on the edge of the waterfront, and sipped their hot soup in quiet companionship, watching the other fishermen return from their treks or head back out for another go. The harbour was its usual bustling self and the streets were quiet with only locals and dog walkers to be seen.

"Seems we have quite a bit in common," Charlie began, extracting a chunk of artisan bread from a paper bag and offering some to Paige to dunk. "We've both left behind the fast-paced hamster wheel that is the big city."

"Well you did, coming from London," Paige pointed out, watching with satisfaction as the red soup clung to her bread. "Bristol isn't quite as massive."

"Bigger than here," Charlie argued, chuckling as Paige stuffed a huge chunk of bread into her mouth. "You were always so delicate."

Paige shrugged and chomped down on her food without shame.

"I mean - we both left pretty big jobs in the city and have returned to our roots for a slower paced life in this beautiful village. I'm trying to remember why I left it in the first place."

"Because you wanted to make a name for yourself in the law industry. You would never have got it in this place," Paige scoffed.

"Maybe. What made you want to come back?"

"Didn't have much choice," Paige shrugged, though she inwardly reprimanded herself at the bitter way she said it. She washed her bread down with a healthy slurp of soup, a warning eye on an approaching seagull. "I don't mean it like that. I'm actually enjoying being back home - surprisingly."

"Why surprisingly?" Charlie probed, his curiosity distracting him from his soup.

"It's complicated."

"I'm listening... "

"But I'm not sharing."

Charlie frowned but nodded to respect her privacy. Suddenly, he shuffled along the bench, pressing his leg up against hers and placed an arm around her. Paige stiffened at the intimacy.

"If any of it is to do with your mum's passing, you know I'll always be a sounding board."

"Thank you," Paige managed to say, though her cheeks were blazing and she was now staring into her almost empty cup of soup. She felt Charlie's face get closer and a sudden instinct to squirm her way out of his embrace was all-consuming. She stood up, almost spilling the remainder of her soup as she clocked Laura coming from the restaurant, looking withdrawn and upset. "Is that Laura over there? She looks upset. I'd best go and check on her. Thanks so much for a great morning and for the soup. See you soon."

Charlie waved from the bench, forlorn with disappointment as Paige retreated with perhaps a little too much haste. "Yep. See you around Paige."

"Laura! Laura, wait up!"

"He says he wants to fight for full custody," Laura sobbed, blowing her nose into her fifth tissue since they'd sat down in the little tearooms on Church Street. It was a quaint little vintage teashop, with a vast collection of teapots, teacups and delicious homemade cakes. An untouched slice of carrot cake and chocolate cake sat between them as Paige attempted to console her friend.

"He hasn't even seen her properly in months. He still

141

hasn't arranged properly to see her this spring as he keeps promising her, and during the divorce he made it very clear he didn't want any responsibility as a parent. Now he's got this new girlfriend, it's like he's trying to prove something."

"He's just proving what we already know - that he's a giant twat with an ego problem." Paige paused, glancing sideways at the table next to them, where an elderly couple sat, frowning at her with utter disapproval. "Sorry. But he is."

The gentlemen shook his head, whilst his wife relented a little, shrugging and returning to her cream tea.

"What has Nick said about it?" Paige asked, returning her focus to Laura after they both suppressed a smile and silently promised to be on their best behaviour around such delicate ears.

"He's furious. Says he'll call him himself. But that'll do no good. I cannot do or say anything that Scott might try and put against me in court. Oh, god! He's going to take me to court over this!" A fresh new wave of sobs racked through Laura, and Paige rubbed her back in sympathy, feeling utterly useless.

"Can I get you both another pot of tea?" A kindly-looking lady came over, a vintage apron around her middle and a tea towel draped over her shoulder. She smiled in sympathy as Paige nodded in gratitude.

After a few moments, Laura composed herself and started tucking into her chocolate cake. Paige followed suit and started taking small bites of her carrot cake though she was still pretty full from her soup.

"We saw you with Charlie Eathorne by the way," Laura said, sniffing and dabbing her nose with her soggy tissue.

"We?"

"Me and Nick. Getting very cosy there on that bench," Laura managed a cheeky smile.

Paige's heart sank and she could hardly suppress a frustrated sigh. It was bad enough her friend seeing that but least of all did she want Nick to witness that horribly awkward moment. Charlie's closeness had left her squirming and uncomfortable. When Nick had done much the same, her entire body had responded with electrical currents all over.

"It wasn't like that at all," Paige shook her head, feeling a little disgruntled at the accusation. "For some reason he took it upon himself to offer comfort when I didn't need it."

"Comfort for what?"

"Mum. I don't know - it got a bit awkward to be honest. I was glad to clock eyes on you really as it gave me a reason to escape."

"Oh," Laura bit her lip, poorly hiding that she actually looked quite pleased by this. "Poor bloke. That is awkward. He always did have a thing for you in school."

"I know," Paige groaned. "We had a great morning out on his boat. It was great to get out there fishing again. But I promise you, it was completely platonic - until he went all weird on me."

"Well, Nick will be pleased. He didn't seem too chuffed to see you both canoodling on the bench."

"I just told you, we weren't canoodling," Paige snapped. "Can we drop it please?"

Laura put her hands up in surrender and returned to her cake.

"What's it to do with Nick if I was 'canoodling' anyway?" Paige remarked, stabbing her cake with conviction.

"Forget I said anything. You're right, it has nothing to do with anyone. Do you fancy coming over tonight for a few drinks? Rare occasion where neither of us are working a late."

Paige's shoulders dropped in relief from the change of topic and she nodded. "That sounds lovely. I'll bring the gin."

"You'll have to endure watching The Greatest Showman. I promised Lilly we'd watch it."

"Even better. I'll bring popcorn as well."

Chapter Twelve

Nick

That girl, the one with the flowing black hair and the emerald green eyes - she drove him crazy. They argued like cats and dogs. Her sheer stubbornness drove him to madness.

So why? Why did seeing her so close and intimate on the bench with that new skipper have his stomach twisting in knots? It didn't make sense. Surely he couldn't be jealous.

He'd watched with Laura at the restaurant window as this new skipper - Charlie, was it? - had closed the gap between him and Paige, Nick's fists clenched at his sides and his jaw painfully rigid. It was almost nauseating as Charlie leaned in, clearly going in for the kiss.

Nick had to turn away. He couldn't watch.

Only a couple of days ago he'd had her tucked under one arm as he'd comforted her from the drama of Ollie. Her hair had smelled sweetly of an aloe vera and eucalyptus blend, almost intoxicating him into a stupor. He hadn't thought of much else since, only how it had felt holding her.

Now Laura had headed off, leaving him stewing in his tangled mess of emotions, confused as to why this bothered him so much. Laura was upset and all, but suddenly he couldn't focus on that. His mind was too foggy.

So much had happened in a matter of days. He couldn't deny it. Things hadn't exactly been dull since Paige's arrival. Not that he could blame her for a storm and the betrayal of his sous chef. But something in her arrival had stirred something that he didn't realise had been dormant in a very long time. He'd been perfectly happy, in his rather predictable Meva life. And yet, something in

Paige's arrival had his body buzzing.

He'd said it before and no doubt he'd say it again. He'd wanted to hate Elaine's daughter. He'd silently vowed that if he ever met this daughter - the one who regularly cancelled plans, made obligatory contact through wishy-washy text messages, who only made short reluctant visits at Christmas time and some birthdays - he'd have things to say to her.

Instead, like the absolute pillock that he was, he'd fallen almost immediately into those beautiful green eyes of her, disarmed from the moment they met when he hadn't initially realised who she was.

He should have recognised the likeness. She was exactly half of Jacca and half of Elaine.

"Bleddy hell - what's got your knickers in a twist?" Jacca chortled as he came through the front door of the restaurant. "You've got a face like bleddy thunder, boy!"

Nick merely grunted, Jacca's teasing only making him more agitated. He couldn't exactly say, "it's your daughter, Jacca! She's the most stubborn, infuriating, beautiful woman I've ever seen! Can you put a good word in for me and lose Charlie out to sea?"

"You seeing your fa'ver at all, today?" Jacca carried on, accepting Nick's grunt as an acceptable answer. "I've got some money to pass on to him for the scallops."

"Wasn't planning to," Nick said, busying himself now by pouring a coffee. "Not sure I'll get any time now until we close. Paige is off today."

"Haven't see Jerry for a couple of days. S'he alright?"

"Not been too smart last few days, no. Carers are in today though," Nick added, almost unnecessarily. He said this more as a reassurance to himself. His dad lived right up the top of Polkirt Hill, almost as close to Portmellon as he was to Mevagissey, which meant carving some time into Nick's crazy schedule to check on his father proved even more difficult when he needed to negotiate the narrow streets with his VW Transporter. Not merely a quick walk around the corner like most people in his life. But then, his dad had point blank refused when he'd offered for him to move in to the cottage by the harbour.

"Perhaps I'll pop in and have a cuppa with him," Jacca said, mostly to himself. "Leave it to me, dear boy."

"How's the new skipper in town?" Nick inquired, his best attempt at being nonchalant.

"Yeah, seems hardworking enough. Big boat he's got there to man by himself though. Think Paige gave him a hand on an early trawl this morning." Jacca pulled himself up on one of the bar stools and accepted a coffee which Nick had poured for him automatically.

"Paige did?"

So that's why she'd been with Charlie on that bench. Was this a date, then? The gnawing in his stomach continued.

"Don't sound so surprised, m'boy! My little girl has been on boats most of her life. Probably a better sailor than me! Be nice to think she carried on the fishing trade but 'tis no' much for making a living with. 'Tis nice to see her doing so well with you here in the restaurant, really. You work well together it seems, save a few squabbles here and there."

Nick nodded, allowing Jacca to think out loud, a sort of reminiscing expression across his old features. Jacca hugged his hands around his coffee and pondered with a big sigh. No doubt his thoughts were with Elaine.

"Right," Jacca said finally, sliding off the stool and pushing his empty coffee mug towards Nick. "I'll leave you to it, shall I? No doubt you'll have people pressed up against the glass in a bit, seeking out some lunch."

"Hello, Jacca!" Maxine said in delight, as she came through the front door ready to start her lunch shift. "Alright, m'love? Nice to see you in here."

"Hello, Bird. Twas a quick stop," Jacca smiled warmly at his old friend and then turned to Nick. "I'll stop off to Jerry a minute and see if he needs anything. Save you a trip."

"Think the carers have just been, Nick," Maxine informed. "Is it Josie who sees to Jerry?"

"That's the one."

146

"Then, yes. Lovely girl. She cared for my George on his last days. He always did prefer to have her than any of the others."

"Ideal. He won't mind me stopping by then," Jacca said, zipping his brash yellow coat back up.

"Thanks, Jacca. Appreciate it."

With Jacca gone, it was Maxine's turn to scrutinise Nick, his temper not much better than before Jacca had stopped by and probably just as prominent on his face.

"Oh dear, Nick. What's happened, m'love? Don't mind me prying, only I saw Laura with Paige just a minute ago, and she looked ever so upset."

Paige was with Laura now? That made him feel marginally better. She was no longer canoodling on a bench somewhere and Laura was at least being comforted. Then again, she and Laura were probably sat somewhere now, gossiping away about this morning's date.

"Scott's reared his ugly head again," Nick replied, steering things well away from his own little troubles.

Maxine's face contorted into a rage that only mothers could adopt when their own children had been served an injustice. "Honestly! That man! I'll knock him off the harbour wall if he causes any more trouble!"

"Join the queue, Max," Nick said, grimly. Heading into the kitchen, he joined Daniel and Jamie now, checking on the progress of lunch preparations as Maxine opened the doors ready to welcome hungry customers.

Later that afternoon, the lunch shift merging into dinner time sittings, Laura wandered into the kitchen with that universal look for food.

"You're looking better," Nick observed, braising a steak and glancing at a much brighter version of his sister than earlier. "Max said you've spent the afternoon with Paige?"

"Yes, and we're having an evening in too," Laura said. "She and Lilly are at mine now, getting tonight's movie ready."

"The Greatest Showman?" Nick asked. Laura

confirmed with a nod. "Thank god for that. Saves me enduring that torture with her."

"Guess what?" Laura said suddenly, pulling on Nick's sleeve like an excitable child. Nick arched an eyebrow, glancing only briefly to give his sister an exasperated look before returning his watchful eye on the steak he cooking to perfection. "Charlie tried to kiss Paige-"

Nick scoffed, shaking Laura's hand from his arm. "I really don't want to hear this, Laura!"

"No-no! Listen, you're going to want to! Charlie tried to kiss Paige and she gave him the shunt. She told me earlier, in those tearooms on Church Street, that she'd only gone on the boat to catch up with him and then he went all weird. She found it totally awkward and said she couldn't get away fast enough! Poor Charlie - I mean, he's a lovely bloke. But she has no interest in him! That's good isn't it?"

"I have no idea what you're getting at," Nick said, feigning distraction and nudging Laura out of the way with his hip as he came through with his hot steak pan. "No interest of mine who Paige kisses."

"Oh, come off it! That's total bullshit and you know it!"

Nick looked around him and checked to see if Daniel and Jamie were listening in. Last thing he needed was to be wound up by those two after Laura finally buggered off.

"Was there anything you wanted? Other than to gossip and pester me while I'm working?" Nick huffed, now garnishing his steak and adding the extras.

"Yeah, can we have a couple of pizzas to go?"

"Ask Jamie."

Two pizzas made up and cooked, Laura was on her way within half an hour. No sooner had she left, Daniel and Jamie pounced.

"So... got the hots for the new boss ave'e?"

"Piss off," Nick muttered, fuming with a heavy sigh through his nose.

The boys chuckled and waggled their eyebrows in amusement, Nick's murderous glares sending them running back to their own tasks. He'd let Laura pay for that later.

Chapter Thirteen

The frosty nature of March soon trickled away with the arrival of a warm spring April, clusters of yellow daffodils spotted all over the village: in plant pots, on Cornish hedges and even in people's window boxes. Mevagissey was shedding its winter coat and looking all the better for it, as fishermen hauled their boats out of the water for repairs and paint touch-ups, the pungent smell of fibreglass in the air.

Paige was very aware that she still hadn't broached Nick about his plans on buying the restaurant prior to Elaine's death yet. The idea of her being the one to have put a stopper in those plans didn't sit right with her and she'd planned to raise it with Nick on multiple occasions during the time they spent together which, with the increasing number of holidaymakers making their early way down on the edge of tourist-season, had been more than usual to keep up with the growing demand for bookings. Since the Easter holidays, the team had been at it with fully booked lunch times and evenings, and it seemed things weren't about to ease for the approaching summer.

So of course, Paige was down with the worst cold she had had in years.

"Alright Bird? How you feeling?" Jacca asked, creeping into the darkness of Paige's bedroom and stepping over the scattering of snotty tissues.

"Like crap," Paige groaned, her face stuck to her pillow with snot and drool.

"Look like crap too."

Paige just about managed to raise an arm to flip her old dad a rude gesture, just as Jacca yanked the curtains open and let in some sea-salt air through the now open window.

"Can you manage some breakfast?"

Paige groaned a response, declining anything that had to slide down her raw, swollen throat. She felt awful, and not just physically. She'd left Nick completely in the lurch. She couldn't remember the last time she'd taken a sick day, let alone a sick week.

"She doesn't want any breakfast!" Jacca called down the stairs, making Paige's head feel as if it was going to split open.

"Who you shouting to?" Paige complained, clamping her hands over her ears.

"The hell she doesn't!" Nick's voice responded from downstairs, followed by heavy footsteps on the small, rickety stairs.

"What the - Nick's here? Don't let him come up!" Paige squealed, throwing herself under the covers. "I'm in my pyjamas and look like crap!"

The sound of Jacca's retreating chuckles gave her a false sense of security just as her bedroom door burst open again.

"You are never going to get better if you wallow in here all day long. You've been cooped up for two days now," Nick said, striding in and pointing an accusing finger towards the lump that was Paige under the covers. "Come on, get up. I have an hour before I need to get to the restaurant and Lilly's watching your omelette."

Paige's inner battles over the growing feelings towards Nick weren't getting any easier, and to have him towering to the ceiling in her dinky little childhood bedroom was just a little too much for her as she wrestled with the butterflies erupting into a frenzy in her tummy.

"Come on!" Nick yanked the duvet from Paige, revealing her tangle of legs in her skimpy black silk shorts. Nick's eyebrows waggled at the sight. The man had no shame!

"Jesus, Nick! Bugger off, will you? This is beyond invasive!"

Nick took himself downstairs to check on the

151

breakfast, his chuckles trailing along behind him, whilst Paige rolled inelegantly out of bed to put something more appropriate but equally as comfortable on for breakfast.

When she got downstairs, Jacca and Nick were huddled around the stove, in deep conversation about lobsters, and Lilly was tucking into her omelette.

"Morning, Auntie Paige."

Since her movie night in with Laura and Lilly, Paige had been honoured with an official position as auntie and it made her heart swell every time she heard it.

"Morning, sweetheart. I've got germs, so I won't get too close. I'll park myself on the sofa."

She'd made a feeble attempt to tame her hair before coming down, her long mane of black hair still sticking up in different directions. She'd replaced the skimpy shorts with thick grey joggers and had slipped on an old hoodie she had dug out from the bottom of one of her old chest of drawers. She looked homeless, but it was a marginal improvement.

"Lemsip. Omelette. Ketchup. Fresh orange." Nick plonked each item on the coffee table next to Paige as she sat up enough to accept the plate with her freshly prepared ham and cheese omelette. Her heart swelled just that little bit more at Nick's efforts to look after her.

Each piece of omelette that Paige swallowed was hot and bruising, but it slid down enough to make eating just about bearable. She could hardly taste what was bound to be a perfectly seasoned dish - knowing Nick - but the heat and the texture was enough to tell her that it was delicious.

She felt Nick's eyes on her as she attempted another dramatic and agonising swallow, her whole body twitching from the pain.

"Do you think maybe you should get some antibiotics?" Nick asked from the table, he and Jacca finally tucking into their own breakfast.

"Tried to tell her that, beginning of the week," Jacca complained. "Used to get tonsillitis all the bleddy time when she were little."

Nick flung his fork down and strode over to Paige, finishing a mouthful of omelette as he knelt down in front of her.

"Look up."

Paige reluctantly tilted her face up towards the ceiling as Nick placed a large hot hand on either side of her neck, pressing down on what she could already tell were very swollen glands.

"Open your mouth."

"Piss off - I'm not doing that. Sorry Lilly!"

"Your glands are the size of bloody golf balls. You need to call the practice and get some antibiotics."

"Doctor, chef and personal wake-up caller. Impressive," Paige attempted to joke, flinching as another agonising but potentially delicious bite slid down her mangled throat. She rolled her eyes as Nick's lips barely twitched into a smile. "Yes, boss."

"No, you're the boss. And I need you back at work! Bookings are going mad."

A slight wave of disappointment rippled through Paige at the idea that it was simply just work logistics related why Nick was being so attentive. Her initial reaction was to scowl like a surly teenager, then she immediately gave herself a mental shake back into reality.

"Sorry, Nick. I've been useless this week. Perhaps you could get someone to drop off the ordering and accounts. I can at least chip away at the paperwork while I'm home."

"No," Nick said firmly, shaking his head. "You rest and get those antibiotics sorted. That's it. Don't worry about the restaurant - we can manage."

Everybody's ears pricked up at that point at the sound of a commotion going on outside on the harbour.

"What's all that shouting?" Jacca grumbled. "It's seven in the morning!"

Jacca plonked his cutlery down with a clatter and strode out of the front door, quickly followed by Nick. Despite feeling as weak as a new-born, Paige's curiosity got the better of her as she shuffled to the window with a blanket draped over her.

"Sounds like Malcolm," Lilly commented, joining Paige at the window. "He sounds very cross."

"Wouldn't want to get on the wrong side of him, that's for sure," Paige muttered as she tried to catch a view of the skirmish. "This is no good. I can't see a thing."

Paige wrenched the front door back open and secured a better view over the wall just outside the house. Nick and Jacca were running up to Malcolm by the fishing market, who was trying to break up an escalating fight between two other fishermen. She caught snippets of the argument, fishing territory being the main theme.

The excitement for the morning fizzled out quicker than it started once Nick and Jacca had got involved, and soon they were both out for their day's work, with Lilly at school, leaving Paige to mope around the house alone again.

A long, hot bath made her feel somewhat human again, soothing her sore skin and aching joints. She was beginning to contemplate heading back to bed again, despite Nick's earlier protests, when there was a sharp rap at the door.

"Oh - hi, Charlie!" Paige wrapped her dressing gown around her tighter, feeling suddenly exposed.

"I heard that you're unwell," Charlie shot her a sympathetic look through the gap in the door. "Jacca told me that you're struggling to eat, so I brought soup."

Paige clocked two steaming takeaway pots from the ice-cream parlour down below, the familiar smell of rich tomato and basil. On one hand, the aroma made Paige's appetite whetted slightly from its hiding place. On the other hand, it all reminded her of how awkwardly she'd left things with Charlie since that day on his boat, a good three weeks ago now. She let Charlie in with a slight reluctance and pointed him in the direction of the kitchen.

"Any idea what all the squabbling was down on the harbour this morning?" Paige asked conversationally as Charlie returned with two spoons and the soups safely in bowls. He returned a second time with a stack of buttered bread.

"Last I heard, somebody intercepted Jim's catch. Mackerel are out in large shoals now, see. Think some bloke from Fowey way muscled in and caused some damage to Jim's drift net."

"Oh no! No wonder he was angry then."

"Malcolm was saying he had to get in there quick. He thought Jim was going to murder the bloke or push him into the water."

"That would have been quite the entertainment," Paige smiled, gingerly sipping at her soup. She had to admit, the warmth of it settled in her chest wonderfully and soothed her raw throat. "Hope somebody reports him though, if this bloke was out of territory."

"Nothing will come of it," Charlie huffed, dipping some bread into his soup. "It's a bit of a free for all out there at the moment. I've caught bugger all last couple of weeks."

"Have you spoken to my dad? I'm sure he'd be happy to help with the otter trawler for a couple of days."

"Well, I was actually hoping you might come out again and help me. That was my best day's work so far," Charlie shot Paige a cheeky grin from across the table. "You must be a lucky charm."

"The myths say otherwise about a female on board," Paige returned with a smirk, before wincing as she swallowed a large mouthful of soggy bread. She held her throat in protest, swearing under her breath.

"You've got it bad," Charlie grimaced in sympathy. "I've never had tonsillitis before."

"You don't want to either. My brother and I used to get it all the time when we were little."

As soon as she said it and as soon as the look of surprise crossed Charlie's face, she could have kicked herself. Suddenly, it wasn't just the soup-marinated bread she was struggling to swallow, but a large lump as well as she felt her heart catching up from its missed beat.

"I didn't know you have a brother," Charlie said, his

eyebrows up to his hairline. "Neither you nor Jacca have ever mentioned him. Does he live far away?"

Paige was momentarily lost for words and simply nodded. She returned to her soup, praying with all her might that Charlie would drop the subject and never ask another question towards her dear brother ever again. She just couldn't bear it.

The front door bursting open was both her saviour and a complication.

"Oh... I was coming to check on you and to make sure you had something decent for lunch," Nick stood stock still in the doorway, blocking out any light from outside, a foil tray of something hot and delicious in his hand. "But I see you're already sorted."

"What is it? It smells delicious!" Charlie asked, seemingly unaware of the crackling atmosphere, Nick seething as Charlie took the trays from him and carried them into the kitchen. Nick shot Paige an incredulous look as she shrugged bashfully.

"It's leftover sausage pasta. There's only enough for one," Nick added pointedly as Charlie came back with the pasta transferred to a dish and a couple of forks in his hands.

"I'll make sure she eats. Don't worry," Charlie said, cheerfully. His fork was already poised over the pasta dish and Nick was now hesitating at the door with a hand clutching tightly on the door frame.

"Thank you, Nick," Paige said in an attempt to put him at ease. "Everything OK at the restaurant?"

"All good," Nick spoke through gritted teeth, his eyes trained on Charlie who was now tucking in to the pasta like he hadn't eaten in days. "I'll leave you to it, then."

Paige let him go, knowing that she would be dealing with whatever that was another time. Her mind was too full of snot and fluff for her to even comprehend what had just happened.

"This is good pasta," Charlie said through a mouthful of her food. Suddenly, Paige felt utterly irritated over Charlie's presence and his inability to read an awkward situation when it was smacking him in the face. She just wanted to be alone.

"Charlie, I'm feeling quite tired. Would you mind... ?"

"Hmm?" Charlie looked up from the pasta dish and the penny finally dropped. "Oh! Yeah, of course. You need to rest."

"Thanks for the soup."

"Of course. Do you want me to pop by tomorrow?" Charlie asked as Paige encouraged him out of the door.

"That's OK... "

Charlie paused in the doorway, waiting for Paige to say something else, but when nothing came he nodded in understanding and gave a final tap on the door frame before heading off back to the harbour. No longer hungry, Paige crawled her way back upstairs and slept for the rest of the afternoon.

The sun beat down in a cloudless sky. A thin sheen of perspiration gleamed on her skin as she drank in her daily dose of vitamin D. Her name was called. It was her turn.

She adjusted her feet to the edge of the harbour wall and braced herself for the jump. She took the plunge and felt her lungs retract from the icy cold of the sea, waiting for that first gulp of fresh air as her head broke the surface of the water.

She waited a little longer, desperate for her lungs to fill with that crisp sea air, but it never came. Panic began to rise within her as the ocean floor formed a seal around her feet, cementing her beneath the water. Her lungs flooded as she screamed without sound, calling for him as his face became visible just above the water's surface. She became still for a moment, her arms floating aimlessly and her hair like wild seaweed. He smiled at her, that boyish grin meeting his twinkling brown eyes - their mother's eyes. Her body continued to fight against the paralysis of drowning, her chest spasming from the lack of oxygen as his smile widened across his face. She cried out his name and reached for him as the distance between them grew and grew, until his features became blurred and forgotten. He was slipping away, and she was drowning.

Suddenly, and with aggressive force, she was torn from her watery grave and rose from a tangle of sheets coated in sweat. Nick's hands were firmly grasped around her shoulders as she fought against him with every bit of strength she had.

"Paige! Wake up. That's it. Wake up. You're OK." Nick's voice was an anchor as Paige pulled herself back into reality, the effects of her nightmare still clinging to her feverish form. She was trembling all over in a cold sweat and sobs came in ragged bursts as she fell into Nick's arms and clung to him for dear life.

"She alright?" Jacca's voice could be heard from the doorway as he stumbled in, a tone of panic in his voice. As she came to, she realised darkness came through her bedroom window, not the afternoon daylight when she'd taken herself to bed. She'd slept right through to the evening.

"Wacky dream, I think," Nick said, now stroking her soaked hair and soothing her with gentle shushing. "She's got a fever."

"Had them terrible when she was a girl. Used to freak me and Elaine out something awful. Like she was possessed or something. I'll pop the kettle on."

Paige heard her father retreat back downstairs, focusing now on her breathing, which settled to a more manageable rhythm. Despite her slight discombobulation, Paige was aware of her cocooned position in Nick's arms and relished in the feeling. It was firm and warm and secure, and for the moment she needed it to hold herself together, her brother's contorted features still etched into the front of her mind.

Neither Nick nor Jacca questioned Paige over the feverish dream incident, for which she was grateful. Nor did Nick mention anything about Charlie being over for lunch during the day, which had clearly bothered him judging by his reactions. Nevertheless, she was very grateful and spent the rest of the week recovering with the help of a course of antibiotics.

"You're looking more human!" Laura acknowledged one afternoon, passing over some flowers and a takeaway box of hot lunch from the restaurant. It was Paige's last day of recovery before her return to work. She was glad of Laura's drop-by as she was now at the brink of climbing the walls with boredom.

"These are lovely," Paige said, admiring the vibrant bunch of tulips, whilst her nose acknowledged the irresistible smell of Nick's famous spag bol. "Do you fancy sharing? I'm not going to eat all of this."

"Go on then. But don't tell Nick. I was under strict instructions to make sure you ate every last bite."

"Is he trying to make me better or fat?" Paige remarked, rolling her eyes as she returned from the kitchen with two forks, some Parmesan and a grater. "He's more of a fuss-pot than my dad!"

"Tell me about it. Don't worry - I get it an' all. He's told me I need to have more time out in the sun because I look like a ghost."

"Charming," Paige chortled, taking a seat opposite Laura at the dinner table. "He's right though. You've been working long hours and lots of nights. You need some daylight."

"God, if you two eventually decide to get it on, I'm going to get it in the bloody neck from all angles!" Laura huffed, stabbing her fork into the spaghetti and making a hash up of twirling it onto the prongs.

"Beg your pardon?!" Paige laughed, incredulously.

"Nothing," Laura feigned innocence. "Although you know exactly what I'm on about."

"No I don't, and I'm not satisfying you with taking the bait," Paige retorted, twirling her spaghetti expertly on to her fork. "Can I show you some paint samples in a minute for my bedroom, while you're here? Finally convinced Dad to let me decorate my room."

"Oh Lord, that made you sound like a teenager. You're twenty-eight years old, and you're asking for permission to decorate your room. Why don't you just move into your flat above the restaurant?"

"Because I don't want to, alright?" Paige replied, a little prickly. "Jeez, what's got your knickers in a twist?"

"Nothing!" Laura cried, a little unconvincing. "It's just, you've got a beautiful flat going to waste over there-"

"Not true. Lilly makes excellent use of it as a private cinema." Laura's deadpan expression was met with another eye roll from Paige. "I'm perfectly happy sharing with Dad for a bit. I feel more at home here than I ever did in that flat."

"Was it because your mum and Giuseppe lived there?" Laura's voice wasn't unkind, in fact her tone was that of someone gently prodding on a sore topic. "Do you think it might be good for you to... you know?"

"Let it go? Man up? Build a bridge? Probably. Look, I'm just not comfortable calling it home - OK?"

Laura pulled a face and harrumphed loudly.

If she was perfectly honest, and Paige didn't like to admit it but she didn't like the idea of living somewhere completely on her own. In Bristol, she had been used to the constant buzz of her room-mates' social lives. If she wasn't being kept alert with their party-animal lifestyles, then she was being kept company by Matthew. Now, back in her old childhood village, she found comfort in Jacca's shuffling around the house in his old, tweed slippers, his snores which could shake the shingles from the old roof, and the rumble of the kettle followed by the loud clinking of a teaspoon against a mug as he made his first tea for the day on his early morning fishing days. She wasn't sure she could cope with rattling around in the silence of the flat.

Paige and Laura sat and ate their shared lunch in silence for a moment, the midday April sun beating through the glass of the living room window.

"Whilst we're giving each other the third degree," Paige began. "What's up with you? Is it Scott?"

"Got it in one," Laura groaned, looking miserable. "Third attempt at making some solid plans. He's agreed to May half-term now. Honestly, Lilly isn't even daring to get excited anymore. She just doesn't believe it's going to happen. It's breaking my heart to see her look so despondent over it all."

"A positive - none of this will do him any favours in court."

"Maybe."

"Tell him that if he turns up, he can have a complimentary meal at the restaurant. Not because he deserves it - because he doesn't - but he sounds like the kind of prick that will play ball with a little incentive."

"Think you're right," Laura grimaced. "Good luck getting him past Nick without having his neck broken."

"If it gets him here and gives Lilly a chance to see her father, then leave Nick with me."

"Yeah... as I said, good luck with that."

As Paige had predicted, the incentive for a free meal was sadly the dealmaker for Lilly's dad, and it equally saddened as well as angered Paige that this secured Lilly's chances to forge a relationship with her father, not the idea of actually spending time with her. Thankfully, it seemed that Lilly was choosing not to see it this way as she finally allowed herself to look forward to it.

The weeks dwindled away fast and now Scott would be arriving in just one week's time, and Laura was right - Paige had completely underestimated how Nick would react to the idea of Scott coming to the village.

"Who the bloody hell made the gnocchi?" Nick demanded, storming into the kitchen with a saucepan of gnocchi in his hands. "You could kill somebody with these fricking bullets!"

Paige kept quiet, not wanting to be the one who threw Lewis straight into the fire. She wasn't much better at making homemade gnocchi herself, but even she could see that the little pellets falling from Nick's hands right now were not up to standard. She chanced a glance in Lewis' direction to see him cowering behind the ancient pasta machine.

"Paige? Did you make these?!" Nick shouted across the kitchen to her.

"Are you going full Gordon Ramsay on us or something?" Paige challenged, shooting Nick a daring look to shout at her again in front of her kitchen staff. "No, I didn't make them. But I agree, they look a bit heavy. Just make some more."

Nick tipped the content into the nearest bin and got to work making another batch in pregnant silence. Slowly, the clinking of pans and sizzling of food commenced as everyone in the kitchen decided the coast was clear for a moment. Paige noticed Lewis looking forlorn and gave him a comforting nudge as she passed him with the pizza dough.

"Sorry, Paige," Lewis whispered, as he followed her into the cool room. "I'm so tired. Been up all night with the baby and Jess has been poorly again, so hasn't been able to breastfeed."

As he mentioned it, Paige noticed the dark circles under the poor bloke's eyes. She hadn't known him for long, with him only returning from an extended paternity leave just a few weeks ago, after his wife had gone through a nasty birth.

"Lewis, if you need to be home right now it's not a problem."

"No, I've had too much time off already."

"What can we do to help?"

"I don't know."

Paige was alarmed to see Lewis's eyes fill with tears as he became overwhelmed by it all. Here was a new dad, desperately tired and trying to hold things together. She wondered how Scott had been in the early days of Lilly's babyhood and whether he too had found things too much and had run for the hills. Paige wasn't a parent, so she couldn't comment. But she was impressed with Lewis who, despite being beyond exhausted, had managed to show up

162

to each and every one of his shifts in the last few weeks. She knew from discussions with Nick on Lewis' return, that things were not straight-forward for him at home.

"Let me have a chat with Nick. Perhaps we can come up with a solution for your hours. Less late shifts or something."

Lewis' shoulders sank down a couple of notches in relief and a small smile crept onto his weary face. "Thanks, Paige. Can you tell Nick that I'm sorry, and that I'll keep practising my gnocchi."

Paige waved him off and took herself straight to Nick to have the chat with him.

"It's Lewis. He's really struggling," Paige explained, now in the office with an agitated Nick. "But I think he's afraid to say anything because of all the time he's already had off."

Nick, who had been on the brink of explosion beforehand, was now somewhat deflated and rubbing his head with worry. His hands now firmly on his hips, he released a heavy sigh.

"Let's go with your idea," Nick grumbled. "Give him nine to five shifts or something, so he can get home at a good time."

"Good idea," Paige nodded in approval, taking the rota off the wall to look at where she could tweak hours to accommodate. She glanced at Nick, noticing that he wasn't making any efforts to move, his hands returning to his hips in an angry stance. "Now for the next issue. Are *you* OK?"

"Yeah, why?" Nick snapped. It reminded her for a moment of Matthew in one of his hot tempers except Nick's demeanour left her more bemused than nervous.

"Oh, nothing," Paige shrugged, "Just the irrational rage and the sudden Gordon Ramsay persona you've adopted. You and Laura are like two grizzly bears fresh out of hibernation. So I'm guessing it's Scott's pending arrival."

"If that little prick steps one toe out of line, I'm pushing him into the harbour," Nick hissed. Paige suppressed a smile and gave Nick a consolatory pat on the arm.

"If he lets that little girl down at all next week," Paige added. "I think you'll have the whole fishing fleet behind you."

Chapter Fourteen

"I forgot how much it stinks here."

Scott had been in the village for less than an hour and was already, in Paige's eyes, saying all the wrong things for somebody who was seemingly years late spending time with his only daughter. Lilly was on her way down with Laura from their apartment on the other side of the village; Nick was at a safe distance at the vets, taking Mowgli for his six-monthly check-up; and Paige had drawn the short straw in welcoming the git to Mevagissey with a hearty lunch and coffee back in the restaurant.

"Can't say I've ever noticed the smell," Paige responded coolly, placing his coffee in front of him as he settled down in a seat by one of the arched windows.

"You're probably nose blind, living here all the time."

Paige wondered whether she'd be feeling this prickly with everything the bloke said if she didn't already have something against him but took a deep breath and chose to remain courteous all the same.

"Actually, I've just come back from living in Bristol for ten years."

"What on earth made you come back?" Scott chortled, tapping away at his phone absentmindedly. He was tanned, but not in a way which suggested he was well-weathered. His speckled beard was sharp and shaped ready for business and the Rolex watch on his fuzzy wrist suggested he was doing just fine as an urban businessman.

"My dad. This restaurant. My mother's funeral," Paige listed off, stopping herself before her voice could get any icier.

Scott cleared his throat awkwardly, nodded his thanks for the coffee and ended the conversation by turning to look out of the window. Paige took her cue and happily returned to her place in the kitchen where she was preparing for a busy lunch shift. She was already starting to regret the free dinner she had offered to get this man back here, in Lilly's life. She busied herself with prepping a batch of tomatoes to distract herself from an unfamiliar sense of lioness protection for the little girl.

May half-term had not only brought with it the arrival of Lilly's estranged father, but Meva's annual tourism chaos as well. Whilst Paige was glad to see the bookings in the restaurant finally creep up to maximum capacity, Jacca grumbled at the sight of his working fishing harbour become a tourist attraction for descending visitors.

"I just got told off by some emit for driving through the bleddy harbour!" Jacca had bellowed through the house one morning. "I bleddy live 'ere! It's a bleddy working harbour, not Disneyland! Bleddy cheek of it! Ten points if I can run 'em over next time."

Paige chuckled to herself at the recent memory of Jacca grumbling all the way to his boat and still being heard exchanging moans and groans with his fellow fisherman an hour later that morning as Paige had walked to the restaurant.

"Have we got all the tables reserved for bookings, Max?" Paige asked, as she leaned over the bar to retrieve a pencil and pad. Really, she was in charge of the kitchen this lunchtime, in Nick's absence, but she couldn't resist finding an excuse to check up on how things were going with Scott after Laura and Lilly's arrival.

"All done, Bird. Though, I don't know how we're going to cater for that group of fifteen, with all those prams as well."

"I know. We'll just have to ask them to fold their prams away and tuck them into the back corridor. Have we got enough highchairs?"

"Think so. I've asked Lauren to clean up the spare ones out the back. What you doing farting around out here in my territory anyway? Get back in the kitchen, you!"

Paige smiled and placed a hand on Max's forearm. She nodded in the direction of the family reunion table, where Laura was making good headway in chewing a hole through her lip as she watched with worry over the father and daughter exchange before her. Lilly seemed shy but happy, whilst Scott was animated in enthusiasm, gesticulating frantically as he told some sort of joke or anecdote, earning a little chuckle from his daughter.

Perhaps this was a good thing.

"You nosy bugger," Max tutted. "Go on then. After that, leave me to it will you?"

Paige approached with caution, feeling both intrusive and necessary at the same time as she caught a glimpse of the tension between Scott and Laura whilst he handed Lilly a gift from across the table. Paige paused about a metre from the table as she watched Lilly dunk her whole arm into the bag and pull out a white box with the famous Apple symbol.

"A phone? You bought me a phone!" Lilly squealed in glee.

Laura's features hardened, her jaw tightening into a sort of grimace as she shot daggers at Scott across the table.

"A phone, Scott?" Laura tutted, folding her arms incredulously. "She's eight years old."

"That way she doesn't have to keep borrowing your phone to call me." Scott shrugged, as if his gift was the simplest resolution for any problem, leaning back in his chair with total ease and satisfaction. His daughter was glowing with excitement.

"What can I get you?" Paige took this as her moment to step in, shooting Laura what she hoped was a reassuring look. "Lilly? The usual spag bol which ends up half-way up your face?"

Lilly giggled and nodded her response, earning Paige a burning hole in the side of her head from Scott's impenetrable stares.

"I'll have the braised rabbit pappardelle," Scott declared, sliding the menu away from him on the table.

"Laura?" Paige prompted as she wrote down Scott's order.

"Panzanella please, Paige," Laura finally responded, not taking her eyes off Scott. "Lilly sweetie, don't open that box yet please. We need to discuss this first."

"Why?" Lilly asked, disappointment in her voice. "I'll look after it!"

"I know, sweetheart. But - but, you're..." Laura stuttered, looking pleadingly at Paige whilst Scott continued to sit back in his chair, one arrogant eyebrow raised.

"I think your mum is just worried you're a little young for a phone Lilly," Paige supplied.

"And thank you! I'll have a Peroni with my meal," Scott said in a loaded tone, waving Paige off like an annoying fly.

Before Paige could think about bashing the man's head against something hard, she spun around on her heel and stormed off into the kitchen. She was silently glad when Nick finally made an appearance, bursting at the seams to pull a 'you were not kidding' face! To her mild satisfaction, her look of utter perplexity was met with a knowing nod followed by a mouthed 'I told you'.

"How on earth did our sweet Laura end up with a piece of dog turd like that?" Paige demanded, as Nick washed his hands and grabbed an apron.

"I used to ask myself that every day while they were together," Nick shook his head, his hands on his hips, and sighed. "What's he done? Or said?"

"He's bought Lilly a brand spanking new iPhone. Completely blindsided poor Laura and everything!"

"She's far too young for a phone!" Nick growled, looking as if he was about to march straight out there. Paige blocked the doorway just in case, her hands landing on his hard arms as she spun him around in the direction of the stove.

"Exactly what Laura and I said. He said it was so Lilly could call him without using Laura's phone."

Nick growled again, threw some oil into a hot pan

168

and started frying some onions rather too vigorously. "Well, that's not bloody happening! Which dish is the prick having?"

"The rabbit. Don't you dare cock it up to spite him! Keep our reputation intact please."

"Spoil sport."

That evening, Lilly was dropped off to the restaurant as usual for Laura's night shift. A troublesome look on Laura's face told Paige that the rest of the day with Scott had not much improved.

"He wants a day with Lilly by himself tomorrow," Laura confided in Paige anxiously once she knew Lilly was a safe distance upstairs. "I'm not comfortable with it. Not with the way he's been so far. He keeps making me feel like some sort of killjoy."

"Then say no," Paige replied firmly. "You're Lilly's mum and Scott gave up the right to make decisions as a parent when he walked away from duties."

"What's this?" Nick asked, the mention of Scott getting the better of him as he passed through with a plate of steaks to braise. He eyed the girls up suspiciously, willing them to tell him everything.

"Nothing that concerns you!" Laura huffed, just as Paige replied with, "Scott wants to steal Lilly for a day by himself."

"Paige! Don't give Nick any more reason to beat Scott up!"

"I'd pay good money to see that," Paige responded, folding her arms and very much mirroring Nick's expression. Together, they looked like parents reprimanding a wayward teenager, Laura finishing the scene with a well-timed stamp of the foot.

"You two are infuriating. God knows what you'll be like when you finally admit feelings for one another!"

"Laura!" Paige and Nick cried indignantly towards her, as she bid them farewell with a defiant shrug. They exchanged perplexed looks and waved away Laura's comment. Both would have liked to say that they didn't have a clue what Laura was implying but the simultaneous blushing said otherwise as they got back into cooking and prepping their dishes for this evening's hungry patrons.

A hectic evening with a fully booked restaurant was soon counteracted with one of Paige's restorative jogs in the crisp golden sunrise the next morning. Running had been hard to return to after having tonsillitis, but Paige had soon returned to the rhythmic pounding of her well-worn trainers against the harbour floor. Mornings had become easier with dark, blustering winter mornings taking their leave, swiftly being replaced by the early morning arrival of the golden rays, throwing into the sky a magnificent spectacle of florid oranges and rosy reds.

It had been almost four months since Paige had relocated back to her childhood fishing village. She'd fallen into a sort of peaceful co-existence with her father, made better with Jacca's slow surrendering of allowing Paige to tidy and redecorate in places around the house. She took comfort from the hazy five o'clock starts with Jacca, as he busied himself with preparing his morning coffee and a crib for later on the boat, whilst she forced down a banana for a bit of morning energy before her run. All these little moments reminded her of a time where grief didn't sit so prominently on the periphery of her emotions.

Paige took pause by the little lighthouse on the end of the outer wall, settling her ragged breathing. It was depressing how quickly she had lost her stamina over those two weeks of recovering from a wretched bout of swollen tonsils.

"So, you're an early morning runner too?" A man's voice from the shadows of the wall made Paige jump out of her skin, her fists pumping straight up in to fight mode. It was Scott, and he was now chuckling away at Paige's reaction. "You're a feisty little thing, aren't you?"

"Being five foot eleven, I've never been called 'little thing' before. What a treat!" Paige bit, sarcastically.

"Laura has done quite the number on making me unpopular around here, hasn't she?" Scott snorted, squinting out to the open ocean, the sun gleaming ferociously at them both.

"Not my place to say. Enjoy your run." Paige tried to bring the conversation to a firm close, readying herself for one last hurdle back to the house, but Scott grabbed her arm gently to seek her attention.

"I just want to make amends. I want a relationship with my daughter," Scott's arrogance melted away for just one moment as his steel blue eyes pleaded for mercy. "You can understand that, surely? I can't set foundations with Lilly if I have Laura, or Nick for that matter, watching me like a hawk. It puts me on edge. They're one of the main reasons I couldn't stick around here all those years ago."

Paige wriggled her arm out of Scott's grasp and eyed him up suspiciously. A part of her knew that it was wrong to deny a father time with his daughter, past context considered. Another part of her knew that this was indescribably painful for Laura.

"I'm only saying this to you because you seem to be very close to them," Scott acknowledged, scuffing his trainer against the pavement and looking a little put out.

"This is hurting Laura, you know?" Paige voiced her thoughts out loud. "She and Lilly are a unit. You're unbalancing the status quo."

Paige's words echoed in the memory of her feeling like the perpetrator of that exact imbalance of a perfectly functioning family. Of how her fears and ego kept her away from rebuilding a relationship with her mother and keeping more in touch with her father. That she had left it too late to realise all of her reasons for staying away had been pride and grief mixed into a horrible ugly ball of nonsense that burned away those final counted moments. Perhaps, despite his arrogance and condescending tone, Scott deserved to have another chance with his daughter.

Coming to the realisation that she had just talked herself out of her own argument, Paige's folded arms

171

flopped to her sides in defeat.

"I'll talk to Laura."

Scott celebrated with a little fist pump. "Thank you... umm... "

"Paige," she supplied, before holding a finger up in warning. "I'm not promising anything and I'm certainly still on Team Laura. But I also want what's best for Lilly."

"You're a sensible girl."

Grinding her teeth at yet another one of Scott's backwards compliments, she turned to go, shouting her final words over her shoulder as she ran. "Just don't cock it up! Between the two of us, Nick's the softy!"

"You want me to do what?" Laura gasped, as Paige finally worked her way around the proposal even she couldn't believe she was presenting to her best friend. It was the traditional post-night shift breakfast now, back in the restaurant, and Paige was starting to see why her running stamina was taking such a hit these days, whilst adding a healthy dollop of brown sauce to her bacon sandwich.

"*I* don't want you to do anything. This is your decision. I'm just offering another perspective on this," Paige said, screwing her face up at Laura's reaction. "Feel free to tell me to bugger off."

"Bugger off," Laura offered, deadpan as she bit into her own bacon butty. "I'm sorry, I'm just not comfortable with leaving my daughter alone with someone who has made himself a complete stranger to us the last four years. I don't trust him."

"And I don't blame you," Paige soothed, looking down at her plate and feeling her cheeks heat up in shame. "Forget I said anything."

Paige and Laura shushed each other unnecessarily as Lilly skipped into the restaurant from the kitchen, closely followed by her uncle who was holding the biggest, most colourful heap of pancakes they had ever seen.

"I decorated my own pancakes!" Lilly sang, proudly.

"It looks like a unicorn puked up on it!" Nick added,

172

his expression somewhat unimpressed. "Quick Lilly, take it before someone puts my name and reputation to this monstrosity."

Lilly giggled gleefully and tucked into her glittery, pink stack of marshmallows and pancakes. Paige couldn't help noticing the spring in Lilly's step at the arrival of her dad and hated herself for needing to have another go at convincing Laura once Lilly was out of hearing range.

"It doesn't have to be for a whole day," Paige muttered sideways to Laura behind her sandwich, once she was sure that Nick had Lilly's full attention as he took a photo of her practically sticking her whole face into her breakfast.

"I'm going to bleddy thump you one in a minute," Laura hissed back. "Why are you so set on this all of a sudden? You witnessed it all yesterday!"

"I know. I just..." Paige began, but shut herself down as she realised she didn't want to share that part of her right now. She lowered her voice to the smallest of whispers, as Nick began to eye them suspiciously from across the table. "If he stays here in the harbour, you'll have plenty of eyes on him. It's probably quite nerve-racking having you watching his every move."

Paige studied Laura's evolution of expressions, the odd sideways glance at Lilly who was so far none the wiser of their conversation, whilst ignoring Nick's penetrating stares.

Finally, Laura slammed her sandwich down and released a heavy sigh before addressing her daughter. "Lilly, serious conversation now. So step away from the E-numbers for a moment."

An anxious Lilly set down her fork as she read her mother's expression.

"Your Dad would like to spend a bit of time with you... on your own. Would you like to?"

There was a pause as Lilly considered this for a moment, more calculated than any eight-year-old over a situation like this.

"Laura, I don't think this is a good idea," Nick warned.

"Neither do I, but Paige seems to think it is."

"Why are you getting involved with this?" Nick shot at Paige, his brow creased in agitation.

Paige blushed as Lilly took in the scene of worried adults.

"I don't have to spend the day with Daddy, if it's going to make everybody this nervous!" Lilly spoke out, her bottom lip wobbling.

Nick dropped his glare from Paige and wrapped an arm around his niece, whilst Laura let out a defeated sigh.

"No, it's OK. Sweetie, why don't you show your dad a bit of crabbing on the harbour this afternoon while Mummy catches up on some housework. Uncle Nick and Paige will be here if you need anything."

The absence of 'auntie' in that last sentence bothered Paige more than it probably should have but she didn't dare challenge the matter as both Nick and Laura simultaneously glared at Paige over their breakfast, as they all ate in loaded silence.

Things remained strained between Nick and Paige all the way through to the early part of the afternoon, when Paige could no longer stand the pregnant silence between them. She slammed a tray of fresh lobsters down on the counter and addressed Nick with hands on her hips.

"Go on then, get it out of your system!" Paige challenged Nick, ignoring the confused looks of her kitchen staff.

"Bit forward, Boss!" Nick teased, knowing how much it annoyed Paige to be called that. He glanced sideways at her for a moment, the usual playful smirk absent from his mouth. He returned to his dish, refusing to add to the discussion.

"You think I was bang out of order," Paige supplied, waving a hand at Nick to continue from there.

"You *were* bang out of order," Nick corrected, his words curt.

Paige harrumphed and took herself off into the cold store to retrieve more shellfish. On her return to the counter, unspoken words hung in the air between them as their cooking skills suddenly became more vigorous.

Lauren strode in from front of house with a food order and immediately stopped, as if she had walked into the tension between Nick and Paige like a hard wall.

"Everything OK here?"

"Yes," Nick and Paige snapped in unison.

"Alright, calm your tits! You two need to have sex already."

Before either of them could retaliate, the kitchen staff chuckling behind them, Lauren stormed back off in the direction of the customers to take more orders.

"I wasn't trying to cause any trouble, obviously," Paige restarted. "I just think... a separation doesn't have to deprive a child of a relationship with both parents."

A snort erupted from Nick as he shook his head in tempered amusement, slapping a steak into a pan, the sizzling matching the crackling of tension between them.

"You're right," Nick finally said, braising his steak perfectly on each side. "A separation *doesn't* have to deprive a child of a relationship with both parents."

"Right," Paige agreed, warily.

"So why did you deprive yourself of a proper relationship with your mum when Elaine and Jacca separated?"

A coldness trickled through Paige. She glared at Nick, his words biting through.

"Now *you're* bang out of order."

"Nick! Paige! There's an issue on the harbour!" Max hollered, running through to the kitchen. "Jacca and Scott are having a to-do out there!"

"Shit!" Paige cursed, both abandoning their dishes to exit out of the side door.

They ran towards the commotion, which took them to the far end of the harbour, by the lighthouse. It seemed that Jacca was giving Scott a piece of his mind, while a shell-shocked Lilly looked upon the chaos in tearful worry.

"-bloody irresponsible!" Jacca roared at Scott, despite being almost a foot shorter. "You put her in danger! She could have been killed!"

"What's going on? Dad!" Paige grabbed her father's hi-vis jacket before he could throw the bloke a punch.

"Oh great! There's me thinking I was getting a couple of hours with my daughter, and I've got the whole bloody village on me!" Scott shouted, addressing the whole harbour. "No bloody wonder I couldn't stick a life here! Lilly and I were just going to enjoy a nice day on the harbour."

It was then that Paige realised that Scott was wearing a wetsuit and that Lilly had stripped down to shorts and a t-shirt, both their feet bare.

"Please tell me you were not about to involve Lilly in tombstoning!" Paige said, her voice trembling.

"He bloody was!" Jacca cried, the same quiver in his voice. "He's got no idea of the dangers he was about put that little girl in! They never do when they come down here! No respect for the mercies of the sea!

"Oh come off it! What's a matter with you folk?" Scott scoffed, throwing his arms up incredulously and looking around at his audience.

Nick grabbed Lilly into a safe embrace, attempting to comfort her as her entire body began to shake.

"You lot are sniffing too much sea air. You're all a bunch of superstitious idiots! People do it all the time. I was just trying to have a bit of fun with my daughter."

"It's nothing to do with superstition! Tombstoning is banned for a reason around here," Paige informed, her voice on the brink of breaking and tears threatening to fall. Scott shuffled on his feet, eying Paige up warily as she became increasingly upset. "I convinced Laura to give you and Lilly some time together, and you've put her in danger."

"We were just going to go for a quick swim for fu-"

"No, you were going to throw your eight-year-old daughter into unknown depths from a harbour wall," Paige snapped, her voice rising and her patience wearing thin.

"People have been…"

Could she say it? Could she say it out loud?

"People have been… killed - people have been killed jumping off rocks and harbours just like this one!"

As Scott took an aggressive advance, closing the gap between them, she desperately held her resolve, holding her hand out to Nick who had practically launched himself towards them.

"Do you really think I would put my only daughter in that sort of danger?" Scott hissed, his tone threatening and nasty, as he looked Paige up and down in disdain. "You've been a meddling pain in my ass since I arrived. I've got enough trouble with this one."

He nodded towards Nick, who was practically burning up with rage, being kept out of harm's way by Jacca.

"I'm a bloody good swimmer and you bloody crackpots haven't got a clue what you're talking about!" Scott finished.

Something snapped in Paige as she rounded on Scott with all her might and shoved him hard out of her face. "I'm talking from personal experience, you asshole! Tombstoning killed my brother!"

Her words echoed across the harbour, the very words she had not wanted to speak out loud for all those years.

"My brother miscalculated his jump and I had to watch as he crushed himself against a rock," Paige sobbed. She gestured a shaking arm towards her father, his eyes brimming with tears. "My dad's son. And he was one of the best swimmers from around here. So you'll excuse us if we have strong opinions about your 'quick swim'!"

Paige gathered her sobbing father and muttered to a stunned Nick that she would meet him and Lilly back in the restaurant. He nodded solemnly, a silent Lilly in the crook of his arm. Paige tried to comfort Lilly with a quick squeeze on the arm but her efforts were feeble as her heart ached from old cracks forming. Scott simply stood defeated, no longer angry, and the small crowd soon dispersed into nothing.

Paige walked her father back to their cottage, her heart heavy and her throat sore from the large lump currently wedged inside. Content with Lilly being in her uncle's capable hands, despite her restaurant being abandoned during a busy lunch shift, Paige popped her father's old kettle on nevertheless.

She felt wretched to the core. Not only had she put Laura in a difficult position, angered Nick and put Lilly in grave danger thanks to Scott's naivety, she'd opened up a very deep wound in her father's heart in the process. She watched in despair as her father, not for the first time, succumbed to heavy sobs over his dead son. He sniffed and looked up, then held his arm out to hold Paige as she too gave in to a good cry.

"I'm sorry, Dad," Paige sobbed after a while.

"What for?" Jacca sniffed.

"For mentioning it."

"You must not apologise for speaking about your brother, my love. It's your mother who found it difficult to talk about him. But we must," Jacca said fiercely. "We must talk about him. We've let him be a taboo topic for long enough, we have."

Paige nodded, a small flicker of relief to be granted that permission. It had hurt deeply to not mention his name, to almost deny all memories of him for so many years.

"Did Nick not know?" Paige asked, recalling Nick's expression when they left.

"Don't think so. His father knows and his mother knew before her passing," Jacca said, his voice steadying as he reached for a handkerchief in his pocket. "But Elaine and I asked for it all to be kept private, you understand. Neither Laura nor Nick will probably remember."

Paige certainly did. The day was etched into her mind like a scar, playing the accident on repeat to torment her all those years. She recalled the nightmare she'd had only a few weeks ago. Just one of many versions of the day. Her darling older brother, Billy, showing off to his friends in a contorted rage over something he would not share with his little sister. The chants and dares from Billy's mates as he drew closer to the edge of that jagged rock on the cliff-side. The screams of terror from herself and Billy's mates as his body broke on impact against the invisible rocks beneath the water's surface. The deafening, warped sounds of emergency service sirens filling the sea air and Billy's cold body being dragged out of the water.

Paige fell into a fresh wave of sobs and they held each other tightly as the kettle rumbled to a slow finish.

Paige did not return back to the restaurant that day.

Chapter Fifteen

A brisk morning brought about a rapid knock on the cottage door. Paige rushed downstairs, mid-brushing her teeth, and wrenched the door open, half-expecting to see an irritable Nick at the door, demanding of her whereabouts yesterday evening. That was a conversation she hoped to leave for as long as possible.

Scott stood in the storm porch, casually admiring Jacca's fishing equipment, a grim smile on his face as she opened the door fully.

"Morning. I'm sorry to bother you so early. Have you got a moment?" Scott asked, his arrogance from yesterday utterly subsided and a sort of pleasantness about him.

Paige reluctantly offered for him to come inside but luckily he waved away her offer.

"No, thank you. I won't be too long and I need to catch Laura before I leave."

"You're leaving already?" Paige asked, shifting herself against the door frame and crossing her arms.

"Think it's best," Scott declared, screwing his nose up. He paused for a moment. "I'm sorry for your loss."

"Oh… umm… thank you. It was a long time ago."

"I lost my brother too, years ago. Leukaemia," Scott said, his voice strained suddenly. "I understand what a terrible hole it can leave, losing a sibling. I honestly didn't come down here to cause lots of trouble."

There was another pause as Scott gathered himself a little, Paige beginning to feel quite sorry for him.

"I would like a relationship with my daughter. But something about this place gets me a little agitated. Too many people watching over me all the time, waiting for me to step over a line."

Paige shuffled slightly as she glanced down at her

feet in awkwardness. He wasn't entirely wrong.

"I regret, more than anything else, not being a part of Lilly's life."

"So why did you leave?" Paige couldn't help herself. She stared him down, waiting for an answer as he chuckled nervously, running a hand through his perfectly styled salt and pepper hair.

"Partly what I just said. I felt like I was on constant trial with that brother of hers - Nick. Even after Laura and I got married. I couldn't breathe. Then, when we found out we were having a baby, I felt like the walls of the harbour were closing in on me. If I'm honest, I started to feel a little suffocated."

Before she could stop herself, Paige was nodding her head in understanding. Because she did understand. She knew that feeling of the walls closing in on her, like the whole of Meva was watching and scrutinising her every move. Was this how Elaine had felt with Jacca?

"But wasn't keeping the family together enough?" Paige voiced her thoughts out loud, dragging herself out of her own memories to focus on Scott's scenario.

"Don't you think that sometimes staying together for 'the sake of the children' is more damaging?"

Again, Paige nodded. Yes. There had been times when her parents' arguing had been so loud and miserable that perhaps being apart had been the better option.

"You still left Laura to raise Lilly on her own. You can hardly come down and make too many demands."

Now it was Scott's turn to nod, a slow bob of his head with his mouth set in a grim line. "I can see that. So, I'll go and let the dust settle. I'll stay in touch with Lilly, on Laura's terms. But yes, we need to approach this more carefully."

Paige and Scott said their awkward farewells, Paige a little perplexed as to why he chose to justify so much to her. The conversation left her pondering all the way to her dreaded return to the restaurant.

She'd contemplated out loud to Jacca last night of

calling in sick and avoiding Nick and Laura for as long as she could. She knew very well that she had overstepped a mark yesterday when getting herself involved in the Laura and Scott situation. She knew she'd got herself on the wrong side of Nick and at some point he would be having it out with her properly. Not the reserved conversation they had had in the kitchen just before the tombstoning fiasco.

But that wasn't what was stopping her from facing them back in the restaurant today. What she refused to see was the look on Nick's or Laura's face over their new-found knowledge of Billy's death. It was what she had hated the most just after the terrible incident which had taken her dear brother from her forever. The looks on people's faces. The pity. She couldn't stand it and it made her skin crawl with resentment.

She caught sight of her darling father, who was loading nets onto his boat for the day's haul. Her heart ached as she thought back to last night again, where her and Jacca had finally spoken about Billy over a glass of whiskey. There had been something quite restorative about the whole evening, and she and Jacca had departed to bed feeling utterly exhausted but perhaps peaceful.

She skulked through the front door of the restaurant. It was almost eight in the morning now, and much later than she would usually rock up. But she hoped that Nick's usual morning routine would have him in the cold room stock counting the meats.

Her predictions of his whereabouts were confirmed as she heard rustling and shifting of produce in the cold room at the back of the kitchen. She took the opportunity to dump her bag in the office and make a start on the pizza dough.

Making pizza dough and fresh pasta had quickly become one of Paige's favourite tasks since moving down. She'd completely underestimated how therapeutic it could be to put all her energy and might into working and kneading the dough every morning.

She had just entered the stage of falling into a full

kneading rhythm, her hands and arms already coated in a thin layer of flour, when she finally heard the cold room door shut. She focused her full attention on her kneading technique, something that had made a huge improvement from her first week back down here, given that the menu in Garlands hadn't required her to make pizzas. She felt Nick's presence in the room as she used the heel of her hand to stretch her dough, willing him to refuse all acknowledgment of her. No such luck.

"Thought that was you just a minute ago," Nick commented, washing his hands thoroughly after handling the meats.

Paige didn't answer, placing her first ball of dough carefully into the tray for proving.

"So, are we going to talk about yesterday? Or are we just going to pretend nothing happened and focus on the fact you left your own restaurant in the lurch last night."

In an odd way, Paige could have kissed Nick for his compassionless approach. She'd choose a bollocking on her absence over pity of her brother's death any day.

"Sorry," Paige mumbled, her focus still on the dough. "I'll make up the hours."

There was a resigned sigh behind her as Nick set to work on shucking a fresh batch of scallops, shaking his head impatiently.

"Laura wants to speak to you as well, by the way," Nick added from the counter behind her, leaving them back-to-back in a sort of protest. "She called just a minute ago."

"Suppose she'll want it out with me as well, because I'm such a terrible person for wanting the best for everyone," Paige spat, throwing her second ball of dough into the tray with a clatter.

"Oh Paige, stop being a pillock and talk to me properly will you?" Nick said, spinning around and coming to stand next to her.

A heavy pause fell between them and Paige cursed a couple of teardrops that had dared to escape, wiping them away furiously with the sleeve of her chef whites.

"I didn't know about your brother." Nick's voice was soft and tender now, his frustration subsided. His hand was hot and weighted on her back and it took all of Paige's might not to give in to the desire and fall right into his arms for a good cry.

"Not many people our age did," Paige responded curtly instead, silently begging him not to continue.

"Yeah, but I'm embarrassed to admit that I didn't even know you had a brother. I don't understand why I've never heard about him from Jacca or my parents."

"You won't have heard anything from my father because we haven't spoken about him properly in almost seventeen years." The next ball of dough was now being kneaded to within an inch of its life as Paige put her whole weight behind it, trying with all her might to keep her voice steady.

"Oh, that's healthy," Nick drooled, not unkindly.

"Tell me about it." Paige paused reluctantly from her laboured task, wiping her brow with the back of her hand and most probably coating her forehead in dusty white flour.

"Did you want to talk about it?"

Paige thought for a moment. In all fairness to Nick, his mannerisms towards the whole thing had been easier to swallow than anyone else's. But she'd spoken more about Billy last night than she had in seventeen years, and it was enough for the time being. Her heart was fit to break all over again.

"No," Paige said finally, a shuddering sigh escaping as she resumed her kneading process. "No, I don't think I do."

A small, silent sob escaped her lips as Nick's warm hand squeezed her shoulder, the signature gesture that told her that they were alright and that she had the time and space she needed to get by. She couldn't ask for much more than that.

"Nick said you might be avoiding me, which really

184

pisses me off. So I've bought booze and you're going to let me in, and we're going to sort our shit out. Alright?"

Laura's feisty outburst rattled through the empty cottage one evening, on Paige's night off. She wasn't wrong. Paige had been avoiding Laura and she wasn't proud of it. A large part of that had been the minor detail of working, but Paige couldn't deny that being an excellent excuse.

"Come on in, then," Paige said, stepping to one side to let Laura in. "Where's Lilly?"

"With Dad tonight. I need a night off."

Aside from being a ball of fury at her first arrival, Paige couldn't help but notice how tired Laura looked. She'd been overdoing the night shifts again.

Paige retrieved some glasses from the kitchen, set them on the coffee table and watched in awkward silence as Laura poured from the bottle of red she had brought with her. Paige used the time to brace herself for the wrath Laura was about to release on her.

"Right, go on then. Go for it! Give me what for," Paige said, finally. Throwing her arms out as if offering herself as a target. "I shouldn't have got involved in the whole Scott thing."

"What?" Laura's eyes were round as she stared at her friend incredulously. "This isn't about Scott, for God's sake. You were right, in a way, about that - we'll come to that! I'm more devastated to hear from Nick about... about your brother. Paige. All those years."

"Laura, please," Paige begged, her leg bobbing up and down furiously as she tried to hold it together. "I can't... "

"I'm so sorry, Paige. That it ever happened. Dad said the whole fishing community was asked to keep it hushed. But I remember you having all that time off from school. How did I not know?"

Paige nodded in response. Desperate to change the subject, Paige leapt up to retrieve a bag of salt and vinegar crisps for them to share and began asking Laura about what had happened with Scott in the end.

185

"We've been quite civil with each other so far," Laura explained, in between mouthfuls of crisps. "He's going to make more of an effort to remain consistent in Lilly's life and I'm," Laura gave Paige a pointed look, "going to back off a little when he does come to visit."

"Sounds fair."

"You made quite the impression on him before he left," Laura stated. "He seemed much more humble when he came to say goodbye. Like the old Scott I fell for at the beginning."

Paige knew that it probably had everything to do with him losing his brother too from a young age, but she wanted to avoid that side of the conversation the best she could. "He'd had the full Jacca treatment when I turned up."

"Oh heck! No wonder, then," Laura chuckled. "Anyone on the receiving end of an angry Jacca is in for it!"

A huge sigh of relief escaped from Paige as the prickly atmosphere between Laura and her melted away from their chuckles. They topped up their glasses and sat back to enjoy a well overdue evening's catch up. Laura respected Paige's wishes and dear Billy was not mentioned again that evening.

The busy nature of another tourist season boomed as Feast Week approached closer and closer. The week of celebration, where Mevagissey was dressed to look its very best, had been one of Paige's favourite village events growing up. A week of festivities, street games, boat races and of course a delicious range of food and drink. For as long as she could remember, Feast Week had been one big party for all villagers, business owners and visitors alike - and it was approaching fast.

Scott's visit had soon become a distant memory and Paige had been grateful to fall back into a form of a routine, hers and Jacca's tragic past being put on the back burner of conversations. It wasn't that she was avoiding talking about him again, it was that she needed time to deal with the fact more people knew about it. It was that she and Jacca had to

186

deal with this entirely alone now, one half of what their family once was.

Now, the restaurant was in full swing to get prepared for Feast Week alongside an increase of bookings from a growing number of visitors.

"What do you usually do for Feast Week?" Paige asked Nick one morning as they sat in their usual spot by the curved window to make notes on their festival plans.

"Well, back in Giuseppe's day, he had us out there providing a full Italian experience. Gelato desserts, pizzas, huge stacks of cannoli. Those cannoli! The best I've ever tasted!" Paige laughed as Nick drifted off into splendour of the memory.

"Did Giuseppe make them then? Did he leave a recipe?" Paige asked as she wrote the ideas down. There was a pause and Paige felt Nick's eyes on her. She looked up, her pen poised. "What?"

"You make it sound like... do you know what, never mind."

"No, go on. You clearly have something to say," Paige challenged, sitting up a little straighter and placing her pen down.

"Sometimes, you just don't sound like Giuseppe's stepdaughter. Hey, don't get all uppity with me! I'm just stating something that's bothered me for a while."

"Me not acting like Giuseppe's stepdaughter has bothered you for a while?" Paige asked, an eyebrow raised.

Nick shrugged and waited for Paige to respond.

"Well, I wasn't," Paige shrugged back, irritable.

Nick leaned in remarkably close, his arms caging her in where she sat as he scrutinised her with all his might through those stormy grey eyes.

"You're telling me that for the five years your mum and Giuseppe were together, you didn't have a single ounce of a relationship with him?"

Another shrug erupted from Paige's shoulders, utter defiance on her part. What was it between them that just made her turn into a belligerent teenager?

"Giuseppe was a top bloke!" Nick burst, leaning back in his chair incredulous.

Another shrug. She was starting to annoy *herself*. Of course Giuseppe was a top bloke. He was utterly delightful, and it had irked the heck out of her how wonderful he had been. It had crushed her darling father, who had lost more than just a spark inside of him after the death of his only son, to see his wife find happiness again with the man who had the brightest spark of all within the village of Mevagissey. It had infuriated Paige to the core when her mother had declared that Giuseppe was full of life and made her feel young again, that Jacca aged her and dragged her down in his misery. Not allowing him to grieve properly.

She couldn't deny though that she felt shame for pushing a lot of that resentment onto Giuseppe, essentially an innocent in this whole mess. But in the eyes of her teenage self, he had been the invasion, someone to ruin what was already a broken family.

Paige released a heavy sigh, "I know he was. So can you make the cannoli or what?"

"Yup," Nick said, resigned. "Leave it with me."

"What's this?" Maxine asked as she came through the front door for the start of her shift, a little puffed out from her hot walk through the village.

"Feast Week plans," Paige replied, glancing in Nick's direction and jolting slightly as her eyes met his for a moment.

"Ooh, I do love Feast Week," Maxine cried, wistfully. "Giuseppe's famous cannoli!"

Paige rolled her eyes as Nick shot her a smug look. Maxine grabbed a seat next to Nick as she too reminisced past Feast Weeks.

"The outdoor pizza oven is always a big hit too!" Maxine recalled, her eyes lighting up. "I quite enjoyed manning that. Had a right little batch line going last time, didn't we Nick?"

"Sure did."

"That sounds like a great idea," Paige agreed,

writing it down. "We can always have our main one going in here at the same if we get backlogged. I think we have enough ideas for food. We just need to sort out the bar now."

"I usually get an old rugby mate of mine to come and man that side of things," Nick said.

"You used to play rugby?" Paige asked.

Nick feigned looking affronted. "Don't sound so surprised. I was fit and active once! His name is Tom and he's the owner of Trengrouse Cider Farm. He supplies the ciders behind the bar. He'll be expecting a stall."

"Great," Paige noted this down on her list. "In that case, we're all done."

"If you don't mind, I have scallops to shuck for lunchtime reservations," Nick declared, departing and leaving Paige with Maxine.

"How are you, love?" Maxine asked, her voice gentle and maternal.

Paige looked up and smiled awkwardly, a little surprised by Maxine's question.

"I'm all good, thanks Maxine. You alright?"

"I'll just get straight down to it, shall I? I don't like faffing around too much. Your dad asked me to have a little chat with you. Says he's worried about you."

There was a pause as Paige waited for Maxine to continue, her eyebrows raised in anticipation.

"Is it true you haven't been upstairs into your mother's apartment since you moved down here?" Maxine's tone was one adopted for a mother reprimanding her child, as she eyed Paige over her glasses.

"Yes, of course I have. Lilly uses it, doesn't she?"

Maxine scoffed and gave Paige a little flick with her tea towel. "I don't mean to give Lilly some food or to retrieve her at the end of an evening, you silly girl. I'm talking about you going in there, in the apartment you now own, and starting to route through your mother's things."

"What is it with the third degree at the moment," Paige muttered in irritation. "No, I bleddy well haven't. So what's Dad worried about?"

"It's been five months, my darling," Maxine soothed, reaching for Paige's hand.

"So?"

"Most girls your age would be falling head over heels at the idea of their own harbour view apartment, and you have one up there collecting dust as speak."

"Actually, I'm paying Lauren on the sly to go up and give it a little clean twice a week," Paige rebutted, a matter-of-fact tone followed by an irritated sniff showing her annoyance at the topic. "When I'm ready, I'll start thinking about getting it redecorated and I'll rent it out or something. No big deal!"

"What are you so afraid of, my girl?"

They stared each other down for a moment, Paige chewing the side of her cheek as she contemplated a multitude of responses - a snarky comment, a downright lie. One thing she knew she couldn't respond with - the truth. Because, if she was honest, she didn't really know what that was.

"Come on, Maxine. We've got another busy day ahead."

The sun's beams bounced off the surfaces of the bobbing boats in the harbour. As always, Paige spotted her father and his fluffy, white hair straight away and negotiated her way through the growing crowd of visitors to get to him.

"Alright, m'love?"

"Everything alright?" Paige asked, her hands on her hips as she waited to find out why her father had requested her so urgently. "Only, it's been a busy lunch period and I have an even busier evening ahead."

"I won't keep you long. I'm a little worried about Charlie."

Jacca took a quick glance around him, in fear of being overheard. He beckoned his daughter onto his boat, and so they clambered on - Jacca more gracefully than Paige. Despite the weight of the next six hours of busy dinner reservations, Paige took the moment to soak in some rays, Jacca's boat proving to be much more peaceful than on the harbour itself.

"I hate this time of year," Jacca grumbled. "Give me a thunderstorm and pissing down rain any day if it means I don't have to fight my way through these bleddy crowds every time I want to get to my boat."

"You never were a fan of tourist season, were you Dad?" Paige teased, a coy smile on her face as she watched her father roll a cigarette.

"Silly season, don't you mean?" Another grumble, making Paige want to grab him for a big hug out of pure amusement and affection.

"Right, grumpy. What's a matter with Charlie?"

Jacca shook his head gravely, popping his cigarette into his mouth and lighting it up.

"Poor boy. You know he took a heavy loan for that boat of his, don't you?"

"He mentioned something about it, yes," Paige replied, not liking where this was going.

"Well, he's not admitting it but I think he's struggling big time. I've helped him a couple of times on the otter trawler, but other than that, he's completely on his own. His father was as much use as tits on a fish!"

"You went to his dad?!" Paige asked, remembering what Charlie had said about his family not being too happy about his lifestyle change.

"Yeah - said that the daft boy shouldn't have chucked his career away to play around on a boat! Good to know the man respects a fisherman's living. Where does he think his cod and chips come from, stupid pillock."

Paige rolled her eyes as Jacca fell into another one of his rants, making time for her to scour the harbour for Charlie's boat.

"Where is he then?"

"He's past the inner wall," Jacca stored his cigarette between his lips and turned the engine of his little boat on. "Hang on, I'll take you over to him."

Paige glanced at her wristwatch nervously and, as soon as they reached Charlie's boat, Paige jumped into the vessel. She'd quickly check on him, settle her dad's worries then head back to the restaurant where a fair amount of preparation for tonight was still in order.

The main deck was littered with nets, buckets and other fishing equipment, whilst the door to the cabin was wide open and emitting loud snores from within. Surely, Charlie couldn't be sleeping right now. It was in the middle of the afternoon. Paige rapped on the door, the rhythm of the snoring undisturbed.

Inside, the air was stale and fermented with spilled booze. Empty cans and bottles took up every surface around the cabin and cocooned in an old sleeping bag was Charlie in a deep slumber.

Paige sighed through her nose and shook her head at the state of the place, a spot of worry growing in the pit of her stomach.

"Dad," Paige called down to Jacca's boat as she stepped back out into the fresh air. "We have a much bigger problem here."

Chapter Sixteen

"You did what?"

Jacca and Paige had spent almost an hour coaxing an exhausted and intoxicated Charlie out of his boat and into the cleanliness and warmth of the apartment above the restaurant. It had been no easy task, negotiating the thick crowds of tourists whilst praying that Charlie wasn't ill all over the harbour floor. With Charlie fast asleep in the bed upstairs, Nick was now questioning Paige with surprising agitation, following her around the restaurant kitchen as she prepared some food for the drunken skipper.

"I've told him he can stay in the apartment, just until he finds his feet," Paige repeated herself, slicing some fresh bread and adding it to the small platter she was compiling. "Though not sure how much he actually took in of what I said."

"And you've given him some hours here, in the restaurant?"

"Yeah," Paige shrugged, matter-of-factly. "But not right now, he's pissed as a fart."

Nick scoffed. "Great. That's great. So we hire pissheads now? And where is Lilly supposed to go during Laura's night shifts? She's not sitting up there with him!"

Paige bit her lip, not wanting to admit that she hadn't thought of that. "We could always put a TV in the office. Or perhaps Dad could watch her?"

"I'll let you have that conversation with Laura and Lilly, shall I? You have not thought this through at all," Nick said, storming off in the direction of the cool room to retrieve some ingredients, the sounds of his tutting and huffing following in his wake.

Paige chose to ignore him, knowing she'd done the right thing even if it meant evicting Lilly from her private headquarters for the time being.

It was a small gesture in her eyes, to counteract some of the guilt she felt for not realising her friend had been living on his boat for the past four months, being unable to pay his utility bills and being evicted from his little flat in St Austell. Charlie had told Paige that things were difficult the time she'd accompanied him on the boat, but he'd been chirpy and had clearly downplayed his predicament entirely. She should have taken him more seriously, but as usual she had been too caught up in her own affairs - and of course Laura and Lilly's with the whole Scott thing.

She groaned, mortified by her ignorance, as she recalled the day he'd visited her when she was poorly. How he'd looked tatty, his eyes strained with stress that Paige hadn't understood at the time, and how he'd brought soup for her but ferociously tucked into the hot pasta dish that Nick had brought - like he hadn't eaten a decent meal in weeks. It seemed more likely now that this had been exactly the situation and she'd simply turned him back out on the streets, purely for being inconvenienced.

Jacca had, of course, given himself an equally hard time, wringing his hands in worry after they'd deposited Charlie into the apartment. "I've helped him out here and there with the otter trawler, and I never even noticed that he's been bleddy living on that boat. In all that horrible weather back in March and all!"

In the last couple of hours since, it had been heart-warming to see the fleet of fishermen come together to see Charlie was looked after, some even coming into the restaurant later that evening to check on him.

"Do you mind me popping up to see him, Paige?" Malcolm asked, popping his head into the kitchen, Maxine rolling her eyes behind him at the invasion.

"Go ahead. He might be awake now, if you're lucky."

Malcolm's heavy boots were heard on every creaky step leading up to the apartment as Maxine gave Paige an appraising look.

"Well, at least I found a use for the apartment," Paige quipped, earning a passing swipe from her mother's old friend. Paige chuckled and returned her focus on her dish, glancing up at Nick just in time to see the sourest look on his face. "What's the matter with you?"

"Wish you had run it by me that he'd be working here," Nick grumbled, his eyes on the steak he was braising. "I don't like the guy."

It was Paige's turn to have an appraising look about her now. She waited for an explanation to follow, which never came.

"Any particular reason?" Paige probed, one eyebrow raised.

Nick seemed to be battling with a multitude of things to say, eventually settling with a defiant shrug. "Just don't. Don't trust him. The way he ogles at you as well - it's creepy. I think you should be careful around him."

Despite her frustrations towards Nick, her face broke out into the smallest of smiles, her stomach clenching and her heart swelling. She blushed ferociously as she realised they had an audience.

"What are you two grinning about?" Nick growled at Daniel and Jamie, who's cooking had momentarily ceased. They waggled their eyebrows at Paige and even she had to turn away to hide her expressions.

"You're all a bunch of children," Nick grumbled.

"He's just an old school friend. Relax," Paige assured, rolling her eyes at her kitchen staff as they elbowed each other in amusement.

She had to remind herself though, Nick's natural default was to care for everyone around him. She was nothing special and she was sure this sudden protective nature was more brotherly than anything worth getting herself worked up over. The sheer disappointment of that thought dissipated the feelings quickly and she returned to her work with nothing more to say on the matter.

The evening shift was worked with very little words exchanged after that, and once all the other staff had headed home, Paige braced herself for something she had been dreading doing since her return.

"You can head home you know? I'm just going to check he hasn't choked on his own vomit or something?" Paige reasoned as Nick planted himself firmly against the door frame leading out to the front of house, just by the bottom of the stairs leading to the apartment.

"I'll wait here, thanks," Nick said, adopting his usual stubborn stance with his arms across his chest.

She climbed the narrow stairs, every step with its own unique creak or pop of the floorboards. The same outdated framed images of Italy and holiday snapshots taken by Giuseppe and Elaine on their many trips back to his home country. It did seem absurd that they were all still here, given how much they bothered Paige. Perhaps she could convince Charlie to do a spot of redecorating as rent money.

When she finally reached the bedroom, she found there was no explosion, or anything else equally sinister. The world didn't come to an end. In fact, it really was the biggest anti-climax of the century.

Charlie was sat up in her mother's old bed, his floppy, blonde hair sticking up in all directions, and red circles around his eyes. She didn't remember much of the decor from when she'd last ventured up here all those years ago but it seemed familiar. From the plain marigold walls to the understated cream curtains and loud, floral duvet cover.

"Bit of a funny time to be finally waking up," Paige teased, standing awkwardly at the foot of the bed. "The whole village will be heading to bed in a minute."

Charlie was looking sheepish and downright miserable. "Paige, I'm so embarrassed. I don't know what came over me," he groaned, rubbing his face gingerly. "I must have drunk a whole bottle of whiskey."

"Christ. No wonder you were steaming," Paige attempted an amused chuckle, edging her way cautiously around the bed towards the side table. "Do you at least remember our conversation earlier?"

197

Charlie nodded and grabbed Paige's hand as she placed a glass of water and painkillers down next to him. "You don't need to do any of this. It's my mess."

"Just how much mess are you in right now, with the bank?"

Charlie's grave expression was enough for Paige that she didn't need an answer. She gave him a feeble yet comforting rub on the arm and instructed him to grab something to eat before heading back to bed again.

"There's a pasta bake on the kitchen side. Just give it a quick ping in the microwave and eat it steadily." She pointed out the provisions on the bedside table. "Paracetamol. Water. I'm knackered. Goodnight."

"Goodnight, Paige. Thank you."

The week before Feast Week, tensions were running high in the restaurant, Charlie and Nick being no exception. It had quickly come to light that Charlie was terrible at waiting tables, often getting orders wrong and offering dishes to the wrong customers. When Paige had diplomatically removed him as Maxine's burden and placed him in the kitchen to do basic kitchen portering, it had turned out to be grave mistake, resulting in testosterone knocking about the room like a pinball between him and Nick. She couldn't deny the poor man's resilience however, as he showed up for every shift with enthusiasm, despite Nick's blatant impatience towards him. He'd even offered to do extra hours during Feast Week, asking if he could get involved in the pizza stall.

"If you say yes to him manning the pizza stall, I'll kill you both," Nick warned, not having the desired effect as Paige burst into laughter, along with Maxine, who was just glad to have him off the front of house.

That morning, Jacca came rushing in, all ready to answer Nick's prayers.

"Where's Charlie?" He asked without any form of greeting, Paige looking up from the diary in alarm.

"He's in the kitchen. Why, what's the matter?"

"Nothing a matter, my dear girl!" Jacca sang, clapping his hands together and strutting a merry little walk towards the kitchen to retrieve Charlie. "Charlie! Grab your waders, boy! We've got fishing to do! You can spare him, can't you Paige?"

"Of course. Summer species finally coming through?" Paige asked, remembering what her father had said about warmer waters bringing in the money.

"You better believe it - ha! Come on, Charlie! Hurry up, m'boy!" Jacca shouted down the corridor to the kitchen, then turning to Paige again, "Malcolm's just got back from a trawl. There's some prime fish out there. John Dory, Dover sole, lemons, turbot - you name it!"

"That's fantastic! Happy fishing, both of you," Paige said, as Charlie came running down from the apartment in his fishing gear, a wide grin plastered across his face.

"Sorry to jump ship on my hours here today, Paige."

Paige thought of Nick and how relieved he'd be to not have Charlie knocking about in the kitchen today and waved Charlie off. "Not another word about it. We'll be fine - go!"

She watched as Charlie and her father rushed to his boat, pleased to see the alliance they had formed together - both for Charlie's sake and for that of her father's. As they were swallowed up by the dense crowds of tourists, she turned her attention to the view before her, right from the door of her own restaurant. The azure sea glistened in the sunlight as the harbour trustees busied themselves erecting the famous Feast Week flags along the inner wall, a splash of added colour against the aqua blue of the cloudless sky. Paige smiled at the long queue of people forming in front of the Wet Fish stall to buy their own fresh fish for tonight's dinner, whilst visitors lined the waterfront as they tried their hand at crabbing on the quayside. The harbour had really come to life in the last month and Paige could not deny feeling very grateful for such a view from her own business, something she had been so reluctant to take on at the beginning of the year.

Paige's view was suddenly compromised as a man holding a box of clinking bottles stood before her, his sheer height and size plunging her into his shadow.

"Morning. Looking for Nick?" The man inquired, his deep voice gentle and oddly soothing.

"He's in the kitchen. I'm the owner - Paige - can I help you at all?"

"Ah sorry. Yes, Nick mentioned the restaurant was under new ownership. Nice to meet you. I'm Tom."

The man shifted the weight of the box to one arm and offered his hand to Paige in greeting. Paige's hand disappeared into Tom's warm grasp before she led him through to the bar, a slight blush on her cheeks.

"Nick said I could start bringing some of next week's stock over early, so we have less to shift on the day. Hope that's alright," Tom explained, as he brought a second box in from his 4x4, which was parked outside. Paige hoped one of the harbour masters wouldn't be along in a minute to clamp his wheel for obstruction.

"No problem at all. I'll start taking them through and let Nick know you're here."

Paige grabbed a box of clinking cider bottles and carried them through to the kitchen where Nick was getting Maxine to taste test a batch of cannoli.

"Oh my lord - Paige, you have to try these. Nick has outdone himself. Here."

Relieving her arms of the box of bottles, Paige took a cannoli the size of her face from the plate, her eyes round. "Nick, your mate is here from the cider farm. Tom. Oh my bloody god, this is delicious."

Nick chuckled and took himself off in the direction of the front of house, whilst Maxine and Paige tucked into the test batch of cannoli, offering one to each of the kitchen staff as well. Paige bit through the crispy shell of her second cannoli, the creamy, sweet ricotta filling oozing out of the other end. Her mouth and hands were coated in icing sugar dust, making her an utter mess. She had absolutely no regrets on the matter, until she heard the approaching footsteps of Nick and Tom.

"There might not be much left for you to try, mate. As you can see, the boss has nosedived straight into them."

Maxine chortled as Paige attempted to clean herself up with a nearby cloth, the dust migrating to her black top and increasing her look of gluttony.

"How did you eat them so gracefully, Max?" Paige turned to her, trying not to look as mortified as she felt.

"Years of practise, my darling. You remember, I was here in the Giuseppe days, where I swear we ate cannoli for every meal of the day."

Paige cleared her throat awkwardly, abandoned any last attempts at tidying herself up and held the depleting plate towards Tom. "Cannoli?"

As Tom gladly retrieved one, Paige was surprised to see Nick's eyes on her with what could only be perceived as affectionate amusement, his features soft and almost gooey. It made a change from the glowering she had received from him of late, so she'd take it whatever it meant.

"I'm just going to show Tom where he can store his kegs for next week," Nick finally said, giving Paige a pointed look. "Try not to eat all of them before I get back."

Once Tom and Nick were out of earshot, Paige turned to Maxine with wide eyes.

"Bloody hell - he's gorgeous!" Chelsea exclaimed, as she came hurtling into the kitchen as if bursting to declare this statement.

Paige nodded in agreement, now tucking into her third cannoli without even realising, her and Chelsea eying the door where Tom and Nick had disappeared through.

"Oh for goodness sake you two, get a grip! I heard he's got engaged to a young American maid, so don't either of you waste your time. Besides, Paige - don't give poor Nick more bleddy competition."

"Oh, don't start that again," Paige scoffed, her cheeks colouring instantly as she gave Chelsea a quick swipe on the arm for laughing in agreement to Maxine. Maxine had made countless comments about this fabricated infatuation she seemed to think was brewing between her and Nick. Not counting the odd looks that even Paige couldn't deny noticing, Maxine had clearly not noticed how much they infuriated each other most of the time.

"Why do you think Nick is so worked up about Charlie working here?" Maxine said, her eyebrows raised in a knowing look.

"Because Charlie is shit in the kitchen and gets in the way," Paige whispered, feeling a little shameful for voicing the fact out loud. This time, Chelsea nodded her agreement, her mouth now entirely full of cannoli. "All Nick and I do is argue and piss each other off, so you've got it all wrong."

To Paige's infuriation, Chelsea and Maxine exchanged knowing looks.

"We'll see," Maxine trilled. "You can do a lot worse than Nicholas Stone, that's all I'm saying."

Maxine simply shimmied her wide shoulders knowingly and skulked back out to the front, coaxing Chelsea out of the kitchen with her. Paige now officially feeling sick from her indulgent sweet tooth made a start on a new seafood fideuà that she had recently been working on. If she was being completely honest with herself, she was desperately bored with the menu, which hadn't seemed to change much since she'd taken over in February. She sensed another conversation was needed with Nick to allow her to make changes to the menu, but as she'd quite accurately pointed out to Maxine, their discussions usually exploded into an argument.

She could hear the deep tones of Nick and Tom's voices echoing from the back storeroom and hoped that none of Maxine's words had travelled that far. She listened to snippets of conversation about 'good ol' rugby days' mixed in with the logistics for Feast Week. Something about Nick's big plans particularly caught her attention.

Well, if Nick could have big plans - so could she. It had been four months after all since she'd taken ownership of Giuseppe's. Perhaps it was time she started putting her own stamp on things.

"Can I take a couple of those cannoli back with me?" Tom asked, as he and Nick returned to the main kitchen area. "My Emily is from Brooklyn in New York, so she'll love these."

"Why? Because everyone from Brooklyn is Italian?" Nick joked, slapping Tom on the back and gesturing for him to help himself. Tom thanked them both and was on his way with promise of much more cider for next week's festival.

"Nick?" Paige began as soon as she heard the restaurant's front door close, deciding how best to throw herself into another potential argument over menus.

"Yeah?" Nick replied, leaning over Paige to examine the beginnings of her new dish. His chest pressed firmly against her back and it suddenly took all her willpower not to lean back into him. "What's this?"

"Seafood Fideuà," Paige answered in her best nonchalant voice, despite the flurry of excitement clenching in her stomach. She could blame Maxine for putting these ridiculous ideas into her head.

"Isn't that Spanish?"

"Can be."

"That's not on the menu tonight."

"I know. I just wanted to test it out," Paige replied, tartly. "That's what I wanted to talk to you about. The menu. I want to change it."

There was a pause as Nick examined the ingredients lined up for the new dish, a slight frown on his face. It wasn't looking promising.

"Okay. Good idea," Nick said, finally.

Paige turned to find Nick on the other side of the counter now, stretching pizza dough out with his hands, no more to be said on the matter.

"Really? You're not going to get all protective over your current menu and pick a fight?"

"Why would I do that? You're the boss. About time you started putting your stamp on the place."

Paige's jaw practically dropped to her chest and she

flung her arms up in the air in frustration, nearly sending a bowl of mussels flying.

"Are you kidding me? You kicked right off at me when I last suggested changing the menu!"

Again Nick paused, giving her an appraising look from across their stations. His eyes glinted slightly - a challenge.

"I hardly kicked off. Besides, it was your first day. You hadn't even decided whether you wanted the restaurant yet." Nick's voice was beginning to rise as they faced each other in a stand-off. "And you came waltzing in demanding changes because it wasn't living up to your fine dining."

"See? This is why I'm so bloody afraid to bring up any changes with you. It always results in... in this!"

"I just said 'good idea'!" Nick exploded, almost sending his pizza dough hurtling up to the ceiling. "What more do you want me to say?"

Heavy footsteps were heard approaching the kitchen as Maxine stormed in, pointing a large finger at both of them as if they were children who had been caught taking biscuits from the jar. "Will you two pack it in? Every time I leave you alone, you're at each other's throats for goodness sake!"

Paige scoffed, raising an eyebrow at Maxine. "Told you that you were way off."

"What's that supposed to mean?" Nick demanded, as Paige walked away to retrieve some fresh shellfish from the cold room. She returned with her goods, Nick looking irritated and perplexed.

"It seems people around here are a bit delusional and think there's something going on between us. I told Maxine she's way off because all we do is argue." Maxine had the right mind at least to look sheepish as all the building frustration from Nick fizzled away like a deflating balloon.

"Oh."

"I'll draft up some ideas for the new menu and run

it by you next week," Paige said, all the fight in her gone and just leaving a sort of sadness behind. "Max, please can you add Seafood Fideuà to the Specials Board for tonight?"

Despite the crackling tension returning between her and Nick in the kitchen, Paige was at least pleased to hear that Jacca and Charlie now had had three successful trips with the otter trawler, walking away with a healthy earning which brought Charlie straight to Paige's office, offering her rent.

"I don't want rent yet," Paige insisted, waving off the offer. "Use the money to pay off some of the debt."

"I can't live upstairs for free!" Charlie exclaimed.

"You can for the time being. The apartment was vacant anyway. Be good for it to be lived in for a bit."

It was clear on Charlie's face that he, like lots of people, couldn't understand why the apartment had been vacant all this time, but she was quietly grateful to him for not taking his curiosity further.

"Do you want me to work at all tonight?" Charlie asked, hovering in the doorway, his shoulder casually leaning against the frame. Paige noticed, over Charlie's shoulder, Nick glancing in their direction, his attention on his work compromised.

"We've got a full team tonight. However, I wouldn't mind your fishermen's opinion on this draft menu I've put together."

Paige handed Charlie the piece of paper on which she had scrawled all over with ideas, dishes, local fish - anything she could think of.

"Some expensive fish on this menu. Not very Italian, either."

"Who says I'm keeping it Italian?" Paige shrugged, a little more aggressively than she had been aiming for.

"Just saying - people like having their own little Italian in the village. Something an average family can afford. I get the idea that Giuseppe made a great impression on the people of Meva, which is why people return."

"So it would seem," Paige muttered, through gritted teeth. "Forget the theme for a minute. Do the dishes sound OK?"

Charlie shrugged. "They're OK. Sound fancy anyway. Probably too fancy for me, so asking the wrong person. What does Nick think?"

Charlie turned his body as if to include Nick in the conversation, and at that moment Paige felt like she could have throttled him. She hissed at him to give her back the page and waved him off, saying she had invoices to do.

If she was going to do this new menu justice, she needed to speak to somebody who wasn't biased towards the old Meva and Giuseppe's legacy. She needed somebody with a keen eye for excellent food and fine dining, and she knew exactly who that person was.

Chapter Seventeen

Feast Week had arrived in Mevagissey, the whole village exploding in colour with the weather putting on its best show for a week of celebrations.

Given that the streets and quayside of Meva were already cluttered with stalls, marquees and staging for the festival, it made Paige's usual running route somewhat difficult. A diversion up to the top coastal path towards Pentewan had her gasping for air on her return, where Nick was locking his door to head for the restaurant.

"Alright?" Nick asked, a mix of concern and amusement in his voice as Paige grasped her side from a stitch.

"That coastal path… is a bitch," Paige panted, now leaning her head on the rail of Nick's steps whilst taking a glance at her watch. "You're going in early."

"I was going to knock on your door actually, see if you wanted some breakfast before the madness begins," Nick said. "Should have known you'd be out on your torture jog."

Paige smiled wryly, nodding her agreement and asking him to give her ten minutes to change.

"Come in for a bit, while I change. Dad's in here," Paige said as she opened the cottage door, Nick following close behind. Jacca waved from his spot at the table, where he was currently mending his watch over a morning coffee.

"Alright, boy? Kettle's just boiled. Help yerself."

Paige left Jacca and Nick to have a chat as she ran upstairs to change out of her sweaty gear, only to throw on her chef whites for a day of alfresco cooking. When she returned downstairs, Nick and her father were in full swing in their conversation, their sides splitting from laughter over an anecdote that Jacca had just shared. It was then that it occurred to Paige how long it had been since Nick had been over for their little dinners or even just for a quick catch up.

"How come you don't come over as much as you used to?" Paige asked, as she and Nick walked down to the restaurant, stallholders getting in early to set up for a busy first day.

Nick shrugged a response. "Just don't have time."

"You didn't have much time before," Paige pointed out, reminding Nick of what he'd said on her arrival. "But, by the sounds of it, you and my dad used to spend a lot of time together before I rocked up. Don't stop on my account."

Nick stopped in his tracks, his key poised by the door as he stared at Paige.

"Is that what you think?"

"Just a wild guess. What else am I supposed to think?"

Nick sighed impatiently and unlocked the main door into the restaurant.

Paige stuck the coffee machine on and followed Nick into the kitchen where he started gathering ingredients to make them both a hearty breakfast.

"My dad values your company. Just saying," Paige continued, cracking some eggs expertly with one hand in to a hot pan.

"I know. And I value his. But we're both very busy men. It's not like we ever met regularly," Nick rambled, buttering the bread and lining rashes of bacon on the grill.

"Yes, you did. Every week. You and Jacca quite openly said this when I first moved down. And not long after, you stopped. Why?"

Nick responded with another shrug, clearly uncomfortable with the conversation - and yet, Paige continued.

"I just think it's weird that -"

"Look, Paige - I'm really trying to get through just one morning with you without us getting into some sort of fight, OK? Can we just drop it?"

208

The air crackled between them, like it seemed to on a daily occurrence. They combined their ingredients in pregnant silence and constructed two perfectly stacked egg and bacon sandwiches, taking them through to sit and watch the first signs of Feast Week commence. Colourful paper lanterns hung like bunting between the lamp posts, while right in front of their restaurant, the large Feast Week staging had been erected, surrounded by metal barriers. The harbour looked very different and would be entirely different again in just a few hours when the streets filled with villagers and visitors alike.

As they people-watched, eating their sandwiches in companionable silence, Jacca and Charlie passed by the window, carrying a couple of crab pots each. Paige waved at them, whilst Nick offered a simple nod of acknowledgment.

"Is it Charlie?" Paige asked, thinking back to Maxine's comment about Nick seeing Charlie as competition. Come to think of it, Nick had openly said he didn't like him. Could it be possible that Nick was jealous of Charlie and Jacca's new working relationship.

"Is what Charlie?" Nick huffed, impatiently.

Paige chewed and swallowed the last bit of sandwich, pushed her plate forward in front of her and, leaning her elbows on the table, gave Nick her full attention.

"Is Charlie the reason you've stopped spending as much time with Dad?"

"No!" Nick scoffed, though his eyes gave him away almost immediately.

"It's OK for Jacca to have other friends, Nicholas," Paige teased.

Nick's chair scraped loudly against the chequered floor as he stood up abruptly, clearing the table. "You're insufferable, woman."

"Oh come on - don't be like that. I'm sorry, I'm just trying to work out what's changed."

"Lots has changed, Paige. But I'm not saying anything, because you never like what I have to say. And it's naff - so, just forget it."

Before Paige could probe him any further, Nick was up with the dirty dishes and setting off to the kitchen to start the day's work.

"Tom and Emily will be here in a minute," Nick called over his shoulder. "Help me get the marquee outside."

Later, on Tom and Emily's arrival, Paige decided immediately that she liked Emily very much. Her benevolent and jovial demeanour was catching and soon Paige was finding herself having the most fun she'd had at work for a very long time.

"Your father," Nick said to Paige, his eyes wide in amusement, "has signed me and Tom up for the bleddy raft race. Will you be alright?"

Paige laughed, trying to imagine both Tom and Nick's large physiques squeezed into a tiny raft. "Absolutely. We'll be fine. Good luck!"

Nick and Tom ran off like two giant excited schoolboys and a fresh cluster of customers soon approached the stall for their fresh pizzas.

"How long have you and Nick been together?" Emily asked, as she competently drafted a pint of cider for her customer on the neighbouring Trengrouse Cider Farm stall.

Paige rolled her eyes and blew out an exasperated sigh.

"Oops - sorry, have Tom and I misjudged the situation?"

"Not the only one, don't worry," Paige said, sliding a couple of pizzas on to her paddle and taking them over to the outdoor pizza oven. "If you saw how we work together most days, you wouldn't be assuming any romance between us."

"Oh, I don't know," Emily chuckled. "I only assumed you were together by the way he looks at you. But then again, I am a bit of a romantic these days."

"Paige, can you cover me for a moment, m'love?" Maxine called from the cannoli stand. "I need to bring a chair out here, my legs are killing me already."

"Oh, Max. I'll grab you one. You stay there."

Paige ran inside and grabbed the nearest chair just as Charlie and Laura came through from the stairwell leading to the apartment, chuckling away and with Laura's arm slotted through his. Their arms dropped immediately as they caught sight of a bemused Paige, the chair suspended in her arms.

"Need a hand with that?" Charlie asked, clearing his throat loudly and trying to grab the chair.

"No, I'm good. I can manage." Paige looked slowly between them, a slight smile playing on her features. "Whatcha doing? Actually, don't answer that. I have pizzas to make."

As Paige carried Maxine's chair outside, it was everything she could do not to burst in to a fit of uncharacteristic giggles. She also could not deny a sense of relief and happiness for her two friends, if her instincts were to be trusted. For a reason she didn't quite understand, this could be the answer to their current Charlie problems and she almost wished it to be true.

The festival was taken up a notch as local musicians took to the stage, making for a fantastic atmosphere, but difficult working conditions.

"Sorry! Say that again! You want what on your pizza?!" Paige shouted over particularly loud classic rock music to a customer who was now shouting their order for the third time.

"This is bloody hard work," Daniel grumbled, when they'd finally worked out what the poor customer had wanted and slotted his pizzas into the oven. He helped Paige bring out another batch of ready-made dough balls, taking the opportunity to talk at a normal volume in the quiet of the restaurant, which was currently closed on the inside for the public.

"Have you seen Nick? Him and Tom buggered off about an hour ago," Paige asked, turning to Emily who, to give her credit, had been working endlessly since the start. Emily shrugged, looking tired all of a sudden. "Emily, why don't you take a break and have a look around the festival. Maybe try to find Nick and Tom while you're at it. Daniel, are you OK to manage for the cider stall for a bit?"

Emily and Daniel agreed to Paige's instructions, Emily grateful for an opportunity to explore the festival a little more. She agreed to bring the men back as soon as she found them, declaring they'd had quite enough fun by now and needed to pull their weight.

In a way, Paige was pleased to see Nick lightening up and having some fun for once, but on the other hand, she'd wished he'd timed himself a little better. Another twenty minutes passed before he finally returned, flushed in the cheeks and with a giant grin on his face.

"Have fun, did you?" Paige asked, her tone loaded. "Don't worry about us! We're good here!"

"I know you are," Nick smiled, planting an unexpected kiss on her cheek and reaching for a bottle of water on the staff provisions table. "You're a very capable woman."

Paige scoffed and told him that flattery didn't work with her, despite her insides raging with sudden desire and her cheek burning blissfully from his touch. In a flustered haste, she ordered him to grab his apron and get on with it. She contemplated sharing with him what she had seen between Charlie and Laura, thinking of what Maxine had said, but reminded herself quickly that Laura was his little sister and that he might not find it as amusing as she did. Besides, she thought to herself, why did she feel the need to reassure Nick of his lack of competition in Charlie? Nick was a confident man: if he really wanted more with Paige like Maxine suggested, he would have surely done it by now.

The rest of the afternoon and evening went off without a single glitch, and Paige was astounded to discover how much money they had made on pizzas and cannoli alone.

"Right - that's it, I'm closing the restaurant and we're going mobile," Paige cried, locking the money away in the safe and bringing her cash flow sheet out to show Nick.

He was cleaning the indoor pizza oven, his T-shirt and arms covered in black ash. "We'd save ourselves a lot of money on bloody VAT."

"You're funny," Nick replied wryly, wiping himself down and washing his hands of all the soot. "Not sure about this pizza oven. Think we need it looked at. Look here."

Nick pointed at where the wall behind was slightly darkened in soot behind the oven, the plaster blistering.

"Know anybody who can service it? How old is this thing anyway?" Paige asked, dragging her finger through the soot and tutting. "Not being funny, look at the state of this wall anyway. All the walls. The whole place needs redecorating."

Nick nodded a slight approval, looking at their surroundings with his hands on his hips. "We can discuss it. Check the finances for a refit."

"You don't sound massively committed to that," Paige pointed out, smiling grimly.

"You might not have fond memories of Giuseppe and everything he did here, but the rest of us do."

He hadn't said it unkindly, and he even gave her an uncharacteristic nudge with his shoulder to keep his words light, but those words still stung. She'd been on the outside of this little world that Giuseppe and her mother had created and she'd been positively fine with that - up until now.

"Right, come on you," Nick said from behind the bar where he was wiping away the dirt from his arms with a towel. "We agreed to shut the stall slightly earlier than the rest to give ourselves a chance to actually enjoy ourselves. I'll treat you to dinner - something we didn't cook for once."

The next morning, for the first time in a long time, Paige woke up with a huge smile on her face and a kind of spring in her step. Since she'd moved back to Mevagissey, it had been all work and no play. No wonder she'd been miserable as sin recently - at least, that's how she'd felt. She'd also seen a new side to Nick and she'd liked it very much.

Yesterday evening, in the sheer splendour of a warm summer's evening, she and Nick had explored the streets of Mevagissey as if it was a brand-new place to be explored, involving themselves in the festivities and celebrations of the evening. They'd indulged in more than enough Trengrouse cider and had become very merry and giddy in each other's company as they'd swayed their way to the evening's show of local music, dancing the night away without a single worry or argument between them. Laura and Lilly had joined them at one point, even Jacca, and it had been the perfect set up.

She felt a little flutter as she recalled the small moments and gestures shared between her and Nick. Fingers interlocking when they were sure nobody was looking, eyes meeting and connecting, Nick's arm a warm cocoon when he caught her shivering in the twilight breeze. Something had shifted between them last night, and it felt like nothing she'd ever felt with Matthew.

Speaking of Matthew, she was pretty sure he'd messaged her late last night and had to check her phone to see if she'd imagined it. She hadn't and his name on her screen almost brought her heavily back to earth.

It had been amicable enough. The obligatory start of asking her how she'd been, followed by the real reason for his sudden contact - would she be willing to share with him her recipe for her signature beef wellington dish, something she had been well-known for back in Garlands. Back when she'd been excited about creating new dishes and experimenting with ingredient combinations.

She couldn't complain. She too had been on the brink of contacting him for opinions on her new menu but had chickened out on more than one occasion half-way through composing her forced nonchalant text message to him.

But things here were good. They were. She'd promised herself last night that she would be more grateful for everything that had been sent her way. She may be a little stuck on the food passion front and she may not be making the big changes she had imagined when she'd taken ownership - but she had her dad close by, she had a real friend in Laura and, for all his faults and grumpy ways, she had Nick.

As she entered the restaurant just an hour later following her morning run, she found Nick scrutinising the indoor pizza oven with a worried expression on his face. For a small moment that worry melted away as he and Paige exchanged shy smiles, memories of last night's intimacy causing spots of red on both their cheeks.

"Hey," Nick said.

"Hey," Paige returned.

Nick soon pulled himself from his stupefied state, giving himself a shake and returning his concerned attention the pizza oven.

"Everything alright?" Paige asked, following his trail of vision and sticking her head under the brickwork to see what the problem was.

"We can't use this today. I've had it lit this morning to see where the main damage might be and I've been checking the co2 levels. Look - this is bloody lethal."

This was bad news for their trade. Second day into the Feast Week and they were going to be as busy as ever. Being down one oven for their pizzas was going to prove to be tricky.

"Bugger," Paige huffed, feeling the lightness of yesterday evening disappear almost instantly.

Nick grabbed his phone from his pocket and began dialling. "Don't worry. A friend of mine fixes chimneys - he might be able to take a look at it for me as a favour."

Nick disappeared into the office to make the phone call whilst Paige unlocked the front door to let Emily and Tom in, who had just arrived for another day of cider selling.

"How are you feeling?" Emily asked, an amused look on her face.

Paige looked confused and smiled awkwardly, "I feel fine - why?"

Emily and Tom both looked impressed as Tom said, "Crikey, you can hold your drink then. You nearly had a whole keg of cider to yourself last night!"

"Not quite," Paige scoffed. "Slight exaggeration." As if she needed to add the explanation, she added, "I'm my father's daughter. Holding your liquor around him and his fisherman crew is a rite of passage."

Tom and Emily chuckled, and Paige ordered them to sit while she fixed them a coffee and a quick breakfast.

"Have you thought about getting a barista machine?" Tom asked, as they settled into the spot by the window that everyone seemed to always fight over.

"Every day since I took over in February. But they cost more than a small car. Why?"

"My sister, Sarah - she runs the tearooms back on the farm - she's looking to upgrade her machine to a triple station. You've been getting really busy, haven't you Em?" He kissed his fiancée on the side of her head with pride and it was all Paige could do not to pull a face.

"Yes, since we started the wedding business and providing tours around the farm, the tearoom has started doing really well," Emily confirmed. "The machine is only about four years old. It might need a service but other than that, it would be perfect for a restaurant. I expect you'll sell less coffee in an evening when a bar is available."

"It would be great to be able to offer proper coffee. I couldn't believe there was only filtered coffee available. Considering the previous owner was Italian!" Paige rolled her eyes at the irony.

"Well, we'll speak to Sarah about how much she wants. But it'll be mate's rates," Tom said. Paige smiled and thanked them both, before getting on with their breakfast. Nick came out of the office looking disappointed.

"He won't be able to look at the oven until Thursday."

"That's helpful," Paige said, sarcastically. "We'll just have to make do with one oven for a bit then. Customers will have to wait."

"Both you and I know perfectly well that customers don't like to wait for anything these days. That's why I'm glad our menu is so pasta and pizza orientated. Quick and easy!"

Paige made a non-committal grunting sound, catching Nick's attention with a suspicious look.

"And what did that little grunt mean?" Nick asked, nudging her gently with his elbow.

"Nothing."

"Oh, no you don't!" Nick grabbed her gently by the arm and stopped her from leaving the kitchen with Tom and Emily's breakfast rolls. "We had a great evening last night and I felt like we really got somewhere. Don't go all weird on me now!"

"Their breakfast is going to go cold!" Paige complained, trying to bypass him with the plates.

"Tom! Your breakfast is ready!" Nick hollered through the door. "Out with it. Let me guess, it's about the menu again."

"What kind of shit service is this, mate?" Tom said, stomping in and giving Paige a wink to show his good humour. Tom took the plates from Paige and carried them back through for himself and Emily. Meanwhile, Paige looked in every direction but Nick's, willing him to drop the subject.

"I'm waiting," Nick said, his arms crossed.

"Oh, piss off with that tone!" Paige snapped. Nick threw back his head and erupted in a hearty laugh. Once he was finished, he gestured patiently for her to continue. Paige released a massive sigh and took the plunge. "Since I moved back down and took ownership of the place, I've completely lost my passion for cooking. The menu doesn't excite me. In fact, it bores me to tears. I miss cooking the dishes I designed back in Garlands. I changed the menu every season. You won't let me change a single thing, even once. I'm frustrated as hell."

Nick was no longer smiling, his brow creased in concern and his arms slowly unfolding.

217

"You've been complaining about the menu, but I didn't realise you felt like that," Nick said. "Why haven't you explained this sooner."

"I've tried," Paige muttered, defeated. "But we end up arguing."

"That we do," Nick nodded in agreement. "You're right though. I haven't let you change anything. When I heard you were taking over the restaurant, we were all worried you were going to change everything and that the place would be unrecognisable."

"A bit of change is good though," Paige reasoned, feeling that closeness she had felt last night seeping back in. She looked up into Nick's steel grey eyes and neither of them spoke for a moment. The time paused between them and stretched until it felt it would snap. She caught his eyes glance at her lips a couple of times and this only made her lick them self-consciously.

"Let's come up with a new menu. One we're both excited for," Nick said finally, taking a step back to create a distance between them. He cleared his throat, rubbed her arm in awkward reassurance and took himself off to make a start on today's preparations, leaving her totally deflated.

Chapter Eighteen

Keeping up with public demand with just one pizza oven had proven to be the precise level of stress that Paige had predicted it would be. But somehow, with sheer determination and Emily's ability to charm customers into waiting that extra twenty minutes for their pizza, they'd managed it - earning themselves another humble income for the day.

Evening rolled by again, and this time a quiet evening at Nick's cottage was on the cards, giving them a prime elevated view of the festivities continuing on the harbour below. The windows were thrown open to let in the delicious scent of a summer's evening and the sound of the music and cheery chatter on the quay. Nick and Paige were unwrapping the fish and chips, whilst Tom brought in a box clinking with cider bottles.

"I know we have a perfectly good restaurant to stretch out in," Nick said, addressing the six people squeezed around his dining table. "But Paige and I agreed that we see enough of the inside of that place as it is."

"Plus, you can guarantee that we'll have customers pressing their faces up against the window or trying the door because they think we're open," Paige pointed out, taking a seat next to her father, whose intoxicated swaying was enough to question his sea legs.

"Keeping you up, sis?" Nick teased, as his sister failed to stifle a yawn behind her hands. She blushed and mouthed a sorry to the table.

"Sorry, I'm exhausted. I start nights again later and honestly, I don't think I'll make it to Lilly's bedtime, let alone to next morning."

Paige and Nick exchanged worried looks as everyone else tucked into their dinner. It was clear by Nick's grave expression matching hers that they'd both noticed the effects that these sporadic hours had had on her health.

"So, you're the face behind this delicious cider," Jacca boomed, holding his own bottle up to Tom in thanks. "One of the best ciders around, m'boy! I've been drinking your cider for years!"

"Thank you very much," Tom nodded, humbly. "You should all come to the farm one day, for a tour of the orchards. Jacca, I'd be happy to arrange for a taste testing afternoon. You seem like a gentleman who knows his cider."

"How did you guess?" Paige muttered wryly, cussing as her father squeezed one of her knees in jest, something he always used to do to wind her up as a child. She hated it by equal measure now, his bony yet strong hands clamping down on her knee cap. "Dad! Bugger off - that hurts!"

There was a knock at Nick's door and, being the closest to it, Paige got up to see who it was, glad to get her knee at a safe distance. On the other side of it, Charlie gave her a nervous smile.

"Charlie? You OK? What you doing here?" Paige asked, stepping to one side to let him in, glancing in Nick's direction to gauge his reaction. To no surprise, his face was set in stone.

"Oh, I invited him," Laura said, suddenly waking up from her sleepiness at the sight of him. Paige watched Nick closely, his facial expressions altering by the second. "Hope that's OK."

Charlie edged himself around the room towards a seat next to Laura, Nick burning a hole in the side of his head the entire way round as he glowered at him in utter confusion. Paige shut the door and returned to her seat, placing a warning hand on Nick's arm and willing him to tone down the glaring.

"You never responded to my text, so I didn't order you anything. But you can share my chips," Laura said to Charlie as he seated himself at the table. He couldn't have looked more uncomfortable, sinking under the attention.

"It's OK, I'm not massively hungry," Charlie

muttered, his back rigid as if the chair he was sat in was going to electrocute him at any given moment.

Everyone resumed eating their dinners, except Nick who continued to observe his sister and Charlie with intense interest. Paige elbowed him and shot him a loaded look, gesturing to him to eat his food. Reluctantly, Nick stabbed a chip with his fork and returned to his own meal.

After the food was consumed, Paige helped Nick take the dirty plates to the kitchen where he immediately jumped on her for answers.

"Is that bloody Charlie boy dating my sister?" Nick hissed, pointing his finger in the direction of the dining room, where everybody was in full chatter.

"I think so," Paige chuckled, amused by Nick's extreme reaction. "So what? Why do you sound so appalled?"

In a noisy rage, Nick started chucking the dirty plates into the sink of hot, soapy water, only to amuse Paige even more.

"What have you got against the poor bloke?"

"Well for one thing," Nick began, pausing to think as Paige raised an eyebrow at him.

"Go on."

"Well, I have to question his loyalty, for one. He was head over heels for you at one point. Bloody obsessed for one minute - now suddenly he's dropped you and pursuing my sister instead. Excuse me for being a little suspicious."

Paige wasn't sure if it was the three ciders she had already consumed or the buzz of the evening with friends, but she felt her heart swell just a bit for this ridiculous man.

"Well, look on the positive side. Less competition for you now," Paige pointed out, boldly. The frown on Nick's face dropped suddenly and he stared at her in mild shock for a moment. Satisfied with that outcome for now, Paige retrieved the ice cream from Nick's freezer and ordered him to bring the bowls.

The air of brotherly protectiveness to one side, it was an evening of laughter and togetherness. Jacca called it a night around the same time as Laura put Lilly to bed in Nick's spare room upstairs, declaring himself too old for these late-night shenanigans. In his merry, cider-induced state, he'd wrapped Paige up in his gangly arms, calling her his precious little girl.

"Love you lots, daughter of mine," Jacca slurred, barely maintaining a vertical stature.

"Love you too, father of mine," Paige puffed, trying to keep balance from his unsteady weight, her eyes rolling to the ceiling at Nick who was watching in amused fondness. "Think I'll walk you to the door, you old fart."

The summer evening was holding on amicably, only just beginning to darken around the corners from the setting sun. The evening's Feast Week celebrations were showing no signs of dwindling for a while and Paige smiled as she recognised some familiar faces down below enjoying the evening's line-up of entertainment.

She monitored her dad's descent of Nick's steep concrete steps before steering him in the direction of their much more gradual storm porch steps. Once she'd unlocked the door, ordered her father to go straight to bed, and kissed him goodnight, she walked back over to the Cornish wall looking down at the quay and did a spot of people-watching. How anyone around here was supposed to sleep over this wonderful racket, Paige did not know, but she was sure that Nick and Lilly would give it a good go, looking at how tired they both were at the dinner table.

From next door, she heard Nick and Tom roar with laughter over something and was about to go and join them when her phone buzzed in her back pocket. Checking the screen, she could see Matthew's name flashing at her in mild warning.

She groaned, involuntarily. She'd forgotten to respond to his text the other day about the recipe.

"Hello?" Paige answered, her tone a question even though she knew exactly who it was.

"Hi Paige, it's Matthew." There was a pause. "How are you?"

Despite her initial groan, she couldn't deny that it was good to hear his voice again.

"Matthew, hi. I've been good, thanks. How are you? How's the competition going?"

"Gruelling. I've never been so stressed in my entire life," Matthew chuckled, in good humour. "But I've learned loads along the way and made some great connections. I can't tell you exactly how it's going, obviously. I've had to sign one of those contract things to stop me giving away anything before it airs."

"Sounds official," Paige smiled.

There was a pause at the end of the line, and Paige's eyebrows creased slightly.

"You still there?" Paige asked.

"I miss you, Paige."

She wasn't expecting that, and going by the uncomfortable squirming in her tummy, it wasn't what she wanted to hear either. *Don't complicate my feelings,* Paige thought. *Not when I'm finally starting to figure out what I want.*

Nick chose that time to release another eruption of laughter from inside his cottage, Paige's heart swelling just a little at the sound of his voice.

"Guess that silence tells me it's one way," Matthew chuckled awkwardly, sounding hurt.

"No - I do ... miss you. I just," Paige turned towards the ocean, as if it was going to give her the right words to say. "I just don't want to go there."

"Fair enough. It must be going well down there. How's the restaurant? I bet you've worked your magic and started to make it your own."

"Not exactly," Paige replied, pulling a face. "But it's about to get better. I've made some headway this week with the head chef, who was digging his heels in a bit. But we're going to look at menu changes next week, after Feast Week is finished."

"Paige!" Matthew cried in exasperation. "You're the owner. Don't pander around this head chef of yours. You

223

want to change the menu, you change the bloody menu. If he doesn't like it, show him the door."

Paige cocked an eyebrow. That was Matthew all over. It was mighty rich of him to say this, considering the amount of arguments he used to have with the owner of Garlands.

"It's not as straight forward and brutal as that, Matthew. Nick holds a lot of loyalty and history with the business and I'm not about to charge in like a bull and piss everybody off." Even though she'd done that a few too many times already.

"You always were far too considerate of other people," Matthew sighed in disappointment. "You'll never get anywhere by being like that. Sometimes you have to be ruthless to succeed."

Paige's eyebrow was in danger of disappearing into her hairline all together as she scoffed at her ex's cock-sure attitude.

"You can tell you're in a cooking competition at the moment. It's not my style, but good for you. You do you, I'll do me."

A little burst of frustration erupted in Paige and before she knew it, she was snapping down the phone.

"Was there something you wanted, by the way? I know you didn't call me to give me management tips."

"Oh yes," Matthew continued, seemingly unaware of Paige's tone. "Can I use your beef wellington recipe on the next round? I did text you about it."

"Sure. Go for it."

She ended the call after that, wishing Matthew luck with the rest of the competition and promising to send him the recipe by the end of the evening. A little bit of her hated him for bursting her happy little bubble this evening, a phone call for his own personal gain but leaving her deflated and thoughtful. And to think, she'd considered contacting him herself for approval of her new menu. Now, she even felt tempted to slip away from the small gathering she had been so ecstatic to be involved in just ten minutes before, to sink into her bed with her thoughts. Then the door to Nick's cottage opened to shake her out of it just for a moment.

"I'm off to work," Laura declared, looking far from pleased at being dragged away from the evening for her night shift. "Lilly is reading in bed with Mowgli sprawled across her stomach. It's the cutest thing."

"Do you want me to walk you to your car?" Paige offered.

"Thanks, but I'm alright. I'd rather you got back in there to make sure my brother doesn't give poor Charlie a hard time."

Laura then paused and gave Paige a side-glance. "I was going to tell you. I promise. It's just been going so -"

"Laura, Laura. You do not have to justify yourself. It's your business," Paige smiled and gave her friend a reassuring nudge, "and I couldn't be happier for you."

A huge sigh of relief escaped from Laura's lungs and she smiled nervously. "It's just - you and Charlie were -"

"There was literally no me and Charlie at any point. We're just friends."

"But he really liked you," Laura muttered, clearly voicing her insecurities.

"And now he likes you, for good reason. He has excellent taste. You're going to be late for work in a minute."

Laura was about to make tracks, then paused again at the slope leading down to the quay. She spun on her heel and walked back towards Paige.

"Promise me you'll give my brother a fair shot."

"Laura!" Paige whispered loudly whilst blushing ferociously. "I've just said that you and Charlie is your business. Return the etiquette please!"

"Sorry, sorry. I know! Just … he's so smitten with you."

Paige grabbed Laura's shoulders and steered her in the direction of home. "OK, that's enough from you. Have a good shift, don't fall asleep on the way and we'll see you in the morning for breakfast."

225

Paige sent a babbling Laura on her way to work and returned to the warmth and brightness of Nick's dining room, where Charlie had Tom and Emily fixated on a card trick. Paige wandered to the bottom of the narrow staircase and could hear the low rumble of Nick's voice, reading a story to his niece. The smallest of things to send Paige's heart racing, something in a man she'd never realised would have that sort of effect on her. She found herself hovering on the bottom step, listening intently to his words, whilst taking in her tasteful surroundings.

There was something calming and homely about Nick's cottage. Where Jacca's cottage was a time capsule of her childhood, encasing everything that was familiar to her, Nick's provided that fresh new start sort of feel. The white-washed walls, the hessian carpets throughout, the minimalistic decor which made it look like the place was ready to be a holiday home at any moment, if not for the small reminders of Nick's inhabitancy, his jacket left abandoned on the console table in the hallway, some of Mowgli's toys scattered in random places, Nick's recipe books in the kitchen.

Perhaps Laura was right -irritatingly. Perhaps she needed to open herself up more to the possibility of something new here. She'd arrived so waspish and ready for a fight with her past back in February, and she'd spent a lot of time butting heads with Nick ever since. She didn't care what Matthew said, she wasn't willing to be that kind of manager - someone who bulldozes through people to get what she needs at the expense of a decent working relationship.

But perhaps it was definitely something more than just a working relationship with the man upstairs, reading a bedtime story to his niece so that his little sister can earn some money as a single parent.

"Alright?"

Paige had been so occupied with her thoughts, she hadn't even noticed the murmur of Nick's voice stop as he finished reading, tucked in his sleeping niece and descended quietly down the narrow, creaking stairs.

"Why are you sitting on the stairs?"

She had no decent reasons without sounding ridiculous, so she opted for the truth. "I was listening to you read," Paige admitted, blushing. "There's something rather endearing about a big burly man like yourself reading a story to his gorgeous little niece."

She'd called him 'a big burly man' before, out of jest and to annoy him, but this time the words nearly faltered on her lips as he joined her on the bottom step, the side of his body pressed up against hers from the narrow width of the staircase.

"Harry Potter. First one. I bought her the illustrated copies for Christmas and - not going to lie- I'm reading them to her for my benefit."

Paige snorted with laughter and Nick smiled.

"They're good books, they are - aren't they?" Nick continued, earning himself more laughter from Paige. "I reckon Professor Quirrell set the troll in the dungeon."

They chuckled and sat comfortably in place for a moment, listening to Tom and Emily gasping at Charlie's card trick.

"I can't believe he's dating my sister," Nick muttered, sighing and shaking his head in exaggerated torment.

"Oh stop!" Paige laughed, bumping her shoulder against his. "It's sweet!"

"Everything alright with Jacca? You were gone for a long time." Nick's voice was low for Lilly's benefit, but it only added to the intimacy of the moment, their faces so close she could smell the peppermint toothpaste on his breath.

"Fine. Actually, Matthew decided to call me just as I was coming back." Paige didn't know why she was sharing this, but she continued all the same. Nick responded with a simple 'oh', looking uncomfortable.

"Matthew? As in your ex-boyfriend?"

"Mmm. He wanted a recipe for his chef competition." When Nick gave her a bemused look, she added, "Back in February, he qualified for the National Chef of the Year competition. The reason he bailed from Mum's funeral."

"The reason you broke up too?"

"No," Paige scoffed. "We outgrew each other way before that. It was a just a timely reminder for us both that we didn't fit in to each other's lives anymore. Then, of course, the restaurant. He encouraged me to go for it. We parted on friendly terms though, so I'm glad of that."

Nick didn't speak but nodded his understanding.

"Well, I'm glad he encouraged you in our direction," Nick finally said, clamping his hand over hers, his fingers intertwining with hers. "I'm very glad you're here."

"Me too."

There they were again, his steel grey eyes scanning hers, holding her in long enough for their lips to draw closer. A light citrus smell invaded her nostrils in a delicious welcome as he leaned in, his breath of fresh mint. He must have brushed his teeth with Lilly in her bedtime routine and she was acutely aware that she had not had such a handy opportunity.

Their lips were only inches from meeting when the scrape of dining chairs snapped them out of their moment.

"We're going to head back to the farm," Tom announced as he walked through to the hallway, his eyebrows slightly cocked at the sight of the two of them squeezed together on the bottom step. "Sarah finally got back to me about the coffee machine. Yours for four-hundred, if you want it."

"That's a giveaway!" Paige exclaimed. "I've got to give her more than that."

"That's what she wants," Tom said, spreading his large hands out in front of him. "I'd take it if I were you. You don't want to get in a debate with my sister - she's terrifying."

Paige laughed and turned to Nick for confirmation. "Barista coffee machine for four-hundred-pounds?"

"Ideal - yes, we'll take it. Thanks mate."

Nick got up from the step to shake Tom's hand in a farewell, his warmth being taken with him and leaving Paige suddenly cold. She got to her feet too and wrapped her cardigan around herself to contain her heat. The warmth of the day had finally dissipated, making for quite a chilly evening now.

Paige reached out for Emily and they hugged each other goodbye, just as Charlie sneaked into the hallway and made his excuses to scamper. Paige didn't blame him wanting to make sure he wasn't the last person left behind with Nick.

Before Paige and Nick knew it, everyone had dispersed and they were entirely alone, an antique clock clunking the seconds away on a nearby wall.

"Is Charlie seriously dating my sister?" Nick finally spoke, following a long pause. Not for the first time that evening, Paige erupted in involuntary laughter and patted Nick's arm in mock pity.

"'Fraid so. Come on, let's have a nightcap outside."

With a healthy measure of whiskey in two glasses, Paige and Nick stood side by side outside the cottages, gazing at the quietening harbour below. The sun had finally called it a day and in its place, the full moon glowed majestically over the inky black sea, the small ripple of waves glistening white in the moonlight. The rainbow stream of paper lanterns hanging from post to post along the quay were like a string of sweets, swaying gently in the late evening breeze. It was a calming scene, made better in small company as they both tenderly sipped their nightcaps.

"I've been quite enjoying these spare evenings," Nick admitted, leaning on the Cornish wall and taking in the scenery. "Not something we're used to."

"I know. It was a good move, although I dread to think how much more the other restaurants and pubs have made in the evenings with us being closed."

It hadn't taken a lot of convincing from Nick for Paige to agree to shut the restaurant in the evenings during Feast Week. Almost all of the staff had declared their desire for time off to enjoy the event, and Nick himself had admitted to not wanting to miss the entire thing like he had done for the last six years. Despite her concern for a huge loss in evening trade, her heart had won over her business head, and that had been that.

"We've more than made up for it in takeaway pizzas, pasta pots and cannoli. Much better way of working through the Feast Week."

Nick sipped his whiskey gently, whilst Paige took slightly bolder gulps.

"Don't think I've ever come across a woman who drinks whiskey without grimacing."

Paige looked into her glass, at the amber gold liquid, the words on the tip of her tongue to say that she was her 'father's daughter', but she stopped herself short of repeating herself from earlier. Best not to encourage that reputation.

"How long do you reckon Charlie and my sister will last then?" Nick said, filling the silence that had fallen between them.

"Just to piss you off, I'm going to say forever. Then Charlie will be your brother-in-law!" Paige said cheerily, laughing as Nick pulled her in to him, pretending to strangle her. "Just let it go, will you? Charlie is a nice bloke and will treat Laura like a queen. He's a skipper too, so I'm sure your father will be pleased."

Nick rolled his eyes and scoffed behind his whiskey glass as Paige checked her phone.

"I think I need to head to bed," Paige admitted, though it was the last thing she wanted to do right now. "Dad wants me up at an ungodly hour tomorrow morning to check his lobster pots." She threw her arms in the air and pulled a face which cried out 'why me?'. Nick smiled and took the whiskey glass from her and for a moment they stood face to face, drinking in each other's features.

"I've had one of the best evenings I've had in a long time," Paige surprised herself by admitting.

"Me too," Nick replied gruffly, his eyes deepening

into hers. She should have just walked away by that point but a sort of invisible thread between them snagged and threatened to snap if she didn't close that gap and place the smallest of kisses on his cheek. So that's what she did, a slight spark of energy igniting between her lips and his stubbled cheek as she did so.

"Goodnight," Paige murmured, turning and making her way up the stairs before her insecurities could be unmasked under the protective blanket of the alcohol she'd consumed that evening. Something had crackled between them for a while now, an electricity of some sort - but now, a fire had been ignited and Paige couldn't help but worry about how things might be in the morning.

What if she'd imagined things between them and it had been all one-sided? Would she return to work tomorrow to find him mortified over her boldness and do everything in his power to avoid her thereafter? She wasn't sure she could handle that sort of rejection.

There was something quite torturous about Nick living next door, too. Climbing into bed, her muscles practically screaming in protest over such labour-induced work over the last few days, she heard the odd muffled shutting of doors as Nick moved about his cottage. From her rear-facing bedroom window, she heard as Nick opened the back door to let Mowgli out for his final toilet stop before bedtime, Nick whistling a local sea shanty which echoed into the night.

Paige smiled and gave herself a mental poke to be more kind to herself. She hadn't imagined it and the feelings she felt between them had not been one-sided - she needed to remind herself this.

Just as she thought it was going to be a long night of torturing herself over unrequited kisses, she fell deeply into an untroubled sleep which saw her seamlessly to dawn the next morning.

Chapter Nineteen

"Are you sure it's a good idea leaving Jacca in charge of Lilly?" Paige asked anxiously, as they rowed further out into the bay, the village getting smaller with every stroke.

It was midweek, and no sooner had the doors of the restaurant been locked up for the evening, had Nick brandished a fully stocked cool box from nowhere and whisked Paige off on his father's old boat. Her body humming with uncertainty, she'd clamped her hands tightly between her knees, reeling off all the feeble excuses she could muster to Nick as to why they probably shouldn't be out exploring St Austell Bay right now. In a more exaggerated version of this scenario, she'd have been dragged on that boat kicking and screaming, Nick kidnapping her against her will. Instead, she'd gone with hidden reluctance, not wanting to be rude or hurt Nick's feelings. He'd clearly put a lot of effort into whatever he was up to.

The whole idea seemed utterly romantic in fact, and had it not been today of all days, she might have even allowed herself to indulge in such a gesture by a man who had literally turned her insides into mush recently. It had to be one of those catastrophic coincidences that they should be heading in the very direction she'd hoped against. There was no way Nick could know.

So did this mean she was on some sort of unofficial date?

All the signs had been there. She could hardly be blamed for assuming so. Nick's cool box was filled to the brim with homemade picnic bites, sandwiches, quiche slices, as well as a couple of bottles each of Tom's cider. A perfect little set up for a first date, perhaps.

Her wandering thoughts continued, a ferocious

attempt to busy her mind and ease her nerves.

As they got further out into the bay and started bearing right towards Portmellon, Paige's nerves burst into full blown anxiety as the direction they were heading in was confirmed.

No, not today. Please not today.

"Maybe we should do this on a night when Laura is home," Paige declared, trying not to look at Nick as her eyes pricked from threatening tears. They couldn't be going there, they just couldn't.

"Jacca and Lilly will be fine," Nick said firmly, clearly unaware of the emotional turmoil Paige was experiencing, his muscles contracting as he pulled on each stroke against the water. "Believe it or not, Jacca is quite responsible with Lilly. He's even babysat a couple of times in emergencies."

Paige rolled her eyes, her go-to response when being told what-for about her own father, slightly shameful that she doubted her dad's abilities to care for a minor.

Her chest restricting and her throat tightening painfully, she fought back the tears as the very spot she'd wished not to see again came into view, the rocks as inky black and sharp as razor blades as she remembered. She looked away, focusing on the open water and willing the tears to go away.

Please don't stop here. Please don't stop here.

She shifted her focus over to Nick's rhythmic grunting, as he put all his might into rowing them along the coast.

"Should have borrowed a boat with a bloody engine," Nick joked through great puffs of excursion. Despite the tears beginning to roll down her cheeks and the heavy sorrow that was threatening to fill her from the inside, Paige managed a hollow laugh.

Relief washed over her as she realised they were now passing the rocks and turning a corner to a little cove with the smallest little shingle beach. The bottom of the boat scraped against the ground as they reached the shore and Paige was only too glad to jump into the shallows of the

233

water to help pull the boat in. The water was blissfully cool, the heat from the day still detectable as Paige massaged her feet into the lumpy bumpy terrain of the seabed. Her eyes still damp from her moment along the way, Paige hovered in the water to observe some little crabs scuttling near her feet, the water crystal clear. Nick got straight to work in preparing his picnic and within minutes was pushing a prosecco glass in her hand.

"Happy birthday," Nick smiled, clinking his glass against hers, the elegant shape of the flute looking precariously fragile in his large, meaty hands.

"Fuck sake," Paige cursed under her breath. "Did Dad tell you? Bloody twat. I hate my birthday."

"I know," Nick said, chuckling at her expletives. "He did warn me this might be your reaction. Which is why it's just the two of us. No one else. No fuss. Just food, drink and the open water."

Paige looked out to the view in front of them and relented a little, her tense stature relaxing as she allowed herself to be led to the little picnic area that Nick had set up. Low slung camping chairs had been set up either side of a small folding table which was overflowing with every picnic delicacy imaginable.

"This is actually really nice," Paige admitted, sinking into one of the chairs and sipping her prosecco. The water rippled under the burning orange sun, a spectacular sunset promised in just an hour or so.

"Yes, well that was the idea," Nick said, lowering himself into his own chair and passing Paige a plate. "Birthdays aren't meant to be torturous."

Paige tried and failed to hide a slight bitterness in her expression, but if Nick had seen it, he chose to ignore it. They consumed their food with eagerness, both having barely eaten anything all day, dipping in and out of conversation about the stall, about Tom and Emily, about Charlie and Laura - to Nick's reluctance. Their conversations were easy, the pauses between comfortable silences to drink in the peaceful ambiance of their little spot.

234

Once on drink number three, Paige began to feel that blissful fuzziness around the edges where the pain from their journey there became dampened in its efforts. She allowed herself to fully relax in the moment, the odd side glance in Nick's direction to appreciate his tanned arms, the ink she'd noticed on their first meeting on show in full this evening.

"Right, I have to ask," Nick began, taking a swig from his cider bottle. "Why do you hate your birthday so much?"

"Dad didn't say? Blabbered enough about my birthday - surprised he stopped there."

"Ah, don't be mad at him. He was worried about you and seeing as you've been away for the last four or five birthdays, I think he wanted to make sure you celebrate this one." Again, he chose to ignore the face Paige was pulling behind her glass. "So come on, what's the beef against your birthday."

"Billy died on my birthday."

Like a plaster being ripped off with haste, she said it. It was out there, in the open and she looked away, not wanting to see Nick's reaction. She hated people's reactions. They never made her feel any better, only worse.

She heard a simple grunt from Nick's direction and chanced a look at him as he looked into his bottle awkwardly.

"I had a horrible feeling you were going to say that. And I still asked! Fuck." He shook his head in what looked like anger, swigging violently from his bottle. "Right. OK. I've got a confession."

Paige looked at him, utterly perplexed as he sat up straight in his camp chair, his brow furrowed anxiously.

"I think I might have been there, on that day."

A cold shiver ran through Paige, despite the warm air. She didn't move, waiting for him to continue.

"I wasn't sure before but gauging how quiet you were over here, I'm pretty sure now. We passed the spot on the way, didn't we? The place where he died?"

Here were the tears again. She nodded violently.

235

Nick cursed under his breath again and the atmosphere shifted between them as the sun was sinking towards the horizon.

"When you told us in May about your brother, I didn't make the links. Bit stupid that I didn't to be honest, because it all seems pretty obvious now. But I remember I was invited out Portmellon way for a meet-up with some mates. I didn't know Billy all that well, but I knew Tim - his best mate."

Paige remembered Tim very well, him being her first kiss, much to Billy's anger and disgust. There had only been about four years between herself and her brother's year group. But considering that she had been in year seven the night she shared a cheeky kiss behind the crab pot pile one idle afternoon, whilst Tim was starting his GCSE year, Billy had been fuming over the idea and had rushed in as protective big brother. She'd been mortified at his 'heroic gesture' and vowed dramatically that she would never forgive him. She did of course, and his accident had been only a week later.

"Anyway," Nick continued. "I was running late to meet everyone because I had to help my dad unload the pilchards he'd caught that morning. When I got there, the road between Meva and Gorran was filled with emergency services and the coast path was blocked off to general public. I never actually got down there and heard vaguely down the grapevine of someone losing their life."

Paige listened intently, the pain surging through her chest as someone other than her replayed the worst day of her life. Nick brought his hands to his mouth, a moment of distress.

"Shit! You were down there, weren't you? I remember Tim being off school for a couple of weeks. He was broken. He'd said something about Billy's little sister being the one who dragged him out of the sea."

Paige sniffed, the tears taking over. Her voice was thick and unsteady. "I'd stolen Dad's little boat and taken it to find Billy. It was my birthday, and I was furious that he'd pissed off to go … to go swimming with his mates without me. So I'd planned to find him and gate crash his fun."

A pause. Only the gentle, soothing motion of the lapping water against the pebbles could be heard.

"To be fair, I was the annoying little sister he couldn't shake."

Nick smiled and placed his warm hand over hers, covering her jittering knee as he did so. She took a long, unsteady breath and continued with the hardest story she'd never told out loud.

"I started calling for him from the boat and he was furious at me. Mostly for turning up uninvited but also for taking the boat out on my own. He was already halfway up that cliff edge - you know the …" Paige caught her breath, her heart hammering. "… you know the bit just around the corner from…"

"Yeah. I know which bit."

"Anyway. Out of pure defiance I think, he started climbing higher up the cliff edge, telling me to go home."

'Go home, Paige! Fuck sake - Dad's going to kill you!'

She could hear his words as if they were yesterday, spat out in uncharacteristic nastiness from the alcohol he'd consumed with his friends. She recalled the other boys, some larger and older than him, jeering at her and making fun of Billy for having his little sister cramp his style.

"I begged him to come down. I needed him home."

"Why?" Nick asked, not unkindly.

"Because it was my birthday," Paige repeated, drawing her knees closer to her chest. "I'd come home from school. Dad was away on a long-haul and Mum was working late. He'd promised me a birthday evening. I could tell by the way Billy was behaving that something had happened. He'd had a couple of drinks and he was angry. So angry. I started to realise that his anger wasn't fully at me and that Billy wouldn't have buggered off like that on my birthday unless something had truly annoyed him. Then again, he had quite the temper so it could have been anything."

"Sounds like a family trait," Nick joked gently,

earning a sharp dig in the ribs.

"His friends were egging him on, all equally as drunk." Fresh tears rolled down her cheeks as his voice echoed from her memories.

"Last chance, Paige. Go home!"

"Billy, what's the matter with you? You seriously going to let me spend my birthday alone while Mum works late?"

"Working late, my ass!" Billy had shouted, spitting his words out with venom. "Watch this!"

"Before I'd even processed what he'd said, he'd … he…"

"Jumped," Nick finished.

Silence. Then a seagull cawed overhead, dragging Paige back to the present day.

"Don't you see? That's why I couldn't forgive Mum," Paige wailed. "Her affair with Giuseppe killed my brother! He'd walked in on them… having a moment and… he… "

Nick was horrified. Utterly speechless. Paige succumbed to the tears and allowed Nick to pull her in close, clamping her in tightly against his chest. He rubbed her arms and back uselessly as he floundered to find the right thing to say.

"Paige, I'm so sorry. I never would have brought you here if… shit, why do I get the impression your dad set me up here."

Paige felt herself laughing through the tears, allowing the last few waves of heavy sobs to pass through until her body was still and peaceful.

"Sounds like the kind of thing Dad would do. He doesn't like to talk about his own emotions, so gets someone else to do it for him."

Even as her breathing slowed back to a steady pace, Nick's grip on her did not waiver and she found herself closing her eyes and taking in the calming and familiar aroma of him which she had become so accustomed to in the last four months.

"Do you really blame Elaine for Billy's death?"

It wasn't a judgment or an accusatory tone, but Paige thought about her answer carefully.

"I did. Right up until her own last breath." A fresh new wave of sadness washed over her, and she held her heart as it ached terribly. "Now I'll never get a chance to make things right with her or to remove that blame I hung over her head for all those years."

"She loved you. She talked about you all the time."

"I know. But did she know that love was returned? I certainly didn't show it half the time."

It was like she was lighter than before, though her heart lay heavy in her chest. She listened intently to Nick's heartbeat, using it as a steadying anchor, the strong regular beats calming her breathing.

"You know, it's like I've been afraid to heal," Paige said, a sort of revelation shedding some light on her tangle of emotions. Nick was still, listening with intent. " It's like my entire identity has been centred around the trauma of Billy's death. I'm not sure I know who I am outside of it all. I don't think Dad does too. But Mum? It's like she found hers immediately afterward his death and I resented her for that."

"Grief does strange things to our emotions," Nick muttered softly into her ear, his arms a vice around her.

"Grief is terrifying."

The sun was taking its leave and Paige felt a shiver run through her despite the cocooned warmth from Nick's embrace.

"It's getting quite dark now," Paige said, sitting up and finally breaking the hold. "Can we go home?"

Nick smiled, but it did not meet his eyes. He reached his hand to her face, his thumb caressing her damp cheek. "Of course. Paige. I'm sorry."

"It's OK. I'm actually glad I told you."

Nick's cottage was a welcoming beam of light when

239

they'd finally returned to the harbour, moored the boat and walked up the hill to their homes, the evening of festivities coming to a close for another day. Where Jacca's cottage was plunged into darkness, vacant with him playing babysitter next door, Nick's white-washed cottage was radiating with lights, warmth and all things new. Paige remembered it in its more dilapidated days and suddenly appreciated the sheer size of the work Nick had undertaken to get his home the way it was now.

"You really transformed this cottage," Paige noted. She still sounded slightly snuffly from her tears back on the little beach, the sea breeze on their return journey contributing to that. She had her scarf wrapped around her shoulders, despite being offered Nick's coat a dozen times. "I hardly recognised it when I came back."

"Thanks," Nick smiled fondly, looking up to its roof and down again. "I'd had my eye on it for a long time. When it went to auction, I had to pay way over its value to avoid second-home owners nabbing it under my nose. Spent another fortune on top renovating it, but hey - it was worth it."

Paige was about to tackle the staircase when she felt Nick's grip on her elbow.

"I gave you a hard time when we first met. About your mum. I didn't know the full story and I made unfair judgments. I'm sorry."

Paige reached out and stroked her thumb along Nick's bristled cheek. "You need to stop apologising. I get it. I lived up to those judgments, so... I really don't blame you for that."

Nick shook his head, his brow furrowed as he placed his hand over Paige's, her thumb still tracing a line down his jaw.

"I should know more than anyone not to judge without the full picture."

The clattering boats down below and the cawing of nesting seagulls filled the silence between them as they locked gazes, Paige's chestnut eyes a pool of warmth.

"Well! Hell of a birthday celebration this turned out to be," Nick said, his voice loud and jovial. "Shall we go inside and get pissed?"

Paige broke into a laugh, both grateful to Nick for lightening the mood and desperately disappointed that yet again a moment between them had come to nothing.

"Happy Birthday my darling girl," Jacca sang, wrapping his gangly arms around her shoulders in a tight embrace as soon as they crossed the threshold into the warmth of the cottage.

"Thank you, traitor," Paige replied, wryly. She patted her dad on the back awkwardly and pulled herself away. "Not happy with you by the way."

Paige took herself off into Nick's kitchen for a glass of water, the sound of Nick and Jacca's voices rumbling through from the other room. The creaking of the floorboards upstairs stopped her from returning to them straight away, and she decided to check on Lilly and let Nick have it out with Jacca for setting him up for an evening of tears.

When she found Lilly's designated room, Lilly was sat back in bed looking a little sheepish.

"Is it true it's your birthday?" Lilly asked from the darkness as Paige peered in. She sighed and entered fully into the room, perching on the end of the bed and nodding slowly.

"Yes. It is."

"Mummy didn't tell me. Happy birthday."

"Thank you, sweetie. Your mummy doesn't know either. I like to keep my birthday a secret."

Lilly's brow creased in confusing as she pondered over this for a moment.

"That's a really bad idea. If people don't know about your birthday, you won't get as many presents."

Paige laughed and nodded for Lilly to climb back under the covers. "That's very true."

"That explains a lot. Why Uncle Nick was all dressed up this evening and seemed really nervous. He's never

241

nervous. I think he likes you."

Paige was grateful for the lack of light in the room as her cheeks flushed with colour. She tucked Lilly in and gave her little hand a squeeze.

"Well, I like him too. He's a good friend."

"No - pretty sure he wants you to be boyfriend and girlfriend. I heard him talking to Mummy about it and she said he needs to stop faffing around and get on with it. Not sure what that means, but Uncle Jacca said something about Uncle Nick needing to know the truth...or something like that."

Paige half-listened to the little girl as part of her mind wandered. It seemed as if everyone was in on this - Paige couldn't help but feel like it was a kind of ambush of sorts. An ambush of her feelings. She screwed her face up a little in annoyance, told Lilly to get some sleep and bid her goodnight.

When she was downstairs, Jacca and Nick were having a drink in the living room, the fire lit despite it being a warm summer's evening. Nick offered Paige a glass, which she refused politely.

"Thank you for a lovely evening Nick. I'm off to bed."

The men fidgeted slightly in their chairs, Nick leaning forward in concern.

"Wazzon, maid? It's only ten o'clock. Have a little birthday tipple."

"I'm alright," Paige declined stubbornly. "I'm a little exhausted from my story-telling this evening, if I'm honest - thanks to your little tip to poor Nick here to take me there of all bloody places."

Nick's hand was straight up to his forehead in embarrassment, whilst Jacca at least had the good will to look a little bashful. He shrugged all the same, in irritable defence.

"You need to talk about it with someone," Jacca argued. "You don't talk about it, my darling girl. T'int right. You got to talk about these things. And if you and Nick are going to make something of it between you -"

"Didn't realise you became a match-maker overnight, Dad. Good for you. I'll leave you two to plan the next evening which ends with me in tears, shall I? Good-night!"

It was a swift exit out of Nick's cottage to jump the wall on to the storm porch next door before she could say anything else that she might regret. Furious with her father's meddling, and now a little peeved with Nick's willingness to go along with it, she took herself off to bed to end her birthday like she always did - alone and with her thoughts fully on her dear brother.

Chapter Twenty

Jacca

"Bloody hell, Jacca!" Nick exclaimed, almost as soon as Paige had shut the door on her swift exit from Nick's cottage. "What were you thinking, man? Dragging me into all of that!"

Jacca shrugged. A rather defiant shrug, he would admit. He knew very well that his charades this evening came with its risks. But he'd been worried about his little girl for quite some time now.

Or more, his not-so-little girl.

Paige had grown up to be just as beautiful and just as strong and fierce as Jacca had hoped. From the very first day when he'd held her in his arms, a tiny baby with the same jet-black hair as both he and his dearest Elaine. The same olive-toned skin. Elaine's sea green eyes to boot.

Every father says it, but she really had been exquisitely beautiful.

It pained him to see that, after all those years, she still held elements of this bitterness from what had happened. He knew full well that there were still certain things she struggled to talk about, to set eyes upon, to even hear about.

"She told you about it all then?" Jacca asked, apprehension in his voice. This was hard for him too.

"Yes! She told me! Jesus, Jacca. On her birthday and all," Nick fumed, raking his hands over his head and leaning back into the sofa. "I was kind of going for the romantic beach picnic sort of set up. Not an ambush on her past."

"Ah, geddon with you!" Jacca waved a dismissive hand in his direction, though secretly his stomach tied in knots. "She'll be alright in the mornin'. Will do her good talking about it with someone. She clearly trusts you enough. She ain't talked about any of it to anyone. T'int right."

"You're a sneaky old man," Nick said, though a small pull of a smile told Jacca he wasn't completely out of a friend. Nick heaved himself up and fetched the whiskey, topping up his and Jacca's glass. "A bit of warning next time, eh?"

"Right you are," Jacca said, tilting his glass in promise and taking a swig. Smacking his lips in appreciation for fine whiskey, he leaned back into his chair and crossed one leg over the opposite knee. The faint sound of a door slamming in Jacca's cottage had them both exchanging nervous glances.

"Maybe I should go over there and check she's alright," Nick pondered, staring at the wall connected to the cottage that Paige was currently storming her way through.

"Best not. Best to give her space when she's in one of her rages. You'll do good to remember that if you and her make something of each other."

A roll of Nick's eyes told him he didn't want to believe in his credentials for such advice. He couldn't say he blamed him.

"Her mother was the same. Terrible temper," Jacca shuddered. "Caw! I was terrified to come home some evenings - that is, if I'd worked out I was in the dog house before it was too late and I'd already crossed that threshold. Know what I mean!"

Jacca chuckled, the whiskey adding to the alcohol already in his system and making him a little giddy. Nick was clearly smiling his amusement in politeness and looked down at his scarcely touched whiskey glass.

"I'm sure you were no saint, Jacca," Nick said, his smile lingering in place unnaturally. Jacca's own laughter died in his throat and he cleared it awkwardly.

"Certainly wasn't dear boy. For all the trouble it may have caused tonight, I'm glad she's told you. It needed to come from her."

Nick's expression showed some agreement in that and he finally sipped his whiskey. "I'm a bit surprised I've never heard about Billy from you or Elaine, I'll admit that. Nor my own parents."

"The Meva community has always been very discreet about Billy's death. Elaine and I were very grateful for that. Of course, it was never much of a secret but everyone's discretion allowed us to protect Paige through her last years in school - know what I mean? I di'nt like the sound of her and Billy being the source of the gossip for years to come. As for your parents, they were just being respectful of our wishes. I hate to say it my love, but your dad probably doesn't much remember of dear Billy himself these days."

"No, you're probably right," Nick relented. "She blames Elaine. For Billy's death. Did you know that?"

The whiskey glass nearly slipped from Jacca's liver-spotted hands as he gaped at Nick with a pained expression.

"Never!"

Nick nodded regretfully as Jacca processed this, a slight sob caught in his throat.

"Oh, my dear girl. Mind you, she gave her m'uva some bleddy trouble when her and Giuseppe were together. One of the main reasons she stayed away I think." Jacca tutted, like the truth of what he was saying cut through him suddenly."

Then was silence for a moment and one more, rather final, slam of a door which Jacca recognised from past experiences as Paige's bedroom.

"And how did you cope? With Giuseppe and Elaine?"

Jacca appraised Nick over his glasses and Nick shrugged in response.

"Hey, you wanted me to get to know your family's past and secrets this evening. You started it!"

Jacca chuckled softly and nodded. "Well, as you can imagine, I dinne much care for it at the beginning. Bleddy torture if you is wanting the full truth. But as I've always

246

said, she always deserved better than what I have 'er when I woz away fishing all the time. She found better in Giuseppe and that's that."

Nick shrugged, leaning back into the sofa with an almost disinterested demeanour. Like the story disappointed him in some way. "And that was that?"

"Listen! It sounds daft! But that's how it woz! When Billy died, the whole family shattered into pieces. My darling Elaine had to grieve and deal with Paige's grief all on 'er own whilst I woz out to sea. I should 'a been 'ere, but foresight's a wonderful thing, eh? I don't ever blame 'er for taking comfort in someone more present - as much as it pained me."

Nick, now leaning forward with his elbows on his knees, shook his head in wonderment. "You're a better man than most, Jacca."

"That couldn't be further from the truth, m'boy!"

A sad silence filled the air, Jacca now staring into the bottom of his glass and thinking of nothing more than his late Elaine.

"Right, well. Only fair. You've had Paige spill her guts out this evening. Your turn. Tell me about him. Your son."

Jacca's heart wrenched slightly in his chest, the very wind knocked out of him for just a moment. And yet, he very much liked the idea. He wanted to talk about his Billy to a young man who had always brought him comfort in the many similarities he held with his late son.

"Quite right," Jacca smiled. "Pour me one more whiskey and I'd be delighted."

Despite the scorching red sun beaming down from a clear sky, there was a bitter nip in the air out on the bay on Jacca's little Martha. The small vessel rocked to and fro as Jacca dragged in yet another empty lobster pot from his spot. The catch this morning was a sorry sight.

"Alright Jacca?!" Malcolm shouted from his own boat just a hundred yards away. "How's the catch this mornin'?"

"Bleddy feeble, Malc! Beginning to wonder if someone's been 'ere already and emptied me pots!"

"They'd 'ave a bleddy death wish, wun't 'em me 'ansome!" Malcolm chortled. "Mind if I board? I have the wife's heavy cake if that should seal the deal."

Jacca and Malcolm negotiated and closed the gap between them, with one of Jacca's oldest fishing friends taking a surprisingly elegant step from one vessel to the other. Jacca started pouring some tea from his trusty, old flask, whilst Malcolm separated the heavy cake into two large wedges.

"Bleddy love your wife's heavy cake," Jacca said, gasping in bliss as he took his first bite. Malcolm plonked himself down on a turned-over lobster pot and the two of them looked back towards Mevagissey which was practically vibrating from a distance with all the little swarms of tourists dominating the waterfront and harbour walls. "I do despise this time of year."

"Can't do without it though, can us Jacca?" Malcolm said, not completely disagreeing with Jacca's notion. "Meva's a bleddy ghost town in the winter, thanks to all these empty second homes."

"That's what irks me! These second-home owners don't want nuthing to do with us in the colder months but they'll keep us good and empty during them. Then, come summer, we can hardly get to our boats to make an honest living! I'm telling you now, if Paige hadn't inherited the restaurant from her m'uva, she'd have afforded bugger all 'ere if she'd wanted to come home."

"She's done alright, your maid," Malcolm soothed. "Don't have to worry about that one. She's got a strong head on those shoulders. Wazzon between her and Nick, then? Or am I not allowed to ask?"

"There be something cooking between 'em," Jacca confirmed, nodding his head in approval. "Can do much worse for a son-in-law. Shan't boo-boo that match up at all. I woz in the doghouse last night, mind."

Malcolm chortled knowingly, as if it was a regular

occasion for Jacca to be in there.

"Nick took Paige on a little picnic for her birthday and I sent him… you know… over there." Jacca pointed in the direction of the location, unable to speak out loud the meaning the place held. Perhaps he wasn't much different to his daughter after all.

"Ah." Malcolm drew in a sharp breath, knowing exactly where Jacca had meant. "And what made you do a silly thing like that?"

"Not silly. Well, maybe it t'was. Nick didn't know n'uthin' about - you know - Billy's passing. And Paige don't speak about it enough. Thought it would be an opportunity, is all."

Malcolm blew out another breath, sitting his cup of tea on the swell of his belly and looking in towards the harbour again.

"You're braver than me, Bird."

As it always did, completely unexpected, a sudden dash of tears welled up in Jacca's eyes and a sob caught in his throat as he tried to speak. "Just worry about 'er - you know? I'm all she's got left now and she's all I have. I need to know she'll be alright. I won't be 'ere forever!"

Malcolm, a man of little ability in comforting someone, settled for a simple pat on Jacca's bony knee. Jacca reached inside his breast pocket and pulled out his old handkerchief, blowing his nose like a trumpet.

"Oh, sorry Malc. I'm going soft."

"You daft bugger. You've always been soft as get out and haven't I seen you cry enough times to be used to it by now?"

Jacca sniffed into his handkerchief and nodded, looking at his old friend with a gratifying smile. "You've been very good to us, Malc. I'm forever indebted to you."

"Christ - you're going to have me welling up in a minute. As I've said - don't you go worrying about Paige. Got plenty of people here to watch out for her if you should fall of your perch tomorrow!"

"Oh - thanks very much! Not sure if that was

supposed to comfort me or not!"

Malcolm threw his head back and let out an enormous belly laugh, clapping Jacca on the back as he joined his old fishing friend in his mirth. And there they sat, in companionable silence, their boats rocking gently side-by-side to one another as flocks of seagulls cawed in the clear sky above.

"Suppose we best head back in a minute. Ain't catching n'uthing more tonight. First pint's on me at the club, ol' boy!"

"Lovely job!" Malcolm said, heaving himself up and gathering up the tin foil from his wife's heavy cake. "You owe me at least three pints, I reckon!"

Chapter Twenty-One

It was Friday before they knew it, with the end of Feast Week drawing near and bringing in the weekend crowds. Trade was booming, and any initial concerns Paige had had over the restaurant being closed in the evenings had dissipated during the cashing up of each day's earnings.

Despite their prime location on the quay, their small line of stalls just outside the restaurant, the growing crowd was like a thick swarm of busy bees, all pushing and elbowing around each other, wandering aimlessly from stall to stall. From their spot, the Giuseppe crew could just about hear the preparations for today's raft race, the favourite amongst many villagers which involved teams of people racing on precariously homemade floating platforms with creative and comical themes. In snippets, Paige had caught sight of racers dressed as the Flintstone family, Ghostbusters and even a T-rex or two. Somewhere on the water was a team of Storm Troopers and, as predictable as it was, Jack Sparrow had walked past not long ago to complete his team's Pirates of the Caribbean theme. It was clear to see why the event was a firm favourite in the village, but alas Paige, Nick and the rest of the crew would have to miss it as fresh new swarms of hungry customers formed chaotic queues around their stalls.

"This is insane," Paige stressed to Nick as they rushed inside to retrieve more dough. "We're going to run out before mid-afternoon. Why can't more people have the pasta? I need to make up more dough. Can you cover me?"

Nick agreed and rushed back out with a replenished tray just as the flare gun was heard, announcing the start of the race. Somewhere on the water, her dad and Charlie were on Jacca's boat, a prime view of the race as precaution for anybody in the race who might come into a spot of bother. Meanwhile, Paige was in the quiet of the kitchen, both relieved to have a breather from the bedlam outside and subdued from missing out on all the fun.

The air was strained between her and Nick the moment she set foot in the restaurant that morning. They hadn't spoken about yesterday and Paige had no plans to unsettle the dust. She did however receive the full wrath of Laura over breakfast, as her friend laid into her for her lack of birthday spirit.

"Why am I having to find out from my eight-year-old that it was your birthday yesterday?" Laura had demanded as soon as she sat down for her post night-shift breakfast. "I feel like a right shit friend now! Happy bloody birthday for yesterday. Here, have a bottle of wine. It's all I had in my house."

What Paige couldn't decide was whether to be fuming at Nick for filling Laura in on the reasons behind her birthday incognito whilst Paige was out of the room, or whether to quietly thank him for saving her the task of explaining herself. She'd quickly found reasons to stay out of Laura and Nick's way after that, so as to avoid the uncomfortable pity looks that she so dreaded from her friends.

Now, as she made up the pizza dough, a mundane but therapeutic process, she was reminded of what she got out of being fully focused on a task. Where her mind would be racing, there was something about keeping her hands busy that quietened those thoughts. It was just a shame that she had lost some of her passion for food recently.

"We need the second oven," Paige declared an hour later, their pizzas backlogged by almost thirty minutes as they failed to keep up with peak lunch time demands. Nick grimaced, considering the little options that they had. "Your mate said it might just need a new lining soon, but he never said we couldn't use it."

"I don't think he recommended it, though!" Nick pointed out.

Blowing out a lungful of air and rubbing the back of

his neck in agitation, he nodded and went inside to light it up. After twenty minutes, the previously redundant oven was back in business and they were back to working on all four cylinders, so to speak.

"Daniel, can you and Lauren do these orders out back with the second oven?" Paige asked, handing Daniel a handful of orders.

"No problem, Paige."

"Need a hand?" Tom asked, side-stepping from his cider stall to their pizza stall.

"Brilliant mate. Can you make up some more pizza boxes ready for the pizzas coming out?" Nick asked. Tom nodded and soon there was a smooth production line of pizzas heading out to the hungry customers in no time at all.

"Thank you for your patience," Paige repeated for the tenth time as she handed another pizza over to a relieved customer, just as Jacca elbowed his way to the stall, closely followed by Charlie.

"Got anything left, Maid?"

"Depends," Paige muttered, scowling at her father. He held his hands up in mock surrender, giving Charlie an affronted look as if to say, *'see what I have to put up with'*.

"What's he done?" Charlie asked, returning Jacca's expression with a wagging of his finger. "Been meddling, have we?"

"Good guess, Charlie."

"Don't be a wretched child. Get your old man a pizza, will you?"

A smile crept on to Paige's face as she shot him daggers.

"Go back to your boat. I'll bring it over when it's ready."

"Something normal please. Not your fancy hippie fig and goat's cheese nonsense."

"Thanks a lot!" Paige laughed, waving him off and quickly taking Charlie's order, a simple meat feast. "Glad my new menu hasn't been wasted on either of you boring farts."

She was chuckling her way over to the toppings station when she caught a glimpse of Nick's expression, not realising that he had been watching the conversation closely. A mixture of annoyance and sadness crossed his face before he replaced it quickly with something more impartial.

"When do I stop getting the cold shoulder, then? Your father's been forgiven, it seems," Nick said quietly to Paige as he helped her prepare Charlie and Jacca's pizzas.

"I'm not giving you the cold shoulder," Paige said, bashfully. Nick scoffed and Paige's work seized for a moment as she placed a hand on his arm. "I'm sorry. I just didn't like the whole cloak and dagger of it all. But that was Dad's doing, not yours. You were just trying to give me a good birthday."

"And a grand job I did there," Nick muttered.

"I love that you tried."

She dared to hold her gaze with him for as long as possible, as a small smile tweaked in the corner of his mouth. He nodded as he placed a warm hand on her shoulder, her heart jolting in her chest as the same hand migrated up to tuck a small lock of hair behind her ears, before taking the ready-made pizzas to the oven.

Mevagissey Harbour was a burst of energy, colour and celebration. Paige weaved in and out of the busy crowds, the pizzas high above her head and a warm smile for every person she locked eyes with. A delightful mix of young and old, fishermen and teenagers, local and tourist - everyone was welcome.

When she reached her father, accompanied by Charlie on his fishing boat, she smiled at the sight of him, totally at ease. Leaning with his elbows on the edge of the gunwale, his glasses twinkling in the sunlight, he chatted freely - something Paige rarely saw in her father.

Come to think of it - the only times she had seen him so relaxed was either with Charlie or Nick.

Not with her, she noted sadly.

"Got yourself a pretty cushty little spot here," Paige

pointed out, passing the pizzas over the water into Charlie's hands. With his other hand, he grasped hers and helped her on board.

"Dear life, Maid. I won't eat all of this!" Jacca gasped, opening the lid of his pizza box.

"You a man or a mouse?" Paige teased, echoing a standing joke of Jacca's.

"Pass the cheese," retorted back her father, a wide grin across his face as he tucked into his first slice.

"I made extra so I can actually sit down and eat something for a change. Pass me a slice - I'm starving, and I have ten minutes until the stall gets engulfed again."

The boat was definitely the more peaceful location in the harbour, and she could see why so many boat owners took refuge in them. She'd never seen the fleet of fishermen so resourceful in luxuries on their trusty vessels. Even Malcolm was taking comfort on main deck, soaking up the rays.

"Laura just messaged," Charlie said, reading from his phone. "Oh dear, Lilly isn't feeling very well."

He clicked on the call button immediately, putting the receiver against his ear. Paige acknowledged him in approval - he certainly cared for Lilly just as much as he cared for Laura.

"Hey babe. Poorly little girl?"

They were on pet name terms now, it seemed.

"Bless her. I'll ask her now a minute - she's right next to me. Yeah, she's fattening me and Jacca up on pizzas."

Paige jerked her head curiously.

"Laura was wondering if she could bring Lilly over to the apartment to sleep. That's OK, isn't it? It's just, Laura finally has a day off and she doesn't want to miss out on the festival."

"Of course!" Paige agreed, through a mouthful of pizza. Charlie returned to Laura on the phone and confirmed the arrangements before ending the call.

"She'll be down in twenty minutes. Do you mind if I go and check on them in a bit, Jacca?"

"No problem, m'boy. Not much going on now for the rest of the afternoon."

Paige was in deep thought all of a sudden, on the brink of an idea. "Have you and Laura talked about living together yet?"

Charlie grimaced. "We've been dating for a month, Paige." A raised eyebrow made him relent. "Well, yes - we've talked about it. Indulged slightly."

"Great! You guys should live in the apartment above the restaurant."

This time, both Jacca and Charlie sent her incredulous looks.

"Think about it. Laura is always saying about how out of it she feels being on the other side of the village. Her flat is tiny and her landlord sucks. Mum's apartment is plenty big enough for a little family, which is what you'll be Charlie - in Lilly's eyes.

Charlie's face contorted between fear and annoyance at her meddling, and finally settled on a sort of contentment. He smiled to himself.

"I'll talk it over with Laura," Charlie said, thanking Paige with a squeeze on the arm which definitely didn't have the same effect. "But you have to start charging me some kind of rent."

"Definitely, you bleddy squatter!"

Charlie laughed, followed by Jacca, who was charging his way through the pizza despite himself.

"Thank you so much," Laura cried, grasping Paige in a hug once she'd tucked Lilly into the spare bed upstairs. "It's chicken pox. She's got a bit of a fever with it too. But I just didn't want to miss out on the whole bloody week. I'm going to grab a cider from the lovely Tom, a pizza from you guys and sit upstairs in that lovely window which faces the harbour. Bloody bliss after the week I've had."

"Sounds perfect," Paige smiled, thinking about her idea from earlier whilst making a start on Laura's pizza.

"Oh, you've had chicken pox before, right?" Laura

added. Paige nodded in amusement. "Oh good. Better check with Charlie too. Thanks again, Paige!"

"Wondering whether we should open later tomorrow evening for the fireworks," Nick voiced his thoughts out loud as he entered the kitchen, passing his sister on the way out. "Laura looks suspiciously happy. What's she up to?"

"She's spending the rest of her afternoon in the apartment upstairs with your niece - who has chicken pox by the way."

"Yeah, she said. So, tomorrow? Open for fireworks?"

Paige nodded her agreement. "May as well. We'll still be able to see the display whether we're serving food or not. What do Tom and Emily say?"

"Yeah, they agree. Tom needs to sell out to make ends meet, so he's pleased for longer trade time."

Paige finished Laura's pizza - caramelised onion, goat's cheese, spinach and field mushrooms, sprinkled with chopped hazelnut. Her dad might not appreciate a quirkier style of pizza toppings, but she knew her friend would give it a whirl. She scooped the pizza up on the paddle and delivered it straight into the oven, which was still blazing away next to the bar in the main restaurant area.

"Oven is holding up alright, isn't it?" Paige asked Nick, as he followed her to check on it.

Nick examined the surrounded brick work, all the way up to the exposed section of the flume. "Seems to be."

"Good, if today is anything to go by - we're going to need it."

Paige hadn't been wrong in her predictions. By the next afternoon, a few hours before the fireworks were due to start, their stall resembled something that had been burgled and the staff behind it looked equally frazzled.

"Remind me why opening for another four hours was a good idea?" Nick said, earning a weary laugh from Paige and the rest of his small brigade.

"I've sent Maxine home," Paige informed him. "She's had quite enough of the week and looked like she was going to keel over."

"Her and me both."

"Yes, but you're not nearing seventy."

"Bloody feel like it after this week," Nick retorted, groaning as two more customers approached the stall for their Italian fix. "I'll check on the dough front. I've ran out of customer service."

The girls who approached the stall looked mildly familiar as they gleefully ordered a large pizza to share between them, Paige feeling pleased to see that her quirky new toppings were a hit with the younger generation.

"We've literally had about three pizzas from you this week," the brunette mentioned, handing some cash over. "Literally never tasted such delicious pizzas in my life!"

Paige beamed, handing the girl her change. "I'm really glad you like it. We've bolstered the menu recently and added new styles, so it's great to get feedback."

"Will you be offering delivery in the village one day?" the red-headed girl asked. "It's just, we live up past the primary school and sometimes it's a bit of a mission to walk down or drive and park. I'd pay a small delivery fee, wouldn't you Fay?"

"Totally! Especially if that chef with the crew cut delivers it."

"Fay!"

Paige chuckled and pondered over this for a moment and smiled at the prospect. "That's not a bad shout actually. Thanks girls! Here, have a cannoli each - on the house."

The girls wandered off to wait for their pizzas, gleeful over their freebie as Paige's mind did a bit of wandering of its own. Ways in which they could modernise Giuseppe's without her being accused of taking the originality of the place away.

It had to work. She'd tasted a bit of what it could be like to have the restaurant run the way she wanted it, with new flavours, a new menu - not to be dictated by Nick's unwavering loyalty towards the old ways in which Giuseppe and her mum had run it. Though, to give him credit where it was due, he had been much better recently and seemed happy with the changes that had made it through.

"I think we should start offering a delivery service," Paige announced to Nick, Daniel and Jamie as they came back out with a replenished tray of dough.

Nick's face fell into a deadpan expression, as he thumped the heavy tray of dough onto the table. "Like Dominoes? I'm not driving around on a little moped, if that's what you're suggesting."

"Pity. The two teenage girls over there just suggested the idea and they offered to pay extra for you to deliver it."

Nick's face contorted uncomfortably just as Paige, Daniel and Jamie fell apart with laughter. His ears pinked and he wandered off, muttering something about checking the pizzas.

"He's always so uncomfortable when a girl fancies him," Jamie chuckled.

"Really? Surely he must be used to it," Paige scoffed.

Jamie and Daniel waggled their eyebrows menacingly, elbowing each other in amusement.

"Like what you see, Boss?" Daniel teased.

"Oh bugger off, both of you."

The extra hours paid off and soon their expeditious trade slowed to a steady trickle as villagers, visitors and business owners alike settled down for the fireworks display, which would end a triumphant Feast Week for all involved.

The summer evening drew in and with it a slight chill on the sea air, encouraging Paige to put another layer on. She watched in contentment at the cosiness of the scene before her, something she admitted she never got back in her life in Bristol. Perhaps she would have, if she and Matthew hadn't worked so much - but here, with the restaurant perfectly poised on the water's edge, it didn't feel quite as arduous as Garland's concrete jungle surroundings.

With the display starting any moment now, Paige told her crew to make themselves a pizza for their dinner and demanded they find themselves a prime viewing spot to take a well-earned break. Tom even offered the Giuseppe crew a cider each, and soon it was just Nick and Paige manning the station.

"Personally, I think we're far too soft on our employees," Nick said, wryly.

"Yes, definitely. No-one likes a happy crew," Paige joked, both mock cringing in unison and clinking their bottles together in triumph.

"We did it," Nick said, smiling down at Paige softly. "We got through a whole week of crazy Feast Week trade without killing each other."

"And - we introduced a new menu, with huge stamp of approval from our customers."

"And I only made you cry once this week. So, win-win."

Paige rolled her eyes to the little gazebo's ceiling and nearly jumped out of her skin as the first set of fireworks flew into the sky. The whirling, spiralling, glittery array of brilliance and colour filled the inky black sky as a symphony of well-placed 'oohs' and 'ahhs' echoed through the crowds. The odd boom and bang ricocheted from the surrounding buildings and lit up even the drabbest of grey pebbledash in radiating beauty.

"Hope Mowgli will be OK with all this noise," Paige suddenly worried, catching a glimpse of their cottages up in the hill.

"You're kidding, right? That cat would sleep through a world war. I love that you worry about my cat though," Nick added in a dopey manner, draping his arm around Paige's shoulders in a strangely natural way.

"He's a good cat," Paige offered, lamely. "Me and him, we're like that." She held her hand up, her fingers crossed in demonstration.

The fireworks were suddenly background noise as her ears hammered with the rush of blood pumping around her body. Nick's arm pulled her in slightly as his lips drew nearer to hers.

They were going to kiss. She knew she'd wanted this for a very long time and allowed her eyes to close, bracing herself for her own set of fireworks, her subconsciousness wondering why people's gasps of awe were suddenly turning into those of horror.

"Paige! Nick!" Charlie roared, as he fought his way through the dense crowd, more and more people turning their backs on the spectacular display in the sky to turn their attention to Paige and Nick's direction.

"Paige! The apartment!"

Stepping out from behind the stall, Paige clapped her eyes on the most catastrophic sight. The windows ablaze from the apartment upstairs and smoke billowing out from the seams, it was all Paige could do not to scream.

Giuseppe's was on fire.

"Nick!" Paige gasped, grasping his arm for support. "Laura. Lilly. They're upstairs!"

Chapter Twenty-Two

"Call the emergency services," Nick ordered, shoving his phone into Paige's hands as he vaulted the stall and ran into the restaurant. Her hands shaking madly, she thumped the numbers into the screen, just as Charlie ran in straight after Nick.

"Charlie! Wait!" Paige cried, her heart crashing against her chest as she connected to the operator. "Fire brigade, please!"

Flashes of white intermittent lights rippled across the harbour as people turned to their phones to record the scene. Friends and locals alike edged forward to offer their services to Paige, Malcolm taking immediate action to dispel the encroaching mass.

"Paige, m'love! What can I do?"

It was Jacca, and Paige had to physically stop herself from giving in to the little girl inside her who just wanted to collapse into her father's arms and let him sort all her problems. Instead, she gave him the phone, asking him to talk to the operator whilst she went in to help Nick and Charlie.

"Don't you dare!" Tom bellowed, coming out from nowhere and grabbing Paige by the arms. "It isn't safe!"

"Laura and Lilly are in there!" Paige sobbed, the rising panic spilling from within as she ripped herself from his grasp. "Nick and Charlie have gone in after them! I have to help!"

Emily was by her side, talking comforting words as they all backed away from the burning building, the heat intensifying by the second. Sirens could be heard from the near distance, the dark sky filling with the flashing of blue lights.

"Dad!" Paige cried, falling into his bony arms, his

grip tight and secure. "Dad! They're all in there!"

"It's going to be alright, m'love!" Jacca growled, his voice tough but quivering. "You'll see. It's going to be alright! They're going to make it!"

Long, ragged sobs coursed through Paige, her chest aching in agonising pain at the loss she'd suffered and the loss she was afraid to face right here and now. She muttered viciously under her breath, willing the people to whom she'd opened her heart up to be safe, just as glass shattered from one of the top floor windows, raining shards down on to the pavement below. The flames licked the guttering and fascia boards up above as great dark swells of black smoke engulfed the night's sky.

"Nick!" Paige screamed, paralysis taking over as she felt glued to the spot, her father gripped to her side with fierce loyalty.

They had to make it. They had to make it. This couldn't be it.

Another round of fight in Paige was about to take over just as a form came into view through the arched window of the restaurant floor. A large figure carrying a small load shaped very much like an eight-year-old girl.

"Lilly!" Paige wept in relief, racing forward to help Nick reach a safe distance. His skin sooty and blistered, he stumbled as large hacking coughs released the smoke from his lungs. In between splutters, Paige planted kisses on every part of his face until she sealed her lips against his, every part of her quivering with gratitude for his safety.

Somewhere in her peripheral vision, she could see Tom helping Malcolm and some of the other fisherman disperse the crowds, making way for the fire engine which was noisily crawling its way to the burning remains of Giuseppe's restaurant. A glimpse of Laura and Charlie's figures exiting the restaurant door had Paige's legs almost collapsing from under her in utter relief as she took blankets from a lady in the village, wrapping them clumsily around Lilly, around Nick and then around Laura and Charlie. She, Jacca and Emily guided them away from the blazing building,

263

the firefighters getting straight to work to control the fire.

Her heart broke into shards to watch the restaurant she had once resented but had grown to love in the last few months crumble from the inside before her very eyes. She gripped hold of Nick and Lilly like they could disappear at any moment, overwhelmingly grateful for their safety, her father a solid entity by her side.

Emergency service vehicles were now coming in from every angle as two more fire engines crawled onto the harbour. The chopping and whirring sound of a helicopter up above filled the air and soon the sight before them was almost surreal.

When the ambulance arrived, Paige numbly ordered Nick and Charlie to lead Laura and Lilly to the paramedics to be checked over, whilst all she and Jacca could do was wait on the side-lines. The crowds of people began to disperse on police orders, the fireworks display cut short, and the evening being shut down to a deadly stop. Most of the nearby residence and business owners hovered, most of them keen to help in some way. Paige was offered numerous hot drinks and at some point someone had placed a thick blanket over her shoulders as shock had begun to set in.

In a strange way it felt like Paige was losing her mother all over again, a part of her life which Paige had never originally accepted. She felt confused by the sheer grief she was experiencing over a building filled with only memories and things which had caused so many arguments in the past. A little time capsule of that part of her mother's life she had never supported, suddenly she wished it wasn't being destroyed right before her eyes. Suddenly she wanted to explore the apartment and get to know that side of her mother she had allowed herself not to be a part of.

She couldn't have felt any more the fool.

"How did you know when you had forgiven Mum?" Paige asked her father, her eyes never leaving the flames.

There was a pause as Jacca thought deeply about his answer. "Not sure, Maid. Hard to say. I just had. Why?"

"Because I think this is it," Paige muttered, her voice wobbly. "And I wish it had come sooner. Dad? I wish I could take it all back. Everything I said. I wish I could take back those moments I just threw away when she was alive. I was so, so stubborn and ignorant and angry. I didn't even try to accept her new life. Oh, Dad - I've been such an idiot. Nick was right all those months ago - I am a spoiled brat!"

"Stop. Stop that right now, m'love," Jacca growled fiercely, grasping her around the shoulders and giving her a gentle shake. "You mustn't think like that for one second. She loved you something sore, even through those difficult times. She knew you were hurting and she didn't blame you for how you were even for a moment. You hear me, my girl? Don't you dare start beating yourself up over what happened."

"I just..." Paige sobbed, her heart aching in her chest. "I wish I could tell her how much I love her."

"She knew, m'love. She knew you loved her, but she also respected that you needed time."

Another hot tea was placed in Paige's hand by a friendly by-stander. She barely registered the face but hoped she'd remembered to thank them.

"How do you know all of this? How can you possibly know?" Paige said glumly into her tea.

"Because your mother and I talked about these things. We may have been divorced but we were still in each other's lives. After Giuseppe died, I was there for her. We spoke about many things, gained closure over many moments in our past. When she had her fall, I was there for her again. We spoke about you. We spoke about ... we spoke about our boy, Billy."

A sob caught in Jacca's voice and Paige grasped her father's hand and squeezed it fiercely. She smiled meekly, encouraging him to continue.

"We spoke more to each other in the last year of her life than we ever did in the whole twenty years we were married to each other. She may have left me all those years ago for a hunky Italian with big biceps..."

Paige couldn't help a slight snort of amusement.

"...but my goodness did we find that true friendship between us that had been lost all those years ago. I don't think we ever would have had those moments if we were still married. And I'm so grateful for those last moments with her. Even if I was no longer her husband."

Paige could almost not believe what her father was saying, and yet she resonated with every word of it.

"Miss Yelland?"

Paige and Jacca turned out from their own little moment to respond to one of the firefighters on the scene.

"Are you the owner of the restaurant?"

"Yes," Paige replied, her voice not sounding like her own. Not strong and wilful as it usually was, but timid and vulnerable. She cleared her throat and tried to sound more in control. "Yes, I'm the owner."

"Looks like we've gained control. I have some officers in there now just checking the stability of the building. The apartment upstairs has mostly smoke damage, but the main restaurant floor has taken quite a hit, I'm afraid."

Paige's heart could quite easily have sunk to the ground and slithered away into the ocean.

"We think the fire probably started up in the chimney of your pizza oven."

Paige nodded, knowing exactly where the fire would have started and feeling like an utter fool. Of course it was the pizza oven. Hadn't Nick warned her that it was dangerous without the flue being looked at? Did she listen? Of course not. She never did.

"Do you have somewhere you can stay tonight?" the firefighter was asking kindly, his voice sounding a million miles away.

"I - I don't live above the restaurant. I live with my dad."

There was that voice again. Juvenile. Vulnerable.

"My friend lives up there." Paige turned to Jacca. "Where's Charlie going to live, Dad?"

266

"So, are you his landlady? Can I speak with this Charlie?"

"He's over with the paramedics. I'll take you over," Jacca offered. "Paige, sit down. Sip your tea, love."

She did as she was told and perched on one of the benches along the water's edge, one knee jerking violently. As she scanned the scene - the scene entirely on her hands - her eyes fell on Nick, who was talking to a paramedic, perched on a stretcher and having his blood pressure taken.

How on earth did he look so calm right now?

No. Heroic. He looked heroic.

He was heroic.

He had run straight into the burning building without hesitation and extracted his niece and sister as if saving lives was a regular occurrence. When Ollie was stealing from the restaurant, he was there by her side and had dealt with him like dealing with crime was his day job.

Her gaze stayed locked on him all the way through his check-up, a new-found gratitude for having him in her life. She had realised almost immediately, when he'd been in that burning building, that she'd never want him out of her life ever again.

Nick shook the paramedics hand and checked on his niece, Paige's heart skipping a beat as he sought her out in the crowd and closed the gap between them.

"Are you OK?" Paige asked, her voice small and breaking.

"A bit sore, but I'm OK."

Sitting beside her, his warmth radiating through her, they simultaneously looked up at the remains of their restaurant.

"Paige, I'm so sorry."

"It should be me who is sorry. I did this."

She felt his eyes appraise her from the side, but she held her resolve.

"How the hell can you say that? This wasn't you."

Paige nodded furiously. "You warned me there was a fault and yet I insisted on using that damn oven. Shit - I mean, look at it!"

A fresh wave of tears consumed her and in one smooth sweep, Nick had wrapped her in his arms, the strong smell of smoke very much lingering on his clothes and in his beard. Clamped in tightly, she allowed herself to succumb to the sobs for just one moment, before pushing herself away for fear of allowing herself any kind of luxury tonight. She was too furious with herself for that.

"So, what do we do now?" Paige asked, the streets emptying around them.

"For now, we go home, we go to sleep, we recoup. Tomorrow, we come up with a plan."

With barely an hour's sleep behind her and with the smell of burning rubble still lingering in the air, Paige began her day in a sorry state. She'd hoped with all her heart that last night's events had been a horrible dream, but when she'd looked out of the bathroom window and caught a glimpse of what was left of her restaurant, her fears had been confirmed. Giuseppe's really had burnt down to the ground last night and it was all her fault.

To say she wasn't in the mood to come downstairs and find her father's cottage filled to the brim with her friends for breakfast was an understatement. But with her guilt still eating away inside and given that she blamed herself entirely for everyone needing to find a new place for breakfast, she attempted her best go at being welcoming.

"Morning, Paige," Charlie spoke first, after Paige greeted everybody with a tight-lipped smile. She was suddenly very aware of her untamed black hair barely holding on in its messy bun from last night, not to mention the dark circles under those dark brown eyes. "How are you?"

"I'm alright. Are you guys OK?" Paige said, directing her question to both Charlie and Laura, who was sat behind him at Jacca's breakfast table. "And since when did Dad have such a healthy stock of breakfast stuff lying around?"

"We're OK. Honestly. As for all this, I brought it with

me this morning to make sure you and Jacca ate something. Should have known Nick would be here already, cooking you both breakfast."

Sure enough, there he was. As usual, his size not quite in ratio with the dinginess of Jacca's old kitchen and yet perfectly suited to his surroundings. Paige felt a little tug in the corner of her mouth which she pushed down immediately. Her restaurant died a sorry death last night - now was not the time to be getting giddy.

Paige took a seat opposite Laura and Charlie, on their orders, and wrapped her arms around Lilly in greeting.

"How are you, Lilly?" She shot Laura a worried glance, as she checked the girl's face and arms for any injuries.

"She's absolutely fine, aren't you sweetie? We're all fine. I knew you were going to do this."

"Do what?"

"Worry yourself over all of us," Laura reached across and grabbed Paige's hand. "Are you OK? Because it's alright if you're not."

Paige was going to reply with some sort of vague response about her being fine when Nick's arrival in the dining room, his arms lined up with plates of hot breakfast, took the unwanted attention away from her.

"Someone should let Jacca know that breakfast is ready," Laura pointed out. "He's down on the harbour."

Charlie got up from the dining table, thumped his way across the old floorboards in his heavy boots to the front door and hollered down to the waterfront. "Jacca!! Breakfast is ready!"

Everyone stared at him in disbelief for a moment, as he casually took a seat and made a hungry start on his breakfast.

"I meant text or something," Laura sighed. "Jesus, Charlie! You're like a fog-horn!"

Having said that, it had had the desired effect and moments later Jacca was storming in through his tiny cottage front door, a wretched expression on his face. He gave his daughter an unexpected kiss on the head and nudged her sternly.

"Eat up girl. You'll need your strength today."

"Please, can everyone stop fussing over me when you lot were the ones extracted from a burning building last night! Nick, you shouldn't even be near a hot plate right now with those burns on your arms and face."

Laura tutted and gestured at Paige impatiently, sharing a look with her brother. "You see? Paige, in case you forgot I am a qualified nurse. I've checked Nick's burns over this morning and he's fine. I've seen a lot worse."

"See how much my sister cares about me?" Nick teased, taking his breakfast to one of Jacca's armchairs to save the little breakfast table, designed for four at best, from being completely overwhelmed. "Honestly Paige - physically, everyone is fine. But your father is right, we all need to eat well and keep our strength up. Today isn't going to be easy."

Nick's words could not have rung truer later that morning as she gripped his hand tightly walking through the blackened remains of their restaurant. His hand was large and firm, enveloping hers with warmth and comfort. Their noses twitched in synchronised grimace over the congealed mix of burnt plastic and rubber, the floor crunching from the debris under their feet. Giuseppe's famous red and white chequered table-cloths singed at the corners and the Mediterranean yellows of the walls scorched and blackened.

Nick was equally silent and still beside her and Paige knew this had to be just as devastating for him. She squeezed his hand but didn't dare look at his face. No matter how much her friends had tried to deny it to her, she had done this.

Their trailing stopped for a moment at the foot of the stairs leading to her mum's apartment and Paige gazed sadly at the dated Italy photos now coated in a thick layer of soot - unrecognisable.

"You want me to come with you?"

Paige thought for a moment. Most of her wanted him very much to remain by her side and to hold her hand all the way round that apartment she'd been so adamant to avoid. But she knew that this was a long overdue tour of her mother's old life and now she owed this to her.

"It's OK."

"I'll give you a moment. Need to check the kitchen."

Every creak and groan of the floorboard was still intact, with perhaps a few added extras. The door was wide open and the only inlet of pouring sunshine was from the broken window in the centre of the living room. Other areas of the small apartment were plunged into shadow, the light compromised from the blackened panes.

To give Charlie credit where it was due, his short residency in her mum's apartment was subtle and practically unnoticed. The odd item of clothing and a small sports bag in the corner were about the only items Paige could spot intruding on the time capsule that was her mother's life beyond her marriage with Jacca.

Gingerly sifting through things, Paige knew this was something she should have done months ago. If she had done it sooner, she wouldn't be doing this knee deep in black soot and ash - a small punishment for being so stubborn.

She approached her mother's bureau, a relic she remembered once being in the cottage - something she must have brought over after her separation with Jacca. Paige got ready to bite back the bitterness but found there was none, only sadness as she gently pulled on the tiny handles to open the little drawers in the writing desk. Amongst all the greying ash, the treasure Paige came across in those little drawers glistened in the sun beaming through that broken window. A wonderful array of sea foam green, turquoise, teal, aqua - even reds and yellows of all shades thrown into the mix.

"Good news! Kitchen is fine! Almost untouched."

Nick's voice boomed through the frail building,

271

breaking Paige's train of thought and making her jump out of her skin.

"What have you got there?"

"It's Mum's sea glass collection," Paige said, her voice quiet and small as she ran her hands through the smooth stones. She sniffed inelegantly and wiped her nose with her sleeve, unable to take her eyes from them for even a second. "I can't believe how much the collection has grown. She'd been collecting them for as long as I can remember."

"I know," Nick said warmly, coming up to stand beside her so he too could admire the collection up close. The small contact of his arm brushing hers coursed through her like warm treacle and it was all she could do to control her breathing from hyperventilation. He held a few of the rarer reds and yellows out to the beaming sun, admiring the way the light travelled through the opaque, coloured glass. "She still walked down to the little beach, every morning, to find more. That's what she was doing when I... "

Paige scooped the handful of sea glass back into the drawer and turned to look up at Nick, his face contorted in pain. Her right hand reached up and stroked his cheek, his beard tickling her wrist as he leaned into her warmth.

"You were the one who found her, the morning she died. Weren't you?" Laura had mentioned it to Paige on that first morning for breakfast, but selfish as ever, she'd not bothered to think about it any further. "That must have been so awful for you."

He cleared his throat, a gruffness in his voice as he wiped at a single tear daring to escape his eyes. "After my own mother died, she and Jacca were there for us - me, Laura, my Dad. But it was Elaine in particular who got me through the times when I could have gone pretty dark, so to speak. Kept me on the straight and narrow with a job here and before I knew it, I was Head Chef and... "

"Setting out to buy the restaurant."

It wasn't said unkindly, only as if Paige was finishing his sentence, but she cringed all the same as Nick's body

272

became still.

"I didn't mean to... sorry, I shouldn't have said that. Bad time to bring it up."

"How do you know about?"

"Ollie," Paige said, that one name enough of an explanation as she shot Nick a look of apology. "I overheard him saying it to his partner-in-crime over the phone that day. How I got in the way of you..."

"No, Paige. It's not like that."

There were no tears. No anger. Paige simply looked at Nick, willing him to be real with her.

"But you *were* going to buy the restaurant."

Nick paused, a grimace passing over his worried features. Rubbing the back of his neck, he chucked out a heavy sigh before relenting.

"Yes - I was going to buy the restaurant. Back when I was under the impression Elaine's daughter wanted nothing to do with this place, where I didn't think I'd be stepping on any family shoes. When Elaine died, obviously everything changed. So, that's that."

An attempt to draw the conversation to a firm close, Nick walked away and quietly paced the rest of the apartment, paying particular attention to the many frames hung dirty and sooty on the walls.

"It explains why you were so hostile with me when I first came down," she said, throwing her hands up in front of her in surrender as she caught sight of Nick's expression. "I'm not picking a fight, I swear. I'm just piecing things together. Because, honestly? I get you being pretty shitty at me for turning up and pissing on your parade."

"The sale fell through the moment Elaine passed away," Nick began, looking as uncomfortable as he did wretched. "When I discovered that the restaurant was tied into Elaine's will and that her estranged daughter was the main beneficiary, I thought at the time she couldn't be less deserving. So, I suppose I was a little unwelcoming at first."

The words cut through her, despite her pretty much guessing the reasons that were going to leave Nick's mouth before they actually did. She nodded, perhaps more than she needed to and did her very best not to show the hurt on her face. "You weren't wrong."

Nick's hands were suddenly cupped around her face and he was locking her into his steel grey eyes, a fierce look on his face.

"I couldn't have been more wrong, Paige."

Chapter Twenty-Three

Nick

The bacon and sausages sizzling in the frying pan, Nick had an extra spring in his step as he prepared breakfast for two in his small but versatile gallery kitchen.

Despite the traumas of the past couple of days, this morning he'd woken up with a new thirst for life. Something happened last night which he knew deep down he'd wanted for a very long time and now he couldn't think of anything else.

Outside his kitchen window, leading out to his little courtyard garden, he watched in amusement as Mowgli lazily attempted to round up some little songbirds, who were feasting on a pile of seeds Lilly had set out on the little tabl

e a couple of nights ago - less than interested in their feline predator. They clearly knew just how incapable Mowgli was of simply getting off his fat behind, let alone springing into action to cause any harm.

Nick turned down the heat on his sizzling pan and got to work with preparing the egg mixture just as there was a frantic knocking on the front door.

"Have you seen Paige? She didn't come home last night!"

It was Jacca, and Nick had never seen him so frantic with worry.

"This isn't like her at all. She wasn't down for breakfast or getting ready for her run, so when I popped upstairs to check she wasn't poorly or anything, I found her bed empty. Don't think she's slept in it at all! She stayed at Laura's d'ya think? Can you call her, m'boy? I'm worried something fierce here!"

Nick could barely get a word in edge-ways as the poor old man ranted his way into Nick's front room, shuffling further into the kitchen to follow the delicious scent of cooking breakfast. Nick rubbed the back of his neck uncomfortably, listening out for signs of movement upstairs. A creaking floorboard. Or mattress.

How could he put Jacca's mind at ease without making his mind race?

"Jacca. Paige is fine."

"You've spoken to her? Where she to?"

"She's umm... well, she - uhh... "

"Hi, Dad! What are you doing here?" Paige asked, as she seemingly floated into the room, her hair unkempt but thankfully, fully clothed, albeit skimpy in those jogger shorts of hers. God, he blessed the company who designed those shorts.

Jacca's face was set in a hard line as he pieced together the easiest cliche puzzle in history. "Oh, well... just having a minor heart attack trying to find my missing daughter! Don't mind your old man! Where the bloody hell have you been? Why are you over here so bloody early - do you know what, don't answer that! I know exactly what's going on here - don't take your old man for a fool. I have fish to catch - 'scuse me!"

With that, Jacca exited the cottage quicker than he could say Mevagissey chicken and it was all Nick could do not to crawl into one of his cupboards from mortification, whilst Paige ruptured into a full set of hysterics, crying from mirth.

"Oh my god! Did that seriously just happen? That could not have been more cliche! Should have thrown on one of your T-shirts as a nightdress!" Paige laughed.

"Stop! This isn't funny," Nick groaned, rubbing his face and sinking on to the kitchen side on his elbows. "Fuck sake. Jacca's never going to look me in the eye. You're his baby girl!"

Paige pulled an affronted face and grabbed a coffee mug, "I'm twenty-eight. He'll get over it. Coffee?"

Not entirely disregarding his humiliation, Nick gave in to the pull and placed his hands on her hips, grazing her cheek delicately with his lips. "So, keeping the cliches going - last night was... "

"Amazing," Paige smiled, leaning into his kisses as she continued to prepare two coffee mugs, the kettle rumbling in the background. "Breakfast also smells amazing."

"Shit, the breakfast. Surprised it's not burnt already from all the disruptions."

"That would be a sad day for us all if Nick Stone burnt his meal!" Paige teased. Her smile faltered a little as she placed a mug of steaming coffee on the counter nearest to Nick whilst he rounded off his breakfast items, her two hands wrapping around her own mug for comfort. The slight change in demeanour didn't go unnoticed by Nick and he watched her with caution as she leaned her back against the kitchen side. She did this a lot, he'd noticed. The smallest of things could have her mind a million miles away.

"So, what's the plan for today?" Nick asked, moments later. He'd separated all the perfectly cooked items on to two plates and gestured for Paige to lead the way into the dining room.

"Well, some insurance bloke is meant to be coming to the restaurant next week to open up a claim, so I guess we need to start sifting through to find things we can save. Give the place a bit of a clean. Then there's Mum's stuff to go through." Paige's voice sped up the more she listed and she soon had both her hands poised on either side of her plate, taking in deep breaths as the stress of it all took over. Nick really did feel for her. He squeezed her hand, keeping it cocooned in his warm hand long enough to see the tension fall away from her soft features.

"It's going to be OK," Nick said, losing count over how many times he'd already said those words the night before. Perhaps a few more wouldn't hurt. "Why don't you go for one of your torturous runs after breakfast and I'll bring in a couple of the kitchen lads to help me clean and box up some glassware. I was thinking - there's a lot of meat in the freezer and fresh produce in the cold room. It's all going to need using up. I could send Maxine around to some of the other restaurants and pubs to see if they'll buy it all for a reduced rate."

"That's a great idea," Paige groaned again, looking more downtrodden than reassured - not the affect Nick was going for. "You're so good. So calm and collected. You should be running this restaurant, not me."

His loaded fork poised in front of his mouth, he glowered at Paige now, his patience wearing thin. "Will you stop? We went over this a thousand times yesterday. You and I make a good team. Not just me. Not just you. Us. Now, stop moping and eat your food."

Paige chuckled softly and resumed her meal, but Nick couldn't help feeling niggled by the thoughtful expression on her face.

As promised, Nick had everybody on a job by mid-morning and soon things that could be rescued by a simple soak in some hot soapy water was cleaned, dried and boxed up for storage. Maxine had counted all the stock available for reselling and was making her way around the other businesses in the village. Even a couple of the girls from front of house had offered up some of their time to sweep and mop up the worst of the debris and water damage on the main restaurant floor. Nick was beyond grateful to see everyone pitching in as they did and could have even been in danger of getting emotional when he saw Tom's four-by-four pull up into one of the parking spots on the harbour.

"Tom mate, you've got a farm to run!"

"S'alright mate. My brother-in-law, Steve, is on the case. I come bearing baked goods, and dinner for tonight as well," Tom said, opening the boot and revealing a crate of homemade goods. "As you can see, my mum sends her regards."

By midday, a skip arrived in the harbour, courtesy of Malcolm and so Nick, Tom and Charlie began hauling all the

278

tables and chairs which were damaged beyond repair.

"You took photos of everything before the mass clean-up, right?" Charlie asked, as they made their fourth trip to the skip.

"Yes, Paige did yesterday. Why?"

"The insurance company will want evidence of the extent of damage before opening up a claim. I used to be a lawyer," Charlie added, as a form of explanation.

Nick almost stumbled as he halted in his tracks to glance in Charlie's direction.

"Lawyer? Really?" Nick couldn't help sounding surprised, but he couldn't picture Charlie in a suit with any form of authority. "And now you're a fisherman."

Charlie shrugged, clearly used to people's reactions to his strange career jump. "My boat on the wide ocean is a far better office than four walls in London, don't you think?"

Nick nodded, still a little stunned but finding he had a new-found respect for the bloke dating his sister. He knew he didn't really have a reason to dislike Charlie - perhaps it was just a natural reaction as a protective brother. But then he did get in the way at the start with Paige too, so Nick was keeping that as a justified reason. But lately he had started to like Charlie, which of course annoyed him further.

"Wow, you guys have done loads already!" Laura commented as she stepped across the threshold into the restaurant, a somewhat tidier room than it had been a few hours ago. "Anything I can help with?"

"You can go and see how Paige is doing," Nick offered, passing through with a damaged table. "She headed out of her mum's apartment about an hour ago with some personal stuff she wanted to take back to Jacca's. Between you and me, I don't think she's doing too well."

Laura's sudden change in expression only strengthened his worries, making him pause again and causing his muscles to rip and ache from the weight of the table currently suspended.

"Nick, I've just seen Paige. She was walking to her car and she was on the phone," Laura explained, looking as

279

if she didn't want to tell Nick the next part. "I over-heard her saying something to the person on the phone and it sounded like legal stuff. Something about deeds."

At risk of dropping the table on his foot, Nick thumped it down on the floor and shot his sister a worried expression. "You what?"

She shrugged, her worried expression reflecting his own. "She saw me and seemed flustered. Said she was just heading to Truro for something. Got in her car and drove off."

"Her solicitor is in Truro," Nick confirmed, his brow creasing more by the minute, his hands on his hips. "You don't suppose she's... "

"I don't know. She seemed quite agitated." Laura's hand rested on her brother's arm, his jaw set in a hard line, the tension in his face visible even through his beard. "Try calling her."

He nodded, grabbing his phone from his back pocket as Laura went in to find something to do. His thumb hovering over the call button, hesitation took over and he suddenly didn't know what to do.

Solicitor? Nick wouldn't be so worried by this if it wasn't for the growing complex Paige was tormenting herself with last night and this morning. What did she need to see the solicitor for? Nick's mind wandered to one possibility - but surely she wouldn't be so drastic.

Nick's thoughts trailed off to the time they spent together last night and how just the thought crossing through his mind made him weak at the knees. The girl he'd thought was tight-lipped and dour turning out to be the most real person he'd ever got to know. Authentic and unapologetically so. He'd been falling for her for weeks now but - last night? Last night sealed the deal. He couldn't let her turn her back on the restaurant now, just because things had got a little complicated with the fire. And surely it didn't bother her that much that he'd been lined up to buy the place all those months ago. If he was honest, he'd have been up to his eyeballs in debt anyway.

His thumb finally made the call and, to his utter frustration, it went straight to voice mail.

A flash of anger came over him at the cowardice of Paige. After all the progress they'd made. Pizza oven fire to one side, they'd landed themselves a great working team. How dare she turn her back on that?

Then again, he couldn't speculate. He didn't know the full story yet and for all he knew she was seeing the solicitor for insurance purposes. But then, why the secrecy?

"Nick!" Laura's shrill voice broke through his thoughts and he focused on her irritated expression.

"What?"

"You were a million miles away then! Larry from the chip shop is here, offering a portion of chips for everyone for lunch."

His anger seeped away and was replaced quickly with the reinstalled feeling of gratitude at another member of the community coming to their aid. He nodded and headed over to greet Larry with a firm handshake.

When Paige finally returned, the chips had been demolished and all hands were back on deck again for another round of clearing and cleaning. Nick watched her cautiously as she stepped through to the restaurant floor, scanning around to gaze at the progress that had been made as she clutched on to a brown envelope.

"You guys have made a serious dent in the place," Paige said in awe.

"Well, you've been gone for almost four hours. I was ready to send a search party out for you," Nick responded, his tone much more irritated and much less cool than he'd been aiming for.

"Sorry, it was a last-minute trip to Truro."

Nick watched as her fingers drummed on the envelope, her eyes giving her away as she seemed deep in thought. She seemed both vulnerable and defiant at the same time and Nick so desperately wanted to close the gap between them and have her in his arms just like this morning - merely hours ago. Suddenly, she seemed untouchable.

"Need any help down here or shall I crack on with upstairs?"

"Crack on with upstairs if you like," Nick said, almost dismissively. His eyes fell on the envelope again. "What's in there?"

The uncomfortable expression which crossed over Paige's face confirmed it all for Nick and his jaw immediately stiffened in a hard line as he watched her squirm for an answer. "Later, Nick. We'll talk later."

All he could do was nod as blood rushed through his ears like a noisy river. She took herself upstairs into the quiet sanctuary of Elaine's apartment and suddenly Nick needed some fresh air. He threw a piece of chair spindle across the room and shouted to Tom that he'd be back in five.

He was about to take a fast, vigorous walk around the harbour when a familiar man approached him with haste.

"Excuse me - are you Nick? Head chef here?"

Nick nodded.

"My son - Lewis. Works in your kitchen."

"Yeah, I know who you mean," Nick said, probing impatiently for the man to continue. He really needed to pound the pavements - in silence, preferably. Suddenly, he was starting to think Paige was on to something with that running business, but he wasn't about to admit that to her.

"Well, you've been so good to him. What with the baby and Jess not being well. Really appreciate it, mate. Well, I heard about the fire." A sympathetic expression was shot at Nick as the poor man rambled through what he needed to say. "I'm a contractor and - well, I'd like to offer up my services to help you get back on your feet, so to speak."

"Oh." Suddenly Nick felt awful for being so impatient and changed his demeanour immediately, taking the card that the man was offering to him.

"Name's Dave. That's my business card there. Run it

by your team, business partner, whatever - happy to help."

Nick offered his hand and shook Dave's firmly. "Thanks very much. Appreciate it. I'll speak to Paige and we'll be in touch. Waiting for the insurance company to give us a clear picture."

"I understand. Listen, my labour will be on the house. Just materials you've got to worry about."

Nick expressed his extreme gratitude once more and continued on his walk around the harbour, his stomping perhaps much less murderous than it would have been about three minutes prior.

"Hello, Nick m'love," Hetty, a little old lady who made regular visits to the restaurant during the quieter months, said as she passed him near the Aquarium. "So sorry to hear of the restaurant, my darling. What a fright for all of you."

"Thank you, Hetty," Nick said, his politeness back in place for one of his favourite regulars. "Don't you worry - we'll be up and running again soon."

"Oh, I do hope so," Hetty said, her kind and aged features looking up at Nick in such sympathy. "Awful for you all. Lovely to have Paige on board as well. Lovely Jacca was made-up when she came down."

At least fifteen years Jacca's senior, the gooey expression which crossed Hetty's face didn't go unnoticed by Nick, his hardening heart at risk of warming to her.

"She's a beautiful young lady - I'm sure that hasn't gone unnoticed with you," she winked. "Exactly like her mother. Lovely long black hair, olive skin. Ooh, to be in my twenties again. Anyway, best get a move on. I have an appointment at the GP's and it takes me twice as long to walk across the village now. Especially with these emits around, blocking the streets."

Nick chuckled and gave her a heart-felt farewell, promising to invite her personally when the doors reopened again.

The dark cloud above his head lifted just a little more and he found he was at least able to breathe easier, maybe even think more clearly. With his new-found determination, he turned on his heels and headed back to 'face the music'.

Chapter Twenty-Four

Paige was both excited and nervous to present her surprise to Nick later that evening. The nerves stemmed from the fact Nick had been behaving strange all day. She only hoped he didn't regret last night.

She certainly didn't.

Every time her mind even so much as wandered she could feel his touch again, his lips grazing against her bare skin, their bodies intertwining and forming a connection she felt would never break. The very memory quite literally took her breath away.

Today however was a different day.

They'd finished their days work at 4pm and Nick had gladly sent the team home not a moment after before disappearing off without a word to his cottage. Paige had of course let him, deciding he was probably tired and upset with the upheaval of his beloved restaurant, so she'd given him space. If there was to be a 'them' she wanted to start it on the right foot and not be too needy.

That said, she really needed to speak to him and so at 5pm she lost her nerve and was tapping cautiously at his door. It was wrenched open only seconds after, and she knew immediately something was wrong.

"Nick, what is it?"

Despite his stress, Paige still detected an element of hostility, something she hadn't felt from him for a good few months. Without those emotional barriers in place, the ones which had crumbled spectacularly last night, she was left much more susceptible to hurt. She didn't like it one bit.

"What's wrong?" She repeated, trying to put her own concerns to one side.

"It's Mowgli. I came home and found him on the kitchen floor, lying in his own mess. I'm on the phone to the vet practice now. Hello?"

Nick's attention was back on the phone, his hand running across his head wildly as he walked off and left Paige stranded on the door-step.

"Yes. Yes, of course. I'll leave now. Newquay. Okay, thank you!"

"Nick, what can I-" Paige began, Nick storming around the downstairs of his little cottage to retrieve things for his journey to the vets.

"Paige, not now. I can't deal with you right now. I need to take Mowgli to out-of-hours."

He couldn't deal with her right now? His words stung more than she wanted to let on and she clutched the envelope with a new resolve as she watched Nick stuff a delicate Mowgli into his travel carrier.

"Dammit, his medication," Nick cursed, turning on his heel and heading for the kitchen.

"Nick, let me drive you to the vets. You're upset and it's a long drive."

"I'm fine."

"I'm driving you. No arguments."

The drive to Newquay was long and tense and Paige was beginning to wonder what on earth she had done wrong, or if this was Nick's temperament when things got rough. Mowgli meowed in misery on the back seat as Paige negotiated corners as carefully as she could, the radio on to fill the heavy silence. Multiple times, Paige considered breaking the ice, only to quickly retreat from that idea as soon as she caught a glimpse of Nick's thunderous expression. He was beginning to remind her of the version of Nick she'd met back in February and she didn't quite know how they didn't kill each other back then.

The static silence officially exhausting the car of oxygen, she couldn't have been more relieved when the vet building came into view, just as Nick couldn't have jumped out of the car fast enough if it was on fire.

"Nick Stone here, with Mowgli," Nick said through

the intercom at the door, then rounded on Paige. "You don't have to come in. You can just wait in the car."

Paige didn't bother to respond and followed Nick into the building all the same as soon as the door was buzzed open. A young vet was stood in the reception area, her hand out in greeting to welcome them in.

"Mr Stone. How is our Mowgli doing?"

"He's vocal but weak," Nick replied, sounding vulnerable himself. It was all Paige could do not to reach out to him and comfort him. But she didn't fancy having her hand bitten off at this moment. "Thanks for seeing him so quickly. Sorry, we've probably just caught you right at the end of your shift."

"It's no trouble at all, not for this little dude," the vet said, turning to smile warmly at Paige, a golden tanned arm stretched out in front of her. "Hi, I'm Dawn. Nice to meet you."

Despite her growing concern for whatever downward spiralling moment happening between her and Nick, Paige couldn't help but smile back at this easy-going vet, her caramel voice cool and calming. Perfect for dealing with stressful scenarios between owners and their pets.

"You too," Paige returned her smile, though it didn't reach her eyes quite like Dawn's did. Her mind was just too foggy. "I work with Nick at the restaurant."

"Oh, Giuseppe's! One of my all-time favourite places! So sorry to hear about the fire. It didn't take long for it to be spread all over social media, did it?" Dawn said, her voice and expression deeply sympathetic.

Paige glanced nervously at Nick, who was still avoiding her eye-contact. Could it be that he'd had time to really think about what had happened and did he now resent her for the fire. She wouldn't blame him, though it hurt her to the very core to think it. She sighed and smiled meekly at Dawn. "No, it didn't."

"Shall we go through and check Mowgli over?" Dawn said, gesturing to the nearest open door.

To Nick's annoyance, Paige continued to follow and

in seconds they were squeezed into a consultant room, Mowgli mewing on the consulting table and unspoken words hanging in the air. Seemingly unaware of the tension in the room, Dawn unclipped the lid of Mowgli's carrier and made her silent introductions to his quivering form. He looked weak, nothing like the strong feline she was used to cuddling. Despite his ailments, it was clear from his delicate purring that Mowgli was familiar with her.

"So, you found Mowgli this afternoon?"

"Yeah, just after four-thirty, when I got home from work."

"Any unusual behaviour before that? Eating and drinking normally?" Dawn asked, now checking Mowgli over, looking in his mouth and listening to his heart through her stethoscope. Everything was like one smooth, choreographed movement, almost mesmerizing as Nick answered the questions.

"There's signs of cyanosis in Mowgli's mucous membrane, which may indicate diminished oxygen in the blood. Was there any diarrhoea when you found him collapsed?"

Paige waited for Nick to respond but nothing came. When she glanced in his direction, he looked a million miles away.

"Yeah, Nick mentioned finding Mowgli in his own mess," Paige interjected.

"Yes, thank you!" Nick snapped. "I'll answer questions about my cat, OK?"

A blow in the chest, Paige threw him a dirty look and crossed her arms, her cheeks pinking as she locked eyes with Dawn.

"OK, so if he has diarrhoea then there's several possibilities here. My first guess is an infection in his gastrointestinal tract. But I wouldn't rule out other things." There was a pause as Dawn appraised the two people in front of her, Nick chewing ferociously at his cheek and Paige tapping her foot at a hundred miles per hour. "Are we OK here?"

"Yep, yep. Fine. Continue," Nick said, waving his hand in mad gesticulation. "Not going to rule out other things…"

"Mr Stone, there's a large possibility that this could be cancerous. With Mowgli's age against him and his existing medical conditions, we need to prepare ourselves. I'm going to take Mowgli to the back with the nurse team who will put him on intravenous fluids for the night, and then we'll begin some tests from there." Dawn paused again, a little exasperated by the distracted pair before her. "I'll give you both a minute."

As soon as the door was closed, Paige seized her opportunity.

"Nick, I know it's been a tough couple of days - what with the fire and Mowgli… but… "

"You're right," Nick interrupted, his eyes narrowed and unkind. "It's been a shit couple of days. But I'm not the one doing a runner when things go pear-shaped."

Paige didn't even know how to answer, staring at the clinically white wall in front of her and then turning her attention to a graphic poster on fleas and worms in cats and dogs, attempting to work out what Nick could possibly be going on about.

"I am so confused right now," Paige mumbled, mostly to herself. "Last night… "

"Was clearly a mistake," Nick jumped in, not looking her in the eye.

He may as well have reached into her chest, yanked her heart out and squeezed it into dust right before her very eyes.

"That's really how you feel?" Paige said, her voice dangerously low, Nick's shrug almost sending her over the edge. "What the hell happened between now and this morning for you to turn into such a prick again! You are so hot and cold - I swear, I never know where I stand with you!"

"Yeah - well, I could say the same about you. There's me thinking there was something good between us and just like that…" Nick's raised voice faltered to barely a whisper as he took in a deep breath.

"Just like what?" Paige shouted. "You're not making any sense! Did you fall into the frickin' skip earlier and bang your head?"

"Do you know what - I can't do this right now. My cat might be dying - and I don't need this right now!!"

"OK!" Dawn swept into the room, a look of annoyance and utter bewilderment across her face. "Things are getting pretty loud in here! Listen, Mowgli is settled and comfortable for the night. Why don't you guys head home... please. We have lots of sleeping patients in the back."

The air crackled as Dawn bounced a pleading look between the both of them, her hand poised on the door.

"Sorry, Dawn," Nick said, rubbing his chin and looking wretched. "Thank you for taking care of Mowgli. Keep me informed?"

"Of course," Dawn smiled, glancing nervously between Paige and Nick, as if they were about to set off on a fresh batch of shouting wars again.

Without Mowgli's meows breaking the pregnant silence between them, the journey back to Meva had been nothing short of torture. By the time Paige's little car had pulled into her space on the harbour, her knuckles were white from tension as she'd gripped the steering wheel, willing Nick to say something that would explain the change of heart.

Switching the engine off, they sat in the stillness for a moment, the sun beginning to dim into an early summer evening. All the anger building inside Paige from Nick's behaviour had seeped away on the car journey home and now she was only left deflated and disappointed.

"I'm going to go inside in a bit and finally get out of your way," Paige said, staring through her windscreen to watch a couple of seagulls devour some chip wrapping between them. "But just do one thing for me. Open the glove compartment and pull out that brown envelope from earlier."

To her surprise, Nick did as he was told and silently

reached into the glove compartment to retrieve the envelope. Breathing heavily through his nose, his brow furrowed, he prised open the seal and pulled out the forms Paige had been so excited to show him earlier, before everything had changed. She watched intermittently as he read the words, the brow loosening on every word and slowly being replaced by lines of anxiety and guilt. At one point, he closed his eyes and pinched the bridge of his nose, before continuing to read her solicitor's words. When he'd finished, his arms dropped in his lap and his breathing steadied.

"I thought..."

"I know what you thought," Paige interrupted, her voice stern, let down. "At least, I made a guess that it was what you thought, somewhere between Summercourt and Trewoon, because I genuinely ran out of ideas as to what else I could possibly have done to piss you off so much."

Nick squirmed in his seat and for a moment Paige's resolve faltered.

"I wasn't about to abandon the restaurant Nick, just because of the fire. If I was ever going to abandon the restaurant, it would have been back in March when you were being a total tosser. When I was adamant I didn't want it."

She felt ashamed to admit that last part, but she couldn't deny it. She'd wanted nothing to do with the restaurant all those months ago, but a lot could change in that time. A lot *had* changed in that time. But right now, Paige couldn't decide if she was glad of these last five months or whether it was something that only put her delicate heart at risk of pain once again.

"I've been in conversation with Katrina from my solicitors for a little while now, but after everything we'd been through in the last few days... last night... I knew I had to get it finalised, so I rushed down to Truro to gather the paperwork and I was going to surprise you with it over dinner tonight."

Swearing under his breath, his hands wringing in his

291

lap, Paige had never seen him look so vulnerable and shameful.

"I just thought... you were being so secretive about it," Nick's voice was small. "Laura said you were being weird when she saw you and I started worrying. You had such a complex about everything last night. Paige - I'm sorry, I jumped to conclusions."

"I did have a complex - you're not wrong there," Paige relented, her gaze back on the seagulls, whose collaborative chip wrapper picking had escalated to a full-blown scrap over the last chip. "I was only secretive because I didn't know how you'd feel about it. Whether you wanted to go into partnership with me. I just thought... I thought it might start to make up for the fact I practically stole the restaurant from you. If I can give you fifty percent, it's a start... right?"

Their eyes finally met, and Paige almost sighed with relief as she saw that gentleness return to Nick's eyes.

"You listen to me, you ridiculous, stubborn, wonderful woman," Nick began, turning his body towards hers. "You never stole anything from me. Although, you've made it very difficult to be away from you. When I thought you might be leaving, I panicked. But it wasn't a concern over the restaurant, it was pure selfishness. I didn't want you to go because I don't know what I would do without you around." Realising he was being far more sentimental than he was perhaps used to, he cleared his throat and checked the progress of the fighting seagulls in front of them. "I've become somewhat fond of you."

"You talking to the seagulls now, or me?" Paige teased and she laughed as Nick nudged her on the shoulder and squeezed her knee, making her squirm in her seat.

"You, you daft woman!"

As she ripped his vice like grip from her knee, their fingers intertwined and they soaked up the returned companionship between them, Nick tracing a small circle on the flesh between her thumb and her forefinger.

"So, what now?"

"Well, I'll decide if you deserve your fifty percent or not," Paige smiled, ensuring Nick that she was teasing and earning herself another squeeze of the knee. "Then you sign, we file and we wait for this insurance visit next week."

"That's going to be fun," Nick said, wryly. "Let's just hope they don't find a reason to decline our claim."

"They won't."

"I'm afraid I am going to have to decline your claim."

It was just under a week later and Nick and Paige stood before a dour man in his mid to late-fifties, a permanent bored expression fixed to his face. It was a particularly misty day, the sun retiring behind the clouds for the day and the restaurant itself was feeling especially gloomy.

In agitation, Nick's arms folded menacingly across his chest, whilst Paige's hands were wringing frantically in front of her as they both tried to process what the man in the tweed suit was saying.

"Decline. You're joking, right?" Nick finally said. "On what grounds?"

"The pizza oven," the man said, his attention on his clipboard, not bothering to look up. "Cause of the fire. You knew there was a fault with it, yes?"

Paige and Nick exchanged a look between them and Paige's heart sank.

"We had a friend take a look at it," Nick said, taking the lead. "He was booked in to get it fixed… "

"But you decided to light it in the meantime," the man supplied, dotting something on his form and closing the clipboard up. "There's nothing we can do. The oven hasn't been officially serviced in years, so your insurance is void anyway."

Paige stood grounded to the spot as Nick practically chased the man out of the door, demanding the right forms for appeal and muttering his way back into the restaurant moments later.

"We're appealing. Bloody rip off. Pay all this money

to be insured and these companies never want to pay out when it comes to it," Nick ranted. "We're changing insurance companies. That's it!"

"Don't think any insurance company is going to take on a restaurant that just burnt down, do you?" Paige reasoned, her stomach lurching in all directions. She buried her face in her hands and released a groan of frustration. "What are we going to do? A refit is going to cost thousands."

They looked around them, the restaurant looking tidier but sad. That was the only way to describe it.

It just looked sad.

The old wallpaper singed and peeling, the exposed brickwork scorched. The previously white ceiling charred and blistered.

Paige was set to dabble in a round of outspoken self-pity when Nick's phone trilled into the empty space.

"It's the vets," Nick sighed, looking like a man at the brink of breaking. Paige reached for his hand and squeezed it and he smiled weakly in return before taking the call. "Hello? Hi Dawn, how is he doing?"

Nick's voice disappeared as he exited through to the kitchen, leaving Paige to stew over the impossible.

What were they going to do?

Thousands of customers had walked through these doors, hundreds of thousands of dishes had been enjoyed in that very room - years and years of happy, successful business under the hands of Giuseppe and Elaine.

Less than five months in Paige's hands and it was burnt to a crisp, without any insurance money to resurrect it, her staff without work for the unforeseeable. It should have been enough to floor her, but instead she swayed on the spot, her mind racing and yet numb all at once.

"You okay here for an hour," Nick said, coming through to the front, sliding his arm into his jacket. "Mowgli can come home."

"That's good news," Paige braved a smile. "Did Dawn say what was wrong with him?"

"Some sort of infection," Nick shrugged, seeming to be a million miles away as he checked his pockets for key, phone and wallet. "Antibiotics. Lots of rest. I'll see you later."

Despite her troubles, her heart did a little jig as Nick leaned in and placed a gentle kiss on the top of her head, the smallest of squeezes on the shoulder before he departed.

"What about a fundraiser?" Paige offered, staring out of the window of her father's cottage that evening, the freshly falling rain on the scorched summer's ground creating that delicious petrichor smell. Jacca was dishing up a bowl of soup for each of them, his tattered green fishing jumper hanging off him as he angled his equally battered saucepan over one of the bowls.

"Could be a start, I suppose," Jacca mumbled. "Though, some might frown upon you setting up a charity like that. You're a business at the end of the day."

"Yeah, you're right," Paige agreed, biting the side of her thumb and earning the bat of Jacca's hand to rip it out of harm's way.

"Don't bite your thumb. You've always been a nightmare for that," Jacca tutted. They sat in their designated seats and made a start on their soups, a part of Paige grateful for some spare time to have dinner with her father.

"I've got some savings, but it's never going to stretch far enough. I can look into a loan I suppose. I'll call the bank tomorrow." Paige set her spoon down long enough to scribble a reminder down on her depleted list of 'ways to save the restaurant'.

"These bleddy insurance companies," Jacca growled, midway through a spoonful of soup. "They'll take your money gladly enough, but when it's time to pay out…"

"God, you and Nick are alike," Paige chuckled, rolling her eyes. "I can see why you get on so well. As much as I want to agree with you Dad, I voided the insurance by making Nick light up the oven that night. It's my fault."

Suddenly the soup didn't go down as easily, feeling as if she was swallowing a huge lump along with her food, her stomach churning as she did so. She felt her dad's scrutinising stare burn a hole in her head as she tried to casually dunk her bread, the slam of a spoon on the table making her jump.

"Bugger this," Jacca said, mopping up the last of his soup with his bread, shovelling it in his mouth and leaving the table. "I just got my old Paigey-girl back, I'm not letting this one back."

"What one?" Paige said, looking utterly perplexed, her bread still poised and disintegrating into her own bowl.

"This," Jacca waved a finger in Paige's direction. "This mopey one who just sits here feeling sorry for herself. You've always been a girl of action. Now, finish your soup, get into some old gear and meet me at the restaurant with a hammer or something."

Before Paige could ask any more questions, Jacca was out of the cottage door, his fluffy white hair speckled with droplets of rain in a matter of seconds, his heavy boots pounding the walkway down to the harbour.

"I haven't seen Jacca Yelland this animated since 1997 when he brought in over seven tons of pilchards in one day," Malcolm said, as he, Nick and Paige marvelled at the man himself round up willing members of the fishing fleet, encouraging them out of their hiding places. The social club. The storage units. Their boats. Their nearby cottages.

"He can't seriously be asking the fleet to pitch in with renovating the restaurant," Paige cried, mortified. "You lot have enough on your plate."

"Ere! When a fisherman in the fleet is in trouble, the fleet come to aid. That's the Meva spirit, me 'ansome," Malcolm growled with pride. "Same goes when it's a fisherman's own blood. Your mother was the heart and soul of this village, and the very same with this restaurant. World's been put to right on many occasion in this place and the fishermen here won't stand to see it go. You hear me, girl?"

Paige smiled, her eyes smarting from tears threatening to fall.

"Besides, if there's free food involved, you're on to a winner," Malcolm added, his thumbs behind his braces as they watched Jacca return with the last of the fleet.

"That will definitely not be a problem," Nick agreed. "All the free food they bleddy want."

At least a dozen fishermen in his wake, Jacca gathered them all outside the restaurant, standing dwarfed between Nick and his daughter.

"Right," Jacca said, facing his beloved fleet, looking tiner than ever amongst his larger fisherman buddies. They stood before him, waiting in anticipation for his next words. "Oh, I'm not doing some speech or anythin'. This in't bleddy Braveheart. Tell Paige what you're good at and we'll make a list."

There was a rupture of chortles and chuckles amongst the men, and Paige rolled her eyes as she opened her notebook she'd been ordered to bring, her pen poised ready.

The weeks rolled by after that evening. Many of the fishermen, despite their own hectic schedules, had volunteered their services, declaring their specialty skills and turning Paige's lack of plan into a full fledging schedule of work.

Paige and Nick spent many late nights elbow deep in dust, dirt and grime as they stripped back the walls, ceiling and floor. There was something strangely therapeutic about nursing the restaurant back to health, even if the progress seemed slow at first. When the walls were rendered and the floor taken up to be replaced, it was only then that all hands were on deck and the restaurant floor became a hive of activity, with the fishermen flooding in with their tools and muscles to get the renovation underway.

One evening, Nick and Paige were pouring over

designs and mood-boards which Laura had cleverly put together. A bottle of wine opened between them and a tapas spread prepared by Paige, the excitement between them became palpable as they started to really visualise the restaurant's new look.

"I'm sure you are a brilliant nurse, Laura," Paige said, shoving a heap of nachos into her mouth and casting her eyes on the latest designs and ideas Laura had conjured together. "But you've missed a vocation in interior design here."

Laura had then nervously placed a separate mood board in front of her friend whilst Nick left the table to check on Mowgli, awaiting her reaction.

"Is this for Mum's apartment?" Paige asked, recognising the layout almost immediately. She had become more familiarised with the place in the last week than she had in the whole ten years of her mum living there.

"Yes. We were wondering... that is, Charlie and I were wondering whether we could strike a deal with you. Where we renovate the apartment and then can rent it from you on a permanent basis. God, I sound like a right scrounge right now! You can tell me to jog on if I am being totally insensitive."

Paige had practically glowed in happiness at the idea that her friends still wanted to make a life together in her mum's apartment, despite everything that had happened, throwing the design down to wrap her friend in the tightest of hugs.

"Are you kidding me? The apartment is yours!" She squealed in delight. "I'm so glad. I thought the fire would have tainted the place for you."

"No way," Laura shook her head, her face beaming now that she'd had her answer from Paige. "We couldn't think of a better place to set up as a new family. And no more late nights for poor Lilly when I'm working night shifts."

In a matter of days, the restaurant had been stripped down to its bare shell and from there the visions had come flooding in for Paige. Suddenly, she could see exactly how she wanted the restaurant to be reborn and the sleepless nights were testimony to her excitement.

"Lewis' dad is here with a bit of a surprise," Nick said, bursting her train of thought, a slight grin on his face. She followed him out to the front, where Bill was skimming the walls with artistic flare. Paige could not wait to start testing colours in place of the brownish mix currently drying in pinkish patches.

"Hi Paige," Dave, Lewis' dad, smiled, shaking her hand in greeting. "Hope you don't mind me dropping by unannounced, but I'm seriously running out of room in my workshop."

Paige almost gasped as her eyes gazed upon the most perfect breakfast bar.

"Dave, this is incredible!"

The reclaimed wood was scorched for effect, with black metal legs shaped into a hairpin for that sleek, modern look.

"The other one's in the van," Dave said, blushing at the compliments Nick and Paige were throwing his way as they admired his work. "I didn't do them too high, as you asked. Should sit perfectly flush with the bottom rim of each window. Here - let's have a look. Nick, give me a hand?"

Nick and Dave lifted the bar, the weight of the whole unit reflecting its quality. It sat perfectly in place before the first window and suddenly Paige could see her and Nick enjoying their breakfast in that very spot every single morning for years to come.

"Is it alright?" Dave asked, nervously, eying up the escaping tears running down Paige's cheek.

"It's perfect."

The restaurant took its slow transformation into early September, with freshly painted walls and a sparkling new polished wooden floor. There was still a long way to go in furnishing the place and bringing in those final interior touches, but the work of the fleet was complete. In appreciation for all their hard work and free labour, Nick and Paige decided to host a free pizza and cider night for the fishermen and their families, the place bursting with life once again.

"Paige, can I have a minute?" Nick asked, poking his head into the kitchen where Paige was kneading more dough, the fishermen having destroyed the first batch of pizzas in less than fifteen minutes. Lewis was back, making up the tomato sauce and Jamie was whistling away behind them, clearing some of the dishes.

"Sure," Paige rubbed her hands clear of the dough and placed the large dome into the tray to prove. It had been so good to be back in the kitchen preparing food for masses of people again and there was a little skip in her step to prove it as she followed Nick through the restaurant floor and into the back storeroom.

It was a tight little space, currently being taken up by a large pasting table covered over with a dust sheet. Nick found the light switch and stood before Paige looking utterly nervous.

"Okay, I have a surprise for you, but this could go one way or another," Nick rambled, tweaking on the corners of the dust sheet. "Now that it's done, I'm worrying that I probably should have asked you, but I really wanted it to be a surprise."

"Stop rambling. Let's see!" Paige said, gesturing for him to lift the dust sheet already.

As the sheet was dragged off the table, the little room glistened in aquas and greens, bouncing off the shadeless down light onto the four magnolia walls. Paige's heart tightened, then leapt, all in one breath and she reached out to stroke her fingertips against the cool, smooth stones. From up close, it was a beautiful mosaic muddle of her mother's entire collection of sea glass. As Paige changed her angle and took it in in its entirety, she realised what had been captured.

"Is that...?" Paige asked, her voice faltering into barely a whisper.

"Yeah. Have I overstepped? Do you like it? Laura did most of the designing and executing, so it's down to her really... or her fault - depending on how you're feeling about it."

The way Laura had encapsulated the shape of the harbour wall with the browns, the reds and the oranges was unmistakable, the slightly disproportionate but utterly charming fishing boat looking suspiciously like Jacca's little Martha. Even the lighthouse was captured with milky white gems, a beacon recognised by all who held Meva close to their hearts.

Paige's eyes panned down to the bottom right of the scene, and once again she brushed her fingertips against the glass, the scatter of noir stones imitating her mother's hair in the gentle breeze.

"Mum," Paige spoke, fondly. She smiled, envisioning her on that beach, letting the world wake up around her as she submerged her bare feet into the smooth shingles, the gentle water lapping in around her ankles. "It's exactly like her."

"It's exactly like you as well," Nick said, fondly. "Though, you don't stand still long enough. You're less in the moment than Elaine was, you're more 'run laps around the harbour like someone is chasing you'."

Paige laughed in humble agreement, digging her elbow into Nick's ribs all the same for the cheeky dig at her running habits.

"So... you like it?"

Turning to face him, her arms snaking around his neck and her eyes meeting his, she kissed him gently on the lips. "I love it."

Their kiss deepened and their arms entwined around one another, momentarily forgetting that just beyond the cupboard door was a pizza party in full swing. Nick's hand migrated from Paige's hip, up her body and through her hair, cupping the back of her head.

Just as things between them were about to heat up a notch, Paige unlatched from the kiss, an idea pinging into

301

place.

"I know what we should call the restaurant!"

"You mean, we're not keeping Giuseppe's?" Nick said, his voice so serious that for a beat Paige believed him, before his face broke out in a charming grin.

"Jesus, I thought we were genuinely on the brink of one of our brawls then!" Paige gasped, taking a deep breath and exhaling dramatically.

"Go on then. What are we calling our new restaurant?"

Paige smiled, the collective word 'our' sending a warm current through her body, a hot treacle filling in the gaps in her heart that had formed from years of grieving.

"Sea Glass."

Nick looked down at the mosaic, at the hundreds of polished clear stones that Elaine Yelland had handpicked from the sea, one by one, every single morning.

"Does that mean we're going to start doing faffy à la carte meals?" Nick joked, earning himself another swift dig in the ribs. He gathered Paige in under his arm and kissed the top of her head, both of them admiring Laura's mosaic work. "Sea Glass it is. Now, let's get out there and replenish the pizzas before we have a hungry fleet on our hands."

Epilogue

The streets of Mevagissey were quietening, another tourist season drawing to a close as locals began to claim the streets as their own again. The sky was heavy in drizzle and little fishing boats were just visible as they returned to the safety of the inner harbour. A flock of purposeful seagulls flew along the curving line of the water-front buildings, a steady herd of hungry patrons heading to the doors of Sea Glass.

Entering Sea Glass Restaurant was like taking a cool dip in the transparent Cornish waters during a hot, humid day. The splash of aqua, azure and indigo from the herringbone tiles bordering the large bar, six wicker lampshades perfectly designed to replicate the crab pots on the harbour. The new private booths taking up the back wall and facing the waterfront were the first to book up every evening, in second place the breakfast bar-style tables at the infamous arched windows. The best seats in Mevagissey was the word on the streets.

At the bar, the stools were occupied by the regular flow of fishermen claiming their complimentary pint and meal - a conversation starter for any visitors coming through those doors.

"Seems we've become a bit of an attraction to these queer folk," Malcolm would say into his pint glass, as diners smiled and waved at anybody donning waders or fishermen jumpers, a novelty to those not from around there.

"Fisherman Friend's gets made into a movie and suddenly we're bloody celebrities!" Bill chortled, secretly enjoying the spotlight.

The feature that started the most conversations was, of course, the mosaic artwork of Mevagissey, made of Elaine's entire sea glass collection, taking pride of place on the wall above the booths, with the lady herself forever gazing out to sea from her favourite spot.

It was another busy night. It had been almost as soon as they'd reopened their doors, only a month ago now. Jacca was taking pride of place at the head of the bar, boasting to every new person he could haul down that this was his daughter's restaurant, Maxine giving him a swift telling off.

"Let our diners eat in peace, Jacca!"

"Can't a father be proud of his daughter?" Jacca chortled, his eyes beaming as Maxine placed a pint of cider in front of him. One of the waitresses passed him, her arms laden with delicious hot dishes. Mixed seafood linguine, beef ragu, baked lobster. To say he was proud of everything Paige and Nick had created here in Sea Glass would be an understatement. He practically glowed in that fatherly pride as he observed the looks of pleasure that crossed every diner's face in the room, every dish practically being licked clean with glorious satisfaction.

"You know, you can have your own meal. You don't have to goggle over our customers' food all evening long," Paige chuckled, coming out from the depths of the kitchen to grab a soft drink from the bar and check bookings. Her long, dark hair was tied and bunched into a neat bun, her chocolate brown eyes glistening bright against her chef whites. She was the happiest Jacca had seen her in years. Before Elaine's passing, before their separation, before Billy's tragic accident. It warmed his soul to have his daughter back again, radiant with that natural beauty she could only have inherited from her mother.

"Go on, then," Jacca gave in, like he always did. "Get your old man a spag bol."

Paige's eyes rolled to the ceiling. "So predictable. One spag bol, coming right up. Might be a little wait, mind."

"Take all the time you need, m'love. Lovely to see you so busy."

Paige squeezed her dear father's warm hand from across the bar and headed back into the kitchen. The noisy

304

chatter of happy diners was replaced with the purposeful clatter and clinking of a full working brigade back in the kitchen. Nick was shouting orders to the line, whilst fresh ingredients hit the hot pans, sizzling away merrily. Paige returned to her station, meeting eyes with Nick and flashing a grin his way.

Things had been good between them. Really good. Just last week, she'd officially moved into his little cottage. The quickest move in the history of moves as she, Jacca and Nick had carried boxes of her belongings from one cottage to the other. She'd immediately felt at home and little Mowgli had helped with that transition, ensuring her lap was warmed at every opportunity. They still had dinner with Jacca often, if he wasn't already at the restaurant, and it comforted Paige beyond measure to have him so integrated into their lives.

"Let me guess, Jacca's having a spag bol," Nick chuckled, watching Paige add some chopped onions to her pan.

"You know it," Paige replied, her smile showing a fondness towards her father's old habits. She checked the diminishing orders on the line. "How are we doing with the orders?"

"Catching up nicely," Nick said, extracting another baked lobster from the oven and setting it on a plate to be garnished. "Our new system is working well. It's like my gorgeous, clever executive chef used to work in a big fancy restaurant or something."

"Hmmm, funny that! And it's true - I am gorgeous. And clever. And gorgeously clever!" Paige teased, browning the mince perfectly.

"Don't over-do it. You're alright!" Nick teased back, catching the cloth Paige had thrown across the room just in time before it hit something hot. "Careful, woman! We don't want to set the place on fire again!"

Before Paige could tell Nick off for his lack of tact, Lauren came in with another order.

"Laura just rang down to the bar. She has another

weird pizza topping craving."

"She rang the bar from upstairs? Lazy git!" Nick scolded, handing the strange order to Lewis, who was in charge of the new industrial pizza oven glistening in the corner.

"Oi, don't talk about your sister like that! She's pregnant with your niece or nephew. She can have as many weird pizzas as she likes. What is it?"

Lewis showed her the order.

"Oh, that is an insult to Italian pizzas everywhere!" Paige relented, patting Lewis on the shoulder in sympathy that he would have to see that monstrosity through.

Like every shift since they'd reopened, the night flew by and Paige was almost surprised to realise it was time to go home, the kitchen spotless and ready for another crack at it the next day. The staff safely on their travels home and the restaurant alarmed and locked up for the night, Nick and Paige took their usual stroll back to their cottage.

Paige loved Mevagissey at night. In fact, she wouldn't be exaggerating if she said it was her favourite time to enjoy the little harbour. Then again, she'd say the very same tomorrow morning when she was up at dawn for her daily run.

At this moment in time though, twilight Meva was her favourite. She looked up at the full moon gleaming down on the inky black water, drawing in the salty air through her nose and sighing with contentment. She hadn't realised that she'd paused, standing on the water's edge to hear that gentle click-clacking of the boats.

"What are you stopping for?" Nick groaned. "Come on - let's go to bed. I'm knackered!"

Despite his complaints, Nick took his spot by Paige's side and clamped her tightly around the shoulders with his arm.

"I'm just trying to remember why I turned my back on this place," Paige pondered, smiling as Nick planted a kiss on top of her head. She turned in to him and surrendered to the warmth of his body, her arms snaking around his middle.

"I'm so grateful that I'm back here. I just wish it could have been for any other reason. And sooner. I wish it had been sooner. When Mum was alive."

Nick's gentle chuckle, as he placed yet another kiss on her head, was a wordless comfort as he too pondered over this. Finally, he straightened up and said, decidedly, "You two never would have worked together."

"No?"

"God, no! It would have been carnage. You're too similar."

"Oh, really?"

"Yeah," Nick said, going along with it now he knew it was safe territory, Paige smiling at his little joke. "Fierce. Stubborn. Absolutely terrifying when you haven't eaten in a while." He shuddered, earning himself a dig in the ribs. "It doesn't bear thinking of."

They laughed and under the moonlight and glistening stars, their lips met. Paige's hand reached for Nick's face as their kiss deepened and suddenly, for all they knew, they could be the only ones around in a twenty-mile radius.

"I love you, Paige."

His voice was deep and husky, his eyes fixed on hers. Her heart clenched tightly in her chest, sending an eruption of flutters in her stomach as she heard those three words from Nick's lips for the very first time. The last of the lights in nearby houses went out and only the streetlamps shone a light on their faces, making them possibly the last ones awake. A perfectly intimate moment in time.

"I love you too."

The next morning, as predicted, Paige set eyes on the beautiful dawn, a heavy mist sitting just above the water's surface, blanketing the boats from view, and declared this her favourite time of day to enjoy her little village.

Twenty laps down around the harbour and Paige was itching to get to the part of her morning outing, a new edition to her routine since Laura had made that incredible mosaic with her mother's sea glass.

Her breath caught in her throat as the ice-cold water hit her hot, bare feet, now released from the sweaty cocoon of her running shoes. It felt exhilarating to cool off, to treat her swollen feet to the pleasures of the wild waters. Suddenly she had never felt so close to her mother, as she bent down and took scoop after scoop of the shingles and sand, seeking out for glimmers of coloured glass in the mix.

There they were. Just two amongst the mix of common stones, but there they glistened blue and green in the palm of her hand, a strangle of a noise heard behind her and ripping her away from thoughts of her mother.

"Oh, m'love." It was Jacca and his eyes were wet with unshed tears. "Thought I'd seen a ghost then."

He traipsed down the little stone steps and joined her on the small patch of sand. "You look so much like your mother."

"I've heard that a couple of times this week," Paige rolled her eyes, not unkindly.

"Don't s'pose… any chance I could…?"

Paige saw the longing in her father's eyes as he gazed at the water's edge, his small little body wrapped up in every layer going, and she smiled.

"Would be rude if you didn't," Paige teased, squeezing his arm in reassurance. She almost burst in joyous laughter as her dear father stripped off his boots, his socks, rolled up his thick overall trousers.

"Oh crikey, I need my sunglasses!" Paige cried, shielding her eyes. "The sparrow legs are out! As white and gleaming as last night's moon!"

And just like that, she was eight years old again, squealing as her dad dipped his hand into the ocean and soaked her from head to foot in gloriously cold water. Pocketing her sea glass into her zip pocket, she ran into the water, no longer dainty in keeping her joggers dry and proceeded to return the favour, spraying Jacca with all the water she could gather in her cupped hands.

Paige could have lapped up another hour of this joy

but alas, Jacca tired quickly and soon they were perched on the wall, their damp legs dangling down towards the sand. Shoulder to shoulder they sat.

"Dad - remind me again why I left Cornwall in the first place?"

"Beats me," Jacca shrugged, his bony arm rubbing up against hers. "You always were an oddball. Anyone who wants to leave this paradise behind… "

She nudged him in response to his teasing and they chuckled softly in unison.

"Were you disappointed? That I left?"

"No. No, not for one blind second." Jacca said it with such fierceness that she had no choice but to believe him. "I admired you. Glad to have you back mind."

Paige smiled, linking her arm in his.

"You can take the maid out of Cornwall… "

"But you can't take Cornwall out of the maid," Paige supplied, nodding knowingly at one of her dad's saying.

"*For this is my Eden, and I'm not alone,*" Jacca sang.

Many years ago, Paige and Billy would have tutted awkwardly, embarrassed as their dad broke into spontaneous shanties as he did. But at this moment in time, this precious little moment - the sun rising above the harbour wall and casting Mevagissey in brilliant light - Paige soaked in her dad's baritone voice.

"*For this is my Cornwall and this is my home.*"

The End

Acknowledgements

The Thankyous

Feels like only a year ago that I was releasing my debut novel into the big wide world... oh wait - it was a year ago!

My goodness has time flown since the publication of Unexpected Beginnings, which has been received so warmly by a growing reading community that I am lucky to receive such wonderful support from.

As always, many lovely people come into the process of creating a novel. I have so many people to be thankful for. I must begin, first of all, with thanking the Mevagissey community. Thank you to all for letting me roam through the village on countless occasions, thank you to some of the harbour masters and fishermen for answering my bizarre questions and having lovely little chats with me on the harbour. It really is a thriving community and I hope I have done it justice in this story.

A very big thank you to Wendy Maynard, my wonderful editor. You have been an absolute rock in the nurturing of this second book and as always you invest in the characters and the quality of the book as much as if it were your own. Thank you for your words of advice and honesty when I needed it the most.

This has certainly not been the first time and it most definitely will not be the last – a huge and heartfelt thank you to my ever-supportive husband, Martin. Without your words of encouragement, without your voice in my head telling me 'you've got this' I really wouldn't be able to achieve what I have done. You and our gorgeous children are what keeps my inspiration alive.

A number of people have been incredibly helpful to me whilst researching and fact-checking this book. My friends and professional colleagues – Chrissi, Leah and Holly – have been the go-to gems in this process, reading extracts and giving the seal of approval for the synopsis. My best friend Dawn, for accompanying me on a walk in Mevagissey, for listening to me bang on about which fictional character lives where and for stepping into the story yourself to be Mowgli's vet. James for giving me advice on the logistics of a restaurant kitchen and Sammy for the correct legal jargon when inheriting something as big as a restaurant.

My mum and dad must also be thanked for not only raising me to be the proud Cornish maid that I am now, but for being my best cheerleaders and believing that I could accomplish anything I put my mind to. Thanks to my whole family for doing their best to look interested when I bore them with little snippets of my story or slip characters into conversations as if they are real people. I really do appreciate your efforts to humour me.

I think it's vitally important that I give a special mention to a number of local businesses in Cornwall who have given me the support and publicity that I could only ever have dreamed of. Duchy of Cornwall Nursery, Haywood Cider Farm, Lost Gardens of Heligan and The Elm Tree tearooms – all of these incredible local businesses have been stocking my books, helping to get them out to all those new readers out there.

Finally, a big thanks to you – my lovely reader. You have either stuck with me from the beginning (having read the first book) or you've just joined me. Either way, I thank each and every one of you for giving me a chance and for investing your time to read my novel. Your support and kind words mean the absolute world to me.

About the Author

Lamorna Ireland

A proper Cornish maid with a rich Cornish heritage, Lamorna Ireland has taken inspiration from the beautiful county from a very young age. Whilst teaching English in a local secondary school and being a dedicated wife and mother, Lamorna has always taken joy from the written word. In April 2020, she released her debut novel, 'Unexpected Beginnings' – a contemporary romance set on a Cornish cider farm, which tells the story of a young American girl finding unexpected beginnings under the nurturing wing of the Trengrouse family. The story gives an insight to the complicated tangles of family love and grief, whilst transporting readers to the tranquil Cornish countryside. In April 2021, Lamorna releases her second Cornish-set romance, 'Unexpected Truths' - set in the thriving fishing village, Mevagissey.

Lamorna's love for coffee and quality food has recently inspired her to write a blog for some of her favourite tearooms and cafés, whilst taking her debut novel on its own unique book tour. Her blog Lamorna Corner can be found bursting with positive vibes and yummy places to visit, including The Elm Tree tearooms and Duchy of Cornwall Nursery.

Lamorna continues to spend her free time adventuring around her beautiful home county, her feet firmly rooted to the place of her ancestors.

You can follow the latest news and updates on Lamorna's work on her website (www.lamornaireland.co.uk), as well as Facebook, Twitter and Instagram. She also sends out a quarterly newsletter with exclusive news for her VIP readers, which is free to subscribe to.

Printed in Great Britain
by Amazon